BACKPACKERS

BACKPACKERS

FEAR ON A SHOESTRING

PAUL BELLAMY

Matador
9 Priory Business Park
Kibworth Beauchamp
Leicestershire LE8 0RX, UK
Tel: (+44) 116 279 2299
Fax: (+44) 116 279 2277
Email: books@troubador.co.uk
Web: www.troubador.co.uk/matador

ISBN 978 1783061 235

British Library Cataloguing in Publication Data.
A catalogue record for this book is available from the British Library.

Printed and bound in the UK by TJ International, Padstow, Cornwall
Typeset in 11pt Minion Pro by Troubador Publishing Ltd, Leicester, UK

Matador is an imprint of Troubador Publishing Ltd

Chapter 1

Andrew was a wreck. Gripping the sides of his dormitory mattress with his fingertips, he was bouncing and rolling on the sexual swell of an uncontrollable, exterior energy. The mattress in the bunk above him was inflating like gasping bellows and expanding towards his face, threatening to consume him with a heavy, hot breath. In the end it was only the straining, rusting bed springs, singing out their despair, which saved him from drowning.

Of course Andrew should have taken a different hotel for the night, or at least a different room. Had he done so, things might have turned out differently. But he didn't. Instead he remained in his bottom bunk and wallowed in misery. And who would have acted differently? Whenever was a fool in love the best judge of anything?

He was in pain. Kirsten was breaking his heart again. She was up there now, fooling around with a drunken bum she'd met in a bar that evening. And here he was, her greatest, most loyal fan, trapped below, frustrated and helpless, going slowly crazy. The pressure was intense. It was 1988, long before email, and this was West Timor in Indonesia, the less troubled half of an island many thousands of miles from home. Andrew felt isolated. There was nobody to talk to, nobody to confirm his well held view that she was mad to reject him. How could she do it to him? She knew how he felt about her.

Their dormitory was how he'd always imagined a tropical jail: too many iron beds in too small a space, laden with strangers, their arms and feet flopping over the sides, their bulk bowing their mattresses like hammocks. That morning he'd scratched his name in the soft plaster wall with a wooden chopstick and, only an hour earlier, he had killed two fat cockroaches with his flip-flops. The heat was suffocating him. He could taste the heavy, earthy moisture clinging like moss to his lungs. Wet towels stuck to chairs where they'd been left to dry. The ceiling fan, his one potential friend, was rotating so slowly that mosquitoes had gathered in clouds around its blades. Any minute now those blood-sucking bastards would be coming for him, whining around his ears, snapping at his feet, tormenting him with their spiteful arrogance, sucking him slowly to death.

But the real cause of his misery was Kirsten. She'd looked right though him as she'd helped her new lover clamber skywards. She was drunk, of course, a poor excuse, but were she sober it would have been impossible for Andrew to bear.

Then, like his washing machine back home, it was full spin in the bunk above. The bed lifted from the floor and Andrew imagined the crockery above his kitchen sink vibrating and smashing onto the linoleum, the old sash windows rattling in their frames. Then, with thoughts of the hose bouncing and unwinding out of the sink, like a rampant cobra, he heard her moan and he wished that he could do that to her. In desolation, he buried himself beneath his pillow.

Re-emerging from the pillow once things felt calmer, he glimpsed movement in the adjacent bunk. He rolled over to see what it was. A large, middle-aged man was grinning right back at him. The man's mouth was ajar and, like that of a thirsty cat, his tongue protruded from the corner. Saliva had dribbled onto his chin. Andrew felt sick. Unexpectedly, the man made a show of grabbing his groin; two quick shakes and then he winked at Andrew; a knowing, conspiratorial wink. 'Me next?' the man joked, and he winked again.

'You dirty bastard,' Andrew whimpered, gasping for air, clawing at the bed frame, utterly defeated. He leapt from the bed and made his escape, past the rows of bunk beds and the piles of sweat-soaked sheets lying discarded on the floor. He tripped over a pair of sandals and dragged the sheets from a top bunk as he momentarily lost his balance. He was at the door when he heard a groan of finality and then Kirsten's exaggerated sigh of disappointment. Lover boy mumbled, 'Sorry,' and

Andrew knew that the man would be devastated. Kirsten had enjoyed another great victory.

Andrew took a seat outside and immediately felt a whole lot better. The palm trees were dancing in the breeze and a bright moon glimmered somewhere beyond them. Andrew imagined Kirsten running her hands through his hair. He could hear bullfrogs and crickets or cicadas, or whatever they were, and wherever they were because he'd never seen one. He could see the stars. In Asia you could always see the stars, that was one of the thrills of it all. It was nothing like the grey skies of London. Asia held everything for a dreamer, particularly a dreamer like him, but it held back, for him at least, when it came to love.

Andrew worshipped Kirsten. She was only twenty-five and she'd been travelling alone for over a year. That was not easy for a woman what with all the wankers about. He'd seen them often enough, leering and groping and whispering "Fuck you." He'd seen her terrify the life out of men who had pushed their luck – terrified him, in fact – and it always took an age for her to calm down afterwards. He once saw her punch a man who had stroked her arm as he walked past. The man's eyes had watered, not with sadness or pain, but with shock and fear. He had been mortally humiliated before his peers. But who could blame her for that?

Kirsten was a confident woman, strong too. Yet she could be weak. Something in the past had hurt her and nothing and nobody was going to do so again. It was her resistance that Andrew loved so much. She stood up to people, yet she was gentle around him. It gave him hope and made him brave. Her blonde hair was cropped short and, when she ran her fingers through it, to Andrew it was like watching a wheat field in the breeze. When she did that after a shower, if she was standing by the window on a sunny day, just for a split second he liked to dream that he could see a rainbow above her head.

As if he'd conjured her up she was suddenly standing above him, grinning wildly. Her obvious freedom was glorious but threatening. With the flick of a hip she could be gone and that was what Andrew

3

feared most of all. She placed a hand upon his shoulder and gave him a friendly squeeze.

As usual he let himself down. 'What do you see in these men?' he whimpered.

'You are right,' she said in her seductive German accent, placing him back under her spell. 'He was no fun at all.'

'That's not what I meant,' he grovelled. 'I meant, what's so wrong with me? What have they got that I haven't?'

Kirsten put a finger to his lips. 'There is nothing wrong with you,' she said. 'You are just too old.'

'I'm thirty for fuck's sake!' Andrew said, like an indignant schoolboy. 'How does that make me old?'

'You know what I mean,' she said. 'I take my pleasure from these idiots. I don't give them what you want. I don't give them love.' She was stroking his cheek now. 'What we have is special. We are best friends. Nobody has a friendship like ours. I love you so much, but as a sister, not a girlfriend. Nobody has done as much for me as you have. You know that I'm grateful. You know that I depend on you.' Then she laughed at his boxer shorts, reached down to take his hand and pulled him up. 'Come inside,' she said. 'You can have a little piece of me now. Take me to bed.'

Even Andrew wasn't stupid enough to think that Kirsten wanted to sleep in his bunk out of choice; her bunk still contained her worn out lover, Andrew's offered a stain free mattress where two could cuddle and snore in relative dryness. Kirsten fell asleep, her head resting on his chest. Seconds later Andrew's hands were cupped around her hot backside. Then he remembered how, only a couple of days before, they were almost in Australia, just across the Timor Sea, heading south.

He still had a vivid image of the smug grin on the face of the fat, red-bearded Australian immigration official who had beckoned him from the front of the queue to his desk. Andrew had wanted to point out the stains underneath the armpits of the official's off-white shirt, but

4

he knew that he was already batting on a sticky wicket so he kept his gob shut tight. For all the good it did him.

'Good evening sir,' the immigration official said superciliously. 'What is the purpose of your visit to Australia?'

'Tourism,' Andrew replied nervously.

'Can you tell me how much money you are carrying with you?'

Andrew told him that he had about $2000, which was complete bullshit and he was beginning to sweat.

'Can you show me please, sir?' the official asked, clearly bored, and Andrew knew that the game was almost up. He prayed that the official was a complete moron because it was the only chance he had left.

But, of course, he wasn't. 'I notice that those are Australian dollars,' the official said. 'And I only count $1000. You must have spent more on dinner than you thought.' He looked back over his shoulder and was joined by one of those ever-silent, narrow-eyed types in a suit who then counted the money with him. The two men nodded to each other knowingly. They'd caught one. 'Yes sir,' the official said, looking up at Andrew with the slightest hint of glee in his eyes. 'Definitely just $1000, I'm afraid. How long are you thinking of staying in Australia? This won't last you long. Are you thinking of working?'

'Oh no,' Andrew said. 'I'm just visiting.'

'Then I don't see how you hope to maintain yourself on the money that you have,' the official said, and the man in the suit dragged Andrew away.

Kirsten was sitting at a desk with the contents of her bag spread across it. A stern looking woman was sitting opposite her. 'Our single air tickets are no good, Andrew,' Kirsten said, in despair. 'They say that we must have return tickets. They will not allow us to stay. We must leave Darwin and go back to Indonesia.'

And that was more a plea than a statement. They were broke.

Andrew's hangover was gone by the time he woke late the following morning, and so was the winking bastard in the adjacent bed. His sheets had been changed and turned up, and a new bag had been dumped on top. The room was silent. The mattress above was lying flat; there was no bulge in the middle. Andrew dragged his right arm free of Kirsten and poked a finger into it. It moved. Kirsten's latest lover had gone as well.

Kirsten was asleep, the little diamond stud in her nose begging to be kissed. As Andrew leant forward she half-opened her eyes and gave him a soft, hot kiss on the cheek, and it turned him to jelly.

Andrew felt better by the time he reached the shower. He knew his luck was in because he found a whole bar of soap on the floor. So, with his newfound bar of soap he washed away the previous night's woes. He scrubbed hard because there was so much to get rid of, but even with a free bar of soap he couldn't wash everything away. Kirsten had slept badly as usual; talking and muttering in German in her sleep. She often had bad dreams and sometimes it seemed as if she was crying, but she never mentioned it and Andrew didn't ask. If she wanted to talk about it, she would.

Andrew was almost out of cash, having paid for both their tickets to Darwin in a last-gasp, futile effort to kindle some spark in their relationship. He had hoped to find work in Australia, maybe settle there for a few years. Lots of people were doing it. He had hoped that Kirsten would realise that he had been their salvation, that he had done it for her. He hoped that she might even begin to love him for it.

But now his plan was in ruins. He didn't even have the money to get home. Anyway, going home wasn't the solution. His travels were supposed to have transported him away from his lacklustre life. When he had finally gathered the strength to quit his job and leave his rented flat to travel, his friends and his parents had scoffed at him. He had left South London in the hope that he would reinvent himself and nobody had believed that he could do it. He had hoped to find work in Hong Kong or Australia. He could not return home now, he would be a laughing stock. And he would never see Kirsten again. It would be the worst kind of defeat.

He finished his shower with a blast of icy water that left him exhilarated and blind. His towel was damp and mildewed and it smelt like something rescued from a sewer, but he wasn't buying another one until he had some money coming in. Things were bad but at least he had Kirsten to himself again – for a while. To celebrate small mercies he changed into a fresh T-shirt.

The dormitory was empty when he returned. Kirsten had left a small note to say that she had gone ahead to breakfast and Andrew hoped that she hadn't gone to meet last night's lover. He stuffed his dirty laundry into the side pocket of his rucksack and looked forward to the day when he could be bothered to wash it. He draped his towel over a chair as far from human habitation as possible, then he clambered onto his knees and stuffed his rucksack under the bunk, out of the way. And that was when he found the money belt.

He had to get low to reach it and when he stood again he was covered in a kind of wet dust. He sat on his bunk and played "zip me, unzip me" with the money belt, not knowing quite what to do. His first thought was to go straight to reception and hand it in, maybe even get some reward. *No chance of that*, he argued, *they'd probably rip it off themselves anyway, and what would that gain?*

He looked up, checked that nobody was about, and opened it.

His head spun and he felt sick. Everything went blank and, for a moment, he was lost in a daydream. It was just too much for a simple man to cope with. His conscience became a warzone. *Should I? Shouldn't I? What if somebody found out? And what would Kirsten think? Yes, exactly, what would she think?*

He came out of the dream, remembered just how poor he had become, partly because of Kirsten, zipped up the money belt, put it into his day bag and walked to breakfast. He had made his decision.

'Andrew what is this?' Kirsten asked as a waiter placed Andrew's breakfast on the table. He had ordered a large pot of coffee and an enormous bowl of chocolate banana pancakes soaked in syrup. 'We can't afford that,' she said, 'and you can't eat so much anyway.'

'Want one?' Andrew replied, like the smug bastard that he'd always wanted to be. 'Would you like some coffee?' And he knew that he'd got up her nose because she just stared right back at him. 'I felt like a decent breakfast for a change,' Andrew said, and he stuffed an oozing slice of pancake into his mouth. 'And anyway,' he added, like a man with no teeth, 'I've come into a little money.'

'What money?'

Andrew raised a finger to his lips, indicating that they were sharing a secret.

'Where has the money come from?' Kirsten whispered.

'I found it.'

'Oh, Andrew, stop playing games.'

'I'll tell you later,' Andrew said. 'But first we've got to leave Timor.'

'Tell me now, Andrew.'

'No, first we should leave.'

Kirsten calmed down. 'Okay,' she said. 'But where do we go?'

'I thought Bali.'

'We've been to Bali.'

'Yeah, and we loved it.'

'Bali is beautiful, but we need work. We need to leave Indonesia. We need a change. Hong Kong would be better.'

She had no idea how smug Andrew was feeling. 'Listen,' he said. 'We will fly to Hong Kong, but, first, I'd like to spend a few days in Bali. We can afford it now.'

Kirsten's wariness returned instantly. 'How much did you find?'

So it took Andrew another twenty minutes to convince her, but she finally agreed – Bali was next.

Chapter 2

Kirsten was right about Bali being beautiful. On their last visit they had travelled around the island, from Kuta in the south, through the idyllic tropical paradise that is Ubud, across the volcanic centre with its lakeside temples and right up to the black volcanic beaches of the north. Best of all were the volcanoes, the spine of the island: Mount Batur and Mount Agung, reaching silently above the mist like gods, threatening any time to explode and bury the island alive.

They went everywhere on their last visit, travelling by bus and *bemo*. They first saw Mount Batur from the rim of its crater, having taken a *bemo* up the narrow winding road from the town of Bangli. 'Wow!' they had gasped in unison as they drove into a clearing at Penelokan and realised that they had been driving up the side of the crater for the past half an hour. Below them the eight-mile crater, beautifully desolate, surrounded Mount Batur, black and green, smouldering and shocking, its conical roof blown off. Beneath the volcano, Lake Batur glistened in the morning sun and some of the pluckiest villages they had ever seen went about their daily business, living off the fertile soil and risking their very existence in the shadows of a silent, fire-spitting dragon. They took a room in a hotel overlooking the crater, bought a beer, put their feet up and settled back for some extended viewing.

A week later they took a bus across the relatively under-populated north of the island and down the east coast to the village of Tirtagangga, to visit a water palace built by a Balinese rajah. The road hugged the barren lower slopes of Mount Agung and it was only having done this journey that they realised that Eastern Bali was, in fact, one vast volcano. To live in Bali is to go the whole way, or you simply have to get off.

At nightfall, as a light, refreshing rain began to fall, somebody played a Balinese flute in the darkness, out of sight. The melody drifted through the rain and across the rice paddies like an echo. Had it not been for sleep, they would have listened to the rain and the music until dawn.

Kuta Beach was not like anywhere else in Bali. The beauty was gone. This was where the Aussies took their summer holidays, a lot like the British in Majorca. Once upon a time, probably about the same time that Andrew first discovered pubs, Kuta and Legian had been blissfully separate little coastal villages. Now they were so close to each other, it was impossible to say where one ended and the other began. They had developed so much that there was no way a sane tourist would think of them as villages.

The attraction had once been the palm-fringed beach and its beautiful sunsets but, over the years, the emphasis had changed to cheap hotels, cheap restaurants, cheap bars, happy hours and discos. You could find all of these in a series of narrow, winding alleys above the beach and along the main road, Jalan Legian, further north. When you went out hawkers selling soft drinks, watches, wallets and sunglasses stuck to you like flies on shit. They'd follow you into restaurants and bars and line up to stop you in the street. If you actually liked shopping, there was the network of maze-like alleys, called *gangs*, which had been turned into tunnels by street-stalls selling T-shirts, jackets, waistcoats, shorts, batiks and sarongs. The drains couldn't cope with the over-development and, during the rainy season, the streets flooded with sewage. What Andrew particularly liked now, though, was the fact that the number of foreign tourists in Kuta made it easier to blend in and disappear until the heat was off.

Kirsten was pleased with their cheap, family-run hotel, a *losmen*, situated at the end of an obscure muddy alley. Their ground floor room was off a tiled courtyard, surrounded by other rooms and a few trees. In the centre of the courtyard was the family shrine; a platform of bowls and prayer flags raised on rickety stilts. The family lived directly opposite. The daughter, a dark-haired girl of six, was the one who filled the temple bowls, usually with her crisps.

Kirsten wanted an answer. As she was emptying the contents of her rucksack onto her bed she aimed her question at Andrew. 'Now that we are finally here,' she said, 'how much money did you find?'

'Well, actually,' Andrew said, fighting between telling her the truth, which would both scare her to death but, hopefully, impress her, and telling a little white lie which would keep things simple. But he'd never been that discreet. 'I found a money belt in the dormitory in Kupang.'

'Jesus Christ, Andrew!' Kirsten growled. 'Just fucking tell me, please. How much did you find?'

Andrew crossed his fingers and blurted it out: 'Two thousand dollars.'

Kirsten convulsed like a retching dog and Andrew considered patting her on the back.

'Two thousand dollars!' she shrieked. 'Are you serious?'

'I told you we didn't need to work yet.'

Kirsten jumped from her bed. 'Show me,' she said. 'I don't believe you.'

Andrew showed her. He closed the door and took twenty crisp $100 bills from the bottom of his rucksack and placed them flat on the bed. He left the winking man's passport where it was, though – just the thought of him gave him chest pains.

'Two thousand American dollars,' Andrew repeated, trying to appear as cool as possible.

Kirsten was stunned. There was quite a delay while she calmed down. 'You know, this money must belong to somebody,' she said. 'For sure they will know that you took it.'

'No!' Andrew shrieked, trying to convince himself as much as Kirsten. 'They left it behind, and loads of people checked out today. Anyone could have taken it.'

'Andrew, this is dangerous. Why would a backpacker be carrying two thousand dollars in a money belt?'

'I don't know and I don't care,' Andrew replied, although he realised that the question was a good one.

'Do you really think that you will get away with it?'

'I have got away with it, Kirsten.' Now he thought that he sounded cool. 'We can stay here for a few days and then fly...' He thought for a moment. '... Anywhere we want. Nobody will catch us then.'

'Catch *you* Andrew, not us. I took nothing.' Then she gave him that crafty wry grin she always did when she knew that Andrew knew what she was thinking. 'Unless some of this money is for me?'

'Of course,' Andrew replied, realising that things were beginning to go his way. 'Half of the money is yours.'

Dreams were made of this: Kirsten lost it completely and grabbed Andrew by the back of the head. She kissed him hard on the lips and pulled suddenly backwards, almost creating a vacuum. 'I cannot believe what you have done,' she said, her eyes wide with excitement, and Andrew's body began to tremble with hope.

Kirsten turned towards her bed and hesitated momentarily. Then, suddenly, she hurled her clothes onto the floor. Andrew was standing rigid, frantic with expectation, watching her closely. 'I'm going to give you something fabulous in return,' Kirsten said, running around the bed, clearing the last of her things. Andrew hadn't moved. Kirsten turned to face him as she pulled her T-shirt over her head. 'You always wanted this,' she said. 'You had better be ready.' Andrew was more than ready but he still couldn't move. Kirsten pulled down her trousers. She was pulling off her knickers.

To celebrate, Andrew got drunk. He had found a handy little alcove table not too far from the bar in Peanuts Disco. Peanuts was packed; tourists were hanging from the balcony, clinging to the iron stairs, crammed onto the dancefloor, fighting for space on the stage just so they could watch themselves dance on the huge video screen mounted on the wall. There were plenty more still fighting to get in and loads more getting wrecked in the bars in the small square outside.

Andrew kept the refreshments simple – no cocktails, just Bintang beer. But it didn't matter; he was drunk as a lord and having great difficulty focusing on the Australian woman sitting on the barstool. *She's probably wet her knickers*, he thought, because she had been sitting up there for at least two hours and she didn't look capable of climbing down. How did Andrew know that she was an Australian? He didn't, but he was feeling bitter towards them for having refused him entry into Australia, and most people in the disco were Aussies.

He really couldn't understand where his rotten mood had come from considering that only a few hours before he had realised his greatest ambition. He had been a sex god in paradise, albeit briefly. *From paradise to Peanuts* he thought, trying to amuse himself, but it didn't help. He was trying to convince himself that back there Kirsten had finally found the one that she had been searching for, but he knew that it wasn't true. She had been happy enough to let him go drinking alone. She had made no effort to keep him in bed and he didn't think that she was actually searching for anyone in particular anyway. He didn't think that she cared.

Now he was drinking for England in a lousy disco, playing lousy music from a lost decade to Bali-shirted, mini-skirted tourists from a lost continent. Finally he managed a resigned laugh when he remembered that he could afford to be so pissed because he had loads of money, and he remembered that he was a great adventurer, a thief in the night, a spy. He felt romantic. He was Raffles; women adored him, men were in awe. *Like fuck!* The truth was that he was squirming with fear because there was an enormous, leering bastard out there somewhere and he was probably searching for him right now. So he staggered to his feet, found the bar, accidentally knocked the Australian off her barstool, and bought another Bintang.

Andrew hated that helpless feeling when you come out of a drunken coma and realise that somebody is shaking you like a wet fish and shouting in your ear.

'Hey Aussie, we're closing. Come on, it's time to go to bed.' It was one of the doormen.

Andrew had been asleep, but he was sort of awake now and he hit the doorman with some witty repartee. 'I'm fucking English, not Australian. The bastards wouldn't let me in and now look at the state of me! Fuck 'em!'

'Okay, bloody Englishman,' the doorman said, lifting him by the armpits, which seemed pretty incredible considering that Andrew was at least a foot taller than he was. 'You fuck the Australians,' the doorman said. 'But do it in your own bed. We're closed. Go home.'

Andrew was convinced that somebody had thrown a bucket of water in his face, but actually it was raining. He turned as the door slammed shut behind him and, somehow, he made it to a wall before he went arse-over-tit in the mud. He got his bearings in the dark and noticed rows of eyes peering at him from the shadows. Somebody said, 'You want company, Aussie baby?' He remembered the sanctuary that was Kirsten.

Tonight of all nights he couldn't find his way. One muddy alley looked like another. But he moved quickly enough when a moped came flying through the shit, spraying filth everywhere, and he was in a doorway in seconds flat. The next lunatic nearly had him, though, and the third got him with a wayward boot up the arse. He cursed aloud as he scrambled up from the floor. However mud surfing was nothing compared to the frustration incurred at the end of the alley when he realised that he was trying to open the wrong gate.

What he liked to call "home" finally came into view half an hour later. It was such a relief to find it. He was feeling like shit; his clothes were encased in a muddy discharge, much of which was from the overflowing sewers; his backside ached where it had made contact with the biker's boot, and there was a piercing throb in his head which sounded like somebody had left the television on. He didn't give a fuck about the money anymore and he wasn't all that bothered about getting back into bed with Kirsten.

The losmen was sound asleep and in darkness, but he noticed that Kirsten had left a candle burning. The door was slightly ajar, which was a bit silly, but, even then, Andrew had difficulty opening it. His

14

head was really spinning now and he knew that, whether he liked it or not, he was about to make a grand entrance. Suddenly he was inside and, for no obvious reason, he raised his arms in the air and announced himself with: 'Tara!'

But Kirsten didn't notice, because there was a fat arse thrusting downwards at her. Her fingernails were tearing chunks out of it and her feet were peddling the air like somebody falling over a cliff without a bicycle. As Andrew began to slide down the wall, heading into oblivion, the head at the top of the arse turned, grinned, and winked at him.

Chapter 3

Bangkok. No place like it. At least that's how it seemed to the thousands of western backpackers for whom the city was the first and, sometimes only, Asian port of call. Bangkok was on the stopover route between Europe and Australia.

As a tourist destination there was plenty to do. There were mind-blowing temples, monasteries and palaces decorated with marble, mosaics, murals and statues of gods, dragons and giant, golden Buddhas. There were snake farms and crocodile farms, a village which still made traditional monk's alms bowls, and floating markets along the canals. There were fantastic museums and galleries, and parks where people flew kites or practised t'ai chi, or set up stalls and sold snake bile as health tonics. There were restaurants and bars and Thai boxing shows and, funnily enough, there was Patpong, one of the most infamous red light districts in the world.

Yet, even with these distractions, what did it for many of the world's great adventurers was Khao San Road, Thailand's big city backpacker heaven. Asia's modern equivalent of Kathmandhu's Freak Street, home to the next generation, a place that required no introduction, Khao San Road was where you went to get back amongst your own. This was basecamp. Here were the cheap hotels and bars and cafés and restaurants and shops and moneychangers and travel agents. Here you could buy counterfeit music and jeans and shirts and watches. This is where you got resupplied for your next voyage. This was the place for press passes and student cards and examination certificates and prostitutes and drugs. You could buy it all, but you didn't have to.

You could strut the catwalk in your fancy ethnic clothes, made by children in India and Thailand and anywhere else labour came cheap.

16

You could watch videos in the restaurants and play snooker in the pool hall, or you could have your photographs developed and get free enlargements. You could phone home or send a fax or even a letter! You could do pretty much anything and have an excellent time as long as you kept your eyes to yourself, didn't get too pissed or too stoned, didn't get into a fight, didn't mistake a transvestite for a woman, and didn't insult the Thai royal family.

Closing time came late, if at all; the self-enclosed, twenty-four hour circus didn't have the time to stop. Late night revellers shared Thai whisky with early risers eating banana pancakes. The only thing that changed was the pace. Strutting was a daytime thing; at night people began to weave and drift.

Bernadette and Monique were in Bangkok for the first time. School was out; university beckoned. They had spent the afternoon and most of the evening smoking hashish in their hotel room, emerging just before eleven to get some air. They were dressed in light summer frocks, flip-flops and little else because of the heat. The hashish had left them wrecked; they barely touched the stuff back in Paris.

'Monique,' said Bernadette, while she played idly with her hair. 'You know what I would like now?'

'A man?' answered Monique, looking over Bernadette's shoulder at two men at a table inside the restaurant.

Bernadette smiled awkwardly. Men weren't the subject on her mind, but Monique did like to tease her. 'What are they like?' she asked.

'You should have worn your glasses, then you'd know yourself.'

'I still wouldn't be able to see them,' Bernadette said.

This was their first adventure without their parents and they had never expected it to be so exciting. Everything was different; France had its café culture but in Thailand people really did live on the streets, and on the canals, in fact. The street markets were packed with fabulous clothes and materials, and they sold the most delicious snacks and drinks. Whenever they bought something they received a huge smile; they had never been made to feel so welcome before.

As they talked and fantasised they became aware of a presence nearby. A man stood motionless on the pavement, like an idling sport's car, its engine growling just loud enough to get attention. He was bathed in arrogance, scanning his surroundings, mentally consuming everybody and everything around him. Only his eyes moved. Even in that unexpected moment it seemed as if the entire world were waiting for him. He raised his head slightly, sniffed the air and swaggered into the restaurant like a visiting dignitary, like a returning hero, and it was no surprise that he moved alone. This was no pack animal: this man was some kind of rogue.

'Oh my God, look at him!' Monique said. 'He looks like he would eat you alive! I bet he's Italian.'

'I think he's French,' Bernadette said, inspecting his sense of style; short-sleeved, white, cotton shirt, sharply-creased, black trousers, quality leather sandals, gold watch on his left wrist. 'He doesn't exactly look like a backpacker.'

'Who cares?' said Monique, staring at the man, her eyes glued to his backside as he sat. She guessed that he was about forty years of age. He had medium length black hair, a hard, well-defined face and the tanned skin of an experienced traveller. He looked like a man who had conquered the world.

The women watched intently as the man examined a menu, his eyes flitting from front to back. Moments later, his choice made, he beckoned to a waitress. She was at his side immediately.

As the waitress returned to the kitchen, the man looked across at the women and swallowed them whole with his smile. It was so unexpected that they had no time to look away.

'Join me,' the man said aloud in French and, without hesitation, they did so.

'I am Maurice,' he said, standing politely and pulling up seats. 'I've taken the liberty of ordering a small meal for three.'

'You are French,' said Monique. 'I thought that you might have been Italian.' She pulled herself as close to Maurice as possible.

'From Marseilles,' Maurice said.

'We're from Paris,' said Bernadette. 'It's so good to speak French for a change. Don't you find? English is difficult, but nobody speaks anything else in Asia.'

'They speak a lot of Thai in Thailand,' said Maurice jokingly.

'Very funny, but I meant the tourists,' said Bernadette. 'Last year we had a holiday in West Africa. Everybody speaks French there, even the Africans. So, for a change, the English must speak French. Have you ever heard an Englishman speak French with an African accent? It's terrible!'

'The dollar is nothing there,' said Monique. 'The French franc is like gold.'

'I have never been to Africa,' said Maurice. 'Perhaps one day.' He laughed to himself and the girls laughed with him, without knowing why.

Maurice looked at them quizzically. 'Have you been drinking?'

Monique laughed. 'Hash,' she said.

'Hmm,' Maurice sighed. He seemed to think for a moment. 'You have some to spare?'

'We have some in our room,' Monique said, smirking at Bernadette. 'Would you like a smoke?'

'You would invite a strange man to your room?'

'You're not so strange,' Monique said.

'Didn't your parents warn you about men like me?'

'Of course, but they're not worried about us. We're good judges of character.'

'Even so, they should be.'

'Bernadette's parents have given her an allowance to buy telephone cards,' Monique said, grinning at Bernadette. 'She has to call them once a week.'

'So your parents aren't afraid?'

'She knows that my parents telephone hers straight afterwards,' Bernadette said, having her revenge.

Conversation halted temporarily as the waitress returned to the table and laid out plates of fried rice and bowls of noodles. She had a particularly warm smile for Maurice, who had pushed himself away from the table to give her room. She left them momentarily and returned with a plate of chicken satay and a bowl of green Thai curry.

'This is fantastic!' Monique said, dipping her nose towards the curry.

Maurice laughed. 'You see?' he said, examining the feast. 'The French do not have a monopoly on good food.'

After dinner they wandered back to the hotel. They hesitated at the end of Khao San Road until the road was clear and then they rushed across, laughing like children as they ran. They walked into an alley and emerged moments later outside their hotel. Maurice hesitated as he examined the two-storey building. All the windows, he noticed, were protected behind wrought iron bars, and the door looked like it would be locked at some point during the night. 'Tell me your room number and I will follow you up. If anyone realises that we are together they may throw me out. After all, I am not a paying guest.'

The women agreed and went ahead of him.

Maurice knocked on their door five minutes later and Bernadette opened it to him. Monique was sitting cross-legged on a bed, smoking a joint.

Maurice glanced quickly around the box-like room. There was barely space enough to walk between the two single beds, but there was an en-suite bathroom. The thin plywood walls were covered in graffiti. *Stupid hippy poems*, Maurice thought. A ceiling fan whirred above, the draught it created unable to stifle the humidity. A Walkman attached to two tiny speakers filled the room with the ubiquitous sound of Tracy Chapman, the most popular musician of the year. The women's belongings were strewn around the room, their half empty rucksacks looking as if they'd had their contents kicked out of them where they lay, half hidden, beneath the beds. A wax candle was melted to the windowsill. There was an empty box of matches beside it.

Maurice sat beside Monique. He removed his sandals and let out a particularly satisfied sigh before accepting a joint from her. He took a long drag and, having publicly considered the smoke satisfying, passed it to Bernadette on the other bed. She took it clumsily, dropping ash across the floor. 'Careful,' Maurice said, 'you will burn down the hotel. There are no fire escapes.'

'What are you doing in Thailand?' Monique asked, without caring what the answer was. She was merely taking comfort in her own voice. She had never been so stoned before. She had never felt so paranoid.

'Just having fun,' said Maurice. 'What about you?'

'We're seeing the world before we go to university,' Bernadette cut in. 'So far we've only seen Bangkok. We're adapting for a while and then we're going to meet some friends in Ko Samui.'

'You call this adapting?' Maurice said. 'Smoking hashish in your tiny hotel room is your way of adapting?'

'We're adapting *slowly*,' Monique slurred and she laughed at her slovenly joke. 'It's not as if we have to do anything. That's the whole point. We can do what we like.'

'How long have you been away from home?'

'A week,' said Bernadette. 'Feels like longer.'

'And you've spent the whole time in your room?'

'We go out to eat.'

'I'm glad to hear it.' Maurice laughed and the end of the questioning was declared. 'I know Bangkok,' he said. 'I could be your guide.'

'Will we have to leave the room?' Monique asked, and everybody laughed.

An hour later Monique was asleep. Maurice sat silently, watching Bernadette struggling to finish off yet another joint. Her eyes were red now and she wore a slightly ridiculous grin. 'You're a very attractive woman,' Maurice said gently, not moving a muscle, but drawing her into him. 'You have such strength for one so young.'

'Thank you,' Bernadette said, unable to further the conversation. 'I'm stoned,' she added, explaining herself, apologising almost, overcome by embarrassment.

Maurice smiled. He was offering her comfort and understanding.

21

He slid across to her bed and sat beside her. He took the joint from her hand and, leaning across her, he stubbed it out on the windowsill. 'Your friend is funny,' he said. 'I like her.'

'She's my best friend,' Bernadette said.

'But I like you more.'

Bernadette turned her head towards Maurice and smiled warmly at him, and as she did so he slid his hand along her cheek and held her close to him. He kissed her and she found herself kissing him back. This was not what she had planned. It was Monique who had joked about sleeping with him, but Bernadette could hardly think straight and kissing him felt nice.

She felt the weight of him against her. Her head was sliding down the wall now, heading towards the pillow, half aware, half asleep. Her dress was above her waist. She moved a hand to cover herself, but Maurice held her away. As she fell further she felt him tugging at her knickers, pulling them down over her knees, and she realised that she was falling asleep, that she was giving in to the hashish, that she was giving in to him.

The room was silent. Maurice sat up, listening for voices or footsteps but, hearing only the distant sound of light traffic, he stood, grinning to himself, and walked to the door to lock it. His clothes were in a heap on the floor. He picked them up and slipped them inside a bag belonging to one of the women. Then he found one of the women's towels and put it into the bag with his clothes. He took their money. When he found their passports he stopped for a moment and examined their personal details and photographs. Monique's dark hair was shorter, but her insolent grin was the same. Bernadette was just eighteen years old, one month younger than Monique. Her photograph was so happy. Maurice smiled; *you had to like Bernadette*, he thought, and he added the passports to his collection. He owned them now.

Maurice took a lock-knife from his trouser pocket and took the women's bag into the bathroom. He stashed the bag behind the door and returned to the bedroom. He found some of the women's shirts, cut them into strips, and tied the strips together.

There was little chance of the two women waking; frankly, there was little chance of them ever regaining consciousness. They had both eaten enough sleeping pills with their dinner to kill them. But Maurice had got it wrong before so he was taking no chances tonight. He knew for a fact that Bernadette was out for the count; there had been absolutely no response from her while he was raping her. He tied up Monique first. She didn't stir. Only when he gagged her did she wake and try to struggle, but it was too late for her now – she was firmly tied to the bed.

Maurice turned his attention to Bernadette, securing her hands first and then her feet. As he stuffed her knickers into her mouth he remembered her passport photograph. It crossed his mind that she might be carrying pictures of her family. It would be interesting to see what they looked like. It would help him to know her better.

He climbed off the bed and rummaged through the women's belongings, irritated by the untidy mess. He found what he was searching for in a small, throwaway photograph album. He sat on the end of Bernadette's bed and while he flicked through the pages he toyed absentmindedly with her feet. Her warmth relaxed him. There were a dozen pictures of friends and family. The one that struck him most was a standard shot of mum and dad and two kids. Bernadette had a younger brother, perhaps fourteen years old. What a spoilt brat he was about to become; his parents would never let him out of their sight after tonight. He snorted. They should have kept Bernadette at home.

When he looked up from the album he realised that Monique was staring at him. Her eyes were bulging with terror. She was snorting like a dying bull; bubbles of mucus belched from her nose and bubbled up against her cheeks. She had lost all dignity. Tears streamed down her face. Her fear excited him. He had an erection, but he was also angry with himself for getting the dose wrong. She could have called out before he'd gagged her; it would have been impossible to escape had a crowd developed in the hallway. Luck was on his side, though, and what was more he really had the perfect victim to toy with now. She was giving him everything. Bernadette was forgotten for the moment; Monique was the apple of his eye now. She was too drugged to struggle much. Her stuffed mouth gasped for air like a fish on the deck of a trawler. The fact that she was conscious at all amused him. This woman was going to take some killing.

He knelt beside her bed, slightly behind her so that she couldn't see what he was doing. Not knowing would terrify her, he knew. It was an old trick. He ran his fingers through her sweat-soaked hair. He talked to her in his kindest voice, sharing his loneliness, explaining that he was misunderstood; that he had never been able to rely on anybody, not even his own parents. But he wasn't bitter, he said. His experiences had made him strong. He depended on nobody, needed nobody, and cared for nobody. Nobody and nothing could hurt him.

'On the other hand,' he said, 'you are going to lose your friend, Bernadette, and that notion breaks your heart. How do you think her parents will feel when the telephone call doesn't come? How do you think your parents will feel?' Monique was sobbing. 'You should have stayed in France,' Maurice said, 'where you would have been safe amongst your own kind, and you definitely should have stayed away from hashish. You've made too many mistakes: your luck couldn't last forever.' With that he knelt to the floor, picked up his knife and, like a man sacrificing a goat, he pulled back her head and, from left to right with a precise, long, hard draw, he cut her throat.

Blood pumped from the wound and gushed onto the bed. It sprayed the nearby wall and formed bright red pools in the folds of her sheets. The room smelt sweet. There was something so peaceful about watching a creature bleeding to death, Maurice thought, something so generous about the moment when they give up the struggle and lapse into sleep. He had watched many a slaughtered goat kicking away its last breaths in much the same way. To share the moment was one of the highest honours anybody could ever hope to enjoy.

It took Monique longer to die than Maurice had expected. He used the time to plan his departure. There was no point in taking any risks. Nobody had seen him enter; it was best that nobody saw him depart. He would wait until the early hours of the morning. At the very least, anybody noticing him at that time of night would probably be too drunk or tired to remember or describe him.

He sat for an hour, relaxing and thinking about the past. He remembered how his mother had died. She had been young, but she could have been mistaken for a grandmother. In death her eyes were closed beneath wrinkled eyelids and the skin around her mouth was taut like a drum. Her hair was long but thin and her wrists, showing from the end of her sari, were no more than skin and bone. Her clawed hands lay upon her stomach, grasping thin air.

She lay in a room which was once a cupboard, the only one the manager of the Calcutta brothel was willing to sacrifice. It was only for a few more hours. There was a blanket across the doorway for privacy. The other girls had come and gone, crying gently. One by one they had held his shoulder out of respect and pity. Some openly hugged him. The attention was nice. His mother had not been able to hug him in months.

Maurice lifted his head and discovered that he was alone with his mother at last. He would be completely alone after the funeral, he realised, and, for a moment, he had wanted to cry. There was no chance of his father returning from France, he knew. His father had left India when his diplomatic posting ended and he had never returned. Maurice had been four years old at the time and he couldn't remember anything about him, other than what his mother had told him. Even then he had realised that his mother had only told him her version of the truth. What he came to realise over time, was that his father had met his mother while he had been on weekend leave from Delhi. He had charmed her with promises that he had never intended to keep. She had been his bit of fun. Nonetheless, to impress him, Maurice's mother had learned French and, in turn, she had taught Maurice. She had even given him a French name. Maurice was grateful

25

to his father for one thing, though; he had taught him the power of charm. In return, and because it seemed useful, Maurice had kept his name.

Maurice's mother was spurned by her family after the affair. Eventually she had fallen into prostitution, but she never surrendered her desire for Maurice to receive an education, even if she provided it herself. Maurice was prepared for what life had to offer a young orphan. After a moment alone with his mother he had gone out into the corridor. He was wearing a thin pair of navy shorts and a torn vest. He had no shoes. He picked up his broom and began to sweep. His mother was dead but he still had to live; if he wanted any chapatis or rice the floor had to be spotless.

After work Maurice had said goodbye to his mother. He had watched, expressionless, as the flames licked, red and blue around the body, hotter and hotter. They rose into the darkened sky, casting dancing reflections across the fast moving waters of the Hugli river.

Maurice had vaguely remembered his father's sudden departure as the flames swept his mother away. He pictured his mother piling up his father's few belongings, and he remembered the expression of delight on her face as she put a match to them and watched them burn. Even now, the smell of burning and the heat of the flames excited him. There was power in fire. Soon his mother would be scattered on the river where she belonged. Momentarily, he had surveyed those around him. Nobody should see how vulnerable he felt, he decided, or they might take advantage of him. He'd learnt that from the women in the brothel. The ones who cried were invariably the ones who were beaten.

There was nobody left in the world who cared for him now. Nobody would share the pain of his loss. Fighting back unexpected feelings of loneliness, he turned away from his mother and walked back to the brothel. He was twelve years old.

The sound of somebody walking down the hallway brought Maurice back to the present. He listened to the footsteps and held his breath as somebody leant against the women's door. There was a sound of drunken sighing and then that of a key in a padlock. Whoever it was let themselves into the room opposite and closed the door behind them. Moments later a bed creaked and then there was silence.

Time had moved on. It should be safe for him to make his departure. He looked at Bernadette. Her breathing was shallow. Perhaps she was near to death herself, he couldn't say. He liked her; he wouldn't destroy her face like he had Monique's. *No, he thought, it would be cruel.* It would be hard on her family. He'd had an excellent evening. Now he was feeling generous.

Once again he searched the room. What he wanted was a plastic bag of some kind, something that most backpackers carried by the dozen. Not these two though – they were far too disorganised, so he settled for a thin leather belt. He sat beside Bernadette and lifted her head from the pillow. He tied the belt around her neck and tightened it as far as he could. He kissed her gently on the mouth. Then he stood and put a foot on the bed, pressing her head firmly to one side. With all his might he pulled on the belt until the blood drained from his fingers and his knuckles turned white.

In the half-light of a Bangkok morning Maurice, a mere silhouette, crept past a sleeping security guard, slipped from a back-alley hotel and walked, unseen, through the light rain, past closed stalls, parked cars and startled dogs. He stared ahead, limiting the chance of the faintest glance from a passer-by, however drunk; a look of recognition that, on a bad day, could put a noose around his neck.

The rain became heavy and Maurice quickened his pace. With the flick of a hip he turned the corner and, like the thief that he was, he was gone.

Chapter 4

Water was all that Andrew wanted: glasses and glasses of ice cold, hangover quenching, life-giving water. But he wasn't moving to get it. He was in bed. It was still early, and he'd found the position that best limited the agony. He was on his back. His mouth was wide open and dry. With his right hand he was pushing down on his forehead and he was squeezing the pain behind his eyes out through his nose. Something else troubled him, though. There was much more to last night than he could remember.

He was planning on more sleep when Kirsten's voice drifted into his consciousness. 'Morning,' she said. 'What did you do last night?'

Andrew rolled onto his side to face her. She was standing in the bathroom doorway, brushing her teeth.

'Was there someone else here last night?' he asked.

'No. I went to bed early.'

'Oh.'

'You don't look so good,' Kirsten said, as Andrew dragged himself out of bed. He tried to speak but, as he opened his mouth, his world turned upside down. So it was hang on and run for it. He clenched his teeth to stem the flow and almost sent Kirsten flying as he rushed into the bathroom.

The last place anyone wants to be when they're feeling like shit is in a strange toilet, and the worst position to be in is on all fours, but that's where Andrew ended up. Thankfully he managed to control his collapse and he didn't actually fall into the toilet. While he was vomiting across the moulded foot rests into the dark hole he heard Kirsten grabbing her shoes.

'I go to breakfast,' she shouted through the bathroom door.

Wiping tears of agony from his eyes and vomit from his chin, Andrew knelt upright. 'Kirsten,' he whimpered, feeling suddenly alone. He was certain somebody else had been in the room last night. Another wave of nausea flooded his trembling framework, and he leant back into the toilet. With a heady mixture of deep thought and daydreaming, a picture of the previous evening developed; the bars, the disco, the rain and the motorbikes. He remembered being kicked up the arse. All that mud. That's how he got so filthy, he realised. And that man. That winking man! 'Oh, Jesus,' he wailed. 'Oh Jesus, that fucking pig is here!'

The bathroom door crashed flat against the wall and, moments later, Andrew's panicked figure rushed outside. He ran, as best he could, from restaurant to restaurant, stopping far too often to retch into the gutter. His face was a picture of horror, a mixture of sickness and dread. Tourists and locals alike stood well back, and even the hawkers avoided him.

The restaurants were crowded for breakfast. Each time Andrew made his entrance startled faces greeted him. Some of the younger children hid behind their parents. Somebody spoke to him. Turning his head he found a middle-aged couple looking up at him from their table. They both looked deeply concerned. 'Are you alright?' they asked.

'Err, yes,' he replied. 'Yes. I'm trying to find a friend.'

'You don't look at all well.'

'No, I'm fine. I had a heavy night, that's all.' Their intervention confirmed what he already knew; he didn't look his best. For the first time he took stock of his surroundings. He was in a courtyard. The restaurant was a paradise of tropical plants, fish ponds and fountains. The customers were well-to-do. The waiters wore smart uniforms and two of them were heading his way. And, amongst all of this, Andrew was wearing no trousers. 'I've got to go,' he said, trying to smile, and he ran back into the street, horrified by the probability that people despised him.

Andrew gave up. Kirsten was nowhere to be seen. He returned to an empty hotel room and, in despair, he sank into his bed and buried his head beneath the pillow. He was not in control. His stomach turned again and he ran back into the bathroom.

Andrew woke up on the bathroom floor an hour later. He was in his favourite foetal position. There was a buzzing in his head and the sound of somebody calling his name. Kirsten! He leapt to his feet and ran outside. Kirsten was standing sheepishly by the door. 'Thank God!' Andrew gasped. 'I was worried about you.'

'Andrew,' Kirsten said, standing to one side. 'This is Carlo.'

The big man filled the doorway. 'We've met before,' Carlo said triumphantly. He put an arm around Kirsten, marking her as his own. He was a colossus; a man as broad as he was tall. He wore a short-sleeved shirt and a pair of baggy shorts. He had straight, dark hair, and unusually blue eyes.

'You've met before?' said Kirsten.

'We were in the same hostel in Kupang,' said Carlo.

Kirsten was suspicious now. She was looking to Andrew for an answer, but Andrew didn't have the strength to provide one. His hangover overwhelmed him again and he ran back into the toilet.

'You would look better with your trousers on, old son,' Carlo shouted after him.

Having wretched thin air for the umpteenth time Andrew crawled back into the room. Kirsten and Carlo were sitting on her bed, examining a map of Thailand.

'Carlo has made us an offer,' said Kirsten.

'Make you rich,' said Carlo.

'That's kind of him,' Andrew sneered.

Carlo hit him, one sharp blow to the stomach. 'Don't laugh at me,' he said. 'I've got you by the balls and you know it.'

'Carlo!' Kirsten gasped, jumping from the bed. 'What was that for?'

'That's because I spent three hours in a Kupang police station yesterday, reporting the theft of my passport and money. And can you guess the identity of the thief?'

Kirsten could.

'How was I to know who the money belonged to?' Andrew said, lamely from the floor.

'From the passport,' said Carlo, standing on Andrew's left hand. 'Too late for all that, now, though,' he said, 'because you are a wanted man.'

Andrew tried to ignore the pain. 'How can the police know it's me?'

'They don't. But they will, and if you think I'm unreasonable, then you should try the Indonesian police.'

'What do you want?'

'Cooperation.'

'What?'

'In my business venture.' Carlo removed his foot from Andrew's hand. 'Kirsten likes the idea.'

'We can make good money, Andrew,' Kirsten interjected, trying to help Andrew save face. But Andrew didn't need to be persuaded. He had no face left to save.

'Things don't have to be unpleasant. If we're going to work together we must try to get along. Agreed?' Carlo was smiling. He had achieved everything, so far, through violence. The way to close the deal, he knew, was to be a little friendlier.

Andrew nodded in agreement.

'Good. Then for starters you can keep the money.'

'Keep the money?'

'Keep the money. The money isn't important. But I mean it; fuck with me and I go straight to the police – if you're lucky that is – if you're unlucky and I'm in a bad mood, I'll deal with you myself. Oh, but can I have my passport back, please?'

'What kind of business is it?' Andrew asked.

'Smuggling.'

Andrew's heart sank. 'Smuggling into where?'

'Thailand.'

'Thailand! Drugs into Thailand?'

'Don't be ridiculous,' Carlo said. 'Nobody smuggles drugs into Thailand. I smuggle diamonds. There's more reward and less risk. It's

31

far more acceptable a practice in today's climate. Drug smuggling can get you hanged.'

'That's okay then,' Andrew said, insincerely. He would agree to anything just to get back to bed. 'What do we have to do?'

Carlo laughed, slapped his thigh, and turned his map around so that Andrew could see it. 'It's too easy. I have most of my stash in Jakarta, but I've got a sample here with me. I want to get the sample into Thailand first. Once a sale is agreed, I can take in the rest. Naturally I'm not going to trust you with the bulk, but I do want you to take the sample in. Simple.'

'Seems easy,' said Kirsten.

'But why me?' said Andrew.

'Because you're all I've got. I spend too much time on planes already and I don't need to be seen flying in and out of Thailand too often. Foreigners stand out, you know. Even with my connections there's no need to take unnecessary risks. And, frankly, I don't have anyone else. Oh and talking of risks, Kirsten will be staying in Jakarta with me until you phone to say that you're okay.'

'Why can't she come with me?'

'Your references aren't that good, Andrew. Once the diamonds are delivered we'll come together.'

Kirsten walked to the doorway. She was watching something across the courtyard. 'What will you pay us to do this?' she said, without looking back.

'Pay you?'

'Do you think we will do this for nothing?'

'Listen lady. I'm doing you a favour. You could do with a sense of gratitude.'

Andrew agreed with Carlo. He didn't fancy a Thai jail, but an Indonesian one didn't sound any better. The Indonesian one was guaranteed. At least he had a chance in Thailand, but Kirsten clearly didn't see it his way.

'We will make you a lot of money,' Kirsten said. 'You have been reasonable so we will be, too. Give us two thousand dollars.'

Andrew was stunned and he could see that Carlo was too. But instead of punching Kirsten in the mouth, which is what he seemed eager to do, he laughed. 'You've had two thousand dollars already,' he said. 'I'll give you another thousand, but only once the diamonds are delivered. But if you do well – who knows what you can make?'

And with a brief series of handshakes they were in business, whether they liked it or not.

'Andrew,' said Carlo, now totally in charge. 'You will be on tomorrow night's flight to Bangkok. We're going to Jakarta this afternoon. When you get to Bangkok take a hotel for the night. Somebody will contact you.'

'Which hotel?'

'Don't worry. Somebody will contact you.'

'How?'

'Not important. Somebody will contact you. You don't have to worry about anything. As long as you follow instructions you will have an easy time, and as long as you do as I say Kirsten will have an easy time. It's that simple, and we will all get rich.'

'That sounds a little threatening,' Andrew suggested stupidly.

'Yes, it is. Do you have any objections?'

'No,' said Kirsten. 'It is understandable.'

'Once you've been contacted you can travel down to Ko Phangan. Fly to Ko Samui if you like and take a boat from there. We will meet you in Hat Rin.'

'Will I be followed to Ko Phangan?'

'If you are you'll never know.'

It seemed to Andrew that he wasn't his own man anymore.

Chapter 5

The smog-grey skies of Jakarta offered Kirsten no hope. From the tenth floor of the Borobudur Intercontinental Hotel she watched clouds of petrol fumes rising from the stationary traffic. Vehicle horns honked above the deafening chatter of road drills. The stench and the pollution appalled her. She closed the window and shut it out.

There was so much to do in the hotel; swimming, jogging, tennis, squash. She could even have a sauna and a massage if she cared. But she didn't care. She was thinking about Andrew. He had looked so shocked and so upset when Carlo announced that they were leaving for Jakarta. Why had she done it? Why had she taken things so far this time?

Well, there was money to be made. Not money for expensive hotels and first class air fares, but money for a little independence; no more desperation. No more trying to sneak into Australia; no more picking lover's pockets or running from hotels while the management sleeps, or suffering the indignity of accepting Andrew's desperate generosity. She missed Andrew in the kind of way you miss your favourite coat. She enjoyed their understanding. They were friends. Andrew would never be her lover, not in her mind at least, but he was good company and he made her laugh. And he was weak enough for her to manipulate. Not like other men – he didn't want to control her – possess her yes, but not control her. He was as close to a decent man as was possible to find. They would have a good time once the smuggling was done. It would be worth the trouble.

She definitely wasn't missing Carlo, though, he really was a pig. He had certainly proven that! In the morning he'd gone out to arrange a new passport at the American Embassy. The one Andrew had stolen from him was apparently almost out of date anyway and needed changing. 'My old pal Anthony will look after me,' he'd crowed.

Anthony wore the tidy look of the civil servant; short-sleeved white shirt, black slacks with a sharp crease, shiny black shoes. His tie was loosened and his top button open. His brown hair was thinning and to compensate he had grown a tidy moustache. He poured purposefully from a bottle of bourbon and passed a glass across his desk. 'You've put on weight, Carlo,' he said, patting his own stomach, which was beginning to spread. 'I didn't think that you were in Australia long enough.' He laughed but noticed that Carlo remained grim-faced. Best move on, he decided. 'So are you making progress? Is our bait on the hook?'

'The gullible bastard is primed, that's for sure,' replied Carlo admiring his variously disguised features in the collection of passports procured by Anthony for him. 'These are good. They're better than your jokes, for sure. It's going to be difficult for people to trace my movements with this lot.'

'Our bait?' said Anthony.

'They're a couple of destitute backpackers. I spotted them being deported from Australia; I just couldn't resist it. I knew that my wallet would tempt Andrew but I had to make sure, so I invested an old passport and two thousand bucks: he had to have enough to get away from the scene of the crime.'

'Two thousand is hardly pushing the boat out,' said Anthony.

Carlo grinned as he looked up from the passports. 'I sat in a taxi outside the losmen until they ran.' He laughed. 'They took their time. They'd just stolen two thousand dollars and they still stopped for breakfast! They're perfect; so gullible, so damned stupid. Anyway, they were easy to follow from Kupang. I even took the same flight and they didn't notice me.' He swallowed the bourbon and pushed his glass back across the table. 'They're convinced I've been to the police. And I've convinced them that they'll spend the rest of their lives in prison if they don't do as I say. I'm using the girlfriend as insurance to keep Andrew hooked.'

'How long before you can start?'

'I've already begun. Andrew is on a flight to Bangkok tonight and Kirsten is here with me. I've made arrangements in Bangkok and, if my information is correct, Maurice should be onto Andrew within hours.'

'Might I ask how?'

'I've set Andrew up. My people will ensure that Maurice notices Andrew's arrival in Bangkok. He will be convinced that Andrew is working for me.'

'Your people know about Maurice?'

Carlo laughed. 'No.'

'Then what?'

'One of their colleagues is photocopying documents and passing them to somebody. They have no idea who Maurice is. They've seen him and they've described him to me, but they don't know who he is. They certainly don't know *what* he is.'

'Just as well – they'd probably want out.'

'Probably.'

'Any idea how Maurice figured things out?'

'We worked together long enough. I must have let something slip on one of our night's out. These things happen.' Carlo sniggered. 'Especially if you've got a mouth as big as mine!'

'I've told you about your drinking,' Anthony said, half-jokingly, knowing that he was risking Carlo's anger. He hesitated for a moment to ensure that Carlo hadn't taken offence. 'And you're convinced that this is how he intends to find you?'

'You can never tell with him, but I'm not taking any risks. This way, if Andrew winds up dead, I'll know for sure, and I might even be able to get to him before he gets to me. I've sent Andrew onto Ko Phangan. It should take Maurice a couple of days to find him there. And Maurice won't be able to resist a trip to a tourist beach; it's like a candy stall to him. I'm flying out in a couple of days. Ko Phangan would be a damned good location to catch up with him.'

'What if he gets to this Andrew before you arrive?'

'I can't help that. I hadn't planned for this to happen so quickly but, once I'd found Andrew, I just wanted to get on with it. Anyway, I can live with it. Once I know for sure that Maurice is onto me I might be able to trace him back to Bangkok.'

'And what will you do with the girl?'

'Lose her, of course but, for now, I'm enjoying her company. And she likes my bedside manner.'

'Vanity, Carlo,' said Anthony. Anthony couldn't remember how their relationship had begun. He would never call it a friendship; Carlo scared him almost as much as Maurice did. They had gone to the same university, albeit a year apart, and Anthony had met Carlo at a party or two while they were there. But when he'd bumped into Carlo out of the blue in a Bangkok café during his previous posting, Carlo had seemed so pleased to see him that he had convinced himself that they must have been friends at one time or another.

Then one day Carlo had appeared unannounced in Jakarta and suggested that they could both benefit from Anthony's position of trust. The idea had terrified Anthony at first and he had even considered reporting it to his security manager but, when Carlo indicated how much he was willing to pay for false passports and how many passports that he was likely to need, Anthony's will was overcome. So far Carlo had kept Anthony's identity a secret and, to his relief, Maurice didn't know he existed. However, until Carlo got rid of Maurice there was always the possibility of his discovery. Anthony didn't want to contemplate the result.

'Maurice killed two more tourists in Bangkok,' said Anthony. 'It was on the news, and it was no accident either. He butchered them.' A serious tone entered the conversation. 'He's getting worse, he's really quite disgusting. They said the walls of the room resembled a Pollock masterpiece. He cut the head off one of them and left the other hanging naked across the doorway for the cleaner to find. You will have to get lucky soon, Carlo, or somebody else will get to him first. He's scared off all your couriers now. When you can't even find couriers you know that business is dying. He's costing you a fortune, and he's a great embarrassment to say the least. You know, I've never understood why you went into business with him in the first place?'

'I went into business with him because he's a risk taker and I love that. He lives close to the edge.'

'Over it, I'd say,' interrupted Anthony unwisely.

Carlo ignored him. 'He lives close to the edge and comes up with results that nobody, absolutely fucking *nobody*, including me, could ever manage. I went into business with him because I knew he'd make me a lot of money.'

'Until he started killing everyone.'

'Until he started killing everyone,' Carlo agreed, trying to disguise the embarrassment in his voice. Greed had got the better of him and he had taken to banking part of Maurice's share in his own account. Nothing could have prepared him for Maurice's reaction, though. Maurice had killed eight of his couriers, leaving their bodies charred and unidentifiable, always somewhere where they would be easily discovered. The bodies were warnings to Carlo's associates and they'd taken heed. One by one they'd cancelled business with him. Maurice was slowly ruining him. For a moment Carlo became reflective and then he looked up. 'Don't worry,' he said. 'As long as Maurice stays in Thailand, I'll get him. I've spent good money on this. Once he finds out that Andrew has a sachet of my diamonds on him, he won't be able to resist the opportunity to get back at me. He'll be convinced that Andrew is working for me and he'll be after him like a greyhound after a rabbit. He won't stop to think.'

'You believe that?'

'I have to.'

'You're an optimistic bastard, Carlo.'

'Well one thing's for sure, Anthony: I'm going to fuck that bastard, Maurice, before he gets to either of us. Then I'm going to get my business back on the road, make my fortune and live long and fat. When the time finally comes I'm going to die in bed, and on my terms. If you hang in there with me, you'll do the same.' They laughed so loud that the ambassador's secretary stopped typing and stared at the door. The sudden silence penetrated the door like a physical slap. Carlo sniffed hard, shook Anthony firmly by the hand, gathered up his passports and headed back to the hotel.

Chapter 6

Maurice was not Maurice. He was anybody but Maurice. Of course, he would be crazy to visit Khao San Road otherwise. Carlo, or even one of his people, what was left of them, would spot him in an instant, so he wore a disguise. Nothing much; disguise was not Maurice's speciality. He didn't go in for plastic surgery or sticky moustaches. He just relied on a long black wig, dark sunglasses and a cheap, locally made cotton suit. He looked slightly ridiculous but, to Maurice, everyone looked slightly ridiculous in the Khao San Road.

The risk was exhilarating. Risk was the difference between him and Carlo and just about everybody else he had ever met. Nothing comes from nothing and little comes from hard work, he thought. He'd made money in the brothel but none of it came from working. The money he had made as a child barely served to feed him and, as an adult, he made only slightly more. It was when the brothel owner put him in charge that he finally started making money, and the real money didn't come until the brothel owner was too old to notice that Maurice was trading in women himself, and pocketing the profits.

Maurice was sitting at a table in a large, half-empty restaurant, unlit and dark at the back near the toilets, bathed in sunlight up front where it was open to the street. Ceiling fans whirred above, rows of tables sat empty, covered with checked tablecloths; waiters chatted and laughed, and a woman leant on the counter waiting for business to pick up. It was still only eight o'clock in the morning.

Maurice read the *Bangkok Post* and drank a coffee. His killing of the two French women had sent a wave of anxiety through the local hostels. He took particular pleasure from overheard conversations; trembling, horrified voices discussing the case, discussing security, blaming the women for their stupidity, giggling with fear. As was to be expected there were more policemen on the street, but little had really changed. Opportunities were many. Potential victims were everywhere.

Maurice learnt early on in life that people see only what they want to see and, even when their defence mechanisms are warning them against danger, they tend to ignore their instincts and take the easy option. Tourists confronted with being alone will take up with a friendly face almost every time. To save time Maurice had devised his own personality theory, based on experience, and he could now tell after a few minutes of conversation those whom he could or couldn't dupe.

He dipped his newspaper slightly and peered over the top of his sunglasses as a man at the table on his left unzipped a pouch hanging around his neck. From the pouch the man removed a passport and a wallet of traveller's cheques. He detached three of the cheques, wrote their serial numbers on a sheet of paper and returned the remaining cheques to the pouch, which he pushed back inside his shirt. Maurice watched, delighted by the tourist's casual display of his wealth. *Such naivety*, he thought. The man was probably new to Thailand. There was every chance that he would be open to an offer of friendship.

'You should be more careful,' said Maurice, catching the tourist's eye. 'This town is inhabited by desperate people who would jump at the opportunity to rob you of your valuables. They run around here like rats. Even now somebody is probably telling an accomplice about what he's seen you do.'

The tourist smiled but seemed too embarrassed to answer. He was young, perhaps twenty-five, but prematurely balding. He wore thin-rimmed glasses, a check shirt and trousers that were too heavy for the Thai weather. His shoes were polished. He smiled without opening his mouth and his cheekbones pushed his glasses high on his face.

Maurice held the tourist's gaze. 'Just arrived in Bangkok?'

'It's my first day, yes.' The man was English. 'I suppose it takes time to adapt; I'm a little out of my depth here.' He laughed and searched for something to say. 'It's not what I expected.'

'What did you expect?'

'Something else. I don't really know. Something more basic, more local, less touristy. Times have certainly changed, though.'

'In what way?'

The Englishman frowned. He lacked confidence. 'During the days of European colonialism everyone wore short-sleeved white shirts and khaki shorts and rode around on elephants. Today they're hiring motorbikes and dressing as if Woodstock has found a new home. Ironically the hippies of the sixties opposed the war in South East Asia – now they're invading the region themselves.'

Maurice was surprised by the comment. Momentarily his interest in the man changed to one of respect. 'Not a view I often hear from a European,' he said.

'I'm interested in anthropology. It's one of the reasons I'm travelling. What I'm particularly interested in is why Europeans feel such a need to leave their homes and settle so far from everything that's dear to them. It doesn't seem natural to me. I'm terrified when I'm far away from everybody I know.'

'Greed is the reason,' said Maurice, as if it was the obvious answer.

'That may be so, but I'd like to spend some time with people and find out for myself.'

'What good will that do you?'

'I just find it interesting.'

'Anything that serves to reverse the trend of western colonialism will ensure the survival of so-called minority cultures. If you were to write a study that proves that western economic migration is evil, then you will do some good.'

The Englishman smiled. 'I'm not qualified; I can't even write a decent letter.'

'You could try,' said Maurice and he turned to call a waiter. 'I'm going to have a beer. Do you want one?'

The Englishman hesitated. 'It's a little early for beer,' he said.

'The best time for a beer is the morning,' said Maurice. 'Don't be restricted by other people's rules. Try something new. Be different.'

The Englishman sighed. 'I'm doing something new just by being here.'

'Well don't stop now. Come on, have a beer. Don't let me drink alone.'

'Okay,' the Englishman agreed reluctantly. 'Just the one. Maybe this is a defining moment in my life,' he said and laughed. 'This is the day I did something different, twice.'

'At least you will remember our meeting as the time you drank a beer in the morning. I hope it won't be the most memorable moment of your travels.'

'It probably will be.'

'But there is so much to do in Thailand. You have your guidebooks,' he said, pointing at two travel guides on the tourist's table.

'True enough. Been here long yourself?'

'I'm here on business,' Maurice said. 'Bangkok is like a second home to me.'

'Then can you recommend a few things to do? I'm only here for two days, and then it's onto Singapore.'

'You should hire a guide.'

'They're expensive.'

Maurice laughed. 'They can be.' He hesitated for a moment. 'I used a guide when I first visited Thailand. We've become friends over the years.'

'Do you think he would help me?'

'He has other interests now but I'm sure that if I recommend you to him, he would help you. He owes me plenty of favours. After all, you only have two days. You shouldn't waste them.'

'You're right,' said the Englishman. 'I paid enough to get a stopover. I can afford a guide for a day.'

'Then I will call him,' Maurice said and he stood abruptly. 'Order a beer and I will be back before you finish it.' He smiled kindly and left the table before the Englishman could object. In an adjacent street Maurice found another café, bought a newspaper, and ordered a fruit drink. Things were going well; the Englishman was too polite to sneak away, even if his instincts told him to do so. Maurice would wait twenty minutes and then go back. The Englishman would probably

43

be relieved when he returned. Nobody likes to be abandoned.

Maurice returned just as the Englishman was finishing his beer. The restaurant was busier now. The man smiled with what looked like relief when he saw Maurice. 'Any luck?' he asked.

'I can't contact him,' said Maurice. 'I tried everywhere.'

'Oh well,' said the Englishman. 'It was kind of you to try.'

Maurice sighed. 'I've let you down.'

'Not at all. You've been generous.'

'You think so? Then you don't expect much.'

'You've been kind. I never expected to meet anybody here. I'm hardly a backpacker like the rest of them.' He made a sweeping gesture with his right hand. 'They wouldn't piss on me if I was on fire. It's always been like that: kids with glasses, fat kids, spotty kids, the wrong coloured kids. My name is Nigel, by the way.'

'You're not at school now, Nigel. These people are adults.'

'Adults teach bigotry to their kids. Adults are just children with more hair.'

Maurice laughed. 'Not you, though.'

'Premature balding,' Nigel said, tapping his head. 'I was a fat kid with glasses. When I finally lost weight and they invented contact lenses, my hair started falling out! There just comes a time when you have to accept that life isn't going to be easy.'

'You need another drink,' said Maurice.

'I shouldn't. I don't drink at all, normally.'

'Then it's already too late, and I need one myself after my trek.' Maurice gestured to the waiter and he heard Nigel sigh in satisfied resignation. To Maurice it was confirmation that his judgement was as sharp as ever. Now it was important not to rush him. A few more drinks would ease him into his role of victim.

Two hours passed and Maurice ordered three more rounds of drinks. He paid for them all because Nigel had not yet cashed his traveller's cheques.

'You realise,' said Maurice, 'that you have been sitting here all morning? You have seen nothing of Bangkok.'

'I'll do better in Singapore.'

'It would be a shame not to see anything. There is so much in Bangkok.'

'I'm a little too drunk for sightseeing, to be honest. I would be better off taking a nap.'

'That would be a waste. I tell you what, let's see the city together. I don't get the chance very often these days.'

'What about your work?'

'My work can wait,' Maurice said, slapping Nigel gently on the shoulder. 'I'm the boss!'

Nigel sat up straight in his chair and his face reddened with excitement. 'Okay, but you will have to let me buy dinner. I could never do this alone; it took me two hours to build up the courage just to step out of my hotel.'

'Then I insist that you let me be your guide. I also know an excellent traditional Thai restaurant for dinner.'

Nigel shook Maurice's hand with unaccustomed strength and Maurice felt his body oozing with relief. Nigel was feeling good, at last. He was going to be alright. Travelling wouldn't be so hard. He'd found somebody he could trust. He'd found a friend.

'I was shocked when they made me redundant,' Nigel said, later that evening, as he tried to focus upon a woman spinning around a pole above him. Nigel was twenty-eight years old, slightly older than Maurice had estimated. He had worked for the past nine years as a computer operator in a small mail order company in Manchester. He was high on Mekong whisky and excitement following a marvellous day's sightseeing. 'I decided to use my redundancy money to see the world,' he said.

'Why are you travelling alone?' Maurice asked, adopting his most paternal tone. 'You've never married?'

'Hardly.'

'Girlfriend?'

'No.'

'Why not?'

Nigel sipped from his drink before answering. 'I haven't got the charm.'

Maurice grinned. 'Bangkok is an excellent city for girlfriends, you know. Look around you; they're everywhere.'

'Yeah.'

'I can arrange it.'

'One of these girls? A prostitute?'

'They're dancers, Nigel. There are no prostitutes in Thailand.'

'Of course not.'

'Bangkok is not a city where a man needs to be alone. It is normal for a man to pay for company here. It's nothing to be ashamed about, or to feel guilty about. I have a few girls who keep me company when I'm feeling lonely.'

'You do?'

'Yes, even me.'

Nigel sucked at his teeth. 'I suppose nobody would know about it back home,' he said.

'Not unless I telephone your mother,' Maurice said.

An hour later Nigel was too drunk to stand. Maurice had to help him to the toilet so that he could be sick. Afterwards Maurice suggested that they return to Nigel's hotel room. It was time for bed. First though, he had to cash some traveller's cheques to repay a small loan that Maurice had given him to pay for the meal. Maurice held him upright while he signed the cheques at a moneychangers. The cashier glanced at Maurice but paid more attention to the three hundred dollars that he was counting out.

At the hotel Maurice helped Nigel onto his bed and waited while he drifted into unconsciousness. It took Maurice just two minutes to clean him out: credit cards, traveller's cheques, cash in three currencies, a passport. It was easy money. Nigel would feel betrayed in the morning; his great adventure was finished before it had begun. At least he would be alive to endure the emotion – in many ways it had been his lucky night!

Chapter 7

The tiled floor of the arrivals hall at Bangkok's Don Muang Airport had Andrew's undivided attention, or so it might have seemed. He was praying that his bag would arrive on the baggage carousel, untouched by customs officials' hands.

Carlo had shoved him on the first available flight to Bangkok and, suddenly, he was a smuggler. He couldn't eat his meal on the plane because he was so uptight – that had never happened before. He even turned down a free copy of an English language newspaper because he thought he'd be sick. When it got too much he went to the toilet and sat with his head in his hands for fifteen minutes until somebody knocked impatiently on the door.

When the plane landed he half expected armed police to charge onboard, but that didn't happen. On the way down the corridor he wanted to piss, but he avoided the toilet in case somebody should suspect that he was dumping his stash. It seemed the only place for a nervous smuggler to bail out before customs.

Immigration really got him going. He couldn't believe that he was really smuggling diamonds! There had to be more to it: Carlo could have easily sent them by courier. Something was very wrong. The queues seemed to stretch all the way back to Bali. Normally, Andrew would watch the way each immigration officer dealt with the new arrivals and join the queue operated by the friendliest one. Here, though, they all seemed miserable.

At the yellow line, after fifteen minutes spent slowly shuffling forward, he stopped moving. He stood as casually as possible, but his chest was convulsing and he couldn't stop himself shaking. He was so lost in thought that somebody behind him gave him a shove because, apparently, the official was sick of calling him. All he received was a smart-arsed comment and a stamp in his passport marked "tourist". His Thai visa was endorsed with the word "Used," which was how he was beginning to feel.

At baggage collection Andrew watched suitcases, rucksacks, well-wrapped cardboard boxes and what looked like a collapsible bicycle as they passed through a hole in the wall and out onto the luggage carousel. Trolleys were parked two, three deep and hands were grabbing and dragging at baggage as it passed. One woman wailed in anguish as her belongings slid past, but a young backpacker with a Canadian flag on his bag grabbed it for her and they collided as he passed it back. The backpacker looked, and probably felt, as if he had just saved somebody's life.

At this point Andrew's mind drifted into more comfortable territory. He was thinking how Canadians always seemed to be the ones with the flags on their backpacks and he remembered being told that it's because they don't want people to think they're American. It's typical of people who feel that they live in the shadow of their larger neighbours. New Zealanders are the same; they don't want people thinking they're Australian. The Danes don't like being mistaken for Swedes, so they wear flags as well.

At last Andrew's rucksack appeared. It bounced onto the carousel and slewed sideways, the straps and the rusting buckles dragging along the floor. Andrew hesitated for a moment as butterflies fluttered and danced inside his stomach. He scrutinised the crowd waiting impatiently around him for tell-tale glances of interest. There were none. So, taking a deep breath, he stepped forward, pulled the bag off the carousel, threw it onto one shoulder and headed for customs.

To his horror everyone's baggage was being searched. They were thorough in Bangkok, but that wasn't so bad. The diamonds were in Andrew's shoe beneath his toes, so he was going to be okay as long as they didn't do full body searches. He imagined having to bend over to show his arse. There wouldn't be any winners if he did!

Andrew stopped in line and watched as the Thai woman in front was questioned. She opened her bag and stood back. The official pulled the two sides of the bag apart and looked inside, headfirst, like a vet examining a pregnant cow. When the official stood upright he was holding three bottles of perfume in his hand. With a scowl he questioned the woman again and she began to shake. Andrew didn't need to be able to speak Thai to know what was going on. Then he was called forward by the next official in line and he wanted to burst into tears.

'Please open your bag for me, sir,' said a small man in a green uniform. It was a polite request but Andrew's imagination went into overdrive. He remembered the film *Midnight Express* and realised that he could hear his heartbeat above the noise of the crowd around him. He wanted to scream. He looked to the door and counted the number of policemen he would have to get past if he made a dash for freedom, but then he remembered Kirsten. He held on tight to his stomach and managed a smile as he placed his bag on the counter, but he couldn't let go of the bag and the official looked directly into his face. 'Can you step back from the counter please, sir?' he said.

The search was over in seconds. Just like that! The bag was hardly touched. 'Thank you, sir,' the official said, and Andrew was free to go. He was so relieved that he actually felt like shouting, 'Look inside my shoes!' The desire to do so was so strong that he had to force himself to move on. Carlo was right – nobody smuggled drugs into Thailand.

It was after dark outside the airport and, according to the fleet of taxi drivers, the last bus had gone. It was bollocks, of course! What taxi driver was going to admit to there being a cheap, easy-to-use bus service that dropped tourists right next to all the cheap hotels, when he could drive them himself and drop them at an expensive hotel that was willing to pay him commission? So why, Andrew wondered, did he always ask?

As he arrived at the bus stop, his bus pulled up and he clambered aboard, taking a couple of unwary locals with him. Rucksacks: they're like fishing nets in crowds. The two locals, who were trying to get off, finally freed themselves of Andrew's trap and leapt from the bus. The closing door caught the last of them across the shoulder. Andrew didn't feel guilty, though – it was the way things were in this part of the world.

As the bus drove away Andrew moved sideways and straddled his bag, holding it firmly with his knees. His day-bag with his camera in it was hanging across his chest and he held firmly onto it with one hand, while he grabbed the rail above him with the other. A large crowd had joined the bus with Andrew and, in his paranoia, he suspected them all. Everybody seemed to be watching him, their eyes flitting from his bag to his face and to the floor. Sometimes people bumped into him as they left the bus and his hands moved swiftly to protect his bags. Sometimes they smiled at him and some even spoke to him, not that he understood a word.

Anyone who speaks to you in English wants something, Andrew reasoned. They learn the language so that they can communicate with you, and befriend you. It is people and things that you don't understand that you fear most, so you're most at risk when you feel comfortable. Don't trust anyone, especially if they mention gem stones or card games. Paranoia was his best mate now. Paranoia was his only mate.

Paranoia was generally something that Andrew had come to associate with smoking dope or dropping acid and he couldn't help thinking that his recent drug-taking had affected his mind. He remembered the time he ate some hash on a beach in India and, within half an hour, had been convinced that all the Indians innocently sitting around enjoying the sunshine were planning to murder him. He couldn't understand why his companions were so unaware of their predicament. In the end, before the imagined assassins tore him apart, somebody walked him off the beach and put him to rest in their room. It was hours before he calmed down and, even then, he spent half his time running to the toilet only to discover that he couldn't piss.

The bus journey into Bangkok was as slow as hell, even late at night and with wide roads that you'd expect to soak up the traffic.

Traffic was heavy, so heavy in fact that the only way for pedestrians to cross it was by pedestrian bridge, and they were everywhere. Andrew recognised the Weekend Market, where you could spend hours weaving amongst stalls, eating chicken portions and spicy sweet sauces or kebabs on sticks, and you could buy just about anything you wanted from clothes and toys to opium pipes and Bonsai trees.

Andrew was reminded of his first journey on the Chao Phraya River Express, Bangkok's great river bus. He had taken it the short distance to the Post Office. He found the Chao Phraya River at the end of a short alley, hidden beyond a magazine stall. The river had opened up to him like yet another exciting Asian surprise. Broad and brown, smelling overwhelmingly of fish, from the main road you wouldn't have known that it was there. Crossed by wide concrete bridges and bordered on all sides by orange-roofed temples, houses, shacks, restaurants, five-star hotels, warehouses and narrow, darkened alleys, it was like discovering Bangkok's guts; the city from the inside, harsh, aromatic and vibrant. The river was alive with the comings and goings of residents and workers, traders and shoppers, schoolchildren, saffron-robed monks and tourists. A longtail boat, no wider than a canoe, zipped through the waves, nose up, engine stirring up the water at the end of its long shaft. It disappeared behind a tug pulling a row of iron barges, transporting waste away from the city, sluggish and uncompromising in the water.

The ferry passed the Grand Palace with its green and orange roofing, gilded stupas and tree-lined gardens then, shortly afterwards, Wat Arun, a fabulous temple on the riverbank resembling a space rocket from *Star Wars*. Best of all, though, were the riverside communities; people cooking, washing and playing almost oblivious to the outside world. Bare-footed women in straw hats squatted low and dried displays of fish in the sunshine. Children splashed about in the water, laundry hung out of windows, limp in the humidity, restaurants served food on riverside verandas, small boats clattered together at their moorings and people drifted over them like ants.

Andrew's reverie was interrupted by passengers leaving the bus. One-by-one his imagined oppressors gave up until, finally, in Banglamphu at the Democracy Monument, he left the bus safely by himself. Two minutes walk from where he left the bus was his favourite hostel, around the corner from Khao San Road, the tourist ghetto of Bangkok.

Ordinarily Andrew loved the Khao San Road. It was the place to get back a sense of normality. You could get fed, get read, and get drunk. Popping out for lunch, without knowing what you wanted to eat, was like going into Foyle's Bookshop without knowing what you wanted to read. Andrew could telephone home from one of the long distance booths and sob out his heart to an old friend, but he couldn't think of anyone who would understand the mess he was in. Maybe a night with one of the whores would cheer him up. With so many distractions he thought that he should be able to forget his troubles for a moment, but not so. He had no appetite for food or sex; the best he would be able to manage was a bottle of Mekong whisky and a bloody good hangover.

Following the street away from the main road he stopped in a doorway. Nobody was following him as far as he could tell so he picked up the pace. He needed to get away from the imagined prying eyes. Even if it fucked things up and he lost the person Carlo had arranged to meet him, he needed to get free. He turned down a passage beneath some buildings and slipped along a narrow back road to the hotel. The owner was watching snooker on his portable black and white television. He didn't leave his reclined position when Andrew appeared, but he did give him a beaming smile and a warm welcome. He was wearing nothing but a pair of shorts and a well-worn pair of flip-flops.

'Ah, you come back! You gone long time. Where you been?' It was a genuine greeting. Andrew had spent many an hour chatting with him in the past.

'I've been everywhere,' Andrew boasted with feigned enthusiasm. He had almost forgotten what it was like to chat with an old friend.

'But where your lady friend?'

Andrew hadn't expected the question and it took him a few seconds to compose himself. 'She's in Jakarta. I'm going to wait for her in Ko Phangan.'

'Look,' the hotel owner said, crossing the floor to the keys behind the reception counter. 'I have your old room. It's free. I give it you only forty baht.'

The hotel had an annex around the back, just past a small sweatshop where old Thai women worked late into the night, squeezed tightly between rows of sewing machines and presses and traffic jams of wheeled laundry baskets. The annex was a two-storey block of twenty small rooms. Andrew took the room at the far end of the first floor corridor and threw his bag onto his bed. Usually he only took the things that he needed from his bag, preferring not to clutter up his room. This time, however, he decided to empty his bag onto the bed. He wanted to get organised. There were things he didn't need anymore, now that he wasn't going to Australia. He had two pairs of jeans, for example, bought especially for Australia. They were too hot to wear in Asia. There was no way he was getting rid of both though; he'd keep one pair for flights and sell the other. One of the pouches in his rucksack was like a library and he'd already read three of the four books. Those were heading for a second-hand bookshop. He would have loved to dump more but the rest belonged to Kirsten.

Kirsten's stuff was mostly heavy paperwork and books. Andrew had offered to carry it when he first met her because he wanted to get on her good side and he'd been stuck with it ever since. Even so the contents of the bag had remained a mystery, because he'd been frightened to discover what she really thought of him. But now she was sleeping with Carlo and he was stuck in Bangkok alone. He was feeling reckless. So he took a peep.

Nothing immediately leapt at him. There were two books, both written in German, which was probably why she had hung onto them. There were a couple of letters and her passport details in case her passport was stolen. There was a German-English dictionary, some old crap that Andrew couldn't identify, her vaccination card, and an envelope containing half a dozen moth-eaten photographs.

The photographs looked like family shots, but there were just two people; Kirsten and her mother. Kirsten was about ten or eleven but, even at that age, you could see that it was her. There was something strange about the shots and it took a few minutes for Andrew to realise what it was. Strange, he thought, that in the photographs of Kirsten on her own she was standing rigid and she couldn't raise a smile to save her life but, in the shots of her and her mother, she was so obviously happy. In one she didn't look like she was ever going to let her mother go. The last photograph was the weirdest of all, though. It was taken in London. Tower Bridge was in the background and, judging by the positions of the subjects, there were probably three people in the original photo, but the third has been cut out. Andrew concluded that it must have been her father. *She couldn't have liked him much*, he thought.

But, mysteries aside, there was nothing to indicate her feelings about him. Mind you, there were no photographs of him, either. He decided that no news was good news. Andrew thought about taking a shower after his journey, but he was exhausted. He stuffed Kirsten's things and his own back into his bag and shoved it beneath his bed. The heat was stifling, so he switched on the ceiling fan and lay on his bed. He watched, hypnotised, as the fan revolved faster and faster, feeling relieved that his smuggling adventure was over for the moment. He closed his eyes and enjoyed the breeze on his face. He drifted off to sleep and saw an image of Kirsten: she was making love to Carlo. Andrew's eyes opened involuntarily. 'Wow, I'm going fucking mad!' he said to himself.

He could hear knocking but he didn't make the connection. He closed his eyes and tried to get back to sleep, but there was the knocking again and he realised that somebody was at the door. He wasn't really with it but he remembered that he hadn't signed the register. Why the manager couldn't leave it until morning, he didn't know. Then he remembered that somebody was going to contact him. That's who it was.

But the two men at the door were policemen. They shoved him backwards and sat him on his bed. One of the policemen spoke: 'You are Mister Andrew and you arrived today from Bali, yes?' There was no expression on the man's face and Andrew didn't know whether he'd made a statement or asked a question.

'We are policemen, Mister Andrew. My name is Sergeant Win. Please answer my question.'

'Err yes,' Andrew nodded, open-mouthed like an old drunk.

The second policeman was emptying Andrew's rucksack onto his bed. Then he started picking through everything in minute detail and Andrew's throat went dry. He could hear his heartbeat again and, although the men were speaking to each other, he couldn't hear what they were saying. Everything was falling apart and Andrew's strength was draining away.

'What is inside this, Mister Andrew?' a voice said, and Andrew looked up. The policeman was holding Kirsten's bag. 'Will you open it for us please?' It was Sergeant Win. He was surprisingly, almost reassuringly, polite.

Andrew opened the bag and sat back as they looked through it. His heart was racing and he could feel sweat pouring down the inside of his arms. *Were they looking for the diamonds*, he wondered? They flicked through Kirsten's paperwork, seemingly without interest, but, as Andrew turned to look out of the window, he heard the two men speaking quickly to each other. He turned back to face them as the sergeant started going through his clothes. They were searching everything.

Andrew was finding it difficult to breathe and he couldn't focus on what was happening. They were going through everything, so it wasn't long before they reached his shoes and the sergeant came up trumps. He opened the sachet and looked briefly inside. He said something to his colleague and then he looked at Andrew. 'You must come with us, Mister Andrew,' he said. 'We have many questions. But do not worry – everything is alright.' The sergeant took the sachet and its contents, gave orders and then left. Andrew felt strangely alone without him.

Taking Andrew gently by the arm the second policeman led him outside into the street. They crossed the road and walked into Khao San Road. The restaurants were still full of tourists, some were eating but most were watching videos or drinking. Nobody noticed Andrew as he passed, and he felt like the loneliest man in town. He wanted to scream for help and, for the umpteenth time, he considered running away.

They say that New York never sleeps, but Andrew wanted to challenge any city to outpace Bangkok and still keep going twenty-four hours a day. Even in his current predicament he couldn't help but soak up the atmosphere. Apart from the darkness you would never know that it was after midnight. The humidity, the pollution, the choking fumes, the sound of honking horns and music set to distortion remained long after dark, a concoction of misery thick enough to chew. On the main roads, traffic was bumper to bumper. You could watch passengers cooking in buses like shrivelling food in a microwave, juices bubbling out of them as they dried up. Little yellow tuk-tuks spewed smoke, did U-turns on pavements and raced the wrong way up one-way streets, even motorcycles couldn't always get through. The pavements were packed with pedestrians, child-beggars and street stalls selling curries, fried snacks, kebabs, and pineapples cut into spirals. If, like Andrew had done more than once, you spent the whole night drinking in a restaurant, you could knock back your last glass of poison while somebody at the next table ordered breakfast.

At the end of the street the policeman tightened his grip on Andrew's arm and directed him to the right. They left the chaos behind and turned into an ugly concrete building on the corner that looked half-finished. They stepped over a sleeping dog and passed through a side door. A man sitting at a desk looked up and exchanged a few words with the policeman, who handed him Andrew's passport. Andrew was seen into a small room and made to wait. He was left alone.

There was nothing in the room to occupy his mind: bare, whitewashed walls; a barred window, a desk, a metal cabinet and three chairs, one of which he was sitting on. The chair creaked each time he moved. So now all he could do was think. He didn't have a story to tell, and he didn't want to make public the fact that he had stolen Carlo's money. He could hardly claim that Carlo was blackmailing him, which was what he *was* doing. Either way it would be jail in Thailand as a smuggler, or jail in Indonesia as a thief. And even if he wasn't jailed, what would Carlo say when Andrew told him that he'd lost his diamonds? Whatever happened now, he was right in the shit.

An hour passed and nobody returned to the room. Andrew's story went through a series of changes and not one sounded even remotely innocent. He had also been trying to figure out how events had unfolded. What he couldn't understand was how the police had found him? Why didn't they stop him at the airport? Why did Sergeant Win say everything was alright? He sat forward in the chair, one hand in the other, his shoulders hunched up. He was really tired now. He closed his eyes. As he did so, the door opened and the policeman peered inside. He handed Andrew his passport. 'Okay Mister Andrew,' he said. 'You go now.' With that, the policeman disappeared.

'What?' Andrew mumbled. 'What do you mean?' He'd been sitting there for over an hour, nobody had asked him any questions, and now he was able to leave. It made no sense at all. *It had to be a trick*, he thought. They'd shoot him as he tried to escape. Surely that was it? 'They're winding me up,' he said aloud to himself.

Andrew wasn't having any of it so he shut his eyes and tried to remain calm. Kirsten was out there somewhere, being held against her will until he delivered the diamonds – which he'd lost – and he was sitting on a chair in a police station doing fuck all about it. If he hadn't stolen Carlo's money in the first place she'd be just fine now. What had he done to her? She would never forgive him, he feared. But it also crossed his mind that Sergeant Win could be his contact, which would explain things very nicely, although it made no sense. If that were true then surely there was no way that he'd have dragged him to a police station.

He'd been sitting in silence for twenty minutes since the policeman told him to go and he was finding it increasingly difficult to remain still. He was tempted to take a peep outside. He stood and paced the room with his hands behind his back and his chin raised high in defiance. And then, in a snap, he stuck his head out into the corridor. There wasn't a soul in sight. He closed the door again and returned to his chair.

Immediately he was up again and out into the corridor. He turned right towards the entrance and walked slowly. The clerk was still sitting behind the desk but there was no sign of the policeman or the sergeant, whom Andrew hadn't seen since the hostel. 'Can I go now?' he asked the clerk.

'Yes, why you still here? Go.' The clerk continued with some paperwork and Andrew was rooted to the floor. This was all very strange. Andrew couldn't bring himself to believe that he was free. The clerk looked up again. 'Go!' he barked, and Andrew turned on his heels and through the door into the street in seconds.

Chapter 8

The screaming woke Kirsten, as it always did. She had become so used to the banging on the front door over the years that it no longer reached her, but the screaming still pierced her defences. Father was home from the bar and he couldn't find his key, even though he always kept it in his back trouser pocket. Of course, it was Mother's fault.

Kirsten sat upright in bed and looked towards her bedroom door where a strip of light illuminated the carpet. She wiped sleep from her eyes and hoped that her father wouldn't come to her room tonight. Climbing out of bed, she brushed her long hair back with her hand and pulled up her pyjamas. Kirsten was twelve.

At the door she stopped and listened. She could feel her stifled breathing tearing at her chest, tickling but sharp and cold. She wanted to exhale, but she couldn't in case he heard her. She sat against the door with her knees pulled up to her chin and listened so hard that she could almost hear spiders climbing up the walls.

Kirsten heard Mother open the door and allow Father in. She could hear him blaming her. Why did she always hide the key? Something was hurled against a wall. There was an explosion. It was probably the picture on top of the television again, the one of them on holiday in England last year. He would take it away and have it repaired in the morning. Why always that photograph? Why didn't Mother put it up high on a shelf where Father couldn't reach it? That's what they did to things she could reach when she was a baby.

There was a slap and Mother shrieked. He was chasing her. They were running around the room. Sometimes they did it when Kirsten was in the room and it looked silly. The sound of thumping feet rushed towards her and, suddenly, the door exploded inwards and banged against her head. Somehow the door remained closed but Kirsten's ear hurt where it had struck her. She fought off the need to cry.

Father did the strangest things to Mother. 'It was just a game', he said, but it was the same game he played with Kirsten when Mother was too ill to play, and it hurt. Sometimes mother's face looked like she had painted herself with make-up and, although she always smiled and tried to make Kirsten laugh, she was crying inside.

From the next room came the sound of the breath being choked out of her mother, like a cheetah gripping a gazelle in its jaws. Kirsten imagined her father, the big cat, standing expressionless amongst the dust while the eyes of her mother, the gazelle, stared in horror at the world that it had known, imploring somebody, anybody, to intervene. In the distance, amongst the dried grasses, the herd with which it had run for so long was receding out of striking distance, unable to help, unable to care, simply relieved that this time they had escaped. The gentle world of the gazelle was slipping away in one moment of unimaginable terror. In time, when the cheetah hungered again, the cycle of fear would continue.

Kirsten didn't want to hear anything more. She couldn't help her mother. She could only help herself. She slid backwards across the carpet, pulling herself like a cripple with the palms of her hands. She raised herself into her bed and pulled the blanket up over her head. Mother would come to her soon – that would be nice.

Kirsten looked up and broke away from her childhood when she felt something shaking her. She opened her eyes and found Carlo staring down at her. 'Shut the fuck up, will you?' he said, and Kirsten imagined her father's wicked face in place of his.

She leapt from the bed and stood by the door, staring back into the room. 'You bastard,' she whispered as her body shook with anger.

'Bad dream, lady,' said Carlo indifferently. 'Stop fucking about and come back to bed. Come here and I'll make you feel better.'

Kirsten stood motionless while she fought to control her emotions and her breathing. She didn't want him to make her feel better. He couldn't anyway. But she could make him feel worse, and that would help.

She climbed back into bed and lay flat on her back. Carlo climbed on top of her and spread her legs with his own. He tried to kiss her but Kirsten turned her face to the door. She wanted him to know that he repulsed her, but Carlo didn't seem to care. He forced himself into her and began moving quickly, deeper and deeper like a man hammering a nail. Kirsten remained silent but, inside, her mind was bursting with hatred.

She thought of Andrew. At least he didn't disgust her and, suddenly, she remembered that he had the pictures of her mother. The realisation was like a slap in the face. The thought of losing her mother's photographs sent shudders through her body. She wanted Carlo to stop. She began squirming beneath him, clawing at his back, pushing him away, but Carlo was far too big and Kirsten sensed his increasing enjoyment. The more she struggled, the faster and harder Carlo struck. He began to grunt like a bull as he buried his face in the pillow beside her. The bed was bouncing against the wall and rattling the lamp on the bedside table as the floor squeaked. The room seemed to convulse. Kirsten felt as if she was being forced into the pit of the room below. She gave into him finally and numbed her mind.

When Carlo slept, Kirsten went to the bathroom and vomited into the toilet. The revulsion of the past half an hour couldn't be controlled. It washed through her like a flood and ripped her stomach open. She felt as if she had lost her power; everything she had achieved during the past six months was lost. The men she had humiliated in bed had enjoyed their revenge, her father had enjoyed his. Kirsten remembered her mother's photographs and vomited again. She had to get those photographs back.

Carlo waltzed into the hotel foyer feeling like the million dollars he hoped to make by the end of the year – assuming that he got rid of Maurice, of course. At least Anthony was proving to be reliable. He was too timid to double-cross anybody. Carlo bought a bouquet of

61

roses for Kirsten. Her attitude towards him last night had bothered him. She made him feel like a pig. 'Even fucking hippies like roses,' he said under his breath as the cashier took his change from the till.

He stepped out of the lift and skipped along the corridor to the suite. He threw open the door and marched inside. 'Hey lover,' he shouted. 'I'm home.' He had promised himself that he would be on his best behaviour. He was going to give her a great time tonight and win her over. A great criminal he might be, but his ego badly needed massaging. 'Hey Kirsten,' he said cheerfully. 'I'm back. Sorry I was so long.' He put the flowers on the bed and walked towards the bathroom. Kirsten wasn't there. 'Kirsten, where are you?' His tone had quickly become impatient. *Keep calm*, he told himself. He must not upset her. He sighed. She was out, that was all; probably taking a sauna as he'd suggested. He sat on the bed and fingered the flowers. Then he noticed the chest of drawers, all open, and his suitcase, cut to pieces. The room looked burgled. Kirsten's bag was gone. And so was his recent passport and nearly two hundred dollars.

'You mother-fucking bitch!' Carlo roared, his face reddening. He leapt from the bed and stood motionless, trying to calm himself. He surveyed the room and focused on his shredded bag. 'You fucking bitch!' he growled again, still fighting to control himself. But it was impossible. Fists clenched, he screamed, and tightened his grip on the flowers as if strangling them. The room was like a pressure cooker, boiling, boiling, boiling. Then, suddenly, he tore the flowers to shreds and hurled them at the wall. But it wasn't enough to sate his rage. As the flower petals blanketed the floor he charged at the bathroom door and kicked it so hard that the doorframe splintered. He tore into the bathroom, punching and kicking. The mirror dissolved in a frenzy of blood and shards, the sink was ripped from the wall. A jet of water sprayed the air. He tore the shower curtain down and the curtain rings pinged off the walls. He punched and punched and punched at everything and nothing.

Suddenly he stood still, bent double, hands on hips, gasping for breath. His breathing was out of control and it took every effort to prevent himself choking. His fists were clenched so tight that the veins in his arms bulged blue. With the taste of blood in his mouth he surveyed the chaos around him. In seconds he had destroyed an entire bathroom. Blood dripped from his hands, across his knuckles, soaking his trousers and splashing the debris. But he felt no pain – his rage had consumed him. Rage was his worst enemy.

Chapter 9

Andrew was drowning. He was surrounded by a city of people but he couldn't think of anybody who could help him. He was trying to relax and he was trying to slow his breathing. He was almost hyperventilating and panic was consuming him. He could taste blood in his throat, and he could feel the eyes of his contact and of the police on his back.

The most sensible thing for him to do was to wait for morning, when somebody might hopefully contact him. In the meantime he needed to relax and take stock of his position. Ironically, the idea that somebody was going to contact him was comforting. He needed the company. His position would be stronger, though, if he still had the diamonds. Carlo was going to kill him when he found out that he'd lost his diamonds.

Andrew had been unable to sleep. Images of Kirsten had haunted him. She was staring at him, begging him to help her, but he couldn't help her. He felt naked, powerless, and the more he thought about it, the more he felt the need to scream. He spent hours getting in and out of bed, or pacing his tiny room. In bed he wriggled from side-to-side, clawing at the edges of the mattress. He lay on his back. He rolled onto his stomach and occasionally he sat upright, and then he felt the sweat dripping off his brow. His sheet was discarded on the floor – it couldn't cope with the friction. So, having lost the battle, probably his mind, and definitely any sense of reason, he slipped out of bed, got dressed and went in search of alcoholic sanctuary. In Bangkok there was a lot of it about.

Two hours later Andrew was swivelling on a barstool just feet from the pavement in a bar open to Patpong Road. 'A bottle of Singha please,' he said, and a child-like woman behind the bar turned and stooped into an enormous fridge. Although this was touristville there were no other tourists in the bar, just a load of young drunken Thais playing a noisy game of pool. Andrew had already paid for three games, all of which he had lost. That had surprised him because he had always been pretty good but, towards the end, he realised that his opponent's friends, who had all crowded around the table, were poking balls into the pockets when he wasn't looking. So, after a last beer he left in search of a friendlier watering hole.

The streets were busier than the bars so he tried to keep to the bars. The customers were mostly Thai men but there were quite a few middle-aged westerners. The women clung onto the men or hung around in groups, wearing bikinis and stiletto heels, looking bored. 'Hey mister, come inside. No cover charge. Just pay for drinks.' Everyone seemed to be shouting at Andrew but all that he could think of was Kirsten. By the time he'd walked one hundred metres invitations were ringing in his ears, and his arms bore the marks of eager fingers, which had tried tugging him through half-open doors. A couple of times he'd been tempted to punch somebody.

Occasionally, well quite often, in fact, he allowed himself to be dragged inside bars, where he was greeted by mirrored walls and half-naked dancers. Although the beer was expensive, nobody propositioned him. And he felt more alone than ever.

By the time Andrew reached the disco he was in trouble. Neon lights flickered in his face and video screens flashed images of naked women at him. He was enduring some sort of out of body experience; he knew that he was fucked, but he couldn't do anything about it. His legs were not responding to instructions and his apologies weren't made in any discernible language. Walls had become his constant companions. Sometimes, he crossed roads and staggered into sidestreets without meaning to. 'Beer,' was all he was able to say.

'So, handsome, what you name?'

The question came at him like another wake up call and he almost fell off his barstool trying to turn. He was squinting at the woman who had been generous enough to speak to him. 'I'm Andrew,' he said in desperation. He felt like thanking her. 'Who are you?'

'You can call me Anne,' she said wriggling onto a barstool beside him. 'Can I sit with you?'

'Oh, yes please,' he begged. 'Would you like a beer?'

Andrew's new friend had detached herself from a group of women to be with him. Like her friends she was beautiful; slightly taller than most Thai women, but just as delicate. She was wearing a tight-fitting blue dress. What surprised Andrew, though, was the intricacy of her make-up. She had obviously spent hours painting her face. *Absolutely stunning*, he decided, Kirsten all but forgotten for the moment.

'I would love a beer Andrew,' she said. 'You nice.'

'Not really,' Andrew said. 'I can afford it.'

'You rich man, Andrew! Then perhaps you like buy my friends a drink?'

That sounded like the kind of question only a ponce would ask and Andrew was tempted to tell her to fuck off. 'Yeah, why not?' he said, calming down. 'Call them over.'

'Oh no Andrew. I want you for myself. I just thought that it would be nice for my friends to have a drink. Beer is expensive for us.'

Andrew was touched. 'You really care for your friends,' he slurred. 'I like that.' He was staring at Anne now, seeking her approval. 'It's important to care,' he heard himself say, and he realised just how drunk he was. 'I have a friend, you know,' he continued. 'Her name is Kirsten. I love her, but she's miles away. She needs me, but I can't help her.' At that Andrew slipped off the chair with a jerk. That woke him up and he pulled himself back onboard with a helping hand from Anne.

'You pretty drunk, lover boy,' Anne laughed. 'Maybe I take you home,' she added, but the drinks arrived and the moment was lost.

Andrew paid the bill while Anne took the beers to her friends. They screamed with delight and waved at Andrew, but he barely noticed. When Anne returned Andrew was really in trouble. 'Where's the toilet?' he asked her.

She smiled almost maternally. 'I show you if you like.' She put an arm around him and nudged him through the crowd. The toilet attendant gave them a strange, knowing look and handed them some strips of toilet paper. Andrew thought it strange that he didn't stop Anne going inside with him – it was the gentlemans' toilet after all, but he had also noticed Anne putting some change in the attendant's discreetly outstretched hand. 'Okay Andrew,' she said. 'This the place for you.' She led him to a urinal and leant him against the wall. 'I help you,' she giggled, and she began to undo his zip.

'Thank you,' Andrew said, unaware by now that he was in a toilet. His forehead was resting heavily against the tiled wall and his arms were hanging limply by his side. He was hoping that Anne could direct him and he was falling asleep. But even as he slipped away he could tell that Anne was doing far more than helping him piss. *Strange*, he thought, *how big her hands were.*

Chapter 10

The clerk from the tourist police station wiped his dry mouth and took a sheet of computer paper from his bag. The bar was crowded and he felt awkward. Anybody could see them together here; he wondered why Maurice took such risks. The clerk fought to stop the paper shaking as he passed it over.

Maurice sat back in his chair, satisfied with the uncontrollable terror that he instilled into the man. He unfolded the paper and read it silently before speaking. 'Who do they think they can fool with this stupid story?' he sneered. 'This man had failed to register with immigration! How can he possibly have walked through immigration without them noticing? It is a cover.' He leaned close to the clerk's face and enveloped him with his hypnotic eyes. He dug his fingers into the man's shaking wrist. 'How long did they keep him?'

'Maybe two hours,' the man whispered, 'Maybe longer. They didn't question him. They just checked his passport and let him go.'

'How was he treated?'

'They treated him well. He was left in one of the rooms alone. The door was not locked. Then they let him go.'

'Do you know which hotel he is staying in?'

'Not now. I heard that he left this morning for Ko Phangan. There is no record of which beach he has gone to.'

'So what does he look like? Were any photographs taken?'

'I have this for you.' The clerk passed a sheet of paper across the table. It was a photocopy of page three of Andrew's passport; the page with his photograph on it. 'It is good.'

'This is what I have been waiting for,' Maurice said. He looked long and hard at the photograph. 'He is an Englishman. He is a courier. I am certain of it.' There was excitement in his voice. 'He thinks that nobody can interfere with him.' Suddenly, as if a light had been turned off, Maurice became thoughtful.

'There is one other thing,' said the clerk warily. 'I think that the Englishman may have been smuggling diamonds.'

'How do you know?' said Maurice, slightly agitated by the interruption.

'I heard the others talking. They were very indiscreet.' The clerk smiled weakly. 'I think I have done well for you this time. You are pleased?' It was both a request and a question.

'Yes, I am very pleased,' Maurice said, reaching into a pocket. 'This is for you.' He passed a small envelope to the clerk. 'Count it later. You will see that I reward success well.'

The clerk made to leave the table, but Maurice stopped him with a glance. 'In all my excitement I forgot to ask after your beautiful family.'

The clerk hesitated. He nodded and forced a smile. 'They are well. My wife is grateful for the money you give. She speaks of you only with respect.' He hesitated as long as politeness required and then walked quickly from the restaurant.

A moment later Maurice did the same. His long stride carried him away swiftly. His speed through the crowds made him difficult to follow; he was always aware of the possibility of ambush. His head darted from side to side, his piercing brown eyes picking out potential enemies, his pace never slackening. Suddenly he stepped into the road and hailed a tuc-tuc. His instructions were brief and the tuc-tuc buzzed back into the traffic. Within five minutes of leaving the restaurant he was so far away that he might never have been there.

The tuc-tuc stopped at traffic lights and suddenly Maurice thrust money into the driver's hand and leapt out. He walked for half a mile before taking another tuc-tuc to within half a mile of his apartment. He could be accused of paranoia but to date he had not been caught.

Maurice went immediately to a small safe in his bedroom wall and deposited the new information. Out of habit he checked the safe's contents and removed a large, brown envelope. Placing the envelope in the top drawer of the bedside table he walked to the bathroom, undressed, stood before the full-length mirror and examined his beauty. Satisfied, he stood in the shower and turned the water on with an aggressive flick of the wrist.

Many years before, Maurice had begun his murderous journey in a moment of hatred. It was hard to forget, not that he wanted to, but it proved how easy it was to kill a man and how easy it was to be rid of a body. What had really stood out that night was his utter lack of remorse. The man had deserved to die and that was that. It was as if he'd simply pushed the man out into the street and told him never to return. The man had gone. It didn't matter that he was dead.

Silvery sweat lay on the man's fat, pink back. The droplets were illuminated by a shaft of light from the open window. He moved his body like an elephant seal, rubbery flesh running the length of his back, pounding his neck like waves crashing against a breakwater. With each forward movement the middle-aged Austrian grunted like a pig. He dribbled saliva and whisky and he swore. Below him, sobbing gently, lay Devi.

Devi was sixteen. She had been working off her debt in the brothel for almost a year, ever since her uncle fooled her into leaving her village in Nepal. He had told her that she would be married to a man in another village near Kathmandu. They met another man, who her uncle said would take her to her husband. But the bus crossed the border into India and kept going, for two whole days, all the way to Calcutta. Nobody spoke to her, not even the border police asked any questions.

When she arrived she thought the place was a hotel; so many people coming and going and so many rooms. During the night a man was brought to her, but when she fought him off the manager beat her. She learnt that to survive she must do what she was told. On the streets of the city, people waited for others to die so that they could replace them at their workplace. If Devi was ever to return to her family she had to be brave.

The Austrian was the worst of so many. With a snort, he awoke from his drunken stupor. His eyes focused upon Devi's weeping face and he realised that she was disgusted by him. 'Don't you like me my little cobra?' he slurred. 'Am I not good enough for you? Won't you dance for me?' He sniggered at his own joke and slapped her hard across the face. As Devi winced with the pain, the Austrian glanced at a bottle of whisky standing on the bedside table. Looking down at Devi he said: 'Give me the bottle.'

Devi pulled herself back slightly and the man moved forward inside her, trying to maintain his position. He stared angrily at her. 'Careful with me,' he said. 'I don't like games.'

'I try to be careful,' Devi answered, and she reached out and grabbed the bottle. The man's bulk had engulfed her and was almost crushing her tiny ribs. She passed the bottle up and he snatched it from her. Leaning on one arm, he raised the bottle and whisky flowed into his mouth, puffing out his cheeks and dribbling down his chin. It poured over Devi and she squirmed. She turned her head to the door and prayed that somebody might help her. The fat man noticed. He sneered and lifted himself as high as his sapped strength would allow. He poured the rest of the bottle over Devi's face and threw the bottle at the door. When he slapped her again, Devi screamed and, in that moment, she slipped from the man's grip. She raised her knees high and kicked her heels into his face. The man yelled out. Devi leapt from the bed and slammed, naked into the door. Desperately, she pulled it open and ran out into the corridor. Surprised and exhausted, the man fell back and resigned himself to sleep.

He woke to what he thought sounded like a snorting animal, only to find the manager of the brothel, Maurice, staring down at him. Maurice's fists were clenched and his face was screwed tight as if in agony. He was searching the room for something. He found the empty whisky bottle in the corner. Picking it up, he closed the door.

'Help me up,' said the man. 'I'm not paying that fucking bitch.'

Maurice leaned forward and helped the man onto his back. Without warning his arm arched high behind him and sprang back like a bolt from a crossbow. The bottle crashed into the man's skull just above his eyes and split his forehead. Blood coloured his face and he began to cry. The bottle didn't break.

Maurice said nothing. He hit the man over the side of the head and stunned him, then he climbed onto him and pinned him to the bed. He let the man struggle, surrendering what was left of his strength and only once he'd slumped motionless on the bed, did Maurice relax. He straightened his back and gripped the bottle firmly in front of him. This was to be a defining moment and he knew it only too well. With a hiss, he smashed the bottle, neck first, into the man's mouth, smashing his teeth like a broken comb. The man began to gurgle and hiss, liquid spewing like a burst beer can between the bottle and the side of his mouth. His body bucked hard. His eyes bulged in terror. Maurice leaned hard on the bottle and shoved it in until it stuck.

Afterwards Maurice sat on the bed, grinning to himself. Through the open window he could hear people laughing and shouting in the street below. Somebody was advertising garlands. It was the end of the day and they were cheap. *How easy that was*, Maurice thought. He was twenty now, and everything seemed so easy.

That night Maurice watched the body float down the Hugli River. He'd stripped it naked, shaved off all of the body hair, and smashed in the face so that a cursory half-interested examination wouldn't reveal its western origin. The man's skin was dark, the result of many years whoring in Asia. For good measure Maurice wrapped the corpse in a white sheet. He knew the body would remain anonymous until it sank into the mud and decomposed like a sack of rotten, wet fruit. Even if it were discovered early, nobody would bother it. There were too many bodies in the Hugli for anybody to be interested in this one.

Maurice often thought about Devi when he took a shower. He couldn't help himself. Refreshed, he walked back into the bedroom and lay on his bed. He took the large brown envelope from the bedside table and emptied it onto the bed beside him. Collector's pieces; twelve passports – Monique and Bernadette were there still smiling innocently, albeit long dead, and so was the Austrian from so long ago. There were many more passports in the safe, all intended to hide his identity when he travelled. Stealing passports was so easy, especially if the victim was dead. 'These people are worthless,' he said to himself. 'Even their families don't care where they are.'

The clerk at the police station was worth the retainers when he delivered such good information. Tomorrow Maurice would travel to Ko Phangan and find the Englishman. There could be profit in this as well as pleasure. He would use one of the passports from the envelope and travel as a tourist. Perhaps he could pose as the Austrian from the brothel. The man's skin was almost as dark as his own. Once his own photograph was fixed into the passport nobody would be suspicious or interested enough to question the personal details. He wouldn't use a disguise this time – he would have a simple haircut instead. The Austrian was his first murder. The Englishman would be unlucky thirteen and perhaps Carlo would soon follow. Maurice laughed. He knew that Carlo must have some hold over the man. 'Englishman,' he sneered, 'you will wish that you had never allowed others to control your destiny.'

Chapter 11

It seemed that she would never fall. Spinning and spinning, arms flailing in the air, fingers twitching, eyes closed. Her full-length, cheesecloth skirt floated high to her knees, revealing the bells around her ankles, which hissed as she spun and spun and spun. There was nobody else on the dancefloor: everyone was captivated by her dance and, anyway, with her arms outstretched there was no room.

Andrew was sitting alone with a bottle of Mekong whisky at a table at the edge of the dancefloor. He was mesmerised by the woman's dance, convinced that, at any moment, she would trip and spiral from grace. But no! The song ended before any such disaster occurred and the spinner walked off the floor. She sat alone at a table and stared out across the sandy clearing beside the disco, probably hoping that somebody would turn up. Maybe she was as lonely as he was, Andrew thought, and he considered asking to join her. Instead he swallowed another glass of whisky and looked around the disco, hoping to spot a familiar face – any face would do.

Kirsten was a terrific dancer. Not as tall or as skinny as the spinner, but just as graceful. Her entire existence was choreographed, even when asleep. She floated when she walked, and she swam like a reptile in slow motion. Every movement had purpose, every turn of her head sought out information and recognition. Kirsten was a dream.

So long on the road and so many friends had come and gone. There had been so many goodbyes. Andrew missed them all. He was frequently bumping into people along the way, often months or years further along and in very different countries. On this trip alone he'd met people he had known years before in Israel and Greece. Reunions made the hardships of travel worthwhile and, like any grapevine, there was always news. All those "Hellos" compensated for the "goodbyes". He was pretty fucked up, drinking far too much and he desperately needed an old friend to talk to; somebody to understand and sympathise.

The last person he'd expected to sympathise with him was a Thai woman in a disco in Bangkok. He had a horrible feeling that she'd done a lot more than make him tea and biscuits, and he was not entirely certain that she was a woman! When he'd woken up he was alone in his hotel room with a hangover for company, so she must have got him there somehow. And he didn't think that she'd done it for nothing – he was forty dollars shorter when he checked out but at least the rest of his money was there and nothing else was missing.

A week had passed since Andrew had arrived in Thailand and there had been no sign of Kirsten. Carlo had said that he'd meet Andrew once he'd made contact with his ghost-like friend. Now Andrew worried that, because he hadn't met anybody (unless it was Sergeant Win of course) that Carlo would never come after him. Worse still, what would he do to Kirsten? The scare in Bangkok had turned Andrew into a selfish bastard, but time had passed and Kirsten was back on the agenda. He couldn't get her out of his mind. It took a bottle of Mekong to get him to sleep at night.

He finished the bottle and left the disco slowly, hoping that somebody might appear from nowhere and invite him to their table. Nobody did, so he followed the dirt path alongside two nearby bars, which were packed with laughing, happy people, and he disappeared into darkness. There was a hollow croaking of bullfrogs all around him. Behind him the beat of the music rumbled on and he knew that people were having a great time without him.

His thatched hut bordered the path. Rather than go straight to bed he sat on the verandah and listened to the disco. He could just make out the music. There was a slight breeze and the tall palms around the hut swayed gently. The sea hissed. But Kirsten wasn't going to stroll past the hut tonight and he knew it, and after half an hour he went to bed.

Hours later he listened to laughing voices as they returned from the disco. Vainly he strained for a knock at the door, but none came. People passed the hut as if it wasn't there, and he couldn't stop the tears when they streamed down his face. He didn't care; there was nobody to see him, and he needed to let something out. Once again he thought about going home. What was going to happen once this was all over? Would Kirsten stay with him or would she go off with this Carlo? What would he do if she did? But why did he need her? Why not somebody else, why not somebody who needed him? That would make more sense. What the fuck was he doing? This had to stop. Somehow he had to stop drinking. He had to cheer up. Then perhaps he could begin to think straight. One day things would be better, he reasoned. It was just a matter of time.

Morning brought no relief. There was a time, not so long ago, when morning brought feelings of optimism, but not any more. Depression overwhelmed him. Helplessness and sensations of guilt were beating him up and his forehead felt like it was stuffed with solid concrete, he was so stressed. With nobody to talk to and plenty of time to do it he was beginning to have doubts about himself. Each morning when he woke, an invisible hand grabbed his stomach and squeezed until he couldn't breathe. He knew that the problem was in his head. He knew that, somehow, he had to do something positive.

Ko Phangan was a beautiful island and, ordinarily, Andrew would have found the island heavenly. Having flown to Ko Samui, he had taken the ferry for the half-hour journey across to the small town of Thong Sala and then grabbed a smaller boat to Hat Rin, the party beach on the eastern side of a small peninsula. The island's interior was mostly mountainous rainforest, the highest point, Khao Ra, reaching over six hundred metres. The jungle was full of beautiful waterfalls and gave sanctuary to deer, wild pigs, monkeys and iguanas. Beaches were too numerous to mention. He had already walked into Thong Sala once, using beaches as his pathway. He had to overcome barriers formed by rocky outcrops and cliffs, by wading into the sea, clambering through insect-infested jungle, or sliding across smooth-surfaced boulders and back down onto the sand on the far side. Each beach was home to half a dozen thatched huts, usually with the obligatory hammocks and a small beach café. When he finally came across the furthest reaches of the new road at the bottom of a muddy hill, he took a motorbike taxi the rest of the way into town.

Anybody else living in his wooden hut would feel as if they were in paradise. The hut was big enough for two, raised high above the ground on posts and it had a lovely overhanging thatched roof. The verandah was big enough for a table and two wicker chairs and he had two windows that let in plenty of air but no insects. There was a huge lawn beneath his verandah, spotted with flowering shrubs, surrounded by palm trees and bordered on one side by a winding, tree-lined path, and on the other by the beach. In the distance, through the trees, he could make out a steep, rocky hillside covered by jungle. From the hillside you could see Koh Samui. During the day Mynah birds hopped around on the grass surrounding his hut and sometimes, when they thought that he was not looking, they popped up onto the verandah to investigate.

As usual Andrew ate breakfast at the nearest restaurant and took the only remaining free table. He had taken a book but he read the same line over and over and couldn't take it in. He drank a cup of coffee, but he could only pick at his fruit salad breakfast; papaya, pineapple, bananas. The way he was eating he didn't know why he bothered ordering. He was losing weight quicker than a carcass consumed by flies. If he washed in a bathroom with a decent light bulb he could see the outline of his ribs in the mirror. Any suntan he had was gone. He hadn't shaved in a week.

The restaurant was a little too popular for his liking today and he could tell that a group of tourists were looking at him. They probably wanted his table. He was desperate for somebody to talk to, but not strangers. He couldn't handle strangers at the moment. 'I was just leaving anyway,' he said quickly and haltingly, as one of them was about to speak to him. He was up before they could respond and at the bar paying for his meal, then he followed the sandy path back to his hut feeling as if he needed to run. In a state of near panic he fell into the hut. He stood motionless and fought to gain control of his thoughts and of his breathing. He tried to convince himself that all was well then, with some trepidation, he returned outside and nestled into his chair on the verandah with his book.

Andrew had bought a Robert Ludlum novel when he arrived on Ko Phangan; a good book to watch the world go by with. It was the biggest book in the second hand stall and as book prices related to their quality, not their size, he bought it. Ludlum was pretty good anyway but when you're talking value; in Thailand, big was beautiful. But he needn't have bothered because it had taken him four days to read fifty pages.

As the sun came up over the trees people began to pass by. He watched a woman with a water buffalo pulling a cart full of supplies for the local shops. The woman was wearing a sarong, a baggy striped shirt and flip-flops. She wasn't much taller than the black buffalo, but the animal, with its lovely horns sweeping back to its shoulders, was so passive that a child could control it on its regular daily journey. Other than the creaking of the wooden cart they shuffled along past his hut, between the palm trees, in silence.

Not far behind came the spinner from the disco, drifting along in a light hiss of ankle bells, always alone, always looking like her mind was somewhere else. Andrew couldn't help but wonder whether she had been through the same experiences as him. Would he end up lost and directionless like he imagined her to be?

Then there was the Canadian who spoke to people with such a kind and understanding voice it was as if he had heard that they were dying. Andrew wouldn't want him to be his doctor. He didn't know where he had first met him, either, but it was through somebody on the beach. The Canadian was a nice guy, although Andrew sometimes found him patronising. It crossed his mind that everyone was nice out on the road, mostly because they didn't have to be otherwise.

Morning dissolved into afternoon and Andrew sat with his book and his passers-by. A skinny old man wearing a hat three sizes too big had pulled a barrow onto the grass between Andrew's hut and the restaurant and was serving fruit drinks to a couple of passing tourists. A hippy in a waistcoat wandered past. In his bag was a tin of rice, which he used to keep the beat when musicians gathered to jam. He was a happy-go-lucky kind of guy, the sort of person who would smile at you and join your table simply because he wouldn't consider not joining you. Then he'd roll a joint and pass it around before wandering off to wherever he was heading in the first place – if he was heading anywhere.

Andrew's neighbour in the hut across the path was a German carpenter who sold leather belts and jewellery. He stopped to chat for a minute on his way to the beach. He said that he was waiting for his Thai girlfriend to arrive, but Andrew wasn't convinced that she existed. If she did exist he didn't think that she was coming. The German had told Andrew that he'd been waiting almost two months. The German didn't stop long because Andrew could find nothing to say to him.

A naked man tripping on acid was dancing on the grass, his plonker swinging out of control like a worm on a hook. Andrew imagined him suffering the indignity of his vulnerability. The man headed towards Andrew but he turned back and ran to the beach shouting 'Thank you goodbye!' as he went. Andrew didn't know what to think. The man, like quite a few people Andrew had seen on Koh Phangan, seemed as mad and as lost as he was.

Andrew's worst dreams were the ones where he was naked in public, but his dreams were nothing compared to how vulnerable he felt now. When things go wrong far from home, there's nobody to help you. There were many westerners staggering around Asia high on drugs, some in stinking prisons, trapped without hope. *Who would help that guy*, Andrew thought sadly? As the naked man disappeared Andrew returned to his book but, almost immediately, a woman appeared beneath his hut and distracted him again. She was adjusting her rucksack and looking lost. It took Andrew a couple of seconds to realise what was happening. 'Kirsten!' he screamed.

Kirsten hit the steps to the verandah so hard that the hut shook. She crashed into Andrew, forcing him backwards, against the wall. 'Andrew, Andrew!' she laughed. 'I can't believe how fucking much I've missed you!'

Andrew disappeared in a cloud of utter emotional confusion, not knowing whether to laugh or cry. He couldn't think of a decent thing to say, nothing to suit the occasion, so he searched and came up with the wrong line. 'I'm sorry, Kirsten,' he croaked.

Kirsten looked up at him. 'What are you sorry for? It was my stupid idea to help Carlo.'

Andrew held her tightly and felt the paranoia draining out of him. He led her into the hut and pulled her onto the bed. 'Why did Carlo let you go? I've lost the diamonds but he still let you go. Is he here?'

'He didn't let me go. I stole some of his money and escaped when he went to meet one of his gangster friends.'

'You stole more money from him? You're fucking mad! He'll really be after us now.'

'So we should leave in the morning.'

'We should leave now.'

'No. I want to relax. He will be at least a few days behind me.' She dug into her bag and pulled something out. She held it up for Andrew to see. He was shocked. 'You see,' Kirsten said smugly. 'We have his passport again.' She leant closer to Andrew and kissed him.

Andrew leant backwards and pushed the door shut.

Chapter 12

Carlo finished off his beer and telephoned room service. He had been in Bangkok for a few hours. He hated the place, with all its humidity, pollution and traffic. 'Another beer,' he growled. There was no "please" and, although there was nobody to witness his expression of contempt, his involuntary sneer served its purpose. He found it easier to despise than to respect. These people were here to serve; not to make pleasantries or conversation or to enjoy pointless compliments.

When he wasn't being generally unpleasant, he was thinking about Kirsten and how she had ripped him off again. He assumed that she would feel safe with his stolen passport in her possession, probably thinking that he couldn't travel without it. Now that his anger had dissipated, though, he found the whole affair amusing. The woman had balls, he thought.

He was surprised to hear a knock at the door. There was no way room service could be so quick. When he realised who it was, he opened the door, gave a contemptuous laugh and stepped back into the room, followed by the two tourist policemen. 'Shut the door behind you,' he said. 'I've ordered a beer,' he added, picking up the telephone again. 'What do you want?'

'Beer is okay,' said Sergeant Win.

'So how did it go?'

'As expected,' Sergeant Win replied smugly. 'The fool had no idea what was happening to him. He didn't want to leave when we released him.'

'Did you register his arrest?'

'Yes of course. We listed him as a visitor without an entry stamp. Anybody reading that would know that something was wrong, and

81

we let the receptionist overhear our conversation. He will know about the diamonds.' As he mentioned the diamonds, Sergeant Win took the sachet from his pocket and threw it to Carlo, who caught it in one hand. 'I do not understand why you used real stones.'

'My investment is bigger than some stones. If the opposition found cut glass they would be suspicious and I can't afford that.'

'And who are they?'

'Don't you worry about that. Has anybody seen the record yet?'

'Yes. The record was gone when we checked during the evening and returned by morning. Why anybody would be interested is a mystery, but somebody has obviously paid for the information.' Sergeant Win moved to the window. As he looked out he spoke again, less friendly now; he didn't like to be kept in the dark. 'So you can pay us now.'

A knock on the door interrupted them. There was a moment's tension as Carlo opened it. A smiling waiter was standing in the hallway, the size of his tip the only thing on his mind. Carlo took the beers without letting the man inside. Without tipping or thanking him, he closed the door abruptly and returned to his guests.

'Beers for the staff,' he said, handing them to the policemen. 'My money saves you prostituting your daughters,' he said, putting Sergeant Win in his place. 'It's a display of my social conscience.' The comments were aimed to offend. Carlo's money was simply too good to refuse but, even so, the only way he could demonstrate his authority was through insults. He needed these men as much as they needed him, but he didn't want them to know it.

'You make things very difficult,' said Sergeant Win. 'Why do you always look for trouble?'

Carlo took an envelope from beneath his pillow. He threw it clumsily to the floor in front of Win's colleague and grinned with satisfaction as the man bent to pick it up.

'You are laughing at us,' said Sergeant Win. 'You think that we are stupid and greedy. But it is westerners who are greedy.' He took the money from his colleague and, making a point of not counting it, put it in his pocket. He placed his beer bottle carefully on a table and opened the door. He saw his colleague into the hall before turning for a parting gesture. 'We will see you again, I think,' he said with disdain. 'If we are to continue to do business together it would be better if you are more polite. You have learnt little from your time in Asia. A little politeness goes a very long way here.' He turned and walked from the room.

Carlo looked back out the window. He was pleased with himself. Maurice was hooked for sure. *It should all end in Ko Phangan*, he thought.

Chapter 13

When Kirsten woke it was dark inside the hut. It was just after dusk and the temperature had dropped slightly. She climbed from the bed and stood by the door, looking down at Andrew's sleeping body. His mouth was open. He breathed deeply; his naked body seeming to shrink each time he exhaled. She smirked. She owned him.

Watching Andrew, Kirsten remembered the night that her father killed her mother. She remembered how, afterwards, still holding her mother by her hair, he had shouted that it wasn't his fault, that had her mother not been so ill, so unreasonable, they could have been happy. He was a man, he had screamed, and he had rights. All men had rights.

Kirsten took a deep breath and put the image of her father out of her mind. Her clothes lay strewn upon the floor. She ignored them and opened her bag. She found a new T-shirt and a pair of white shorts and put them on. Then she took a towel and, glancing at Andrew, she walked out of the hut and headed down to the beach.

The beach was beyond a grass lawn, obscured by a line of palm trees. Kirsten stepped onto the sand and lay down her towel. There were few people about but she could hear muffled voices and sporadic outbursts of laughter in the distance. In the darkness the sounds were comforting. She stripped naked and waded slowly into the sea, watching the water lap around her as she moved further, gently, out. Her knees disappeared and the water's soft touch slapped against her thighs and rose like a breath between her legs. She closed her eyes as she felt her buttocks sit on the cold water and she sighed aloud as her body tingled and shook. When the water reached her waist and a wave lifted her off her feet she bent her knees, lowered herself into the water and turned onto her back.

Caressed by the soft rolling of the waves she drifted, listening to the hiss and the silence and the faintly distant hum of conversation. The darkened island lay stretched before her, a collage of silhouettes; palms and thatched huts and towering cliffs. Spreading her arms wide, she ran her fingers through the water and felt the pressure on her palms. Dipping her head backwards beneath the surface, she closed her eyes and opened her mouth. She remembered with surprising satisfaction how Andrew had made love to her, how like the sea he had licked her and caressed her and had filled her with himself, and she thought how pleasant it would be to allow him to love her, and perhaps for her to try to love him.

Slowly, frog-like, she kicked herself further out, opening and closing her legs, making love to the force and the pressure and the weight of the sea. The waves lifted and lowered her in a soothing swell. *Gentle power*, she thought; *it felt so good*. She closed her eyes, lay back and allowed water to flow from her mouth. This was a dream.

Kirsten's head dipped gently into the water and all sound melted away. She remembered the way her father had spoken to her the day her uncle, his brother, had taken her to visit him in prison. He loved her very much, he had said, and he was sorry for the things that he had done to her and to her mother, but it wasn't his fault. Her mother was ill, he had told her, and she didn't care about him, that was why he came to Kirsten some nights. He needed love, just like anyone else.

On the way home her uncle had told her that her father was a good man. She would learn to forgive him in time, she had to, she was all he had left in the world. Kirsten had listened to the words with contempt. She hated her father and she despised her uncle and his family. She could tell that they knew what her father was really like, what he had done to her. The following day she ran away and it was nearly two months before the authorities found her and took her into care.

When she opened her eyes again, a man was walking along the beach. He couldn't see her peeping at him from between her toes. *Good*, she thought. *I will swim in when he's gone.*

The man walked swiftly, keeping to the firmer sand at the water's edge. He occasionally glanced out to sea but, for the most part, he scanned the palm trees and beyond. Kirsten watched as he stopped suddenly beside her clothes. He looked out to sea, trying to spot the owner. He saw her. 'Shit,' Kirsten said. She didn't move.

The man walked a little further and sat down beneath a palm tree. He took out a book and began to read. Kirsten watched him. *He must have the eyesight of an owl*, she thought. He was a lonely figure and he obviously wasn't concentrating upon his book; several times he put it down and stared out to sea. She saw him jump once, when some children ran from the trees. When the children saw him, they ran away.

She had been in the sea, watching the man, for fifteen minutes, and she was tiring of it. The man was going nowhere, but it was darker at least so she swam in. The man looked up as Kirsten waded ashore. She felt his gaze upon her shivering body. When she looked at him he didn't look away. Kirsten stared at the sand, momentarily discomforted by his control over her. She reached her clothes and hurriedly dried herself. Then, recovering her poise, she dropped the towel and stood, naked and grinning, as she considered him. She realised that he was not as young as he appeared; he was probably a little over forty. He looked powerful; lean but strong. His hair was dark and his skin had a strong, natural-looking tan. It was too dark to be sure. He could have been Italian or possibly Indian.

Kirsten turned and dressed.

When she looked again the man was gone. She twisted around, searching for him, but he was nowhere. She was disheartened; the flirtation had been exhilarating. She had planned on smiling at him as she walked back to the hut. She looked again at where he'd been sitting. There was something on the sand. It was his book. She walked over and picked it up. It was impossible to read: the book was written in French. Kirsten sat for a few minutes, hoping that the man would return for the book, but he didn't. She left the book where it was and walked back to the hut.

Chapter 14

The fishing boat appeared on the crest of a mountainous wave and disappeared below another. The journey was scheduled to take less than forty minutes but the boat had been riding waves like a bucking horse for over an hour. Aboard the boat, which acted as a ferry between Ko Samui and Ko Phangan, were twenty nervous passengers and crew. Amongst them sat Carlo, freezing cold and soaked to the skin. He was one of the few who had not vomited but he feared for his life nonetheless. Why he was in such a predicament was beyond him. Each time he looked at the dumb expression on the captain's face he quivered with anger. That man must have known the danger but if he hadn't sailed he would have lost money. 'If I drown it will be with my foot on the bastard's head,' said Carlo, as another wave lifted the boat higher.

Carlo considered his situation. The worst part would be knowing, as he drowned, that he was so close to his goal. Maurice was bound to be on the island; there was just too much for him to resist. Even if Maurice had thought that he was being setup, he would have come. He was that arrogant and, anyway, his desire to kill Carlo would overcome any doubts. No, this was not the time for drowning.

On the bright side, the woman cowering nearest to Carlo was wearing a summer frock, which was now absolutely transparent. To his delight she wore nothing but a skimpy thong beneath and she might as well be naked. She had large breasts and the frock clung to them. Her nipples were erect. She was so rigid with fear that she didn't seem to realise how naked she appeared. Nobody but Carlo had noticed.

While Carlo was lost in thought the boat turned and, as suddenly as they had hit the waves, they left them. Ko Phangan was just a few hundred metres ahead. The transformation was so sudden that Carlo felt as if he'd woken from a nightmare. In the relative calm he listened as conversation picked up and the hum of the boat's engine became audible for the first time since leaving Ko Samui. People who had spent the journey groping about the deck on their knees began to sit upright. Nervous laughter broke out. Finally, the woman in the transparent frock realised that a man was leering at her. As their eyes met, Carlo winked at her, and the woman blushed. She made a vain attempt to pull the frock free of her wet skin, and stared desperately out to sea.

Once ashore, Carlo brushed himself down. He looked back out to a sea that, he decided, was one which kept secrets. From land, in the dark, the waves were invisible. He realised that they could have drowned just a few hundred metres from groups of tourists enjoying an early dinner and nobody would have noticed. Carlo growled and stomped quickly inland; he wanted to dry out and get a drink. The stupid expression on the captain's face and the pathetic reaction of the passengers angered him. He visualised Maurice's face. He had to get away before he beat somebody to death.

He booked into one of the island's more up-market thatched huts and took a shower in his en-suite bathroom. He felt good now that he was back in control. He dressed quickly and walked to a sea-front bar for a drink. He ordered a beer. 'A cold one,' he added. *Not bad work when you can get it,* he told himself, his adventures on the high seas all but forgotten.

He had noticed several posters advertising a full-moon party later that evening in front of one of the bars above the beach. *Good timing,* he thought; *good timing rather than good luck.* Any good luck he enjoyed came homemade; everything that was to happen in Ko Phangan would be a result of his careful planning. It was all about detailed analysis of all the components, an understanding of the basic instincts of individuals, a skill, ironically, which he'd learned from Maurice.

His reverie was spoilt by thoughts of Kirsten. She had broken the mould; a totally unpredictable woman, the one person who could spoil everything. He was no longer certain whether he wanted to kill her or love her.

A breeze blew across the bar and Carlo sniffed the air like a hunting dog. He could sense Maurice's presence on the island. The notion brought him back to life and his eyes lit up beneath the darkening sky, mirroring the exhilarating terror that swelled inside him. He inhaled deeply. The party would attract Maurice like a vulture to a corpse. Only this time, while the vulture tore and consumed the flesh, he was going to pick his moment and send the distracted scavenger screaming back into hell.

I could be on my way home by morning, Carlo mused. He was roused from his dream-state by a waiter arriving with his drink. The man smiled as he lowered the tray onto the table.

'I'll pour my own,' Carlo growled and the man jerked nervously backwards.

The retreating waiter never looked back. Carlo turned his head towards the sea. He raised his glass to the drifting clouds high above the horizon. 'Cheers Andrew,' he said aloud.

Chapter 15

Andrew was in pretty good spirits. He'd had a few drinks and he was sitting with his favourite woman in his favourite Ko Phangan bar, and they had been making love all afternoon, and looking to the future. Kirsten had taken a swim while Andrew was snoozing and she had returned to the hut hornier than ever. He had never known such incredible sex.

She was looking marvellous tonight, Andrew thought. She was dressed in a light summer frock that wafted in the perfumed breeze. She had used a little make-up and she was even wearing a small pair of silver earrings that he had bought her in Bali. He felt good, even though he was still in shock. *Freedom does that to you*, he thought. 'Cheers,' he said aloud, raising his glass.

'Cheers,' Kirsten replied.

'I fancy Nepal,' Andrew suggested, knowing that Kirsten was in a good mood.

'Why not? Kirsten said. 'It is a good idea. I have had enough of Carlo and his stupid games, and Nepal will be beautiful in October.'

'We can go trekking somewhere, maybe go to Pokhara. Pokhara is supposed to be gorgeous; all lakes and restaurants. Then we could trek the Annapurna range. In October the snow-capped mountains are beautiful; the skies are crystal clear and you can see for miles.' At the thought of the mountains Andrew felt hope seeping into his veins. He couldn't believe that Kirsten wasn't arguing. The least she'd normally do was to suggest trekking somewhere else. Instead she was watching Andrew so eagerly that he thought she wanted to make love again.

'And I thought that all you cared about was food,' she said.

'Kathmandu is famous for buffalo burgers,' Andrew replied.

Kirsten laughed, the first genuinely uninhibited laugh Andrew had heard from her in ages.

'That's that then, we're sorted,' Andrew said, laughing at the thought of buffalo burgers. 'Won't it be marvellous when choosing a meal is our biggest nightmare again?'

'But first we have the party,' Kirsten said excitedly. She had her conspiratorial head on. 'How about some acid?' she said. 'Somebody will be selling it at the party.' She laughed. 'It's been so long.'

The thought made Andrew shiver. 'I don't think so,' he said. 'That's really tempting fate. I just know that we would end up thinking about Carlo. Can you imagine his arms grabbing at us through the walls like wriggling maggots, or him smiling and winking in techno-colour? We wouldn't be able to do anything about it all night.'

'Disgusting,' Kirsten said.

'Terrifying,' Andrew agreed. 'I don't even want to think about it. Let's keep things simple. Let's just get pissed.'

They ate late so that they could go straight to the party. Many people did. Others sat for hours on the beach, enjoying the slow pink sunset, smoking dope and talking up the party. Boatloads more crossed from Ko Samui for the big event.

A crowd gathered on the beach and in the restaurant above. Groups sat around bonfires on the perimeter, others sat further out, enjoying the spectacle. There were hundreds of partying westerners, so far from home, all gathered like far-flung clans. There was a bar on the beach but as most people were celebrating with LSD or ecstasy, the most popular drink was water. Music boomed from two enormous speakers erected on platforms on the sand, but nobody was dancing yet. It was still early.

Andrew and Kirsten took a table on the terrace above the beach and settled into a couple of rickety old wicker chairs, with a couple of ice cold beers. 'Will you be dancing tonight?' Andrew asked.

'For sure,' Kirsten said. 'I want to have a few drinks first though – get in the mood.'

As the evening progressed they were joined by a young English couple, Jonathon and Annabel. They were boisterously drunk and Kirsten found them annoying. They had a wild lifestyle, they boasted. 'We're taking some time off,' said Jonathon.

'Yes,' continued Annabel. 'We spend most of our time between Singapore and India smuggling cameras.'

'Smuggling cameras?' *Fucking mad,* Andrew thought. Life in an Indian jail didn't seem any better than those of South East Asia, and he couldn't see how it would be done anyway. 'I thought Indian customs wrote the serial number of your camera in your passport to stop you selling your camera?'

'They do,' said Annabel. She was twenty years old and full of shit, Andrew thought, without the experience to back it up. 'But we fly from Singapore to Delhi on flights that stop in Madras. At Madras, internal passengers join the flight and they don't have to go through immigration or customs because they're not coming from abroad. Everyone books seats at the back of the plane and we store the bags in the overhead lockers. We just swap bags when we get off. At Delhi they take our bags with them and, as they don't get searched, there are no problems. When we arrive we've got nothing illegal with us.' She swallowed her cocktail and coughed. 'We make two hundred dollars a flight each.'

'Aren't you worried that you will get caught?' Andrew asked. They didn't seem like people who had thought things through.

'Not really,' said Jonathon. 'Our only problem is the amount of time we spend on trains between Delhi and Madras. The journey takes thirty-seven hours.'

It seemed to Andrew that Jonathon wasn't overly enthusiastic about being a smuggler, and he recalled the stresses that he had gone through.

'I am going for a dance,' Kirsten said. The English couple were making her nervous. As she walked past Andrew the air was sweetened by a light perfume and he felt drawn to her. For a moment, he wanted to lead her away and make love to her in the darkness at the party's edge. He remained seated, though, and watched her make her way through the crowd until she reached the dancefloor. Kirsten hesitated at the edge of the dancing throng. She needed a moment to prepare mentally. Then, suddenly, she skipped forward into space and joined in.

Andrew loved the full moon parties. The first time he'd discovered one was in Goa and he didn't come across it until five o'clock in the morning. He'd been in Goa for just a few days and in the early hours one morning he woke to the sound of loud music, music that he had never heard before. His initial reaction was: 'What the fuck is that row?' and then he tried to get back to sleep. But it was impossible and, eventually, he dressed and went to solve the mystery. Following the dark, tree-lined alleys, he picked his way carefully over the crawling tree roots and listened for the sound. As he walked, the sound grew and drew him in. Shortly he came across an incredible spectacle: hundreds of travellers were partying to the sound of mesmerising electric music that was booming from stacks of speakers and, all around them, trees were decorated with coloured chalks and fluttering batiks. Andrew was struck by the way these westerners had made their home in a foreign land. They had found something good. They had realised their fantasies, at least for the moment. A guy rolling a joint at the wall had watched Andrew approaching. 'Man, you missed a good one tonight,' he said, and Andrew realised that there was something here that was going to consume him in time to come. He had discovered acid house and it hooked him like a drug. From then on he went to them all.

Kirsten was engulfed by a throng, one hundred strong, moving together, physically linked like the evolving cells of one being. Everything seemed to move in slow motion: arms swayed high in the air like hatching snakes; heads were raised in worship or in awe towards the moonlit sky, far out above the sea. Kirsten was as beautiful to Andrew as ever. Even so, like one of a million bright stars, for the moment, she seemed a little distant.

'Is she alright?' asked Jonathon. 'She looks uptight.'

'She's fine,' Andrew answered, absent-mindedly. The third-party observation surprised him, though. It was so easy to let yourself go so far from home. Strange events were beginning to seem normal, he thought. Somebody had once told Andrew that they thought he was a junkie because he was so pale and skinny. Andrew had checked himself in a mirror the next day once he was sober and only then did he realise how little care he'd taken of himself. He went on a month-long eating binge after that, and spent more time on the beach.

At the edge of the party a bright torchlight illuminated a group of people sitting on the sand. Their startled faces were caught in the powerful beam momentarily and, as they raised their palms to block out the glare, darkness returned. Moments later the beam picked out another group.

The torchlight picked out more and more faces as it moved around the perimeter. There was the outline of a figure beside the light now: a fucking loony, Andrew decided, had to be, pissing everybody off with his paranoid beam. Having identified one and all in the sand the torch died and the man walked into the mass of dancing, tripping, western youth. He passed near Kirsten. He seemed to be watching her feet splashing in the water, but he moved on. Then, suddenly, he looked in Andrew's direction and headed straight for him.

Andrew almost upended himself in shock. The man had him in his sights and was marching steadily towards him. Who the fuck was he? How had he noticed him watching from so far away? He really started to sweat as the realisation struck him: was it Carlo? Then as suddenly as he had begun, the man stopped, and directed his beam back into the throng. 'I'm getting fucking paranoid,' Andrew said aloud.

'What was that?' said Jonathon.

'Nothing,' Andrew said.

'Nothing?'

'Nothing to worry about: just me losing my mind.'

'Everyone's losing it,' said Annabel. 'Everybody's paranoid on Ko Phangan. It's the drugs. Were you talking to me?' she said aggressively, imitating the many dropouts she'd seen since arriving on Ko Phangan.

'Very funny,' Andrew said and, as he turned back towards Kirsten, a beam of light blinded him. 'Fuck!' he yelled, shielding his eyes with his left hand. 'What the fuck are you doing?'

The man behind the beam said nothing. Andrew rose from his chair and realised, with some relief, that it wasn't Carlo. 'Are you hunting moths, or something?' Andrew said. 'Do I fucking know you?'

Suddenly the light was extinguished and a man's face appeared. 'Please forgive me,' he said. 'I thought that you were somebody else.'

'Have you lost someone?' asked Annabel.

'No,' the man replied as he put the torch into his trouser pocket. 'I just hoped that an old friend might be here.'

'Have a drink with us,' said Annabel. Andrew was about to object when Kirsten reappeared.

'We have company,' Kirsten said, and she held out her hand.

The man shook it gently. 'I'm joining your table for a drink. Your friends have offered a lonely soul company. I'm Maurice.'

'Good company is always welcome,' Kirsten said. 'Andrew, please get us some drinks.' She held her smile until she wore through his unspoken objections. She knew him so well. In silence Andrew reluctantly walked to the bar.

Call me sensitive, Andrew thought, *but I'm not keen on people who hunt their friends with torches.* Actually, that was bullshit. He just didn't like the guy. He didn't know why; maybe it was because, even when he was embarrassed about blinding Andrew with the torch, he still seemed cocksure. He was the kind of guy who would steal Kirsten away just when he was doing so well. So he didn't waste time at the bar. He was right back.

'You don't mind me joining you?' Maurice said as Andrew placed the drinks on the table.

'Of course not,' Andrew lied, realising that Kirsten was watching him. He dug deep for some friendly small talk. 'Where have you come from tonight?'

'Nowhere in particular,' said Maurice lightheartedly, and most of his audience laughed.

'Mystery man,' said Jonathon.

'I'm sure I've met you before,' said Kirsten, and Maurice grinned as if to say that she had.

'People ask so many questions,' Maurice said. 'If they don't understand something, they are afraid of it. Sometimes it is nice to accept your surroundings and not worry about the detail.'

'You sound like you've been on Ko Phangan a long time,' Andrew said and, feeling Kirsten's angry eyes on him, he regretted it immediately.

'And?'

'No big deal,' Andrew said, trying to soften the insult, 'but this place can wear you down.'

'I will remember that,' said Maurice and he turned abruptly to speak to Kirsten. 'I saw you this evening, on the beach. You had been swimming.'

'That's right,' said Kirsten, rather too enthusiastically for Andrew's liking. *So that was why she came in so excited and horny after her swim*, Andrew thought. It hadn't been him who had got her so excited: it was this guy, Maurice.

'You obviously take good care of yourself,' said Maurice. 'Don't you agree, Andrew? She is a very beautiful woman.'

'She is,' Andrew answered. He couldn't be bothered to keep it friendly now. 'Too bad you're travelling alone,' he sneered. 'It must be frustrating watching everyone else having a good time.'

'If you are not comfortable with yourself, Andrew, then you will not be comfortable with others. I enjoy my own company.' Maurice turned to Annabel and Jonathon and changed the subject. 'Are you travelling together?'

'Yes,' said Jonathon.

'We're on our holidays,' added Annabel. *She wanted to start boasting again*, Andrew thought, *because she was so naive, so incredibly stupid*. One day they'd tell the wrong person. They didn't know this man. He could be anybody. How would they know?

'You make it sound as if you work?' said Maurice.

'Not here,' said Annabel. 'We work in India.'

'And what do you do?'

Annabel seemed to find words hard to come by all of a sudden.

'We smuggle cameras,' interrupted Jonathon with a slur and with one eye closed.

'Cameras?'

'And walkmans,' whispered Annabel, just for Maurice.

'Not whisky?' he asked. 'Or drugs?'

'No,' said Jonathon. 'Not worth the risk.'

Maurice smiled. 'And if there was no risk? Would you smuggle drugs?'

Jonathon sighed and leant forward until he was just inches from Maurice's face. He gripped the table to balance himself. 'No,' he said, and a ridiculous grin spread slowly across his face.

'Would you?' Andrew said, trying to relax Maurice's grip on Jonathon.

'Drugs are evil,' Maurice answered, smiling condescendingly as he helped Jonathon back into his seat. 'The West has used drugs as a control over the East for centuries. Your fine country created an opium dependency in China, and when the Chinese tried to put a stop to it you went to war with them. Hong Kong is a spoil of war; no different to the Nazis looting from the Jews.'

'We're hardly like the Nazis,' Andrew said, without thinking it through. He didn't like the way Maurice was climbing onto the moral high ground.

Maurice looked at Andrew as if he'd spilt a drink on his shoes. 'Now that the drug problem in Europe is becoming expensive, you want it stopped,' Maurice said. 'So you bribe source countries with aid. No, I wouldn't smuggle drugs and I despise anybody who does.'

Andrew decided to have another go. 'You might be right about the drugs,' he said, 'but is the West to blame for all of Asia's problems? Are all Asians really such kind-hearted, innocent people? Isn't there greed for power and money here? Don't Asians create any homegrown problems for themselves?'

'Greed is a human frailty, but we were talking about drug smuggling. Drug smugglers know the damage drugs can do, but they blind themselves to the problems. Of course the large cartels have no interest in human suffering, but what about people like you?'

'Like me? I'm not a drug smuggler.'

'Perhaps, but so many tourists think that it's okay to smuggle a few kilos; there is adventure in it. They make a few thousand dollars and, somewhere, somebody suffers as a result of their petty-minded sense of self-importance. Westerners who complain that Asians who eat dog are wicked are happy to trade in heroin, an evil that torments and destroys the lives of so many simple and ordinary people.'

Kirsten had kept silent. Secretly she was impressed by the way Andrew was standing up for himself, but she knew that Maurice was too clever for him. Now she wanted the conversation to end. 'Come and dance, Andrew,' she said.

'I don't like him,' Andrew said as they crossed the sand to the water's edge.

'Obviously,' said Kirsten. 'You were rude to him.'

'How?'

'Everything you said was an accusation.'

'Do you like him?'

'He is intelligent.'

'He thinks that you're a Nazi and I'm an opium war lord!'

'But what he says is true.'

Andrew let out a sigh. 'It's hardly our fault, though.'

'He was just making a point.'

'He fancies you, and he knew he was getting up my nose.'

'He has good taste,' said Kirsten. 'And you're just jealous.'

Andrew accepted defeat.

They returned to the table half an hour later. Maurice was still talking. The English couple were listening, red-eyed, with all the intensity of two paralytic drunks hanging desperately onto the pretence of sobriety. 'You dance well together,' said Maurice when he saw them. He nodded at Annabel and Jonathon. 'We have been invited to have a drink at Jonathon and Annabel's. I could do with a break from the noise.'

Andrew was feeling happy, the dance had done him good, and he picked up on Maurice's change of attitude. 'Can't do any harm,' he said, and Kirsten squeezed his hand in approval.

Jonathon and Annabel shared a hut similar to Andrew's, but their's was far from the crowds, along the beach, hidden beyond a rocky headland. The door looked out across the verandah towards the sea, which tonight, at low tide, was silently lapping the sand, twenty metres away. On a stormy day the sea sometimes slapped against the beams supporting the hut, washing coconut husks and dead palm fronds onto the grass beyond. Palm trees hung overhead. The thatched roof was patched where a coconut had crashed through during the rains. There was no electricity. The only light came from a row of flickering candles and the warm glow of a fully rounded moon, which was reflected off the sea.

They carried their drinks from the bar. A borrowed bucket of ice chilled the cokes while Maurice prepared five glasses of Mekong whisky. Jonathon was behind the hut somewhere, supporting Annabel who was using a bush for a toilet. Andrew and Kirsten took time out to test the water with their toes.

'Your drinks are ready,' Maurice called from the balcony, and Andrew and Kirsten walked back along the hard sand. They followed Jonathon and Annabel up the steps to the hut, giving Jonathon a helping hand. Jonathon was barely able to stand but he had an arm around Annabel, who was close to utter helplessness, and, somehow, they reached the verandah.

Even so it was Annabel who emptied her glass first, grabbing it without ceremony from the rattan table where it rested and downing it in one go. The alcohol hit her like a slap and her head rose for a moment before slinking back into her neck. She laughed and, as she grabbed another glass, she almost knocked the ice bucket off the table. 'One more before bed,' she said and emptied it.

'Be careful,' said Maurice, clearly irritated, his pretentious control seeming to slip. 'We only have enough Mekong for one glass each.'

'That's okay,' Kirsten said and she passed a glass to Jonathon, who wasted no time in drinking it. 'Coke will do me.'

As Kirsten spoke, Andrew watched events unfold. Disaster loomed and Maurice was in for an almighty disappointment. Out of the corner of his eye, Andrew saw Annabel lose control of her left leg. It wobbled at the knee and her body scrambled to compensate. She slipped and staggered, her right leg trying desperately to hold her up. Jonathon could only watch through a fog. As Andrew turned to reach for her, she crashed past him in a flurry of arms and legs, heading for the railing around the verandah. She lunged out at Andrew, trying to save herself and crashed onto the small rattan table, her wrap-around skirt billowing like a sail in the wind. Bottles and glasses and ice buckets and ice cubes crashed onto the floor, rolling and sliding over the edge of the verandah onto the beach. There were no survivors.

'Help her Andrew,' said Kirsten, sounding half embarrassed, half amused. Andrew was drawn to the fact that Annabel's skirt had unravelled itself and she turned out to have a very nice pair of legs.

Somehow Jonathon reacted first, but he only succeeded in falling onto Annabel's back and Andrew couldn't help but laugh.

Maurice stepped forward and pulled Jonathon up. He got a grip beneath his arms and effortlessly dragged him into the hut. 'Time for bed,' he said.

With Kirsten's help Andrew got Annabel onto her feet and dragged her through to Jonathon. They dumped her on the bed beside him and stood back to look at them.

'They're finished,' said Maurice.

'For now,' Andrew added. Maurice turned out of the hut and Andrew heard him say 'Perhaps,' as he went.

Kirsten shut the door and they were left standing on the balcony, surveying the damage.

'Never mind,' said Maurice. 'Let's go back to the party. I'll buy you both a drink.'

Andrew had had enough, but Kirsten wanted a drink. With a little persuasion Andrew got his compromise, though, convincing Kirsten to return to their hut for a break. 'I'm almost out of cash,' he said. 'I'll need more if I'm going to get my round in.' Maurice went to find a table. He promised that their drinks would be waiting.

The door to the hut was ajar. 'I definitely locked it,' Andrew said as they mounted the steps. He pushed the door open with the tips of his fingers. There was a candle and matches just inside the door. With a flash and a slowly building flicker, the room lit up. Nothing had been disturbed.

'Andrew, your money?' said Kirsten.

'I lied about the money,' he said. 'I just wanted to get away.'

Kirsten sighed but said nothing. 'Let's check the bags anyway,' she said.

'Nothing has been taken,' Andrew said following a cursory check. 'Maybe I did forget to lock the door.'

'No,' said Kirsten. She was holding the padlock. 'It is broken,' she said. 'Somebody has been here for sure.'

'But they haven't taken anything,' Andrew said. 'It doesn't make sense.'

'Nothing makes much sense these days,' said Kirsten.

'Do you think it could have been Maurice?'

'He couldn't know that this is our hut. He couldn't have got back here before us, either.'

'He didn't,' said a voice from outside.

'Carlo!' Andrew gasped.

'Where did you go tonight?' Carlo said. 'I went for a fucking piss but, when I got back, you'd disappeared.'

Kirsten was stunned, half expecting him to exact instant revenge, knowing the kind of man he was, knowing the limits of his humanity. But her anger overtook her. 'You were spying on us?' she said indignantly.

'Keeping an eye on you, actually,' said Carlo. 'You have been keeping interesting company.'

To his surprise Andrew was first to understand what Carlo meant. 'You know Maurice?'

'Yes I know him.'

'Who is he?' said Kirsten.

'An old friend,' Carlo said. He noticed the padlock in Kirsten's hand. 'Sorry about that, but I had to find you again.' Carlo saw the fear on their faces. He would have to be blind not to, even in the candlelight. 'I'm not here for the money,' he said. 'You can give me back my fucking passport though.'

'How did you get here without it?' said Kirsten.

'Don't worry about it,' Carlo answered as Kirsten handed it over. 'So tell me,' he said, 'will you be meeting Maurice again?'

'He's got drinks waiting,' Andrew said. 'But I can live without him.'

'No,' said Carlo. 'I need you to meet him.'

'Why?' said Kirsten.

'Because you owe me,' Carlo said, his patience wearing thin. 'I want you to get him away from the party. Bring him to the beach. It shouldn't be too difficult for someone like you.'

'Someone like you?' Andrew repeated angrily. 'What do you mean by that?'

'I mean a tart like Kirsten should be able to lure a horny, murdering bastard like him down to the beach. She's made fools of men before – you and me both! What the fuck else do you think I mean?'

Before Andrew knew what he was doing, his fists were clenched and he was on the move.

Carlo was ready. 'Don't try it, chickenshit,' he said, showing Andrew absolutely no respect.

Andrew couldn't help himself. He kept on going even though he knew that he had no chance.

'Andrew, stop!' Kirsten shrieked, pushing him back against the far wall. 'Don't get yourself hurt over me.'

Just as Andrew was thinking that he'd impressed Kirsten without the accompanying pain, Carlo rushed at him and, in a flash of light and a shuddering blur, he landed a punch so hard that Andrew's head almost went through the back wall. Andrew tried to stand but his legs wouldn't allow it. When Carlo followed up the punch with a kick between the legs, Andrew fell to the floor, groaning in agony.

'I'll do it!' screamed Kirsten, and even as Andrew was dribbling saliva on the floor, he smiled at the thought that Kirsten really did care about him.

'Fucking right you'll do it,' Carlo sneered with malice. 'From now on you will do exactly as I say. From now on the police are the least of your problems. Do you understand? I'm your fucking problem now.'

'If I do this you will let us go?' Kirsten said, looking to Carlo for confirmation.

Carlo became thoughtful. 'Lure him to the beach and you will never see me again,' he said.

'What will you do with him?' said Kirsten.

'None of your business.'

'Does he owe you money?'

'Not money.'

'Then what?'

'Absolutely none of your fucking business.'

To Andrew's utter surprise Carlo kicked him again and he squirmed back into his foetal position, the one he did best.

'Just do as I say or I will kick your chickenshit boyfriend to death. And this time Andrew is the one staying with me. You can go alone.'

Maurice was furious. He had taken on too much by involving Jonathon and Annabel. As a result he might have lost Andrew. Andrew had found a way under his skin. He hadn't been afraid to argue, but nothing he had said had been of interest. More than ever he needed to get rid of him. Maurice liked Kirsten, though; something about her reminded him of himself. She had real strength. She didn't say much but she took everything in. It might have been interesting to have known her better.

He put the thought out of his mind when he saw her approaching the table alone.

'Where is Andrew?' Maurice said.

'Gone to bed,' said Kirsten, 'I just came to tell you.'

'But your drink?'

'I've had enough,' said Kirsten. She hesitated and Maurice thought her nervous.

'Are you okay?' said Maurice.

'I'm going for a swim. I wondered whether you would like to come, too.'

So that's it, thought Maurice, *Andrew is out of the way and she wants me. Of course she's nervous.* 'Why not?' he said.

They left the party and headed back along the beach. Kirsten took off her sandals and carried them in her hands. Behind them the noise faded and individuals at the party became a mass of swaying silhouettes, illuminated by flickering bonfires. Small groups squatted amongst the palm trees, smoking, drinking, whispering and laughing. With each palm tree, the groups dwindled. Then there were the couples. Five minutes was all it took for a comfortable silence to descend upon them.

When, at last, the faint sound of the sea could be heard above the booming of the music, they stopped. 'This is good,' said Kirsten, looking back through the trees.

'You seem nervous,' said Maurice, detecting a slight quiver in her voice. 'You weren't so shy earlier today.'

'I just want to be sure that we are alone.'

Maurice laughed.

Kirsten turned her back on him. They were at the agreed spot. Maurice was talking to her but she didn't turn to face him. Where was Carlo?

Suddenly Maurice grabbed her by the wrist and pulled her roughly towards him. 'This was your idea,' he growled, tightening his grip as Kirsten tried to slip free. 'Don't play games with me. Don't waste my time.'

Maurice twisted her wrist and she fell to the sand. She rolled and kicked out with her feet but Maurice knelt over her and held her down.

He slapped her across the face. 'Shut up,' he sneered. He reached into his pocket and found some small capsules. 'These will make you more receptive,' he said. He gripped Kirsten's face with one hand, trying to force her mouth open. He punched her quickly in the stomach, one sharp jab, but Kirsten locked her teeth tight and twisted her face away.

Maurice punched her again. Then he took out a flick-knife. He flicked a button on the side and a blade flashed across Kirsten's face.

She screamed.

Chapter 16

Against his better judgement Andrew was out of cover, like a cork from a bottle, and charging at Maurice. Carlo was somewhere behind him, having fallen on his face trying to stop him. Maurice looked up as Andrew lashed out and he took the blow in the mouth. Somehow Andrew kept on running, his arms flailing wildly for balance, but the fall had to come and one leg went, then the other, then he was on his knees and finally he sprawled chin first in the sand.

Kirsten's hands were set free and she lashed out, clawing at Maurice's face. Maurice yelled as fingers gouged his cheeks and eyes. Defensively he raised himself out of reach and, with a yell, he grabbed Kirsten hard by the throat. Then he punched her hard in the face and knocked her out.

Maurice stood to face Andrew, who was pulling himself up from the sand. Somehow everything had fallen back into place, he thought. He whipped his knife out to one side and strode forwards. As he did so, Carlo charged him from behind.

Maurice heard the snorting charge as Carlo thumped across the sand and he twisted to face him. Carlo was carrying one of those machetes the islanders use to chop coconuts; one blow and Maurice's skull would open, and his coconut brains would spill all over the sand. But as Carlo lashed out with the machete, Maurice stood to one side and put out a leg. With one arm he held Carlo by the wrist, just for a second, and sent him crashing to the sand.

Carlo recovered instantly and was on his feet before Maurice could close him down. 'So, these fools are yours,' said Maurice, and Andrew realised that they were definitely not amongst friends.

'You're the fool, Maurice,' growled Carlo, looking slightly embarrassed after his tumble. 'You took the bait. A quick filleting and it will soon be over.'

Maurice caressed his knife and stepped closer. He indicated Carlo's machete. 'Such subtlety,' he said and, as Carlo glanced down, Maurice rushed at him. Maurice head-butted Carlo with such ferocity that Andrew heard the cartilage in Carlo's nose disintegrate like a snail underfoot. Andrew knew that Carlo would be partially blind now as the searing pain rushed through him in sickening waves, but Carlo didn't seem to notice. He punched and lashed out with the machete, forcing Maurice backwards, but Maurice was weaving and grinning, his knife was high in the air and then low, moving so fast that it was difficult to follow. Carlo advanced, shuffling heavily, flat-footed, dragging the machete by his side, hoping to smother his dancing enemy.

Maurice was in again, this time kicking Carlo in the knee, trying to break his leg, and flashing the knife past his face. Carlo responded with a grunt and a series of wild slashes and punches and, this time, he landed a blow with the flat side of the machete on the side of Maurice's head. Maurice spiralled across the sand, landing lightly on his side, rolling and rolling and up again.

They faced each other, four metres apart; Maurice grinning although looking slightly stunned, Carlo gasping for air, doubled up like a fat old man. Once again Maurice flew at Carlo, his knife flashing through the air once, twice, three times in quick succession and this time he ripped open the back of Carlo's left hand. But even as Carlo succumbed to the pain, letting out an agonised yelp, he followed Maurice with his machete and hit him hard on the back of the head. Maurice staggered on a few paces and tumbled into the sand, only metres away from Andrew. Andrew could see the bemused look on Maurice's face as he spat sand and blood from his mouth.

Maurice staggered to his feet and he stared at Andrew for a second, a second during which Andrew felt drawn to him, like a lemming to a cliff, hypnotised with fear and a longing for everything to end. His entire framework began to tremble. He was rooted to the spot. If the sea came in now he'd drown. Andrew felt strange. Maurice was welcome to kill him now if he wished. He suddenly had no fear of death … only a fear of him.

Carlo attacked and delivered Andrew from the spell. For the first time Andrew realised that he wanted Carlo to win. He knew whoever lost would die and if Carlo lost then both he and Kirsten would die too. The two men were wrapped together, like energetic lovers desperately pulling off their clothes. There were hands and arms and knees and feet and faces shoved into faces, and there was biting and clutching and screaming and panting and groaning and the smell of sweat and of blood. As Andrew listened to the animal sounds and began to hope that maybe they'd kill each other, he noticed something silent and peaceful escaping from them; a piece of paper, fluttering and wafting like a scented petal in the breeze, drifting away from battle, escaping them, landing gently on the sand.

His eyes were glued to it. The fight was in the background, out of focus. Whatever that piece of paper was, Andrew felt that it was important, something to unlock the mystery, and he wanted it desperately. He imagined himself following that piece of paper to the end of the world, running with Kirsten, running from here, running…

Carlo was badly hurt. Maurice stood back panting, as Carlo held onto his stomach. A dark patch spread across his shirt, which was already soaked in sweat. His strength was gone. Maurice was just standing there, at the water's edge, panting hard, wiping sweat from his brow, but doing nothing. Andrew couldn't understand what was happening: he had Carlo now and, then, Andrew realised that Maurice had lost his knife. Carlo could hold him off without it. Panic set in and Andrew's imagination sharpened. Maurice needed to locate his knife. If he was able to finish Carlo, he could do the same to Kirsten. Andrew could run but Kirsten was lying, dazed in the sand.

Andrew could feel the adrenaline rushing to his head and he had to calm himself to think. The knife was in the sand somewhere, probably somewhere near where Carlo was kneeling now, and Andrew realised that Maurice wanted to get there first. Andrew couldn't allow that to happen. He saw the knife, half-buried behind Carlo. 'It's right behind you, Carlo!' Andrew yelled, but Carlo couldn't move. Maurice would get there first. Fighting his fear, Andrew dashed forward and dived upon the knife. He stood his ground as Maurice charged and as he shook with fear, Carlo finally stood with the machete hanging limply by his side.

Carlo was bleeding to death and Maurice was waiting like a jackal for him to die. Andrew had the knife, but it was Carlo who was keeping Maurice away. Like some pathetic hero, Andrew stepped forward and stood over Carlo, like a centurion, fending Maurice off. Then he bellowed into the darkness, shouting for help, knowing that, even if nobody came, Maurice would have to think again.

Maurice stepped back. 'You had the advantage tonight my friend,' he said, a hint of frustration in his voice. 'But I know you now, and I will find you again.' Then he turned and walked back up the beach. It occurred to Andrew that Maurice was referring to him.

People appeared on the sand. They were all Thais. Kirsten was sitting up near the trees and nobody bothered with her. Blood was seeping through Carlo's shirt and soaking into the sand. The piece of paper was beside him. The paper's edge was wet with blood and didn't look quite as enticing as it did earlier, but Andrew stooped quickly and stuffed it into his pocket without anyone noticing.

He realised that somebody was talking to him. 'Is this your friend?' The question was posed by a young Thai. 'You must help him.'

Another man rolled Carlo onto his back. He ripped his shirt and used it to stem the bleeding. 'Do you have money?' the young Thai said. 'We can get a doctor but there will have to be payment.'

'Yes, we have money,' Andrew replied. 'Our hut is at the top of the beach,' he said. 'We can take him there.'

Carlo was laid out on their bed and all but the young Thai departed. 'My friend is sending for a doctor,' he said. 'It will be twenty minutes before he gets here but the bandages have slowed the bleeding. It is not as serious as it looks. He is lucky.'

Kirsten looked pretty sick. 'Thank you,' she said, just to convince herself, by the sound of her own voice, that she was still alive.

Andrew couldn't get over the idea that he'd be spending money on Carlo. It seemed to him that, even if he did steal it from him, he had certainly earned it now. He'd saved his life. 'Will the doctor be expensive?' he asked and he surprised himself. Something in him was listing the possibilities. What if Carlo died? If only they'd killed each other in that fight then they really would be free of them both. But Andrew had an audience and he realised that he needed to be a little more diplomatic. 'Forget it,' he said, 'It doesn't matter what it costs.'

'The doctor will not be expensive. That is not the problem. But you were fighting with knives and that is the problem. Secrets from the police are not cheap.'

The Thai walked out onto the verandah leaving them alone with Carlo. Carlo called Andrew across to him. 'Listen,' he said. 'You must keep the police out of this.'

'How?'

'Come on. In Asia you do everything the same way. You spend money. Don't you ever learn? Money, Andrew, money is what it's all about. In Asia anything worth having costs money. That's why I love the place. I can do what I like here because I have money.'

Andrew looked at Carlo and for the first time Carlo seemed helpless. His eyes had trouble focusing and Andrew felt scared.

'I don't believe that's completely true, Carlo,' Andrew said.

'Andrew, how do you think I got here without a passport? I didn't shoot anyone. I just bought another. Business Andrew, that's what it's all about.' Carlo closed his eyes for a second. He was breathing hard. 'So now I want you to wield some power. Give the man outside three hundred dollars. Tell him to talk to the doctor. No police, Okay?'

Andrew took the money from his money belt and walked outside. The Thai was sitting in his chair. He looked up as Andrew showed him the wad of money and he smiled. 'You will be okay now,' he said, and he walked away without looking back.

Andrew took a deep breath and returned to the others. 'He didn't ask any questions at all!'

Carlo laughed, which was not the reaction Andrew expected.

'You don't have to worry about me any more,' Carlo said. He pulled himself up. 'I will get out of here in the morning. Your contract is terminated. You can go. I suggest you get as far away from Maurice as possible, though. He's a dangerous bastard, and he doesn't like you.'

Kirsten had remained silent. She had been happy to let Andrew deal with things. But there was too much happening and so much that she didn't understand. 'How do you know him? Why did you want to hurt him?'

Despite his obvious pain Carlo couldn't hide his anger. 'I didn't want to hurt him: I wanted to fucking kill him.'

'But what has he done to you?'

Carlo's eyes rolled in their sockets. He wiped blood from the side of his mouth with the back of his hand. 'That man screwed up my life. He's a cold-blooded killer. He's cut me to pieces! He butchers tourists for fun and he would have killed you too if he'd had the chance. I was here to finish him and, until now, he didn't know I was onto him. Fuck knows how I'll find him after this mess!' He was ranting now. 'He thinks you're a fucking smuggler, Andrew. He was here to kill you, you know.'

'What do you mean?' Andrew squeaked. 'Why would he want to kill me? He doesn't know me. You're talking rubbish.'

'What about the diamonds Andrew brought in for you?' Kirsten asked unexpectedly. Things were becoming clearer to her. 'You haven't asked about them. Did Maurice know that Andrew was smuggling diamonds for you? Is that what this is all about?'

Carlo didn't answer. He had worked himself up so much that the wound was bleeding again. He closed his eyes and calmed himself, and both Andrew and Kirsten got the feeling that he'd let something slip.

'Listen,' he whispered. 'Leave me alone, will you? Go down to the beach. I won't need you here when the doctor comes. I need some time alone. I'll talk to you tomorrow.'

There was a moment's silence while everybody considered their position. Carlo's eyes had closed. Andrew and Kirsten were staring at him, waiting for him to speak or die or do something, but he was all done now and so they left.

'What are we going to do now?' Kirsten said, as much to herself as to Andrew.

'Nothing I suppose,' said Andrew. 'If he leaves tomorrow, we'll never see him again and we still have the money. If he leaves we will be fine, although if Maurice is still around I would sooner be somewhere else. Let's get away from here tomorrow.'

'Good idea Andrew,' Kirsten said sarcastically, incredulous that he might have thought otherwise.

The moon was nowhere to be seen but there was still just enough light to find their way along the sand. 'Things will get better,' said Kirsten, and, although Andrew didn't believe her, he was glad to hear her say it. Her strength was something that he hoped would rub off on him. So, as they curled up beneath a palm tree, he didn't tell her that he was actually worried that things were likely to get much worse.

When dawn broke they had the option of sitting tight or returning to their hut. Neither idea was appealing. More than anything they didn't want to see Carlo again, but they couldn't just sit on the beach all morning. They decided to try out Jonathon and Annabel's place. As it was their best option Kirsten put her dislike of them to one side.

They found the hut in silence. It was exactly the way they had left it. After last night's chaos they didn't think that they could wake them up, so they unfurled the hammock above the verandah and climbed unsteadily into it. They fell asleep together.

Three hours later they were awake again. Annabel and Jonathon were still asleep. 'We cannot stay here all day,' said Kirsten sleepily. 'We must wake them up and tell them what happened.'

'I doubt they'd believe us,' Andrew said. 'But we'd better warn them about Maurice. You know...'

'What?'

Andrew thought a moment. 'We came pretty close last night. On the beach I thought he was going to...'

'Me too,' said Kirsten. 'But you stopped him.'

A shiver ran through Andrew. 'Yeah,' he answered, too tired to say much else. He clambered out of the hammock. 'I'm going to wake them up,' he said with a sigh. 'We'll tell them about last night and then we'll bugger off.'

'Where to?'

'Who cares?'

Andrew peered inside the hut. The room was silent and in darkness. Andrew was alarmed by a revolting stench. He couldn't believe that Annabel and Jonathon had been that drunk, although of course they had been. He had to wake them, so he crept inside and pushed open the window above the bed. The two of them were curled up beneath a sheet. Jonathon's back was facing Andrew, but he could see Annabel's face and, in particular, her eyes; her small, round, brown eyes. They were wide open, hiding behind a milky film. She was staring at nothing and he knew immediately that she was dead.

His first thought was to leave the room. Knowing now what the smell was he held a hand over his nose and tried hard not to breathe. He fully expected to vomit, especially as he checked Jonathon. Instead of running outside, which seemed like the obvious thing to do, he blinked hard, swallowed, and walked around the bed to look at him.

Jonathon was wearing the same vacant expression.

Andrew opened his mouth to say something and nothing but dry, rasping air hissed from his throat. He tried to wet his mouth with saliva but it was impossible. 'They're both dead,' he croaked, realising that Kirsten was standing in the doorway. 'That bastard, Maurice, must have poisoned them.'

Andrew stared at Kirsten. He needed to hold her. He had to comfort her. He had to comfort himself. He put his arms around her

113

and pulled her in close to him, but her body was limp, she didn't respond, and Andrew was convinced that if he let her go she'd fall. Suddenly she inhaled so deeply that he loosened his grip. She pushed him away and hit him. She hit him again. Then she rushed at him, her arms flailing wildly, landing punch after punch. She was screaming now and punching harder, but Andrew couldn't see her because his hands were covering his face and he was getting into a crouching position, waiting for the beating to stop. But the blows rained down on him, hard blows to the top of his head, and kicks; she was kicking him, harder and harder and the screaming continued, but it was not Andrew's name she was screaming, just 'bastards'. She was screaming the word 'bastards' over and over and over.

After what seemed like hours, but was probably only seconds, Kirsten suddenly stopped. Andrew was feeling groggy from the assault and he knew that he was going to have two black eyes; one from Kirsten and one from Carlo. He'd never felt lonelier or more confused in his life, but he was sure that Kirsten was just upset. He could hear her panting and gasping for breath, close to exhaustion. *It isn't me she hates*, he thought. *She was just in a state of shock.*

Kirsten certainly was in a state of shock. She felt tainted; it was as if Maurice had killed Annabel and Jonathon simply to prove how easy it was. He had done it as a form of abuse against her. She wanted to kill him, but now she was holding onto Andrew, whom she had used as a substitute, sobbing quietly to herself. She was standing against Andrew's kneeling body and holding his head to her stomach. She was sobbing but saying nothing. How could she have allowed this to happen?

It was some time before they could look at each other. They were comfortable as they were. But Andrew's knees began to ache and he stood. They held on tighter than ever and Andrew could feel Kirsten's wet, hot face dampening his T-shirt. His head was sore and his face ached, and he realised that he was in bad shape.

'Am I so old?' Andrew asked and Kirsten laughed into his chest.

'No,' she said.

'But you don't love me?'

'I don't love myself. How can I love you?'

'But you do care?'

Kirsten was silent. She tightened her grip.

'I know you care.'

'I'm happy that you're alive.'

'Happy that I'm alive?'

'Yes.'

'That's very comforting,' Andrew said, although he really didn't know what she had meant.

'You are a good man. I didn't mean to hit you. You have harmed nobody. You were the only one here. I'm sorry.' It had been a while since she had apologised for anything.

When they got back to their hut a sweat-stained, blood-soaked sheet was all that remained of Carlo.

They stood in silence above the bed, the light from the doorway shining on a pool of blood by their feet. The room smelt of death. They dragged the sheet from the bed and hurled it into the corner of the room. But it did no good: the mattress was drenched.

There wasn't much to pack and what there was they hurriedly stuffed into their bags. 'We should tell the police,' said Andrew. 'We should tell somebody.'

'No,' said Kirsten hurriedly. 'Just pack. Let's get the fuck out of here.'

Chapter 17

Andrew's lungs filled with smoke and his head drifted on a cloud of leisurely escape. He turned his head towards Kirsten. She was laying just a metre away. Andrew exhaled through a glazed smile, then his eyes flickered closed and he laid his head on the pillow. A man kneeling beside him took away the opium pipe and the room emptied. That was enough for now.

They were in a Red Lahu village in a clearing in the middle of a forest in North-west Thailand. The village was a collection of thatched bamboo huts built on muddy clearings cut from the forest, which was constantly encroaching and clambering over fallen picket fences, trying to reclaim its territory. Tall outcrops of green bamboo dwarfed the huts like droopy flagpoles; broad-leafed banana trees huddled together like shy children. Above the village, green hills dominated the skyline, the dark canopy rolling like a mass of impenetrable storm clouds. The hills were alive with the distant shrieks of birds and monkeys. The outside world was kept at bay by a natural barrier of winding rivers and forest that had taken Andrew and Kirsten hours to overcome.

Their wooden hut was raised on high stilts above piles of earthenware pots, bamboo baskets and firewood cut from the forest. The walls were built from bamboo and the roof was thatched with grass. To get up there they had to climb a four-rung bamboo ladder, which led into a living area with an open fire. The ceiling was blackened with soot because there was no chimney, and the walls were thinning in places where they were in need of repair. There was a hint of sky through the roof. There was no furniture; everyone squatted on the floor on mats.

Once inside the hut they had removed their shoes and were led into a darkened bedroom, where they found a row of woven mats to lay on. Tourists had been before; they had left a Walkman behind, probably during a hill tribe trek organised by a tour company to see the 'real Thailand.' After a day spent riding around on the back of an elephant it had probably seemed like the obvious thing to do.

The Red Lahu was one of a dozen or so hill tribes, known locally as mountain people. They grew corn, rice and opium, and Andrew and Kirsten were trying the latter. They were a hospitable people, sharing their meals of sticky rice, spicy noodles and fish, and making conversation with sign language. One old boy gave Andrew a fright when he had stroked his arm. Andrew had shied away with a start and scowled at him, but the man had laughed and explained that the villagers didn't have hair on their arms or legs. He just wanted to know what it felt like.

Two weeks earlier, when Kirsten and Andrew had taken the air-conditioned bus up to Chiang Mai from Bangkok, they were just looking for somewhere to hide away, chill out and escape. They needed time to think, to decide and to plan. First they needed to come to terms with the fact that a man had tried to kill them, and that they had probably been used as bait to lure the man to his death. Two people had died as a result and the killer was probably still searching for them. If that were so, he would probably find them eventually. By the time they reached Bangkok, and Andrew had had plenty of time to think things out, he was adamant that they should fly home to Europe and tell somebody there. The idea was unwelcome but it seemed the most logical thing to do. Kirsten had refused; she would not run away any longer. She had learnt from experience, she said, that cancer should be cut out immediately.

No answer satisfied them so, in desperation, they took a bus from Chiang Mai along the winding road and through dense woodland towards Mae Hong Son, a small market town bordering Burma, so remote from Bangkok that it was known as the Siberia of Thailand. The town's name actually meant "The city veiled by mist" because of the dense cloud that covered it for months at a time.

They shared the bus with villagers and their sacks of vegetables and fruit, and one small pig. It was one of those journeys where everyone seemed to be sitting on their laps, even though they were standing. They left the bus about two thirds of the way to Mae Hong Son and headed into the forest to locate a village, one of many in the forest, where they had been told that they could smoke opium to their hearts' content.

Life was almost dreamlike. They couldn't believe that they had fallen in with such dangerous people, that their lives had taken such an unexpected turn. Andrew supposed it was like winning the lottery. It was something that never happened to you but, if it did, your life changed forever. And you're never prepared for it. He had always felt that people lived on the edge without knowing it. Every day cars almost killed people, while other people were run down. He suspected that the victims lived closer to the edge than the survivors did. Maybe the victims crossed roads more often. In India Andrew had stopped using buses because he'd taken so many bus journeys and somebody told him that, statistically, one percent of buses crashed. Every journey he took was increasing the likelihood of his dying in a bus crash and, whilst he doubted the statistics, he had seen so many road accidents in India, that there had to be some truth in it. Trains were more comfortable, anyway.

Andrew believed that travel was the best way to experience life; on the road, things happened more often. In the last year he'd enjoyed experience after experience, had more fun than in his previous life and met literally thousands and thousands of people. Statistically some of the experiences and some of the people had to be bad. Most tourists had a fantastic holiday, saw the world, only met nice people and returned home mentally exhausted but full of life. But a few didn't. Andrew got the feeling that they were to be the ones who didn't. They were the sacrifice. *Why us*, he wondered? It might have been easier to cope with if somebody had noticed what they were going through and said "thank you."

The first time they smoked opium in the village Andrew had vomited. Many people did. Kirsten said she did her first time. However now they knew their limits and were relaxed enough in the company of the villagers to accept that they had nothing to prove. So once they had had their fill, they dropped their heads into their pillows and grinned at the ceiling. Then they were left alone.

The village made much of its living from opium. Smoking opium in a hill tribe village was all part of the tourist trail. It was not in the brochures, of course, but it was on the lips of every tourist in Chiang Mai. Many of the villagers were addicts. Some children were born addicts. Some of the tourists who visited were addicts. Some were just there for one night of experience. Andrew and Kirsten were there because reality was clouding their ability to make their inevitable decision. Planning a man's murder was easier done without the assistance of reality. Knowing that he would probably kill them first anyway took a lack of reality, verging on insanity. How much opium would that take?

Andrew thought that he might be going through some kind of breakdown. What if this wasn't really happening? Maybe it wasn't. *It's possible*, he supposed. It was certainly possible that he'd overdone the drugs and that they had had some strange effect on him. No question that he'd overdone things; drinking, drugs, mixing with loonies. It was no surprise that he had worn himself out.

He fell asleep some time after dark, listening to the laughter and chatter of villagers outside their hut. He dreamt. There were many people in his dream and sometimes they turned out to be him, but mostly they were unfamiliar and falling in silent, slow motion past him into a void. Some of them, when they saw him, stretched out their arms and screamed in silence for help, but he couldn't reach them and they fell into darkness. There were other dreams, too. He saw his family. He dreamt that he was home and everyone was pleased to see him. He dreamt that he had never been away. He dreamt that he killed somebody. It was a friend, somebody close. But he was forgiven. People understood that it was an accident, but he found it impossible to forgive himself. He was guilty, he knew it. What did it matter what other people thought? He had killed his friend. There

119

could be no forgiveness. There would never be forgiveness. He was going to hell.

The dream woke him with a start and it took a while to realise that he was awake. In the period before his dreams took him away again he remembered how he had broken down in Bangkok the night they arrived from Ko Phangan. He remembered how he had discovered the piece of paper in his pocket, which he had picked off the sand after Carlo had fought Maurice. It was a photocopy of his passport details.

But was it Maurice or Carlo who had dropped it? At the time he couldn't answer the question, but he assumed now that it was Maurice. He had reacted badly, upsetting Kirsten by saying that he felt possessed. He demanded that they find a bar and, after what turned out to be a bout of heavy, all night drinking, he had stormed from the Khao San Road bar as tourists were taking breakfast. He ran ahead of Kirsten, staggering into restaurants, raging at everyone. 'You have no idea, you have no idea!' he had screamed with anger and frustration and drunken confusion. People had stared at him, some with amusement and others with sadness. He finally collapsed into a chair beside a group of bemused women and, by the time Kirsten caught up with him, he was sobbing and apologising like a fool. When he woke, sometime in the afternoon, it was too embarrassing for words, but at least he was in his own bed. Somehow Kirsten had got him there. 'Don't worry,' he told her. 'I won't go home without you, I won't let you down.' But the photocopy of his passport details travelled everywhere with him now.

Kirsten was asleep. Andrew watched her. He thought her beautiful in the half-light. Listening to her gentle breathing was so warming, so comforting to him, and knowing that she was free for the moment, knowing that she would wake in the morning beside him, was a feeling worth living for. And the fact that she was silent was a miracle itself. She was usually the one with the nightmares, not him. She was the one with a past. One of these days, he hoped she would tell him about it. One of these days, he hoped that they would understand each other.

Andrew drifted back to sleep and when he woke again it was light. The only sound was that of the river a few metres beyond the trees, below them. The air was damp but refreshing. There was the smell of wet earth. It took a moment for him to realise that he was awake, and to enjoy the relief. His dreams had left him feeling drained. He was hungry now and, for the first morning in more than a week, he didn't feel like a smoke. Now it was a clear head that he wanted. He was pleasantly surprised to find Kirsten awake. She rolled across the floor and slid herself into his arms. 'I want to leave here today,' she said, and Andrew nodded in agreement.

Although the village was quiet, it was awake. They gathered their belongings and left the hut. Outside, the village was shrouded in a refreshingly cool mist, now beginning to dissipate. Small groups of women dressed traditionally in red and black jackets were gathering together to head out to the fields or into market. Two others were weaving cloth and a group of tiny, naked children were trying to catch a chicken. Small pigs, squealing in excitement, chased each other through the mud, and water buffalo tethered beneath a thatched shelter stood motionless, staring at nothing. A gaggle of brown ducks waddled purposefully across a path, heads twisting and turning on their long necks, searching for admirers.

The owner of their hut looked up as they threw their bags over their shoulders, and he walked towards them. 'Tell your friends that this is good place,' he said shaking their hands. They thanked him and headed out of the village, following the river to the path. Seconds later they stepped through a wall of wet undergrowth and low hanging foliage, and the village disappeared behind them. They had a three-hour walk through the forest to the road. There they could catch a bus back to Chiang Mai.

'How can we find Maurice?' asked Kirsten, unexpectedly.

'Fuck knows.' Andrew answered, after a moment's hesitation. 'Start in Bangkok I imagine, but I don't know where.'

'How would he look for us?'

'His contacts, I guess.'

'What kind?'

'I don't know. People in immigration, maybe, the police, friends in high places, if he has them. Money's the key but I can't see anyone selling information to us. It really is like looking for a needle in a haystack.'

'So Maurice can find us but we cannot find him.'

'Yes.'

Kirsten frowned and Andrew thought that she was trying to get inside his head. She knew that he was opposed to the idea of hunting the hunters but she also knew that he had ideas. She was right, of course: he did have an idea how to find them.

So the interrogation began: 'Andrew?' Kirsten said at the edge of a bamboo outcrop. 'You love me don't you?'

'You know I do,' he answered. 'Why?'

'I didn't ask you to love me.'

'I know.'

'Love is not an emotion I am comfortable with.'

'Yeah,' Andrew said, wondering where the conversation was going.

'You don't expect me to love you?'

'No.'

'But even so you say that you would do anything for me?'

'Yes.'

'Then why will you not share your thoughts with me? I want to find Maurice, but you do not. And you know how to find him, I am sure of it.'

Andrew looked away, focusing on the river where it disappeared around a bend, obscured by trees. The river was finding a path around the hills and they would have to cross it several times before they reached the road. 'If we find him, we'll have to kill him,' Andrew said, like a robot. 'How can we live with that?'

'How can we live with the idea that he is killing people because we do nothing?'

'Maybe we should tell somebody.'

'Who would believe us?'

'I don't know.'

'Who do you trust?' said Kirsten.

'That's the problem, isn't it? I don't trust anybody.'

'Do you trust me?'

Andrew's hesitation annoyed her. 'Andrew? Do you trust me?'

'Of course,' Andrew replied, without conviction. 'Of course I do, but that's not the point.'

'No, the point is that this man is murdering people, and some of these people are our friends. They are backpackers and travellers just like us. And one day he will come for us. You know he will.'

Andrew wanted the conversation to end.

'Andrew what are you thinking?'

He was not strong enough to resist her. 'The photocopy of my passport,' he said.

'Yes?'

'I would bet that it was taken at the tourist police station in Bangkok.'

'And?'

'It was taken by one of the policemen and given to Maurice. They didn't do anything to me there. They just kept me for a while and let me go.'

'So what do you think?'

'I think I was set up. Maurice used the photocopy to identify me; that was why he was shining his torch in people's faces at the party. He was looking for me.' Andrew dropped his bag with a thud. He exhaled and put his hands on his hips. 'But I haven't got a fucking clue *why* he'd want to find me. And why kill me? Why kill Annabel and Jonathon?'

'It was us he wanted,' said Kirsten. 'He killed them because they could identify him. We were just lucky.'

'Yeah, I've never felt luckier.'

'Tell me what you are thinking.'

'I'm thinking,' he said angrily, 'that there was a clerk at the police station who might have done it.'

'Why do you think it was him?'

'He was the only other person I saw. He saw my records and there can't have been that many people who had access to my passport for long enough to photocopy it.'

Kirsten said nothing. She dropped her bag and hugged him. She slipped her hands beneath his T-shirt and caressed his back. She kissed his neck.

'The blokes who arrested me were setting me up for somebody to see me. They made it look like I was involved in something and whoever they wanted to see me photocopied my passport and gave it to Maurice. It wasn't the policemen, I'd bet they were working with Carlo. I heard him laugh at Maurice for taking the bait. I'll bet I was the bait. I think the money I found in Kupang was put there to tempt me. Once I nicked that, Carlo had me by the bollocks. The whole thing was a set-up.' He laughed without knowing why. 'I don't know why he bothered to be so fucking subtle?'

'He is a dangerous man, Andrew, but so is Maurice and I am sure that he is more of a danger to us. He killed Annabel and Jonathon just because they could identify him. He will have to kill us now. We must find him first.'

'Yeah,' Andrew agreed meekly, resigned to the obvious. 'But I could never kill somebody. I'd sooner be dead myself than do that.'

'But what if somebody else killed him? What if we helped Maurice find Carlo? What if we made it happen? Maybe they would kill each other. We would be free again. Isn't that what you want?'

'Of course that's what I want, but not like that.'

'You wouldn't have to. I know how to do it.'

'Don't be mad! They're both as strong as chimpanzees; they'd tear your arms out of their sockets and beat you to death with them.'

Kirsten stepped backwards and looked at Andrew with disdain. She loved his clever mind, although he didn't seem to realise it, but he could also be so pathetic. 'I'm not going to kill them. They will kill each other. What I mean is that I know a way to get them to do it.'

'How?'

Kirsten took a few seconds to get her ideas in order. 'First we talk to the police clerk in Bangkok. He will know how to find Maurice.'

'I'm sure he would, but why would he tell us?'

'We will convince him.'

'That's easier said than done.'

'Maybe, but it is the only way.'

'There has to be another.'

'Andrew, please listen to me.' There was a moment's hesitation while Kirsten waited for him to calm down. 'The clerk will know where Maurice is,' she said.

'But what good will that do us?'

'Carlo has a friend at the American Embassy in Jakarta, called Anthony. He must be the man who gives Carlo his passports. He will know where he is.'

'So?'

'First we talk to the clerk in Bangkok; he tells us where Maurice is. We tell Maurice where Anthony is. Anthony tells Maurice where Carlo is. They kill each other. Simple.'

'That's no different to killing them ourselves. We would still be responsible. Anyway, what happens if one of them lives? Do you think he will ever leave us in peace after that?'

'They won't.'

'I still can't do it.' Andrew stopped to consider his next line, but it was something he had to say – to himself as much as to Kirsten. 'Not even for you.'

The line hit home and Kirsten seemed stunned. Andrew felt as if he'd confessed that he didn't love her.

'You should do it for yourself, not for me,' Kirsten said, her heart still intact. She considered Andrew's comment for a moment. 'So if we can't kill them, what can we do?'

'I don't know. If we were home, we could just tell the police. I don't trust them out here, though.'

'We could tell Interpol?'

'Yeah?' Andrew answered, dubiously.

'Why not tell them?'

'I don't know?'

'We could write to them. They don't have to know who we are.'

'But what would we say? I would bet that Maurice and Carlo aren't their real names. What good would a letter do?'

'We could photograph them, somehow, and send the photographs to Interpol. They might already know about them, but they might not know where they are.'

The idea took Andrew by surprise. He couldn't believe that Kirsten had finally come up with a sensible idea. He was so relieved that he joined in. 'We don't need to get so involved,' he said. 'We can just tell them about Anthony. They could follow him to them.'

'We still need photographs.'

'Why?'

'Anthony won't know where to find Maurice.'

'So we tell them about the clerk, too.'

'No. We don't know for certain that it is the clerk.'

'But they can find that out for themselves.'

'And by the time they have done that Maurice will have escaped and we will be the only people left alive who can identify him. Do you want that?'

Andrew didn't have an answer.

'We must take some risks. We must find Maurice ourselves and photograph him.'

'But the clerk might tell him about us.'

'So we make sure that he doesn't.'

'How?'

'Blackmail.'

'What can we blackmail him with?'

'Let that be my problem,' said Kirsten. She gave Andrew a look that indicated his part in the conversation was over. 'Do this for me, at least?' she said. 'A few photographs and we can be free.'

Andrew wasn't convinced, but he smiled anyway. He didn't mind taking photographs, as long as he was not seen, but he was less keen about blackmailing Thai officials. The only good news, he thought, was that they were no longer planning murder.

Kirsten was standing by the riverbank. She was delighted by the result of their conversation. Everything that had happened on Ko Phangan had come as a shock to her; but now she had a plan and she felt so positive about herself again. They picked up their bags and, together, they waded into the cold water. They would be back in Chiang Mai by the evening.

Chapter 18

The clerk appeared in the alley outside the tourist police station and nervously made his way into the street. Andrew took note of his clothes so that he could spot him again in a crowd; a white, short-sleeved shirt worn outside his long blue trousers, and a belt to keep him tidy. He was a small man, maybe five feet four, and slim. His black hair, cut short, was receding, leaving a bushy strip in the middle of his forehead. He stopped at a crowded bus stop and peered ahead at a line of red buses stuck in traffic. Unseen by him amongst the human tide that was the Bangkok rush hour, Andrew waited on a hired motorbike in the hope that, today, something might happen.

Andrew had been following the clerk for two weeks. He knew where he lived, he knew where he shopped, he knew which cinema he liked to take his wife to and he knew where the children went to school. He also knew where the clerk took an occasional drink after work, depending on what shift he did. But that was it. There was nothing out of the ordinary to work with, nothing with which to blackmail the man.

So Andrew followed him each evening on his motorbike, whilst Kirsten watched the family. The clerk lived with his wife and two children near the main train station in a wooden shack, built on stilts above a canal. Laundry hung permanently over a high balcony, mirrored in the metallic black waters below. The rusting corrugated iron roofing nestled amongst the branches of a group of tall, overhanging trees, which gave the general squalor a sense of freshness and colour. The small community of shacks seemed like a riverside village dwarfed by a modern city that had grown up around it. For miles around there was nothing with which it could be compared.

That the family was poor was good news; they might be bought. If that was so then Andrew could afford what they might ask. But Kirsten didn't want to buy anybody; she wanted an advantage over them and, in Andrew's opinion, she had some pretty extreme ideas. She liked the idea of seducing the man and blackmailing him; no man could ever refuse a woman throwing herself at him, she said. Andrew had to agree that she was right, but the idea terrified him.

The man was not the enemy, Andrew was certain of it; he was just another victim caught up in the web. Because he was poor he was probably easy for Maurice to bribe. He had a family – it was understandable, and if he was anything like Andrew and Kirsten, he was probably terrified and trapped. Surely a substantial sum of money, perhaps a thousand dollars, would buy some information? Maybe if they said that they were getting rid of Maurice, the man might be only too keen to help. But the clerk also worked for the police. What if, in fact, it wasn't him who had supplied Maurice with the passport details? They were in Thailand, not at home. A word in the wrong ear and they were finished.

Then, one beautiful afternoon at the end of the week, shortly after the children returned home from school, Kirsten realised that a change had come about. While Andrew was still trailing the clerk, the man's wife left the house with the children and two bags and headed for the bus station. There she took a bus heading north. Kirsten immediately took a taxi and found Andrew before the clerk left work. They could only guess that his wife had gone away for the weekend, maybe to visit relatives. Even a weekend might be time enough, if they were lucky.

The clerk's bus came and went but, after some hesitation, he stayed where he was. Kirsten kissed Andrew's neck. There was hope, they realised. Ten minutes later the man boarded a different bus. Frustratingly, it took forty minutes to travel five miles. The traffic moved as slowly as plants grow and only pressing fast-forward on a video camera could have given any impression of movement. The air was thick with petrol fumes, which irritated Andrew's throat like raw onions.

Time stood still, but once the clerk stepped down from the bus, things happened quickly. Seconds afterwards he walked through the door of a bar in a neon-lit street and, with the swing of a door, he disappeared. Andrew pulled over quickly and Kirsten jumped off the back. She stood beside him and ran her fingers through her hair. 'I must follow him,' she said. 'He will recognise you.' Without waiting for a response from Andrew, she was gone.

A young Thai girl welcomed Kirsten inside: 'Come in, come in, no expensive, just buy beer.' So Kirsten walked to the bar, bought an ice cold beer and took a seat in a booth with plastic covered seats. She took a swig from her bottle and looked around, expecting to be mobbed, but nobody approached her or even looked at her and, to her surprise, she felt both insulted and relieved.

The clerk was sitting on a tall barstool chatting with one of the barmaids, seemingly oblivious to the half-naked women gyrating nervously around nearby steel poles; nymph-like dancers with tiny breasts and short, skinny legs, tiny backsides and sullen faces. Kirsten assumed that it was probably because they were so familiar to him. She looked at her watch. It was just after seven. *This must be where he always goes when his wife is away*, she thought.

Kirsten sat alone in her booth for an hour, nursing her beer. She was building up the courage to take a seat beside the clerk. His attention had finally moved from the barmaid to one of the girls on stage. The girl was wiggling her sparkling, silvery backside in the clerk's face, and he was laughing. He was already drunk. Suddenly, surprising everyone including himself, the clerk stood, reached forward and patted the dancer's backside. The girl looked down at him and laughed, but the clerk appeared horrified with himself.

As Kirsten feared that the clerk might run from the bar in embarrassment, people in the bar began to laugh. The look of horror on the clerk's face dissipated and was gradually replaced by an ugly, childish, self-satisfied grin. The dancer blew him a kiss and, suddenly, it was him in the limelight, not the girls. He was the star of the show, now. He acknowledged his applause and, in that moment, he spotted Kirsten across the dancer's podium. Without thinking, she smiled at him.

It was what she had wanted after all, but not how she had expected it to happen. Moments later he was standing unsteadily above her, his face tilted downwards, small fingers steadying his unsettled glasses, which were slipping from his nose. 'Please,' he said. 'May I sit here?'

Kirsten slid further into the booth. 'Of course,' she said.

The clerk shuffled across the seat and smiled nervously. 'May I buy you another beer?' he asked, and Kirsten nodded.

The drinks arrived moments later, delivered by a giggling barmaid. She said something to the man in Thai and he turned towards Kirsten. His one small victory at the bar had obviously given him the courage to attempt greater things. Kirsten could feel the eyes of the entire staff upon her. As the barmaid left them Kirsten spoke for the first time. 'You are popular here,' she said. 'Are you the owner?'

The clerk laughed and patted Kirsten on the leg. His hand lingered for just a moment too long. 'No I am just customer like you.'

Kirsten didn't want to make inane conversation with this man but she had to ensure that he was so drunk that he'd not be able to think logically by the time they left the bar. She asked him about his work, about his home, questioned him about his family life, about his favourite dancers. He didn't deny having a wife. It was quite normal, he said, for a Thai man to seek pleasure from prostitutes, not that his wife knew of course. There was no need to make her lose face.

Two of the dancers joined them and the clerk bought more drinks. 'These are my favourites,' he said to Kirsten. 'They like me because I buy them little gifts. They send the money to their families in the north.' The two women had childlike figures, but their faces were worn, and Kirsten guessed that they were of similar age to her. They spoke a series of English phrases, which they obviously used in their work, but they couldn't understand a word that she said. Instead they giggled in unison and hugged each other whenever she spoke to them. Eventually she gave up.

By midnight the clerk was falling asleep and was out of money. Kirsten had cost him a fortune, although she had poured most of her drink into his glass. The evening had been torture for her, but it had been worth it. When she finally thought the moment right she took Andrew's camera from her bag, attached a flash unit to it, and passed the camera to the girls. 'Souvenir,' she said, dropping a ten dollar note on the table. The clerk was too drunk to care and, with Kirsten draped across him, he performed for the camera. Kirsten kissed him on the cheek and then swapped seats with the girls. One last photograph did the trick. The photographs would be suggestive without being indecent – just a night of drunken fun.

The clerk woke the following morning with a thunderous headache. It took him a few minutes to realise where he was. He panicked when he thought that he was late for work, but with the realisation that it was Sunday he sank back into bed and sighed with relief. He wasn't late for work after all. It was his day off.

Closing his eyes to shut out the agony, he recalled the previous night's events. How had he got so drunk? He usually only had a couple of beers. Why was he back home and not at a girl's place? How had he got home? Nobody at the bar knew where he lived. The last thing he needed was for somebody from the bar to meet his wife. He remembered slapping the dancer's backside and he recalled that it had been a popular slap. He smiled at the thought. So why was he home?

Then he remembered Kirsten. What had happened to her, he wondered? He sat upright in bed and looked around the room. He was alone. What had happened to that woman? He climbed from bed and went into the living room where the children usually slept. He was definitely alone. He walked into the kitchen to get some water. On the kitchen table was a line of photographs. He didn't need a second glance to know that he was in trouble.

There was the European woman. She was smiling quite innocently into the camera but she had her arm around him. In the next photograph she was kissing him. That photograph alone would drive his wife to acts of violence. There had been several high profile cases where cheated wives had severed their husband's penises. The photographs of him clutching the two girls would be the end of his marriage, if not the end of him.

He walked slowly back to his bedroom, his head spinning. He felt breathless and beaten. He'd spent years both supporting his family and cheating on them. Now it was time to pay. Why was it happening? Maurice had no reason to blackmail him. Maurice terrified him enough already with the thinly disguised threats towards his family. The woman must be working alone, he thought, but why would she pick on him? He returned to the photographs and took another look. He thought of destroying them, but there would be negatives. It crossed his mind that somebody had set him up for a joke, but none of his friends knew that he used the bar, and nobody at the bar knew anything about him.

He dressed and went out. As he opened the front door he was hit by a wall of glaring sunlight that penetrated the lenses of his glasses, blinding him with searing pain. He stopped dead, feeling sick, and returned to his shack. A moment later he came back out wearing sunglasses. He had to find out what had happened to that woman.

Kirsten was watching from across the road. She was in excellent spirits. 'Come on, my darling,' she said to herself, like a cat ready to pounce. 'You cannot hide from me in those sunglasses.'

Half an hour later the clerk arrived at the bar and reappeared within a couple of minutes, looking more worried than before. The news that he had left with the European woman must have rattled him to the core, Kirsten thought, as she watched him heading for home.

Just after dark, while the clerk was draining the last of a bottle of Thai whisky and wondering how he'd fallen into the woman's trap, there was a knock at the door. He hesitated momentarily, hoping that the visitor would leave, but there was another knock and he put down his glass. He opened the door. In surprise, he stepped sharply backwards and allowed Kirsten inside.

Kirsten didn't speak. She walked through the house and crossed the lounge to the bedroom. She peered inside for a moment and then turned back to the clerk, who was still standing by the front door. He looked dreadful. 'Last night was disappointing,' said Kirsten. 'You were like a pig in there.'

The clerk stared at her impassively.

'You do not believe me?' Kirsten said. 'You have seen the photographs? They are nothing. I have much worse.'

'What do you want?' said the clerk, shaking his head.

'There is plenty of time to discuss business,' said Kirsten. 'But do you not want me again first?' She laughed. 'No, I suppose not.'

The clerk stared at her, unable to comprehend what was happening. He had not seen this woman until last night and now she was taking over his life.

'You should close the door,' said Kirsten.

The clerk pushed the door shut, returned to his chair, and hid his face in his hands. Then he stood abruptly and kicked his chair away. His whisky glass spun from the table and shattered on the floor. 'Who sent you? Who are you?' he growled, clenching his fists and glowering at Kirsten. But Kirsten stood firm and laughed, derisively, and the clerk's courage ebbed away. The woman, who had smiled at him and hugged him and, apparently, slept with him the previous night, was killing him now. Her hatred was unnerving.

'You should watch that temper of yours,' said Kirsten cheerfully. 'The people I'm working for would not like to hear that you have upset me.'

'I'm sorry,' said the clerk. 'I am confused. What do you want?'

'I'm looking for Maurice.'

'Maurice?'

'Yes.'

'I don't know anybody called Maurice.'

'Really?'

'Yes.'

'Then who did you pass this information to?' Kirsten said, handing over the photocopy of Andrew's passport details. She watched with growing confidence as the clerk reached to steady himself against the table. 'Do you understand how much trouble you are in?'

The clerk lowered himself back into his chair and fingered the photocopy. When he spoke it was with the voice of a child. 'You know him? He sent you?'

'This has not been productive for him. He thinks that you have set him up.'

The clerk stared at the sheet of paper and he said something in Thai which, to Kirsten, sounded like a prayer. 'But I have seen him since his return from Ko Phangan. He doesn't blame me.'

'Things change.'

Now he was imploring her. 'This was good information,' he whispered. 'He knows that.'

'You talk shit,' Kirsten snarled. 'Who is this man?' she said, pointing at Andrew's photograph.

'He is a smuggler. He works with the police. This is good information.'

'Why do you say that he works with the police?'

'I told Maurice,' said the clerk. 'There was no reason for the Englishman to be arrested. There was nothing in the register that made sense.'

'Then why did they take him to the police station?'

'I don't know.'

'You do not know? I will tell you why. It was so that a nosey man like you would pass on the information. They know about you, and because of you Maurice was almost killed.'

'No. It was good…'

'It was not good information!' Kirsten screamed, barely able to hold back. She was really enjoying this.

'Why hasn't Maurice come himself?' asked the clerk, beginning to think that something wasn't right. 'Why does he need to send you? Why have you taken these photographs? It wasn't necessary.'

'Perhaps it *was* necessary. He no longer feels that he can trust you.'

The clerk shook his head. 'Of course he can trust me. He terrifies me, he knows that. He will kill my family if I betray him. Even if he doesn't do that, he could inform the police that I am a spy. There was no need for the photographs.'

'Not so,' said Kirsten, accepting that she would have to play another hand to get the information she wanted. 'But I am not Maurice's friend. I work for his enemy, a far more violent and powerful man. He wants you to tell me where to find Maurice.'

'I cannot tell you. He would kill me.'

'Then you have a problem, because I think that he will kill you anyway. The photographs of us together will see to that.'

'You would send them to him?'

'I can do many things with them.'

The clerk opened his mouth to speak but closed it again when he realised how much trouble he was in. He looked to Kirsten for help, but she remained silent.

'How can I tell you?'

Kirsten said nothing.

'He will kill me,' said the clerk.

'You have to consider your family too,' Kirsten said. 'There is a way for you to solve your problems. You can make some money, keep your family, keep your job, and maybe even keep your life, but you have to tell me how to find Maurice.'

The clerk began muttering in Thai. He walked to a cupboard and found another bottle of whisky. He unscrewed the lid and swallowed hard. Wiping his mouth he turned to Kirsten. 'What can I do?' he whispered.

'Tell me how you contact him. Tell me where he is. In return I can give you five hundred dollars and the promise that as soon as he is found I will return the negatives to you. You will never see him or me again.'

'What is the alternative?' said the clerk and he took another swallow from the bottle.

'Simple,' said Kirsten, 'I show the photographs to your wife. I send another set to your employer, together with a little explanation. That way you will lose your family and your job. Maybe you will go to jail. Maurice cannot afford to have you talking to the police to save your skin. When he discovers what has happened he will return and kill you and, perhaps, your family too. There is no alternative.'

The clerk knew he was beaten. 'I will never see Maurice again?'

'Never.' Kirsten spoke precisely, as if she was containing her anger. 'Now... where... is... he?'

'He is in Kathmandu.'

'How do you know?' Kirsten snapped.

'He told me.'

'When?'

'One week ago.'

'When will he return to Bangkok?'

'He didn't say.'

'Then how will you contact him?'

'The poste restante in Kathmandu.'

'What name? Come on, what name?'

'Mister Zimmerman.'

'Zimmerman! Why Zimmerman?'

'Because he says that the poste restante there is very big. There are thousands of letters, but not many names beginning with Z.'

'Is this how you contact him here?'

'He always contacts me. I only contact him when he is abroad.'

'Why is he in Kathmandu?'

'He says he is there for the tourist season.'

'Okay,' said Kirsten. She took two hundred and fifty dollars from her money belt and placed them on the table. 'You must not contact him again. Once we find him I will send you the negatives and the rest of your money.'

The clerk nodded silently, his shoulders bending inwards as he began to slide towards the table. Kirsten pushed past him and left the shack, with the sound of sobbing rising behind her like a siren in a flood.

Moments later she was sitting in the back of a tuc-tuc, yelling across the traffic. 'Zimmerman! Zimmerman!'

The tuc-tuc driver drove on, trying hard to concentrate on the traffic and wondering just who he had in the back seat.

Chapter 19

The bus careered around another hairpin bend and the sleeping passengers swayed in unison like kelp in a swell. There was a dull crack and Andrew opened his eyes. The side of his head ached from repeatedly clattering the window. He turned awkwardly and looked at Kirsten. Her head lolled upon her chest as she swung to and fro. Only the stacked baggage in the aisle and Andrew's aching frame kept her upright.

The Nepalese driver was hunched over the wheel, peering into the darkness ahead. Suddenly he sat upright and dragged the wheel hard to the left as the bus found another sharp bend. He spoke to his co-driver and they laughed. *Bastards*! Andrew let out an ironic sigh and closed his eyes.

Travelling by bus in India and Nepal is hard going. You only have to count the number of wrecked vehicles strewn along the roadside to know that not all is well on India's roads. Sixty people die in accidents daily and just one bus going over a cliff could account for that. Even without accidents, there is the dizzying, bone-crushing discomfort caused by stifling heat, nauseous fumes, rock hard plastic seats, vomiting passengers, ear-piercing Hindi music, videos, scary roadside toilets and the underlying fear of lost or damaged luggage.

So it came as no great surprise to find themselves being transported to Kathmandu by a man who either believed in fatalism or had been diagnosed with a terminal disease. The bus, belching stinking black smoke, thundered along at speeds obviously calculated to compensate for the slow going in the hills. Worse than the speed was the desperate need to overtake on roads designed for one lane of traffic in each direction. Their driver, probably a really nice guy in civilian life, was like any other company timetable slave; accelerator pressed hard against the floor, searching hard for his chance to overtake anything that moved, forcing smaller oncoming vehicles off the road and terrorising entire villages as he assaulted them; horn blazing, sucking up chickens and pigs and boys on bicycles and spewing them out again seconds later, a mass of feathers and bacon and bicycle spokes. Buses run over people often enough but the drivers never stop – killer drivers get lynched in India.

They chased a truck through a village and ran down all the livestock that the truck missed. They spent ten full minutes jockeying for position behind it, weaving in and out of the oncoming lane, tailgating the lorry so close that, at one point, they actually touched it.

As the driver became increasingly impatient Andrew began to feel uneasy. He found himself transfixed by the battle of wits; staring ahead, hoping for a gap in the traffic, hoping for the opportunity to pass safely by. Instead of finding open road, Andrew peered ahead and watched, as a distant spec became an oncoming bus.

The bus hurtled towards them as they weaved back into its path, the opportunity for a successful overtaking manoeuvre too close to call. 'Don't do it, please,' Andrew muttered, not really believing that the driver was that crazy, and not believing either that his eyes were telling him the truth. They pulled further out and increased speed until they were alongside the truck. The truck driver stared directly ahead, refusing to acknowledge them, not giving an inch.

The oncoming bus roared closer.

The engine strained to find speed, the wheels clawed at the road for extra leverage, the driver leant into the windscreen for extra shove.

The oncoming bus hurtled onwards, speeding up rather than down. Somebody would have to give, or somebody would have to die.

They pulled ahead of the truck. The oncoming bus filled the view.

'Fuck! Fuck! Fuck!' Andrew yelled, 'This is it.' His bodily functions went on hold; he stopped breathing, blinking, hearing, feeling, sweating – he was convinced that he was going to die in a head-on Indian road accident, something he had always feared but never really expected. He braced himself against the seat in front but, at the point of impact, instead of catapulting head-first through the crowded bus and through the shattered windscreen, he marvelled at his good fortune as the driver, now standing, knees bent like a jockey, somehow pulled the shuddering bus into the lane in front of the truck, which was breaking hard to avoid them. The oncoming bus whooshed into the vacuum and vanished.

They left the road.

Only then did Kirsten, who had been sleeping, notice that all was far from being well. 'Fuck!' she yelled at nobody in particular as she landed in a heap in the aisle, her face forced into a pile of goatskins.

Passengers were hurled on top of Kirsten; a woman vomited on her bemused baby's head, an elderly man hit his face on the seat in front and baggage tumbled from the baggage racks. The bus ripped into the earth beside the road, tearing at vegetation, hammering through low hanging tree branches, puffing up clouds of dirt and leaves.

The bus returned to the road, crossed it sharply and tore into the earth on the other side. With wheels screaming for mercy and passengers screaming for deliverance, the bus returned to the road once again. Finally, after repeating the dance in a series of ever-decreasing arcs, the driver regained control and, hunched over the wheel, he peered into the distance and prepared to do it all again. Andrew thought that it would have been easier to understand if somebody had called the driver a maniac, but everyone settled back into their seats, the elderly man rubbed his head, the woman wiped the vomit off her baby and life went on. 'This driver is shit,' said Kirsten, closing her eyes and leaving Andrew to his thoughts.

Near-death experiences aside, during daylight the journey had been beautiful. There was the excitement of the sub-tropical Terai, the lowland region of Nepal, where elephants, tigers, deer and one-horned rhinoceroses still roam amongst fields of banana trees and tall grass, and crocodiles lounge upon the riverbanks. After the Terai, as they climbed higher towards Kathmandu they soaked up breathtaking, mountainous scenery, plunging river valleys, forests, wide drifting rivers and torrents. All that remained after dark, though, was a feeling of claustrophobic agony, aching bloodless limbs and the wearisome desire for bed.

In the early hours of the morning the bus began its gradual descent into the Kathmandu Valley. Flickering lights beckoned to them from between distant hilltops. Finally, in the minutes before dawn, the bus entered the city and turned into a walled enclosure, coming to a halt near a collection of boarded-up food stalls. The moment the bus shuddered to a stop the passengers spilled through its doors and clambered, ant-like, up the ladder at the rear. Baggage bounced along the roof, down the ladder and out through the enclosure gate. Before they could catch their breath Andrew and Kirsten were standing alone somewhere in the middle of Kathmandu. There was a chill. Kirsten checked her watch: it was five-thirty in the morning. The silence was exhilarating.

It didn't last. A boy of around twelve ran up to them. He was breathless. 'Good morning! Good morning!' He stopped for a second to catch his breath. 'Do you want hotel? I know good place. Very cheap.' He detected interest – nobody had told him to go away. 'Come. Come, I will show you. You don't like, I know other hotel.' He helped Kirsten with her bag and aimed his conversation at her.

Kathmandu sat in a fertile valley about 1300 metres above sea level, surrounded by hills to the south and mountains to the north. Snow-capped peaks were faintly visible above rooftops although, at first glance, they looked like clouds. There was something faintly mysterious about Kathmandu, as if they had passed through a hidden gateway into a world still living in a previous millennium, which was hardly surprising considering that the first road from India to Kathmandu was only built in the 1950's. Andrew mused that a lot of people probably didn't realise that Kathmandu actually existed – a bit like Timbuktu. But at five o'clock in the morning, the place was very real.

Although there was supposed to be 300,000 people living in the city, there were only a couple of joggers about and one of them had already disappeared around the corner of a large, fenced-off playing field. At the far side of the field was a small spectator stand which, Andrew guessed, was actually for military parades. A short walk to the north was a small Shiva temple, surrounded by a fenced-off, man-made lake. They turned south, passing some deserted, narrow streets of crumbling three-storey houses, their shuttered windows closed against the cold. A small dog sauntered across the road in front of them, sniffing the air. The cold air, the lack of activity and the silence reminded Andrew of all those post-party mornings – all boozed up, self-satisfied and looking for another drink when all you needed was bed.

They had taken to using circuitous routes since Andrew's experience at the airport in Bangkok. They had to assume that both Carlo and Maurice had contacts at the major airports. Knowing that the only way to avoid them was to avoid airports, they flew from Bangkok to Calcutta, but took the bus from there. Instead of spending a couple of hours of relative luxury in the air, they were obliged to spend thirty-six hours of utter discomfort on the road.

Andrew's thoughts subsided as they stopped to cross a road. The boy pointed at him with his eyes. 'I think your friend is English,' he said to Kirsten, 'but not you. You are maybe from Sweden. I know many girls from Sweden. Swedish people are good for business.' He looked at Andrew again. 'English have no money. They buy nothing, always want cheap, cheap.'

'Too true,' Andrew admitted. In Delhi some Indian businessmen, who had introduced themselves as students, were setting up a Scandinavian advice centre to attract more Scandinavian tourists. They had closed their British centre; the British had no money, they'd said.

'I am German.' Kirsten corrected the boy. 'Where are you from?'

The boy laughed. 'I am from Kathmandu. This is my home.' He was wearing old clothes but he sported a new pair of white trainers. The boy thought for a minute and then began a new line of conversation: 'You like hash? I have good hash. It is also possible cocaine.'

'No thank you,' Kirsten said. She wasn't surprised – she had been through the same conversation with children many times before. Asia was still the land of *Oliver Twist*, where children made as much money as their parents; working in factories, begging, pimping, dealing, touting. Children either grew up quickly or they didn't grow up at all.

'Change money?'

'How did you learn English?' Kirsten asked, trying to interrupt the hard sell.

'English is business language here,' the boy replied. 'It is important to make money.'

'You're a businessman?'

'Yes. I can sell you anything. Everything is cheap. One day I will have my own card.'

'Credit card?'

The boy laughed. 'Business card. When I have a business card I will sell more. Then I can have credit card.'

'What do your parents think?' Kirsten asked, but the boy looked away.

They continued in silence. They went past the GPO into a square, where a group of people sat astride their baggage waiting beside a tea stall for the first bus of the morning. The women, wrapped warmly in saris and shawls, were keeping an eye on their children. The men, wearing the traditional cap, the *topi,* and jackets with trousers tucked in at the ankles were talking quietly amongst themselves. In the hush of activity, human breath and steaming hot drinks clouded the cold morning air. Nobody paid Andrew or Kirsten any attention. In the centre of the square was Sundhara, a minaret-like watchtower. They walked beneath it and turned into a series of winding, narrow alleys, the territory of a pack of snarling mongrels. The boy led them to a crumbling wooden door. He knocked loudly and stood back. A minute later they were invited inside by an elderly man, wiping sleep from his eyes. He wore a blanket around his shoulders.

They checked in and were shown to a room with a bathroom. It was simple but enough for their purpose. The boy said he'd see them later. They placed their bags on opposite sides of the bed and while Kirsten checked out the bathroom Andrew reclined on the bed and let out a yawn. Kirsten walked back into the room smiling. 'I will take a shower,' she said, pulling off her dress. She looked suggestively at Andrew. 'And what are you thinking?'

'I'm thinking how good you look,' he said, although what he was actually thinking was that it was because she looked so good that he allowed her to manipulate him. 'And I was thinking how good it is to have finally arrived, and how good it will be to get into the mountains.'

'After we have taken our photographs.'

'I'm thinking that too. I just hope Maurice checks out the GPO soon.'

'He will,' said Kirsten. 'The clerk said that he visits twice a week. It will take four days at most.' She looked earnestly at Andrew. 'You are a little tense. I know how to help you relax.'

Half an hour later Kirsten showered and, while Andrew half-listened to her yelling above the sound of the water, he thought about Maurice. He realised now that, although they had an even chance of finding him before he found them, they were taking a terrible risk to get the photographs. There didn't seem to be any choice, though. At least with his zoom lens he didn't have to get too close – he could get a good shot from thirty metres. He couldn't wait to get it over with, then post the shots to Interpol and get away to the mountains.

The clerk had told Kirsten that Maurice travelled to Nepal every October for the tourist season. It was the best possible time for foreigners to blend in, because tourists came in their thousands following the end of the monsoon. After the monsoon, Nepal was always at its most green and beautiful; the climate was pleasant, the air clean and mountain views were excellent. Maurice travelled in October, not for the views or the weather, but to find a honey pot of gullible victims.

Andrew had fallen asleep while Kirsten was in the shower. Three hours later he woke suddenly. His reactions were blurred by exhaustion and his head felt as if it was bursting. Kirsten was screaming in her sleep. Andrew pulled her close to him and put a hand on her cheek. 'Kirsten,' he whispered as he shook her gently. 'Wake up.'

Kirsten was confused. She stared at him. 'Andrew?' she said.

Andrew gave what he hoped was a reassuring smile. 'You were having another of your bad dreams,' he said, stroking her sweat-soaked hair.

'I cannot get him out of my mind,' Kirsten said, still only half-awake.

'Maurice?'

Kirsten seemed surprised to hear the name. 'Maurice?' she said. She thought for a moment. 'Yes,' she said. 'He is everywhere Andrew, I can sense him, and I dream about him. He will never let me escape.'

Andrew moved back slightly, just far enough to find some space. What he was hoping, more than anything else, was that their information was wrong and that Maurice was anywhere but in Nepal. Somehow, he would like to forget the recent past, but he knew that Kirsten wasn't going to let it go.

'It would be something if we met him in the mountains,' Kirsten said. 'We could push him off a bridge, or trip him over a cliff, or drop a rock on his head, or... or... we could...'

Andrew interrupted. 'We could do a million things. Even if killing somebody is easy, and it isn't... it's living with yourself afterwards that's the biggest problem.'

'I can't live like this. I can't breathe, I can't sleep.'

'I understand how you feel,' Andrew said doubtfully. He thought about his travels and all the horrors that he had ignored; terribly deformed children, some mutilated by their own parents so that they could beg, the beatings meted out on the street, oblivious to passers-by, the abject poverty, abused animals, even dead bodies. It had become easier to ignore the dark side of travel. Accepting things as they were, however awful, not how they should be, created a defensive wall. Until now it had more or less worked.

Kirsten was looking up at him, expecting him to say something.

'We've already agreed that we're not killing anybody,' Andrew said. 'We're just taking his photograph.

'I know,' said Kirsten. 'No killing, just photographs.' She kissed him gently and turned over, leaving him to ponder his reasons for being there.

There was nothing more hopeful and fulfilling to Andrew than a well-spent, well-prepared early morning breakfast. Breakfast was like re-birth; body and soul were freed from corruption, the day ahead was full of promise. Breakfast was also the most enjoyable way to acclimatise on arrival anywhere in the world. Over breakfast they could see a new country through the local papers. They could get a feel for the place through the quality of the food, observe the kind of travellers frequenting the area they were staying in and maybe overhear conversations revealing interesting gossip, travel tips, news. Better still, in busy restaurants where tables were full, people were often forced to cross the cultural barrier and share their space. It was one of the ways travellers met.

Morning arrived with the early songs of urban life; parents shouting at their children, children shouting at dogs, car horns and bicycle bells, builders hauling buckets, neighbours singing in the shower, Michael Jackson thrilling on the radio. The air was still but it was already hot as they sauntered along to Freak Street to start their day. The street was the city's oldest, most notorious tourist enclave, a street without pavements and not quite wide enough for two lanes of traffic.

Andrew's parents had been in Nepal during the early sixties when Freak Street was one of the great Asian gathering places for travellers, synonymous with drugs, hippies and flower-power. Andrew was two years old at the time, so they had dumped him on an aunt. They spent months travelling the length of Turkey, through the deserts of Iran and Pakistan, then up through India. They used to tell Andrew stories about their adventures, about cheap hotels, hash and restaurants, and they never failed to add that they would have loved to have taken him but that it was simply impossible, simply too much trouble. When they planned their trip of a lifetime, they hadn't planned for Andrew.

Andrew considered a journey he hadn't realised that he was on. He saw his parents' dream fading into memory; Freak Street a shadow of its former self, all those stories that frustrated him as a child, all those stories that excluded him and pushed him further away from his parents. For them the dream was over.

Now he was in Kathmandu without them. He had heard that there was a new tourist enclave called Thamel, which was draining the life-blood from Freak Street, but the street still had the charm of the bazaar. There were still enough ancient wooden hotels with dusty, darkened interiors; restaurants with menus from around the world; travel agents with tours to the mountains and the valleys and to the elephants; lazy travellers looking for lazy deals and half-wrecked, furtively whispering drug dealers to give the impression that it was still business as usual. Freak Street remained the place to end any journey, chill out, get fat, get a dream, get a life and get stoned.

Kirsten was studying a menu on a board beneath a rack of gaudy, ethnic, tourist clothes. Somewhere through a small wooden doorway beyond a stone courtyard there was a hidden restaurant beneath a hotel. 'I'm starving,' Kirsten whispered and she laughed. 'I'm going to have everything on the menu,' she said, pulling Andrew closer. 'Chowmein, spring rolls, buffalo burgers, chocolate banana cake and lemon meringue pie… and six pots of coffee.'

Andrew imagined his parents standing on the same spot, reading the menu, their mouths watering after their journey. He felt guilty as he recalled how upset they had been to find a letter from his aunt at the poste restante, demanding that they return immediately because he was making her ill. He couldn't stop them going to Kathmandu, but they never got to trek in the mountains. Perhaps, one day soon, he'd do it for them.

Kathmandu was his to enjoy now. The city was an ancient living culture; a city slowly moving into the modern age but keeping the brakes on. Temples, stupas, monuments and palaces mingled with crumbling brick houses and modern glass-fronted stores. There were the usual main streets and roadways dedicated to motorised traffic, and narrow lanes where a traffic jam might be an ox cart stuck behind a pedestrian. As they turned into the restaurant they gawked at a four-tiered pagoda, which dominated the far end of Freak Street. Normally Andrew would have tingled with expectation and excitement in a city like Kathmandu, but they were on a manhunt. He blamed Kirsten and her obsession with revenge, but he couldn't help feeling that she had a point.

'So how are we going to spend our day?' Andrew asked to get conversation going.

'Let's look around. There is so much to see.'

'That's fine, but what about Maurice?'

'He cannot hurt us in Kathmandu. It is too crowded.'

Andrew couldn't see how they could enjoy themselves, but Kirsten was pissed off with his negativity so he opted for a positive response. 'I suppose that there's nothing we can do about Maurice today, anyway,' he said. 'It's Saturday and the GPO is shut.'

'Yes Andrew,' said Kirsten. 'Let's be tourists.'

It was a good day too, apart from Andrew's constant bouts of paranoia. They spent hours wandering around the ancient city, squeezing through Kathmandu's narrow chaotic streets and fighting for space amongst a myriad people and vehicles. The one-lane streets were bordered by shadowy four-storey buildings, which peered downwards like light-starved trees into narrow ravines. Shopkeepers stared into the streets above from the shadows of their darkened basement shops. From behind racks of clothing, pottery, foodstuffs and ironware they looked like prisoners unable to reach out into the light.

In Durbar Square they climbed the steps of the Maju Deval, a seventeenth century, three-tiered pagoda. Behind them was a twelfth century wooden building, Kasthamandap, the building that gave Kathmandu its name. Like aimless holidaymakers they sat in the sun, high above the square, watching the world go by. Shoppers spent hours haggling and laughing with merchants, squatting amongst waist-high baskets of fruit and vegetables. Children chased each other over the temple steps, around and around rickshaws or between their parents' legs. They gazed at toys and balloons and flutes sold by street vendors. Old men bent double, carried loads on their backs, which should have been on carts. Rickshaw drivers slept with their legs drooping over handlebars. A long-bearded holy man, a *sadhu,* dressed in saffron-coloured robes, squatted cross-legged, eyes closed, nodding gently at a request for a photograph and the drop of a coin. An enormous bull stood motionless in the street, oblivious to his surroundings. The square was an awe-inspiring step back in time and Andrew actually began to relax but, at his side, was his camera, just in case Maurice appeared. They might only get one chance.

Chapter 20

It had been three days since Andrew and Kirsten had first staked out the post office. Maurice hadn't shown up. Andrew was secretly hoping that he wouldn't, but Kirsten was becoming more and more agitated. The night before, while they were making love, Kirsten dug her fingers so hard into Andrew's back that he screamed in agony and had to shake her off. Instead of apologising, she spat in his face and told him that he was nothing to her. Then she turned over and left him staring at the ceiling. As an act of martyrdom Andrew refused to wipe the spittle off his face. In the morning Kirsten shrugged her shoulders when Andrew asked why she had done it. She said that she had just been tired.

Shortly after the post office opened Kirsten ran inside to check whether there was any mail for Maurice. She returned, more excited than ever, to inform Andrew that there was one letter. Surely he would come today. That was two hours ago. Since then Andrew had focused and re-focused the camera on everything that moved. He took a few shots of a man by the gate, refilling throwaway plastic cigarette lighters for tourists, and he took a couple more of the shoe-shine boy as he chatted happily with his only customer of the morning.

Now he was using his zoom lens like binoculars, spying on the world around him, hoping to catch sight of Maurice heading into focus. Groups of people were gathering at the washing *ghats*, a series of steps leading down to a pool, to wash their clothes. There was a pack of dogs fighting amongst themselves, which was hardly surprising in an area known as the "pond of the dogs". Somewhere behind them a pack of twelve-year-old boys were clambering up the ladder at the back of a bus, with bags and boxes and rucksacks, all for a few *paisa* a piece.

Tourists were hovering by the post office gate, some unashamedly gleeful as they read up on news from home, others looking cool and untouched by sentiment. The day was hot and bright, everyone was wearing T-shirts, shorts and skirts, some had hats, some sunglasses. Everyone was on holiday. When Andrew saw him it came as such a shock that he involuntarily took a photograph. Just like that, he had accomplished what he had set out to do. He watched, now, as Maurice strolled into view, looking every part the tourist, and disappeared through the gate into the post office. Kirsten was gripping Andrew's arm with excitement; Andrew was simply holding his breath and peering over the top of the camera, like a soldier who had just shot a man and can't quite believe the brutality of it all.

'I got him,' Andrew said, and Kirsten laughed like a child.

'You got him,' she agreed. 'You got his photograph. He's here. He has taken the bait.'

'Bait?' Andrew asked. 'What bait?'

'Not bait,' said Kirsten. 'Not bait, he is here that's all, like I knew he would be.'

'Now what do we do?'

'Follow him.'

'No chance. I'll take a couple more shots and that's it. Then we're out of here.'

Kirsten released Andrew's arm and took a step towards the post office. She turned back towards him. 'He cannot hurt us here,' she said. 'There are too many people.'

'So what? I don't want him to know I'm here. I want to go trekking after we've done this. I want to enjoy myself for a change, see the mountains, have a good time.'

Kirsten didn't say anything. She stood quietly and gave Andrew room to take his photographs. What surprised Andrew most of all was that he was still able to function. His body was shaking, there was a taste of blood in his mouth and the camera shook like hell when he lifted it to his eye. He was steadying the camera hard against his face, with his elbows tight against his body and the camera strap wrapped firmly around his right hand. His finger was gently but firmly caressing the shutter release button. His breathing was slow. For the first time he felt like a hunter with the power to kill. If he had his way, a photograph of Maurice would see to it that he ended his days with a rope around his neck. One shot. What power! Ironically, for the first time, he felt that he had some understanding of what made Maurice tick.

The post restante section of the general post office was in a small room to the left of the main entrance. Row upon row of letters sat in boxes upon a table, filed alphabetically, the letter A nearest to the door. Most of the tourists, pushing and shoving, and complaining that people were not returning piles of envelopes in the order they found them, were at the near end and the middle of the table. Maurice was standing in an area of relative calm at the back.

But Maurice was not calm. He was standing motionless, transfixed by the opened letter stretched tightly between the fingers of both hands. He stared without reading; the contents of the letter were already spinning around his mind, threatening his entire system with breakdown. There was interference; somebody was threatening him.

Maurice was certain that Carlo had not written the letter; it wasn't his style. Whoever it was, though, knew him well. They had discovered the clerk in Bangkok and claimed that the man was dangerous. They said that the man talks too much. They knew about Carlo. They knew a way to find him. Finally, they had information and photographs that would lead Interpol to him unless he followed their instructions.

Maurice was to return to Bangkok and deal with the clerk, the letter said. Then he must send proof of his actions to four Indian post offices: Delhi; Bombay; Calcutta; Bangalore. Once the proof was received, Maurice would be told how to locate Carlo. Any attempt to discover the author would result in Interpol becoming involved. Maurice must leave directly.

'Must, must, must,' Maurice growled as he thought about the last line. It was the 'must' more than anything that angered him. The clerk was irrelevant at this stage, and so was Carlo. His real enemy was the author of this letter, a letter delivered by hand. 'MUST!' he roared, ripping the letter in half. Faces turned towards him in horror. Seeing the rage in his eyes, those nearest the door left the room. A young woman standing opposite held a pile of letters to her chest and began to whimper. 'Are you okay?' she said in a whisper that only Maurice could hear. 'MUST!' Maurice screamed again, and the woman began to sob. Maurice stared through her, unseeing. He was in a dream. He clenched and unclenched his fists and suddenly, as if nothing had happened, he snapped out of the trance. One thought had come to him: the thought that whoever wrote the letter was probably nearby, trying to gauge his reaction. He smiled at the onlookers, shoved the remains of the letter into a pocket and walked outside.

Ducking through the gate, Maurice scanned the furthest reaches of the crowd He assumed that anybody spying on him would want to have some distance between them. What he found was a sea of movement, people passing through the square, a few looking over a row of stalls, some heading for buses, everybody in motion. But there was something stationary, something clearly out of place, flashing in the sunshine. To his utter delight he spotted Andrew, thirty metres away, taking his photograph.

Maurice had to fight to disguise his reaction. He couldn't let Andrew know that he had been spotted. He laughed to himself, turned away and headed around the back of the post office. *So this was who wrote the letter*, he realised. His position was not so bad after all. If anything it had been remarkably improved. He took a glance backwards. Andrew was changing camera lenses and chatting with Kirsten. He was packing up, satisfied that the job was done. *They were fools*, Maurice thought. They had no idea what they were getting into.

The minute Andrew and Kirsten headed away, Maurice turned back. He stayed close to the walls of the post office and moved slowly. He watched them cross the square before he picked up pace and he caught sight of them turning into a busy street just beyond the square. He followed fifty metres behind, keeping a few people between them, but always keeping them in sight. Andrew and Kirsten kept hugging each other. They didn't seem able to contain themselves. *Christ, are they in for a shock*, Maurice thought. He laughed at the thought of that letter. He had been intimidated by a couple of ridiculous young lovers, enjoying their first date.

As the street widened Maurice caught a whiff of flesh. Huge fish lay on slabs of melting ice, smaller fish writhed, packed like eels into plastic buckets of water. Buffalo heads and goat heads lay in the dust, their eyes begging for mercy, their blood congealing amongst the filth. Black clouds of flies swarmed over joints of red meat hanging from meathooks.

He caught up with them as they ducked into a glass-fronted restaurant near Freak Street, and he realised that he was enjoying an incredible piece of luck. He felt for the letter in his pocket and laughed quietly. They were doing something quite ordinary considering that they had just set a trap for a killer. But how had they found the police clerk? It must have been Carlo; they couldn't have done this without him. He laughed again as he watched them picking up their menus. Perhaps these idiots had been working with Carlo all along? Maybe there was nothing naïve about them after all? Either way they were ordering a meal, and to anyone other than Maurice they looked just like any of the other backpackers sitting around them. Watching them eating together, Maurice was reminded of a time when he had lived simply, a time long before Carlo had appeared in his life, a time, even, when he had considered himself to be happy.

Devi wore a beautiful, long, magenta sari, which clung to her slight figure as she walked. Her hair was parted in the centre and pulled tightly back. She carried a small basket of food in one hand and a cool box in the other. Every Sunday they escaped the city for a few hours.

They travelled in Maurice's favourite black Ambassador. Maurice always drove himself, something that Devi could never understand. He could afford a driver, he could afford many servants, but he employed nobody but his whores and a few boys to fetch for him.

'Whores and animals are all you can trust,' Maurice always answered when Devi questioned him. In truth, he didn't even trust Devi. 'If there were more people around me I would be like an old male langur monkey controlling his harem. All the young males would be waiting for their chance to chase me off the mountain.' He always used that line; it was something he had seen on television. The difference between men and monkeys was purely cosmetic; he was in control, not just of himself, but of all his women. Potential challengers knew to keep well away.

Maurice was wearing a long, white shirt that hung over his black, cotton trousers. He never helped to carry anything and he seldom spoke until they reached their favourite spot on the riverbank. He couldn't relax until he knew that there was nobody else around. The river was half an hour from the road. They had to cross a patch of woodland and pick their way through a field of tall rice to reach it.

Devi placed the basket on the ground above the river and knelt beside it. She arranged a picnic blanket, carefully flattening out the creases, and began to arrange a picnic. Maurice took off his shirt, puffed up his chest, and let out a satisfied roar. They were finally alone and he could relax, so he opened a bottle of beer, threw the lid into the river and watched it sink. Then he sat down, leant back on the blanket and took a drink. 'It used to take me three days to earn enough to buy one beer,' he said. 'How things change.'

'You are a great success, Maurice,' Devi said, to please him. 'And you have been kind to me.' Maurice was vain, she knew, and a compliment was a cheap price to pay for a share of his wealth. He had bought her from the trafficker long ago and had beaten her during her first days at the brothel, but how he had changed towards her!

Trafficking in young Nepalese women was big business in India. Thousands of Nepalese women worked as bonded labour in Indian brothels, sold into slavery by family members and neighbours. Maurice had made his fortune that way, feeding off people's misery. The trafficker had paid Devi's uncle just four American dollars for her, Maurice said. Now Maurice spent more than that each week buying her clothes. Her happiness had been worth less to her uncle than a sari!

Devi had brought along some rice, bread and curried eggs. Maurice ate a mouthful, said that it was delicious and then ate the rest. 'Excellent,' he said when he'd emptied the bowl. He took another swallow of beer and slipped into a hypnotic dream. Devi knew better than to interrupt him when he was like this. She had disturbed him once and the shock in his eyes had terrified her. It had been like waking Kali, the black goddess, fiercest of all the gods. No, it was better to tidy up while he dreamed.

When Maurice woke again he was refreshed. 'I'll take a swim,' he said, and without waiting for a response he undressed. He picked his way across the grass and onto the hardened earth of the riverbank. He felt his way with his toes into the water and when it reached his waist he slipped silently forwards until only his head was visible. He swam out into the river using his muscular legs for power and his sleek arms for guidance. Devi watched him. He was beautiful, she thought; no man his size had such perfect muscular shape and strength. He was so slim and light. She loved to be near him. She unwrapped her sari, stood naked on the blanket and waited for Maurice to look at her. She knew how he loved to watch her.

Devi trapped Maurice in her gaze. She ran her hands over her body, cupping her hands over her breasts and waded into the water. She could sense his power as he weaved towards her, water spilling from his mouth, like a stalking crocodile. She stood with the river tingling between her legs and waited to be taken.

As Maurice lifted her high in the water, Devi closed her eyes and raised her head to meet him. She opened her mouth and Maurice's tongue slid inside. His tongue had power. It ran along the roof of her mouth and licked at her teeth. He coiled himself around her like a snake and squeezed her until she felt dizzy. He was hard against her below the water and she could have screamed as he entered her. In the last moments she held him hard with her legs and squeezed and squeezed and squeezed, and she came with a burst of electricity that ran through her body like a train. She bit hard into his neck and didn't let him go until he too was silent. He loved the shock of pain.

They made love again on the blanket and lay naked until sunset, when they finally drove home. Devi enjoyed a wonderful sense of achievement; she was the only woman he ever took to the river. The others were jealous of her and they had reason to be. Maurice used them all, she knew that, but he only had sex with them. He gave her gifts and shared his rooms and food with her. He allowed her to leave the brothel without an escort. She was trusted that much, at least. Although she knew that Maurice did not love her, she was glad to be valued. The same trafficker, who had bought her from her uncle for four dollars, had sold her to Maurice for one thousand. She would never be able to earn one thousand dollars but, even so, Maurice allowed her to keep some of the money that she earned. She was worth more to him than money, he'd told her. He gave her a sense of belonging. It was something.

Chapter 22

Andrew thought that they must have seemed ridiculous. They couldn't stop babbling and hugging and laughing. Kirsten was talking so quickly that Andrew could hardly understand a word she said. She kept slipping into German and then laughing at his lack of comprehension.

'We must eat quickly,' she said, laughing childishly as she spoke. 'Then I want to eat you in bed!'

Andrew had never seen her so excited, even when he had given her a share of Carlo's money in Bali. Through her T-shirt he could see that her nipples were erect; her face was glowing bright red; she was breathless. As they made themselves comfortable at a seat by the window, she grabbed his leg and kissed him hard on the cheek. 'We beat him,' she said. 'We beat him.'

'Easy Tiger,' Andrew said. 'It's not over yet. We still have to get the photographs developed.'

'You're right. We mustn't forget the photographs.'

Kirsten found it difficult to disguise her sense of accomplishment. She had spent hours planning that letter to Maurice, and it had not been easy hiding what she was doing from Andrew. The message had been simple enough but the tone was what had been important. She had to write something that would get right beneath his skin. She had to take away his sense of control, even for a moment. He had to know that his enemy was strong.

While Kirsten examined the menu, Andrew took the chance to take a piss. In all the excitement his bodily functions had been put on hold, but now he needed some urgent relief. He went to the toilet at the back. Andrew had spent a lot of his time eating in London's restaurants. Whenever he ate anywhere now he always found himself comparing the food and the facilities with those he'd left behind. One feature that never changed throughout the world was the lousy state of restaurant toilets. They seemed to be an afterthought. He was still thinking about one of his favourite restaurants on the way back from the toilet when he noticed somebody outside the restaurant, staring in at Kirsten. Whether the man saw him or not, Andrew couldn't say, because he was suddenly obscured by bright sunlight, leaving Andrew in shock, staring into space.

Nothing worked. He couldn't breathe. Somehow he had to get to Kirsten, but he couldn't move; his feet simply wouldn't walk. He stared at Kirsten, hoping that she would see him, but she was buried in the menu. 'Kirsten,' he gasped, but she didn't hear him. 'Kirsten,' he said a little too loud, and her startled expression surprised him. Andrew felt sick.

Kirsten looked like she was about to laugh, but her expression soon changed. Although Andrew realised that she was confused, he could have killed her for not understanding what was happening. He remained rooted to the spot and Kirsten finally realised that they were in danger. She stood slowly, pushing herself up against the table. 'What is it?' she asked.

'It's him Kirsten, I swear it. He's found us.'

Kirsten swore in German. She looked through the window and then at Andrew. 'We expected this Andrew. We have to stay calm.'

'There's a way out the back,' Andrew said, 'If he thinks that we didn't see him he might wait for us out front. We have to get to the hotel.' He had hoped to avoid this situation but that hope had gone. He considered making a run for it but without Kirsten to give him a shove he didn't think that he could even walk.

'Andrew,' Kirsten said, waking him from his trance. 'We must eat a meal or he will know that we have seen him.'

Andrew couldn't move.

'Andrew,' Kirsten said, coercing him towards the table. 'Come.'

Andrew resembled an old man with a bad back as he lowered himself into his chair. He read the menu but he couldn't concentrate.

He simply couldn't think, so Kirsten took over. She ordered food and drinks, made conversation and urged Andrew on, calming him down with a brief speech. 'We have come too far to run now,' she said. She told him that they were stronger than Maurice. He wasn't invincible, after all. They could beat him if they followed their plan and didn't give themselves away.

Kirsten ordered two chicken curries and rice. She joked that it made a change to eat some Asian food and Andrew forced a grin. However, the chicken was on the bone and, if Andrew had an appetite before, he hadn't now. He picked at a few loose pieces of meat and spooned some rice into his mouth but, even as he did so, he thought of Maurice standing outside just a few metres away, and the thought made him shiver. He suddenly felt a rush of desperate affection for Kirsten. He so much wanted to play the role of protector but she was the strong one, not him. She was eating; hardly ripping the food apart, but she was eating. He didn't know how she did it.

They finished their meal, or rather Kirsten did, and they left the restaurant as confidently as possible. Kirsten was terrified but she was also more excited than she had ever been before. Andrew was simply in shock. Kirsten was holding Andrew's left hand tightly. She knew that he was fighting an instinct to run.

Maurice watched them leave. He couldn't tell whether or not they knew he was there. If they did then they certainly weren't displaying any obvious sign of fear. He was amused by the way Kirsten was dragging Andrew along by the hand, though. The woman wore the trousers in that relationship, he noticed.

Andrew caught a glimpse of Maurice fifty metres ahead of them and a wave of anxiety washed through him. Maurice stepped back behind a public refuse bin, which Andrew thought fitting. He prayed that Maurice wanted to follow them, not ambush them here. He couldn't imagine what they would do if he attacked them now. Edging past the bin Andrew swore that he was going to faint, but Kirsten squeezed his hand and dragged him forward until they were past him.

Maurice followed them into the main street. He was prepared to spend the day following them until they revealed where they were staying, but he wasn't willing to take any risks in the street. There was no point. Once he knew which hotel they were staying at he would find his opportunity to strike.

Kirsten accidentally led them the wrong way but they kept going. From that point there were still two ways back to their hotel; the direct route took them along a narrow alleyway, strangely underpopulated for Kathmandu; the second was back through Durbar Square, but only an idiot would fail to notice that it was a detour of some sort. Andrew liked the sound of very busy Durbar Square, but Kirsten insisted that they take the alley. She wanted to get Andrew home as quickly as possible.

Andrew endured two minutes of abject terror in the alley and it bothered him that Kirsten didn't seem to share his concerns. She was making small talk while he was searching the drains for a hand around his ankle. The alley was so quiet that Maurice could easily have been tempted to charge them. There was no room for manoeuvre, nowhere to hide. If he surprised them they would be finished. Andrew listened to Kathmandu. He listened for steps. He listened for breathing, running, screaming. He looked upwards at the windows, at the balconies, at the rooftops. Then he realised that Maurice could have run ahead of them. He could be any-fucking-where!

But they made it to their hotel alive, and Andrew was posted as guard on the front door while Kirsten checked them out in advance of the morning. By law she had to write their destination in the register. Once Maurice read that then he would be able to follow them to the end of the world. Two minutes later they ran to their room and slammed the heavy door shut, locking it, and wedging a chair against it. Andrew sat on his bed. At least their door was heavy, not the kind of door you could kick in. Then he leapt up and rammed the bed hard up against it, just to be sure. He was breathing quickly and, again, he could taste blood in his mouth. Kirsten was laughing like a school bully.

'He's here. He's here,' she laughed, 'and by now he will be reading the register.'

'We shouldn't have checked out,' Andrew said. 'We should have just slipped some money behind the counter in the morning.'

'Well it makes me laugh,' said Kirsten. 'He thinks that he is so clever but he is falling into our trap. He let us see him. That is so unprofessional. He is just human, nothing more. But you have to be strong Andrew. You have to trust me. We can beat him.'

'But he'll know that we're going trekking.'

'We're not going trekking.'

'No?'

'We can't. Not now.'

'Then what will we do?'

'We'll take the bus to New Delhi and decide there.'

Andrew let out a sigh. 'That bastard's fucked things up for me again...'

'There will be other chances to see the mountains,' Kirsten said, kicking off her shoes. 'Once we have finished with Maurice and Carlo.'

'And what will we do with ourselves in the meantime?'

Kirsten sat on the bed and pulled off her trousers.

'It's the middle of the afternoon and we're trapped in our room,' Andrew said angrily. He couldn't relax. He stood and paced the room like a big cat in a cage.

Kirsten was laughing. 'Relax,' she said. 'Just look at you.' She pulled off her T-shirt and her erect nipples pointed invitingly at Andrew. Kirsten was wearing nothing more than a devilish grin on her face. 'Please don't tell me that you're bored,' she said. 'I can think of a million ways to spend the afternoon. Don't you want to find out what I mean?'

Andrew hesitated momentarily and Kirsten lay down on the bed. 'Come on,' she said. 'Don't tell me you don't feel lucky today.'

'Oh, I feel lucky alright,' Andrew agreed, but if he did feel lucky now, he was pretty sure it wasn't going to last.

Chapter 23

Room twelve was at the end of a narrow corridor on the third floor of the hotel. Maurice stood outside it. There were three other rooms on the floor, one opposite and two further back towards the stairs. The sound of lovemaking emanated from the room, which Maurice found arousing. They could not have seen him after all, he concluded, or they wouldn't be capable of making love. He gently tried the door handle. It turned. He stopped for a moment and bent to take the knife he had strapped around his ankle. With the knife in one hand, he turned the handle again, listening hard for any interruption to the lovemaking. With the handle fully turned he leant against the door. It didn't budge. Immediately he stood upright and slowly let the handle go. The door was locked securely. He wouldn't get them that way. As Maurice bent to look through the keyhole, the door to number eleven opened and a man looked out.

'Lost somebody?'

Maurice was startled but he regained his composure immediately. The man who spoke to him was one of those he hated most of all – a hippy. Maurice smiled. 'I wanted to speak to Andrew but I think that he's occupied.'

'So would you be if you travelled with a woman like Kirsten,' said the hippy. 'They won't be finished for hours. I've been listening to them for days: they're like rabbits.'

'I should come back later then,' said Maurice, and he turned to leave.

'I'll tell them you were here,' said the hippy, and Maurice stopped.

'I had hoped that Andrew might have some hashish,' said Maurice. 'I wanted to buy some.' He waited while the hippy thought about what he had said. The hippy was from the older generation, perhaps fifty years old. Maurice thought him ridiculous in his tie-dye T-shirt, singlet, shorts and flip-flops. His hair was long and thinning. His beard had a gingery-grey tint to it.

'Come on in,' he said. 'We can share a few smokes.'

'Thank you,' said Maurice. 'I appreciate it. You can tell me more about the lovers.'

An hour later, after a brief pause, the sound of lovemaking in the next room was as frenzied as ever. Maurice was becoming irritated. His companion was talking nonsense. 'Astronomy should be compulsory in schools,' the man said. 'After all, it's where we're at in the universe.'

'I wouldn't have thought you'd believe in compulsion,' said Maurice. 'Isn't that against everything you stand for?'

The man just stared. After a moment he continued unsteadily. 'It's amazing,' he said, 'but you wouldn't understand unless you'd dropped acid. If only Grace Slick had dropped acid in the White House punch, it could have changed history. Wow man, I'm talking early seventies. Everyone thought that if Nixon took acid then everything would be okay.'

Maurice looked out of the window at the brick buildings opposite. High above, a kite hovered across his line of vision and dived suddenly towards the ground and then soared again. On the rooftops, amid a sea of fluttering laundry and tall television aerials, dozens of children looked upwards, tugging at strings. As each kite competed for position, the children whooped and leapt and patted each other on the back. Such innocent fun, thought Maurice and he turned back to the man who was slumped on his bed, dragging hard on a joint he really didn't need. Maurice despised him. The man was in Asia to do nothing but smoke hashish and eat cheap food. He needed Asia but Asia had little use for him. 'Why are you here?' said Maurice, suddenly unable to stomach the man. 'What is your purpose?'

'I have no purpose,' the man replied, uncertainly. 'I'm just having a good time.'

'Smoking joints in a darkened room with a stranger is a good time?'

'Yeah man, of course.' He pulled himself upright and smiled. 'The best part of the trip is meeting people. You can meet people out here who become friends for life. You can be strangers one minute but compadres the next.'

'And I'm your compadre now?'

'I thought so.'

'You trust me after an hour?'

'Absolutely.'

'But you don't know me.'

'I don't need to know you. We're the same; we're both on the road. What do I need to know? I've met people on buses and spent the next six months travelling with them. What is there to know?'

'I could be a thief.'

'I've never lost a thing to another traveller.'

'But you've lost things to Asians?'

'Occasionally.'

'So you trust travellers but you don't trust Asians?'

The man looked concerned. 'You should lighten up. I trust you. Why wouldn't I?'

'Because I'm a fucking Asian,' sneered Maurice, as an image of his father flashed before him. 'I'm a fucking Asian.'

'I'm sorry,' the man said, 'but I think you're twisting my words.'

Maurice hit him.

The man groaned, dropped the joint and slumped backwards onto the bed. He rolled onto his side and vomited down the wall as a wave of nausea and fear washed over him. 'There was no need for that,' he whimpered as he choked and spat. He pulled himself upright and shakily held his hand against his bruised eye. 'I don't understand what I've done to offend you? There was no need to hit me.'

'There was every need,' Maurice said and he kicked the man hard across the nose, sending him crashing back against the wall. As the man fell forward, Maurice kicked him again and he slumped unconscious across the bed.

In a rucksack Maurice found a collection of well-worn clothing, an old tin mug, a Nepalese phrase book, a bottle of insect repellent and a small lump of hashish. There was nothing of any value. He moved the man over and looked beneath his pillow. He found a money belt. Inside it was an American passport, a collection of traveller's cheques and fifty dollars worth of Nepalese rupees.

'You can take my money,' the man whispered, recovering consciousness, 'but please don't hit me again.'

Maurice scanned the room until he found what he wanted. He smiled at the hippy to disarm him and pulled his pillow from beneath him. The man tried to return a smile but, as he did so, Maurice straddled him and forced the pillow over his face. The man grabbed Maurice's wrists and clawed at him, scratching his skin with his fingernails but Maurice pressed harder and the man's legs kicked out, his knees pushing desperately against Maurice's kidneys. For nearly two minutes the man fought his new compadre but Maurice pressed harder still and, gradually, the man began to lose strength; his fingers lost their grip and his legs dropped weakly onto the bed. Finally he gave up the struggle and, moments later, he died.

Movement disturbed Maurice's moment of pleasure. The lovemaking had stopped and now he could hear the sound of naked feet slapping across the cold floor of the next room. As he listened a toilet flushed and somebody ran a tap. Maurice walked into the bathroom and looked up towards a grill high on the wall. He realised that like many hotels in Asia the bathrooms were connected. If he was lucky he would be able to see into next door. He skipped back to the bedroom, picked up the chair and returned to the bathroom. He set the chair against the wall. Silently he climbed up and peered through the grill. He was incredulous. Below him, next door, Kirsten was splashing water in her face. She was naked and, even from where he stood, Maurice could see that her skin glowed red. He was that close.

Kirsten saw him. She turned in surprise and was about to shout out when she realised who it was, and she grinned like a Cheshire cat. 'You read the letter then?' she whispered. She was flirting with him.

Her nipples were erect and her skin was flushed. Her breathing was quickening. Maurice felt his heart pounding with excitement and he realised that he had an erection. He felt hypnotised.

Maurice broke from the spell. Kirsten was masturbating. He watched her lean back against the doorjamb and slip her fingers inside herself, harder and harder. 'Who do you think you are dealing with?' Maurice asked, but Kirsten didn't answer. She didn't seem to care. They were having sex together Maurice realised, as he began to touch himself. He couldn't believe it but, at that moment, he would have done anything for there to have been a door in that wall. Suddenly he shuddered as he came unexpectedly. He closed his eyes with satisfaction. When he opened them again, Kirsten had gone.

Maurice went back to the bedroom and sat on the bed beside his victim. He was stunned. He couldn't understand what had just happened. The incident had excited him in a way that the murder hadn't. *Kirsten was crazy*, he thought. She must have known that he intended to kill her, yet she was willing to play sex games with him. What kind of a woman was she?

He stood suddenly, his decision made. He wanted her. He wanted to take her and, afterwards, perhaps he would strangle her, but perhaps he would not. Either way it would be the most wonderful experience of his life. First though, he would play her little game. He would fly to Bangkok as instructed, and he would give her what she wanted. She wanted to manipulate him, but by knowing that and allowing her to do so, he felt that the role had been reversed. He laughed when he remembered the entry in the register. One thing was certain: she wasn't going trekking. Her letter was leading him to Carlo and he knew that she would be there when he found him. One day she would pay for her little torments.

Chapter 24

New Delhi, on a map, was just down the road from Kathmandu but, on a bus, it was a lifetime away. Nonetheless, after a thirty-six-hour journey, with the variety and expectations of any great city, it was a great place to arrive at.

The heaving mass of humanity, the third largest city in India, was where the British had ended their involvement after nearly 350 years of colonial occupation and where, before the British, Shah Jahan, the second last great Moghul emperor, had built his ultimate capital city of mosques, monuments, tombs and red sandstone forts.

They left the bus feeling like somebody had been punching them in the kidneys to keep them awake. After fighting off hordes of motorised rickshaw drivers they agreed a fare with a man with an honest face and spent a few exciting minutes whizzing through the wide empty streets, in a vehicle that sounded like a screaming lawn mower hitting a crazy-paving path. Although the driver insisted otherwise, their intended hostel was not fully occupied, but it was busy. Luckily for them, they were second in the queue behind a backpacker who had spent the past two hours in the hostel doorway, waiting for the place to open.

An hour later, at the top of a steep flight of narrow stairs, they entered one of India's many backpacker havens, where the tired or nervous took sanctuary alongside like-minded souls and spent a few days enjoying lazy conversation, book swapping and club sandwiches. A middle-aged man with thinning hair showed them to a dormitory across a rooftop courtyard. The seven beds were side-by-side along the wall, with just enough room at one end for them to get past. Theirs were the two nearest the window at the far end of the room. The window, a hole knocked into the wall, was obscured by a defunct, grease-covered air-conditioning unit the size of a lorry engine. The unit gave the room the feel and smell of a workshop. Nobody stirred when they entered.

Four hours later Andrew woke with a start and spent a few seconds getting his bearings. A woman in a towel was standing at the end of a bed about four metres from his. She realised that he was awake but she dropped the towel anyway and pulled a T-shirt over her head. 'You arrived during the night?' she asked and Andrew felt his face turning red as he averted his tired eyes from her crotch.

'From Kathmandu,' he said and he could hear Kirsten stirring in her bed. The woman pulled on a pair of white knickers and followed them quickly with a thin skirt. She was as skinny as hell, Andrew thought, with short black hair, tiny tits and long legs, but her face was tender and she had a fantastic mouth. Her accent was French.

'No wonder you are asleep so long,' she said. The woman smiled and Andrew could feel Kirsten's waking presence behind him. 'I was in Nepal one week ago. The journey was terrible.' There was a moment's hesitation while they both searched for conversation. The woman broke the silence. 'Where did you trek?' she said.

'We didn't get the chance...'

'You didn't go to the mountains?'

'There wasn't...'

'But why else go to Nepal?'

'We wanted to go trekking but we ran out of time.'

'That's a terrible shame. Are you going to Goa? Is that why you are in a hurry?'

'Goa?'

'For Christmas.'

'No, we've no plans. Is that where you're heading?'

'Of course. Everybody is heading to Goa. Too many people go to Goa for Christmas. If you want to find a house to rent, you have to go early. It will be fantastic.' She smiled again and turned away to put on a pair of leather sandals. Then she picked up a small cloth bag, gave Andrew another smile, and walked out of the room.

'You were flirting with her,' said Kirsten, giving Andrew a shove in the back.

'I wasn't,' he said, far too quickly.

'She was flirting with you.'

'Nobody flirts with me. Anyway, I don't need to flirt. I've got you.'

'You don't have me Andrew,' Kirsten replied. She sounded offended. 'I don't want you to think like that. One day I will be gone. What we are doing is just convenient.'

'Convenient!'

'Don't be so shocked. We are travelling together. Why wouldn't we sleep together?'

'You didn't let me anywhere near you for six months! If our relationship is purely convenient, why weren't we sleeping together before?'

'I didn't find you attractive before. Things change.'

'So I'm attractive to you now?'

'Yes.'

'That's something, I suppose,' Andrew said, and he reflected upon the fact that Kirsten had almost paid him a compliment. 'Why are you angry with me then?' he asked, remembering that Kirsten had started this stupid conversation.

'I'm not angry. I just don't want you to forget that we must find Carlo.'

'How could I forget that?'

Kirsten pulled back her sheet. 'There's nobody in here now,' she said, looking around the dormitory. 'Let me remind you why you want me so much.'

Two hours later Andrew woke again, this time in Kirsten's bed. The room was empty and Kirsten was asleep. Andrew climbed out of bed, pulled on a pair of trousers and a T-shirt and took his towel and wash-bag from the side pocket of his rucksack. Outside the room people were lounging about in the mid-afternoon sunshine, reading, writing, eating and chatting. Andrew crossed the floor, smiling at anyone who looked up, and locked himself behind one of the warped wooden shower doors at the far side of the roof. The shower smelt of blocked drains and the floor felt like a bed of moss, but the flow of water was strong and cold and Andrew could feel energy and freshness pouring back into his veins.

Succeeding in getting the photographs of Maurice and having put some distance between them so quickly was satisfying. He couldn't wait to post them to Interpol and get on with his life again. It was time to meet a few normal people and have a little fun. That's what travel was supposed to be all about. If only Kirsten would forget about Carlo; just send off Anthony's details with the photograph of Maurice and they were out of it. As he was thinking this he dropped his soap and watched, frustrated, as it bounced once and slid down a hole in the corner of the cubicle. There was no way on earth that he was sticking his arm in there to retrieve it.

Chapter 25

In Bangkok, the police clerk stepped back from the road and hesitated when he saw that the driver of the car, which had almost knocked him down, was Maurice.

'Get in,' Maurice said, flinging the passenger door open. The clerk hesitated and considered making a run for it. 'I'll visit your wife instead,' said Maurice, realising accurately what the frightened man was thinking.

The clerk frowned. Walking unsteadily forward he searched the street, not knowing how to save himself. Then, resigned to his fate, he ducked into the front passenger seat, slammed the door shut and stared through the windscreen as Maurice drove back into the rush hour. *All the years of lying and cheating had come to this*, he thought.

Ten minutes later the car was bogged down in traffic. Drivers and passengers hung their elbows through windows and sat stoney-faced, trying to breathe the stifling air. Cars and trucks and open-backed utility vehicles containing entire workforces and families sat motionless like cattle trucks at the border. Only motorbikes were on the move.

'I had a visitor in Kathmandu,' said Maurice, glancing at his passenger to see if he was listening. 'She told me plenty about you.'

'She trapped me,' said the clerk. 'She threatened to kill me.'

'And you believed her?'

'Yes.'

'Why?'

'Because...'

'Because?'

'She made threats. She said that they...'

'They?'

'She told me that she worked for an organisation…'

'An organisation more powerful than me?'

'Yes.'

'You are a fool,' said Maurice as the traffic began to move. 'There is nobody more powerful than me.'

An hour out of Bangkok, Maurice pulled off the road and drove down a narrow pathway, surrounded on both sides by ditches and rice fields. They passed a group of women with long poles and nets fishing in a ditch, recently swollen by rain. The clerk sat silently, not seeing anything, his fear pervading the car like gas fumes. Maurice was delighted. Ten minutes later he pulled up outside a small house hidden behind a wall of banana trees and turned off the engine. The clerk didn't move.

'Come inside,' said Maurice. 'We can have a drink.'

Maurice had been renting the house as a hideaway for the past three years. He used it because there were no neighbours within half a mile and there was a large garden, surrounded on two sides by banana trees and bordered at the far end by a winding river of brown water. It was almost impossible for anybody passing to see into the garden at night. He unlocked the front door and let the clerk into the house, then he locked the door from the inside and turned on the light. The house was small and undecorated, with barely enough furniture to fulfil the needs of one man. 'Spartan,' said Maurice, 'but I'm not often here.'

The clerk raised an understanding smile but didn't speak. He was fighting his fear but he was close to tears. Occasionally, when Maurice wasn't looking, he wiped his eyes.

'Would you like a drink?' said Maurice, opening the door of a small fridge.

The clerk lowered himself into a chair without answering.

'Whisky, I think,' said Maurice. 'A large one.'

The clerk took the whisky from Maurice and sipped at it. He relaxed slightly and finished the glass moments later. Maurice poured him another.

'We are only here to talk,' Maurice said. 'I'll soon have you back with your family.'

There was silence while the clerk cleared his throat so that he could speak. 'I love my wife,' he finally rasped. 'I would do nothing to harm her. You know that you can rely upon me.'

'Of course,' said Maurice. 'I just need information about the European woman and the people who sent her.'

'You will let me go?' said the clerk, and Maurice sensed that the man was about to be physically sick.

'I will drive you home… and you will never see me again.'

'I'm sorry,' said the clerk, through a series of sobs, 'but I was expecting…'

'What I am really interested to know,' said Maurice, genuinely perplexed, 'is how did they find out about you?'

The clerk was surprised that Maurice didn't know. He wiped his eyes and looked up. 'They found the copy that I made of the Englishman's passport,' he said. 'The copy I gave to you.'

Maurice was momentarily silent and then he laughed. 'Yes,' he said. 'It is my fault – I dropped it. It is my fault.' His error worried him; he was losing control. He'd started making stupid mistakes and now the woman was getting the better of him. 'What convinced you that the woman was working with others?' he asked, as he stood behind the clerk. 'Did she mention a name?'

'No name,' the clerk replied. He was beginning to regain some composure. 'But she said that she worked for your enemy. She had done so much to blackmail me. I couldn't believe that she could have done that on her own.'

'Of course,' said Maurice. What puzzled him was the question of Carlo's involvement. If Carlo did have anything to do with it, why didn't he follow him to Kathmandu? Why send the woman and her boyfriend? It didn't make sense. Carlo could not be involved. The woman was setting the two of them up, he thought. After what had happened in the bathroom in Kathmandu, he knew that she was capable of it. He leant over the clerk's shoulder and refilled his glass. 'Have another drink,' he said.

An hour passed. The clerk finished the bottle and was leaning heavily forwards. Maurice knew that the man would soon be unconscious; the effect of the whisky and the sleeping pills that he'd slipped into the bottle were having the usual effect. Maurice walked into the kitchen and looked out of the window. The garden was in darkness. He filled a large iron bucket with water, took two lengths of rope from a cupboard and returned to the clerk, who was now lying slumped on the floor. Maurice tied up the man's arms and legs with the rope and dragged him through to the kitchen where he dropped him heavily beside the bucket. Maurice lifted him up, pushed his head into the bucket, and drowned him.

Afterwards Maurice changed into an old T-shirt and a pair of shorts. He emptied the clerk's pockets, removing all identification, then he dragged the body into the garden and dropped it a few feet above the river. He walked back into the house and returned carrying an instamatic camera, a white sheet and a large garden spade. He placed the camera on the sheet a distance from the body and began to dig a grave.

An hour later, the grave dug, Maurice was standing unsteadily above the body, the spade hanging loosely beside him. With a sigh, he lifted the spade high above his head and brought it crashing down upon the clerk's neck. There was a thumping sound but, to Maurice's despair, even though blood oozed from the wound, the head remained attached to the body. Maurice swore aloud, hit the neck again, several times in quick succession, and almost cheered as the head severed, spinning and rolling to one side. Moments later the headless corpse was lying in its grave and Maurice was leaning forwards, panting heavily, hands on his knees, eyes fixed firmly on what was once the face of a respected public servant.

Once he had recovered, Maurice washed his hands in the river and dried them on his shorts. He took the camera from the sheet and placed the sheet beside the head. With his feet, he rolled the head onto the sheet until it was positioned facing towards him. There could be no doubt, he thought, that the head belonged to the clerk. Anybody who knew him would recognise that. He stood back and photographed the head in a blast of flashlight and, moments later, the image appeared before him. Yes, he decided, there was no doubt that this was the clerk and there could be absolutely no doubt that the man was dead. Had he photographed the man with his head attached, the man might have appeared unconscious or asleep and he would have wasted a night's work.

He took three further photographs and placed them with the camera beside the back door to the house, then he kicked the head into the grave, threw the sheet in after it, added his soiled clothes to the collection and filled in the hole. He threw the spade into the river and joined it for a bath seconds later.

The following morning Maurice drove away from his rented house for the last time. In Bangkok, he sent a cheque to the owner of the house which would pay the rent for another year and keep the place free of intruders. Then, as instructed, he posted the photographs of the dead clerk to four post offices in India, and returned to his Bangkok apartment to enjoy a real shower and a good meal. It would be a while before he received a reply to his grisly messages. Hopefully, the reply would lead him towards Carlo.

Chapter 26

Kirsten made her call to the American Embassy in Jakarta from a telephone in the luxurious Ashok Hotel, a pleasant ten-minute rickshaw ride from the hustle and bustle of the streets around their hostel. They had been in Delhi for three days. Andrew was still in bed when Kirsten left, although, by now, he was probably chatting with his new friends from the dormitory.

When Anthony answered, he was polite but cagey. Twice he had sent the secretary back to the phone, saying that he was busy. 'Can I help you?' he said.

'Hello Anthony,' Kirsten replied, listening to his breathing at the other end, trying to figure out what was going through his mind. 'My name is Kirsten. I'm a friend of Carlo's.'

There was a brief silence before Anthony replied. 'I'm sorry,' he said. 'Kirsten, you say? A friend of Carlo's? Are you sure you have the right number? I don't know a Carlo.'

'Please don't fuck me about,' Kirsten said, smiling to herself. 'I could write to the ambassador and tell him to check the records to find whether any unapproved passports have been issued recently. What do you think of that?'

'What do you want?' Anthony asked.

'A little cooperation. I need to find Carlo.'

'Why?'

'I have information for him.'

'Such as?'

'Something about Maurice.'

Anthony cut her off so sharply that Kirsten took the phone away from her ear. 'Don't!' he shouted. 'Don't mention him over the phone again. In fact, don't say anymore. I'll contact Carlo and find out what he wants to do. Then I'll call you back.'

Forty minutes later, Anthony called back from a hotel and gave Kirsten what she wanted to hear. 'Goa,' he said.

'Goa?'

'Is that so strange?'

'No, it's perfect.'

'For what?'

'Beaches.'

'Yeah right.' Anthony sniffed. 'He wants you there immediately. Where are you now?'

'Don't worry where I am. Just tell me what to do.'

'Go to Vagator Beach and he'll find you.'

'No,' Kirsten hissed. 'That's no good. I need to know where he is.'

'Vagator Beach. Don't look for him. He'll find you. Take a holiday. Get a sun tan. He'll contact you.'

'If he wants the information then I need to know where he is.' Kirsten's grip on the telephone tightened as the pitch of her voice rose.

'Your choice lady,' said Anthony, feeling as if he was gaining the upper hand. 'But I tell you this – if you call me at the embassy again, you're dead meat. Carlo will see to that himself. He can find you if he wants to. You hear? Don't call me again.'

The line went dead and Kirsten realised that she was shouting. She took a deep breath and replaced the receiver in its cradle. Then, ignoring bemused glances from a number of elderly, check-jacketed tourists, she walked from the hotel and hailed a rickshaw back to her hostel.

At the hostel, Kirsten ignored Andrew and his new crowd who were laughing loudly out on the rooftop. She skipped quickly into the dormitory and opened her rucksack. Pushing her arm through her clothing to the bottom of the bag, she removed a small writing pad and some envelopes. She dropped the bag beside the bed and sat back against the wall. She began to write.

When the letter was finished, Kirsten sealed it in an envelope and addressed the envelope to a Mister Zimmerman, care of the poste restante in Bangkok. There was no way that she was going to let a piece of shit like Anthony talk to her like that. It didn't make sense, she knew, but she wasn't going to wait to receive the letter from Maurice, before sending her reply. The sooner he was on the trail the better, she decided.

Without stopping to speak to Andrew, Kirsten headed back onto the streets and hailed another rickshaw. Andrew watched her go. He was worried by the way she had been acting since Kathmandu but he was enjoying his new friends and he really needed a break from their life of intrigue. Kirsten would have him stressing over her hunt for Carlo soon enough. Even so, he couldn't understand her sudden preoccupation with Post Offices, particularly as nobody had written to her since he'd known her.

The rickshaw did a U-turn across Janpath, the main road, and headed into Connaught Place, New Delhi's business centre. In heavy traffic it took almost ten minutes to reach the Post Office. Buying a stamp and sending the letter took a further twenty minutes and checking the poste restante to find that no letter was waiting took a further five. During that time Kirsten cheered herself up by reminding herself that, with nothing more than a vague threat, she had almost located Carlo. If he could find her on Vagator Beach, then she could find him there too, especially as he probably wouldn't expect her to be so cunning.

She walked back to the hostel and, even when a group of spotty youths shouted abuse at her, she didn't stop smiling. She was thinking about the look on Maurice's face through the grill on the bathroom wall in Kathmandu, thinking that even he had fallen under her spell, and nothing could distract her from that.

Chapter 27

Winter had passed into spring, metaphorically speaking of course, and Andrew was beginning to enjoy life again. The people frantically securing their rucksacks beneath the seat of his sleeper carriage were a mixed bunch of international layabouts, all so poor that, until today, they had been forced to share a dormitory with Andrew and Kirsten. Now they were sharing a second class carriage and preparing to meet half of India. Mixing with the backpackers was exhilarating.

Andrew was thoughtful. The last time he had talked with backpackers for any length of time, they had wound up dead. Even then, the conversation had been of drugs and smuggling, almost like everyone who was anyone was doing it. Now they were talking about the excitement of India and the places they had been to, or were heading to next; Rajastan, the "Land of the Kings" where you could wander around sand-coloured fortresses and ride lazy camels out into the Thar Desert; Himachel Pradesh and its hill stations, where the British used to hide from the heat, and which were now home to thousands of Tibetan refugees including the exiled Dalai Lama; Goa, synonymous with miles of palm-fringed, sun-coloured beaches and midnight parties. This was more like it; this was backpacking at its simple, most uncomplicated, innocent best.

Five days earlier, Kirsten had suggested that they should travel to Goa. There had been no mention of Carlo and Andrew wasn't going to bring him up, so he agreed. Goa was 1200 miles further south of Maurice, and Andrew was secretly hoping that Kirsten had lost interest in revenge, although he wasn't convinced. He had a funny feeling that she had a surprise up her sleeve. The best bit for Andrew, though, was that there was a tribe of backpackers from the hostel heading to Goa with them.

Sylvia, the woman he met on his first morning in the dormitory, had introduced him to the tribe that same afternoon. They were gathered at the top of the stairs to the roof, hidden amongst the drying laundry, sharing a joint in the afternoon sun. The leader of the group was a thirty-year-old Australian woman called Donna. She had a sharp-featured, confident face with a long, thin nose, high brow and high cheekbones. Her black hair was cut short. When she smiled her eyes glistened with fire. She was wearing a thin green shirt and long blue paisley cotton trousers. Whenever she spoke, conversation stopped and everyone gave her their full attention. She had everyone by the balls because she could read and speak Hindi. While the others talked, she read newspapers and, when she found something interesting, she read it out. 'Following recent flooding, roads into Manali are still under repair…' she'd say, and somebody would pass her a joint to coerce her into finishing. 'Which means that Goa remains our obvious destination for Christmas.' Everything was matter-of-fact with her, like there could be no argument. It was obvious that most of the group idolised her. She had a strength that they could only dream of. When nobody else was listening, Andrew got her to check the English football results.

Donna also knew a great house that was up for rent in Goa. She had stayed there the previous year and knew the owner, a woman in Bombay, who said that she could have the place again as long as she booked early. The more people sharing the place, the cheaper it would be. The two other women in the group were Karen, a red-haired American lesbian with fantastic freckles and thoroughly divorced parents, and Jessica, an insensitive Englishwoman who only spoke when she had something spiteful or negative to say. Jessica's parents were diplomats of some kind. It was impossible to tell which of them she despised the most.

At the age of thirty-three, Henrik was the oldest member of the tribe. Being Swedish, he spoke more languages than Donna, but Hindi wasn't one of them. Like the others, though, he was happy to allow Donna to lead, although in his case it was probably only because it saved him doing all the work. Donna was the one who knew India, understood the culture, checked things out, bought tickets and suggested itineraries. Henrik's speciality was buying cheap dope and finding the coldest beer.

The last tribe member was Simon, a twenty-seven-year-old ginger-bearded Englishman, 100% covered in freckles. He didn't have a clue what was going on; his expression was permanently one of confusion, so being led around India was fine by him. The others were always giving him a hard time because his clothes were in such bad shape. 'I'll buy new clothes at the flea-markets in Goa,' was his stock response. Henrik bet Andrew twenty rupees that he wouldn't.

They had all been ready to travel to Goa for ages but Kirsten had wanted to hang on for a letter from a friend in Germany. She refused to tell Andrew anything about this friend, saying that it was personal, and he suspected that she was lying, perhaps because she wasn't sure what she wanted to do next. Then, before most of the backpackers were out of bed one morning, Kirsten returned from the post office with her letter. Within half an hour Donna was despatched to the station with group permission to pay a bribe to get tickets for eight people to Bombay, leaving today. She took Simon along. The rest of them packed and checked out.

So here they were, preparing for their seventeen-hour journey, looking forward to intermittent station chaos, worrying about the safety of their baggage, concerned about the toilets, hoping for a dining car and expecting an experience that could fall anywhere between heaven and hell. This was backpacking as Andrew loved it: a fabulous, expectant chaos.

The only group member who worried Andrew was Kirsten. All the others had their personalities and were sticking to them. Kirsten had so many personalities that he felt that he knew more people than she did. Since she had received her friend's letter, she had been going through the strangest mood swings; talking to herself, laughing, being unreasonably angry, being strangely kind. Andrew couldn't keep up.

Andrew had tried talking with Kirsten several times but he knew that he was skirting around the issue by not mentioning Maurice or Carlo. He simply wasn't willing to go that far. He asked Kirsten if she was ill. He asked if she was looking forward to Goa. He asked her numerous questions, but he avoided asking her the obvious. He decided that short-term misery for Kirsten would be worth the long-term result. Time, he hoped, would be the healer.

Instead, he got into the swing of things, flirted with Sylvia, talked fabulous inane shit with everyone and haggled with the station platform hawkers over the price of chai, bananas, samosas, boiled eggs and packets of orange crunchy biscuits. While the train was in the station it felt as if the entire world had come visiting. Faces appeared at carriage windows; hands and fingers snaked their way through the bars. Men shouted 'Chai, chai,' with universally hoarse voices, nothing like their own. The carriage filled with anxious hawkers, mostly young children with snacks and warm cold drinks, who scrambled over passenger's outstretched feet, trying to make a rupee before the train departed with a jolt. They had to be quick. Sometimes the unlucky ones were carried away to the next station. Quite a few went unpaid.

Station halts were exhausting. Andrew once had the unique experience of being in a station waiting room, rather than on a train, and he was able to watch these goings-on without being involved. The departure of each train created a platform-wide vacuum. The resulting silence was tangible. The combatants withdrew to count their profits, lick their wounds and find fresh supplies.

In seventeen hours they would arrive at Bombay Central Station. They then had to take a taxi or a train across the city to Victoria Station to buy onward tickets to Vasco Da Gama in Goa. Henrik was in the luggage rack, rolling a joint. He was keeping one eye on the rusty fan, just above his head. Donna was talking with some Indian women in the corridor. Sylvia was gazing out of the window. Karen and Jessica were helping Simon with his Walkman. Kirsten was down the corridor somewhere. Andrew expected her to pop back once she got bored. Their relationship was going through its worst patch so far. As usual there wasn't much that he could do about it. The train jolted back into life and, as shouting voices filled the air, he again noticed Sylvia enjoying the view. *Why couldn't Kirsten be like her*, he wondered?

Chapter 28

Maurice watched Anthony drive through the high iron gates to his house. The street was quiet, each house separated by grass lawns and palm trees. There was money here. In this street lived Jakarta's wealthy; locals and expatriates alike. Maurice waited for Anthony to close the front door behind him before flicking the motorbike into gear with his foot. He drove through the gates and parked between Anthony's car and the house.

Maurice had watched the embassy for two days until he chose the man to approach. He was Indonesian, sixty years old and each time Maurice watched him leave for home, the man had looked downtrodden, only too glad to be heading home. This, Maurice decided, was a man who would enjoy deriding his employers, given the opportunity.

Maurice followed him onto a bus and sat beside him on the seat behind the driver. There was little ventilation and the man was sweating profusely. 'The heat will kill us all one day,' said Maurice, and the man smiled. 'You look like you've had a hard day,' Maurice said, trying to elicit a response. The man smiled again and looked out through the window at the traffic, now bumper to bumper and motionless.

Maurice sat back and took an orange from his bag. He peeled it slowly, squeezing it slightly to force the aroma from the fruit, and slipped a portion into his mouth. Out of the corner of his eye he noticed the man turn his head and sniff the air gently. *Hooked*, Maurice thought, and he took another orange from his bag. 'Orange?' he said and the man nodded.

Within minutes they were locked in conversation, the man's gratitude betraying his reticence. He was a clerk at the embassy, working on reception where he had been for six years without any hope of advancement. He enjoyed the job most of the time, certainly he was doing better than any of his friends, so he couldn't really complain. Even so, he was a nobody, whilst the Americans, even the most junior, were flying high, enjoying fantastic lifestyles, belittling him without even knowing it. This was his country, so why was he the poor relation?

Maurice agreed entirely, he said. It was the same all over Asia. The Americans and the Europeans were colonising them with their bank loans, pushing them further into debt, selling them arms, stirring up conflicts, influencing elections, supporting dictatorships. Nothing had changed, said Maurice, and nothing ever would. 'So who annoys you most of all?' Maurice asked the man, taking two more oranges from his bag.

'The younger ones,' the man replied, taking an orange from Maurice and thanking him with a nod of the head. 'The older ones seem to understand our ways.' Maurice didn't interrupt. The clerk was beginning to talk freely. 'The worst of them all are the ones who issue visas. They talk about Indonesians as if we all want to work illegally in the United States. They think that their country is greater than ours, because they have so much technology, but we are also proud of our country.' He mentioned the worst officials by name, describing their faults and listing his grievances against them. The Americans spent their money on luxuries; cars, fine houses, parties, whilst he supported his extended family, sending money to his parents who lived nearly three hundred miles away in the Javan city of Surabaya.

To Maurice's delight, Anthony's name finally came up. Anthony was a single man, the man said, who was known to take Indonesian girlfriends and treat them like prostitutes, discarding them once he'd become bored with them. In his opinion, this was the worst thing that a western man could do to an Indonesian woman.

'What do Indonesian women see in him?' Maurice asked.

'He drives a new Japanese car. They're popular here.' The man thought for a moment. 'And he imports his clothes from Singapore. It's not surprising that women like him. He has everything.'

Maurice laughed. 'So he has everything except good looks?'

'I don't know what is considered good looking in a man. He is quite normal – in fact, he is short for an American.' At last, a moment of satisfaction. 'He is losing his hair too,' he said. 'I've seen him combing it in the staff toilets, trying to spread the hair across his head.'

'Money cannot buy everything,' Maurice said, and they both laughed.

Maurice laughed again as he remembered the conversation. He had remained on the bus until the man had left. Then he had taken a rickshaw back to within half a mile of his hotel and walked from there. The journey in the uncomfortable bus had been worthwhile. The description had been enough to put him on Anthony's tail.

Still thinking about the bus journey, Maurice rang the doorbell and listened to the sound of footsteps approaching the door. When Anthony appeared in the doorway, Maurice punched him hard on the jaw and shoved him forcefully backwards into the hallway. A glass flew from Anthony's hand and smashed against the wall, shattering glass splinters and splashing red wine across the white painted plaster. A flowerpot tipped over, spun sideways and spilt soil and a banana tree onto the parquet flooring. The door slammed shut and sealed the violence within.

Anthony looked up through a fog as Maurice kicked him hard in the right eye and followed the kick with a sharp flurry of kicks to the face, ribs and genitals. He could taste the blood flowing freely now, and his aching nose was obviously broken but he couldn't see the man who was trying to kill him, because his eyes were swollen shut. Blow after blow rained down on him and sent him into a foetal ball. Moments later he realised that, without any reason, the beating had stopped.

He didn't move for fear of precipitating a renewed attack. He had to be careful. Robbery wasn't uncommon in Jakarta, and he had been warned not to resist if he fell victim. People had been killed. Rather than spit to clear his throat, he opened his mouth slightly and felt it drain of blood. With his nose also blocked with blood, it was the first time he'd been able to breathe properly since the attack began. The blood warmed the palms of his hands, which he was still using to protect what was left of his face. Gently he caressed his cheeks and was relieved to find that they were not damaged. What worried him, though, was that because of the buzzing in his ears, he couldn't hear where his assailant was.

Maurice was running quickly around the house. The glass of wine had concerned him: was anyone else at home? Was anybody expected? Nothing indicated that either scenario was likely. The bedroom belonged to a bachelor; there were no women's clothes in the wardrobes. There were no tampons or make-up in the bathroom or toilet. The kitchen wasn't prepared for guests. Indeed, the kitchen was a mess; piles of crockery in the sink and a row of dirty wine glasses and bottles alongside. Anthony, Maurice decided, was a lonely man who drank for comfort.

Maurice locked the front door and hauled Anthony over his shoulder. As he did so, Anthony spoke for the first time. 'If you are looking for money,' he spluttered, 'it is in the bottom drawer in my bedroom. You can't miss it.' He knew as he spoke that he had dribbled blood down his assailant's back and he prayed that the man hadn't noticed.

'What other valuables do you have?' said Maurice. 'Where do you keep them?'

'My wallet is on the kitchen table. I have credit cards. Take them. I won't telephone the police. You can use them. I won't telephone anybody.'

Maurice couldn't withhold an almighty laugh. 'You must think I'm crazy.'

'I don't care about my money,' said Anthony, as he began to cry. 'Please, just don't hurt me again.'

'That is entirely in your hands, my friend. If you cooperate with me, you will keep your money and your good health. If you do not, I will gladly kill you.'

Maurice felt Anthony's body stiffen as he turned into the bathroom and lowered him into the bath. 'Cooperation will keep you alive,' he said, pulling Anthony's hands forward to tie them together. Anthony tried to blink, but his eyes wouldn't open. His body felt as if it was falling apart. He could feel Maurice tugging at him, pulling him into place. He sneezed and a cloud of congealing blood sprayed the back of Maurice's head. Maurice simply laughed and secured Anthony's feet. Then he forced the plug into the drain and turned on the taps.

'You are intelligent Anthony,' said Maurice. 'I'm sure you realise that once the water reaches above your head, you will drown. That is how long you have to answer my questions. The quicker you answer, the quicker I can ask them.' Maurice waited for this to sink in. 'Are you ready?'

Anthony nodded.

'Where is Carlo?'

Anthony didn't respond.

'Where is Carlo?'

'Who are you?' said Anthony, incredulous. This was no robbery, he realised. This was far worse.

'Where is Carlo?' Maurice repeated. 'It doesn't matter who I am. You will drown if you don't answer.'

'I can't tell you where he is. I don't know.'

Maurice grabbed his nose and twisted it until Anthony's agonised body had turned onto its side and blood flowed freely into the rising water. Anthony's horrified scream echoed around the bathroom and Maurice turned and closed the door.

'Please,' Anthony begged, 'I can't.'

'My name is Maurice,' he said. 'You know who I am. You know what I can do. Unless you cooperate I will strip you to the bone and post you home to your family. You can escape Carlo, but you're not going to escape me.'

'I didn't know. I… I am a friend of Carlo's, that's all.'

'Where is he?'

The water lapped against Anthony's chin and he lifted his head higher. 'Why do you want him?'

'Because he ruined my life. Where is he?'

'What will you do if you find him?'

'The same as I am going to do to you if you don't tell me where he is.'

The water lapped at Anthony's mouth and he raised his head again.

'You are about to drown. You will never see your family or friends again. Your parents will die of broken hearts because I will ensure that your face is unrecognisable after you are dead. They will know how much you suffered. Perhaps I will deliver your head to them personally. That could kill them.'

The water poured into Anthony's mouth and he began to splutter.

'Where is he?'

Anthony blinked. 'Goa,' he said as water began to fill his mouth. He could raise his head no higher.

'Where exactly?'

'Vagator Beach.'

'I need the details; address, telephone number, who is living with him?'

'There's an address book in the drawer in my bedroom.' The address book was where Anthony had said it would be. Maurice checked the book and found Carlo's address and telephone number. Maurice could barely breathe. He had him now. He closed the book, located Anthony's passport and money, which he pocketed, and headed back.

Anthony was thrashing about, sending cascades of water over the bathroom floor. Maurice went out to his motorbike and removed a bag from the rack at the back. He returned to the house, locking the door as he went. He stopped in the hallway, outside the bathroom, and placed some clothes from his bag on the floor. He pushed the address book and Anthony's money into the pocket of his spare trousers and threw the passport into the bathroom. Then he undressed and stuffed his soiled clothes into a plastic bag. He placed the plastic bag with the soiled clothes into his bag. From the bag, he took his instamatic camera and a thick-bladed butcher's knife. He placed the camera on the floor with his clothes and returned to Anthony, butcher's knife in hand. He closed the bathroom door behind him. Anthony had slipped beneath the surface but he was still alive. He was holding his breath. Maurice stuck the knife into his stomach and watched as blood seeped from the wound and the last of Anthony's breath bubbled to the surface. Then he unplugged the bath and turned off the taps. Five minutes later, covered from head to foot in blood, his knife cleaned under the bath tap, he stood with Anthony's head hanging by the hair.

He placed the camera on the side of the bath, set it on automatic, and stood six feet away with Anthony's head in one hand and the two bio-data pages of Anthony's passport in the other. The camera clicked and flashed. Dropping the head with a thump, Maurice picked up the camera, waited for the film to develop and, as the image appeared before him, he laughed – the photograph was exactly what was required. The head was clearly the same as the photograph in the passport and, placed casually between them, was Maurice's penis, a bonus for Kirsten to enjoy. He repeated the exercise three times. Then he threw the head into the bath, placed the camera, knife and photographs on the window ledge, the only part of the room which had remained blood free, and took a shower. Four hours later, having posted his four photographs and dumped the incriminating knife and clothes, Maurice was on an aeroplane high above the East Coast of Sumatra, heading for Singapore.

Chapter 29

The first leg of the journey to Bombay passed quickly, although the heat in the packed carriage had been oppressive. Henrik had challenged Andrew to a game of chess halfway through the journey and they had set up on a table in the dining car. It took just five minutes for a crowd to gather around; audience, supporters and critics.

Andrew liked to take his time. Henrik liked to hurry; he played white and went first, picking his piece up and slamming it down. The audience conferred; there were whispers of support and sighs of disappointment. Then, other than the rattle of the train, there was silence. Andrew brought his pawn out to meet the attack head on, and heads nodded in agreement. Somebody patted him on the back. Seeking to dominate support, Andrew glanced around and grinned at the smiling faces looking back. Henrik slammed another pawn into place. Andrew moved a pawn forward. The opening was standard. Outside, India was in darkness and only the lights of well-lit stations were visible as the train hurtled south. Halfway through the game, Sylvia found them hidden beneath a wall of spectators. She squeezed her way through and sat between them.

'Who is winning?' she asked.

'World peace,' said Henrik, referring to the crowd.

'And Henrik,' Andrew added, giving Sylvia a more honest answer. 'World peace needs more help than we can give it.'

Andrew moved a bishop, threatening Henrik's queen, and the conversation disappeared in a hum of excitement. Some of the crowd had seen the move earlier and had been biting their tongues. 'Oh yes,' one man hissed and Andrew turned to acknowledge his support. Sylvia laughed with feigned delight when she realised that Andrew now had Henrik on the run. She gave Andrew's knee a squeeze beneath the table, and he felt a surge of excitement more powerful than checkmate, rush through his body.

Henrik responded instantly. He was in trouble and he knew it. With a growl he attacked like a screaming heathen, slamming his own bishop in front of his queen, threatening all out war. Mathematically Andrew knew that he should win, so he sat back, smiled at Sylvia, still not certain whether he was happy with her hand on his knee, and moved a pawn. His supporters gave a collective sigh of approval and the stand-off began.

It was another hour before victory was Andrew's. When the game was over, Henrik called Andrew a wanker and headed back to his bunk to roll a joint. The crowd dispersed after a few final words and Andrew had received hearty applause. Sylvia and her hand remained behind and Andrew's first test of loyalty had arrived unexpectedly. He really was on a high. Everything was going his way. It would be so easy to respond positively to Sylvia's advances. What did he owe Kirsten, after all?

'Kirsten is sleeping,' Sylvia said, squeezing Andrew's leg.

'And?'

'And I know a guard on the train who will let us use an empty first class carriage for a small bribe.'

Her hand slid between Andrew's legs and his resistance was overwhelmed. The carriage cost them fifty rupees, which was several times more than the guard could normally expect to make in a day. It would have been cheap for a night but there were passengers due at the next station and the guard would have to see to it that the sheets were changed. They had it for forty minutes, but fifteen minutes was more than enough, as it turned out. Just when he thought that there was no going back, Andrew found the resolve he didn't know he had and said no.

'Another time?' Sylvia said, and Andrew gave a non-commital smile.

They reached Bombay in the afternoon, via a chain of wrought-iron bridges that followed a path across an area of eternally flat reclaimed land, which had become an enormous shanty town, a waterlogged cardboard city, home to thousands. They crossed the city by a combination of train and taxis and, once again, Kirsten disappeared, saying that she had to check the post office. She met them again later, at Victoria Station. Andrew liked Bombay. The red double-decker buses made him homesick for London. *Perhaps*, he thought, *going home wouldn't be so hard, after all.*

Donna got them all on a train for Goa, leaving early the following morning. She even picked up two dozen samosas from a stall just inside the station. After their impromptu dinner they crashed on an upper floor of the station, alongside a group of Japanese backpackers. Nobody bothered them.

They changed trains in the middle of the following night at Miraj. They spent three hours sitting around, scavenging for snacks and forcing themselves to stay awake. An old man lay sprawled across the platform and nobody seemed to know or care whether he was dead or alive.

Andrew was in a top bunk as the train rolled into Goa. He felt good. There was movement outside. He rolled onto his stomach and pulled back the heavy curtain. It was just before dawn; the sun was rising beyond the coconut palms and Andrew could make out slow moving figures. As time passed the shadows became clearer. Women were crossing rice paddies with bags and tools slung over their shoulders; men were leading water buffalo. There were bicycles on the roads. A buffalo cart was getting in the way. The paddy fields were glistening in the early morning sunshine and bordered on all sides by rows of tall coconut palms. The ocean was nearby. Everything out there was so languid that Andrew could have been dreaming. He gave a long sigh. The fields were interrupted by a few shacks. The shacks became buildings. They passed a church. They were arriving at Vasco Da Gama, a small town in Goa: the end of the road.

Chapter 30

Although there was a light breeze and the picnic had been delicious, Maurice was tense. The news that Devi was pregnant had cheered him momentarily and he had hugged her. It was the first time he'd displayed genuine affection towards her. He smiled like a child, then he withdrew into himself once more. Devi could only guess what was causing Maurice so much heartache, because he never spoke of it. It was probably the American, the one called Carlo. Why had he come to them, she wondered? Why did he want to take Maurice away? The American treated the girls badly, but he paid well and Maurice had told them to be good to him. Even so, when the American had wanted her, Maurice had refused.

Now Maurice was leaving with the American for Thailand. He would be gone for months and she had become so used to him. What if he stayed away forever? Thailand was a wealthy country where girls worked in wonderful nightclubs with dancing and clean rooms and customers who gave big tips. She was the only one who lived well here. The other girls were like slaves. However, with a baby, life would be harder.

Maurice had always been a difficult man. It was never easy to know what to say to him. Sometimes he'd hit her for the silliest reasons, but now he was worse than ever, almost frightened. She had to please him somehow and she had an idea. She stood, let her clothes fall to the ground and walked into the river. The river was warmer than usual and as her body slipped into the water, she tingled with excitement. In the middle, where the water tugged at her waist, she stopped and turned. Maurice was watching her, but still he didn't smile. He was aroused, though, she was certain of that.

Devi swam the ten metres to the far bank and climbed out. It wasn't yet obvious that she was pregnant. She looked back across the river and cradled her belly gently, knowing that Maurice was watching her. She held him in her gaze as her fingers slipped lower and, as she began to feel between her legs, she lay back in the grass and moaned loud enough for him to hear. Maurice was upon her quicker than she'd expected, almost as if he'd jumped across the river to get to her. She felt the cool of his wet body on hers and opened her mouth to him. He kissed her desperately and entered her immediately. He exploded inside her before she'd even opened her eyes.

They lay together without speaking, listening to a bird singing somewhere behind them. Maurice held Devi against him with one arm. His hand was below her and he played with her still. She felt like sleeping but forced herself to remain awake. She had to get him to say something.

'I'm going to be a businessman,' he said suddenly. 'I will be rich and I will have great power, but I will see little of you.' He paused and Devi heard the bird again. 'I didn't think that I would care,' he said.

'Do you love me?' Devi asked, but Maurice didn't answer. She was pleased, though. There had been affection in his voice even if he couldn't express himself honestly to her. He would love her in time, she was convinced of that. For now, she would seduce him with her body. One day he would want more.

An hour passed before Devi was ready to try again. Maurice had drifted into one of his dreams. 'Come back into the water,' Devi said, and she took him by the hand. They swam back to the shallows at the far side of the river and they kissed. Maurice turned her around. He pulled her close and laid her on her belly in the water. Devi spread her arms forwards and rested her palms on the riverbed as Maurice took her. With each sharp smack of his groin against her buttocks she felt herself shiver.

As Maurice pushed himself into her, Devi dipped her face into the water and opened her mouth to drink and spit. She blew bubbles with her nose. Maurice moved faster and faster inside her and she felt that the river would wash her away. She didn't expect him to be so rough, though. As she raised her head out of the water, she heard him apologising. Suddenly he grabbed her hard by the back of the head and shoved her underwater. Beneath the water, she struggled to break free, but his strength was overwhelming. She fought to hold her breath as a terrible pain developed in her chest. Her splashing hands could do nothing. As the air began to rush from her lungs, it was displaced by water. She begged silently for help, unable to understand what was happening, and her mind clouded over.

Maurice stood still, sobbing uncontrollably. He'd accepted that, after he had gone, other men would have her, but he couldn't accept another man owning his child. This was the only solution for them all. Devi's hair floated on the river's surface, drifting downstream with the pull of the current. Her buttocks rubbed cold against Maurice's thighs. 'I'm sorry, my love,' he moaned.

Maurice caressed Devi's dripping body as he placed it gently onto the blanket, tucking in her hands and feet, stroking her face one last time. He carefully rolled her up in it and then dressed, and packed their bags. Everything done, he circled the clearing and searched for witnesses. There were none. He hid the bags in the undergrowth. Then he picked up Devi's body and carried her to the boot of the car. He would dump her in the Hugli River later that night. He would have to tell the other girls that she had run away.

'All I want is forgiveness!' Maurice roared as Devi's memory returned to haunt him once again. Sleeping faces jerked awake around him as the aeroplane headed towards the South Indian city of Madras.

The aeroplane was in near darkness, light coming only from the galley and the toilets at the rear. Most of the passengers were asleep. Some were startled by the unexpected roar, but their heavy eyelids drifted shut again. Those nearest Maurice tried not to catch his eye, but they found that they were too frightened to look away. Maurice, who had jumped from his seat into the aisle, sat down again. The woman who had been sitting beside him asked for her seat to be changed.

Maurice had murdered Devi in a moment of madness. He had not planned to do it, but he couldn't stand the thought of her or his child being with somebody else. Equally he couldn't take them with him to Thailand; Carlo had forbidden it. It was the one act of his adult life that he truly regretted. It was his one mistake. Devi had given him more than physical pleasure; she had given him what he thought might be love. And because of that bastard, Carlo, he had given her up. Carlo had taken everything from him. He had to take it back.

Maurice felt the silent hum of the aeroplane's engines drowning his screaming thoughts like an enemy shouting him down. All around him, passengers slept on and those whom he had disturbed returned to the sanctuary of sleep. Why was he so alone, he wondered? 'How long are you going to sleep for?' he suddenly yelled at them all, unable to keep silent. He was losing control. 'Why don't you talk to each other? What is wrong with you all?'

He ran down the aisle to the rear toilets and locked himself inside. The lights came on and mirrors and doors and walls surrounded him. He sat on the toilet and put his head in his hands, but he couldn't relax. He leapt up again but couldn't move. He opened the door and set himself free. Outside it was still dark and silent and uncomfortably stuffy. Most of the passengers slept on. Back in his seat, Maurice lifted the window shutter but it was dark outside. He was losing control but he could do nothing about it. He was feeling claustrophobic. His body was beginning to shake like an engine using too much power. He had to do something; he had to get out. In frustration, he punched the window.

A stewardess walked quickly down the aisle towards him. She was older than most stewardesses, perhaps forty, the kind of woman young men would trust. Maurice saw her and knew she was coming to him. He leapt into the aisle and warned her to turn back. She didn't understand his message or understand the danger she was walking into. Why would she? Maurice was a handsome man, sophisticated, gentle even. She didn't realise what he truly was; she couldn't know that she was invading his space.

Maurice thrust out both arms to fend the woman off and she flew backwards with a dreadful jolt. In flight she resembled a cartoon character; arms at her sides, legs trailing, her feet pointing flatly backwards as if she was starched rigid. As she landed, rolled and ran, two male crew members ran past her to confront Maurice, who had returned to his seat. 'No problem, no problem,' Maurice said, and he raised the palms of his hands upwards to express his compliance.

'You should remain in your seat sir,' said the most senior of the men. 'We will arrive in Madras in less than an hour.'

'Okay. No problem,' Maurice repeated, unable to speak clearly. He was shaking as he sometimes did, and there was little he could do about it. He needed to do something to occupy his mind. He would be fine once he was on the ground. People were milling around the galley; a few male passengers and several members of crew. They were there to keep an eye on him; safety in numbers. He left his seat again, edged into the galley and began to lay out plastic cups on a tray. He filled the cups with orange juice from a carton and walked around to the other side of the aeroplane.

Bemused passengers watched him as he served drinks. Conversations stopped, ribs were nudged, and hands were held, the journey all but forgotten. Maurice's terrified expression was contagious and nobody refused a glass of orange when he offered it to them. When the tray was empty, he stood rigidly in the aisle, breathing hard, uncertain what to do next. There was momentary panic: he had no more distractions, but at least time had passed, he was closer to the ground. The thought pleased and relaxed him and he regained some control over his breathing. He took the empty tray to the galley, walked to his seat, locked himself into the seatbelt, and closed his eyes. He couldn't understand what was happening to him. Something in him had slipped and he had to ensure that it didn't happen again. He took a deep breath, opened his eyes and forced himself to smile. He would soon be safe on solid ground.

When the flight landed at Madras, Maurice was refused permission to continue to Bombay. He was advised that he would not be able to fly with the airline again. Only with the arrival of two policemen did he accept his fate. He would continue by train to Goa, but he would travel first class.

Chapter 31

The house was a dreamy, tropical, stone building. It sat like a slightly shabby but loveable child, beneath a canopy of tall coconut palms and mango trees. It had a red-tiled roof and arched windows with green, wooden shutters. There was a verandah at the front, at the top of three red stone steps. Beneath it was a patch of short, dried grass. It was hard to believe that this was going to be home for the foreseeable future. It was absolutely gorgeous. *No wonder Donna keeps coming back*, Andrew thought. You had to admire her; she knew her way around. It was also no wonder that the tribe came with her.

A local family lived next door. They had a couple of enclosures for two lazy buffalo and half a dozen chickens. The family shared a deep well with the house, which was used for drinking and washing water. Most people in Goa get their water that way. It was the reason they hated the big hotels. Big hotels had swimming pools and the water they used drained the water table.

On the other side was their garden and at the far end, beyond the trees, was their toilet; a shack with a deep hole beneath it. The toilet door was covered by an old curtain, which hung just above the ground. Inside, above the hole, two large wooden planks bridged the gap and acted as a platform. An alley ran behind the toilet. There was an alley-level entrance beneath the toilet, which was used by two large pigs. The pigs kept the toilet clean in their own inimitable fashion.

The front door to the house opened directly into the lounge. There was no hallway. The ceiling was high and some of the plaster had begun to crack. The walls were white and bare, not a hanging picture frame anywhere. There was a small wooden coffee table and three wobbly wooden chairs, but nothing more. At the back was a small windowless room, probably once a storeroom, which was used as a kitchen and bathroom, and there were four bedrooms off the lounge; two on either side. The tribe were going into Chapora Village later on to buy mattresses and some cooking things.

Seeing as their arrival in heaven was all due to Donna, it seemed only fair that she got to choose her old room, the one to the right, nearest the front door. Sylvia was sharing with her. Henrik grabbed the room nearest the kitchen and Simon followed sheepishly behind him, almost grateful that he wasn't left to choose between the girls. Karen and Jessica took the back room on the left and Kirsten drifted into the last, leaving Andrew with the bags and the lounge to himself. He was in love with the place.

Andrew followed Kirsten into the room a moment later and dumped the bags in the middle of the floor. Kirsten was poking her fingers through the wrought iron grill in the window to push the wooden shutter open. The sudden infusion of light filled the room with life and highlighted its size; when Andrew spoke there was an echo.

'This is okay,' said Kirsten, going through her bag. 'I am going down to the beach for a while.'

'I'll come with you,' Andrew said, but as he walked to his bag Kirsten stopped him.

'No,' she said. 'I need some time alone.'

'Oh,' Andrew said, disappointed. 'How long will you be? We're going into town in a while to buy some things for the house.'

Kirsten thought for a moment and then she hugged him, and gave him a kiss on the neck. Her hands reached below his waist. 'You could pick up my mattress, couldn't you?' she said, and her fingers began pulling down his zip. Even as he felt the stirring in his underpants, he realised that their door was open and, as much as this was great fun, he simply wasn't the exhibitionist that Kirsten was. 'You go to the beach,' he said. 'When you get back there will be a brand new mattress in your size with a fluffy white pillow at the end.'

203

Kirsten released him with a toothy grin and dug out her beachwear. 'Anyway, you have plenty of company now,' she said. 'You don't need me so much anymore.'

Andrew stood on the verandah and watched Kirsten wandering past a tired old house a little further up the road. A small dog yapped at her from the safety of a tall, iron gate, but she didn't seem to notice it. Her dress lifted on a breeze and, in that instant, Andrew fell in love with her all over again. And then she was gone.

Andrew's thoughts turned to their arrival in Goa. They had taken a bus the short journey from Vasco Da Gama to Panjim, the small capital of Goa, on the banks of the River Mandovi. The bridge over the river had collapsed a few years before so the only way across for pedestrians was by ferry. Road traffic took the long way around. Panjim was one of those soothing Indian towns that you come across from time to time. There were no impossible three lane roads to cross here, and no bumper to bumper pollution. Instead Panjim was a collection of quiet lanes and tiny shops and cafes. There were elegant colonial buildings with balconies, shuttered windows and red-tiled roofs. Portuguese churches, painted white, rose majestically above cascading steps, and dominated pretty tree-lined squares. Chatting locals rested on benches alongside the river and looked upon the broad, brown expanse of water, beyond which, wooded hills rose. And, just for Kirsten, there was a tiny red post office where she could pick up her mail.

The ferry was an experience. People milling about on shore slowly gathered, tighter and tighter, and became a woven mass by the time the ferry neared the riverbank. Meanwhile, onboard, passengers steadied themselves for disembarkation, some climbing onto the outside, others gathering in the gangway. As the ferry landed the more adventurous leapt from the boat like wildebeest fording a river, and when the gangplank was lowered embarking passengers vied with disembarking passengers for the most accessible entry and exit points. Chaos reigned, and in minutes the crowd had disappeared and the ferry was ready to leave again. This continued all day long, from morning to evening.

On the far side of the river, buses packed to the rooftops, were waiting for the ferry passengers. The tribe took one look at them and treated themselves to two taxis. They drove with the windows down, across a vast, flat landscape until, half an hour later, they reached the market town of Mapusa. Roadside hoardings had advertised cigarettes and electric refrigerators on the way into town; on the way out they warned about the risks of drug taking. After Mapusa, the roads narrowed and snaked towards the sea, past rows of coconut palms, acres of rice paddies, hamlets of small houses and roadside stalls. There were occasional clearings, housing stone churches. Anywhere there was a gap in the trees, they were blinded by a backdrop of blue sky. There seemed to be nothing beyond. The Goan coast was at the edge of the world. It occurred to Andrew that he had reached the end of his journey.

There was far more to Goa than beaches. Running the length of Eastern Goa were the foothills of the Western Ghats, a series of forested mountains separating the coast from the Deccan Plateau. Goa's major rivers had their source in the Western Ghats, providing most of Goa's water supply. The area contained a multitude of wildlife including tigers and panthers, jackals and hyenas, porcupines, bison, anteaters and monkeys. There were pythons and boas, cobras and kraits and trinket snakes, and there were crocodiles and turtles and bats. In the skies there were eagles and buzzards, ospreys, kingfishers, woodpeckers, fly-catchers and warblers, so many species that you'd need a lifetime to spot them all.

Henrik interrupted Andrew's reverie with the offer of a smoke. Simon was right behind him and, in minutes, the whole tribe were sitting on the verandah, smoking several joints at once. Sylvia was sitting beside Andrew, her hand brushing his knee. Judging by the looks Andrew was getting, everybody had noticed.

Chapter 32

Kirsten walked lightly but her mind was racing with expectation. Carlo was here somewhere, probably staying in a luxury cottage near the beach. It would be easy to find him. All she had to do was set up camp on the beach and, according to Anthony, he would come to her. But Kirsten wanted to take the initiative away from Carlo and spot him first. That way she could follow him to his home and spy on him for a while. Maybe she could find a way of setting up an encounter between him and Maurice that would finish them both for good. She turned off the dirt path, crossed a grassy clearing and turned left onto the tarmac road leading to Vagator Beach.

The sun burnt the tarmac beneath Kirsten's feet, the heat transferring upwards, melting her flip-flops and stinging the tips of her toes like ant bites. Her neck began to burn. She took a towel from her bag and draped it gently across her shoulders. Goa was hotter than she had expected. She decided to take a cold drink at the first café she found. Fifty metres further down the road, beyond an outcrop of banana trees, she passed a house, set back from the road, which belonged to a local doctor. A tidy row of shoes stood guard outside the front door. Beyond the doctor's house was a small café, its circular mud walls surrounding four small wooden tables and a bar.

Kirsten took the table nearest the entrance and ignored the friendly glances of a western couple sitting at the next table. They were wearing T-shirts and thin sarongs tied around their waists. On their table were two glasses of ice-cold fizzy orange, a packet of cigarettes, a novel and a copy of *Lonely Planet's India guide*. Kirsten ordered an ice-cold lassi from a thirteen-year-old girl who emerged from behind the bar with a smile and a paper menu. The girl watched Kirsten point at the menu, said, 'Thank you,' and disappeared. Ten minutes later her older brother returned with the drink, a smile and a straw.

Across the road from the café, two rickety wooden shacks sold a range of tourist nic-nacs; sunglasses, snorkels, sarongs, gaudy T-shirts and well-fingered postcards. Beyond the shacks, a grassy field fronted a wall of palm trees, which hid the beach from view. Beyond the beach, the sea glimmered in the early afternoon sun. Kirsten sucked hard on her straw, her eyes surveying the scene. Her heart was racing now. Carlo was probably less than a mile away.

Kirsten finished her drink, paid the girl and left. She went down the road, past the field and through an aisle of brightly-dressed Gujarati women, their finery piercing their noses, braiding their long dark hair and draped around their necks, wrists and ankles. The women sold fruit, jewellery, money belts, decorated bags and clothes.

The sandy beach to Kirsten's left stretched for half a mile until it was cut short by palm covered cliffs. Smooth outcrops of dark grey rock reached into the sea, like shimmering fingers, and were colonised by isolated groups of tourists sunning themselves like seals. The beach was bare, except at the far end, where packs of young westerners played volleyball on makeshift courts or sat in temporary palm-leaf tea huts, preening themselves over black tea and hashish. High above, the red-topped hills poked weakly through the palm trees like slowly balding heads. To the right, for almost a mile, the beach reached out towards a rocky hill, on top of which, overlooking the mouth of the Chapora River sat a decaying Portuguese fort. There were three huts halfway along the beach and Kirsten could make out a small group of tourists. A herd of bony brown and white cattle sat in the sand just above the water's edge. Two people played in the sea. This was the quiet side.

Kirsten knelt in the sand and took Andrews's camera from her bag. She unscrewed the standard lens and replaced it with the zoom. She placed the camera to her right eye and began scanning the faces in the distance, the quiet side of the beach first. Once she had confirmed, as best she could, that there were no familiar faces on either beach, she turned to the left and headed back into the palm trees. In the shade, the temperature was cool. She put her towel back into her bag and headed down the beach, stepping between piles of dead leaves and coconut husks, and clambering over fallen palms. Every fifty metres she sat and scanned the beach with her makeshift binoculars, but no familiar faces looked back.

Twenty minutes later she was back at the starting point. The result was as she had expected; Carlo would be crazy to sunbathe on a busy beach because it would be easy for Maurice to approach, unseen. The quiet beach gave little human cover. The quiet beach also failed to provide the cover of palm trees. At this end, the beach was bordered by low grassy hills, dotted here and there by small outcrops of shrubs. Stalking this end of the beach would be hard work.

'Looking for me lady?' somebody said.

Kirsten turned so sharply that the camera fell to the sand. 'Shit,' she swore, unable to decide whether or not to pick it up. 'Where did you come from?'

'Out of your worst fucking nightmare,' Carlo replied. He wore a pair of long white cotton trousers, a white short-sleeved shirt and a pair of leather sandals. His skin was burnt brown. His hair had grown long and was slightly bleached by the sun. Kirsten was surprised by how well he looked. 'You should pick that up,' he said, and he winked at the man standing beside him.

As Kirsten stooped to pick up the camera, Carlo grabbed her bag and pushed her away. When she stepped towards him, Carlo passed the bag to the other man and put an arm out to fend her off. 'Don't,' he said.

'Why do you treat me like this?' Kirsten said. 'I'm here to help you.'

Carlo hissed through his nose. 'Really?' he said.

'Why else would I be here?'

'Just give Thomas here a chance to pick through your personal things, give us a few clues, and you can have your bag back.' Carlo was enjoying himself. 'Then I'll buy you a drink, and you can tell me everything.'

Thomas passed the bag back to Kirsten seconds later. 'There's fuck all in it,' he said in a soft Irish accent. He stood heavily in the sand although he was only five feet eight. Dressed in a red vest, long white shorts and leather sandals, with his black hair closely cropped, he looked like a soldier on leave. His neck resembled an uncomfortable winter sweater pushed into his chin, forcing his head upwards. His arms were forced by muscle away from the side of his body, his rounded forearms supporting two of the largest hands and thickest set of farmer's fingers Kirsten had ever seen.

'Thomas is for my protection,' Carlo said. 'I have reason to believe that I have underestimated my enemy.'

'For sure,' said Kirsten. 'That's why I'm here.'

Carlo led Kirsten and Thomas to the furthest teahouse at the far end of the quiet beach. He ordered three beers from a young boy, who leant into a cool box and removed the bottles from a haven of ice. Thomas sat alone at a table by the entrance, leaving Carlo and Kirsten to talk business one table away.

'I'm not working alone anymore,' said Carlo, tilting his head towards Thomas. 'I have decided that some expense is necessary to maintain my status.'

'Your status?'

'As a living entity. Our mutual friend has gone nuts and I need some protection. Thomas fought for the French in Vietnam, you know. He was in the Legion. He may seem a little old, but he's good, he's got discipline and he can be bloody scary.'

'I am glad.'

Carlo's eyes pierced Kirsten's momentarily and she felt her skin tingling. 'Things change,' said Carlo. 'I have learnt to be more careful. Since the affair in Thailand, I'm letting others do my dirty work. I have other people looking for Maurice now.'

'And have they found him?'

Carlo laughed. 'I shouldn't even be talking to you,' he said. 'Frankly, I should kill you.' He watched Kirsten fidget and he laughed again. 'But not today.'

'Especially as I can be of use to you,' said Kirsten.

'Exactly.'

'So have they found him?'

'No.'

'Nothing?'

'Just a body.'

'Anybody you know?'

'Somebody in Bangkok.'

Kirsten smiled when she detected a hint of concern in Carlo's tone. 'You're scared of him?' she said, picturing Maurice standing above the dead clerk.

Carlo reached beneath the table and grabbed her knee. He clenched his fingers hard around it and Kirsten stiffened with pain. 'I'm not scared of anyone,' he said. 'I've just learnt to be more careful.' He softened his grip and caressed her thigh. 'How is your boyfriend?' he asked.

'Andrew is not my boyfriend,' Kirsten retorted.

'I see.'

'No, you do not see. You are too arrogant to see anything. Andrew is like any other man; arrogant in his own way, and desperate to be loved. Because of that, he has been useful to me.'

'How?'

'He loved me.'

'He loved you?'

'Love is a weakness. He was desperate to please me because of it, and all I took from him was money. Anybody who gives away their love surrenders their soul. There is a lot to be said for owning somebody's soul.'

'You resent him?'

'No. Actually, I like him. He never stopped trying and he never wanted to dominate me, just love me. I have grown to like him. Perhaps in time I will grow to like him more.'

Carlo laughed. 'Now who's weak?' he sneered.

Kirsten stared at him, horrified that she may have said too much. 'You have power and money,' she said angrily, 'but you cannot find Maurice. I have nothing, but I know where he is now and I know where he will be.'

Carlo sat slowly upright and let go of Kirsten's leg. 'You've seen him?'

'In Kathmandu.'

'And what makes you so sure that you know where he will go next?'

'I know his plans.'

'What?'

'He told me his plans.'

Carlo roared. 'Are you for real? What do you mean, he told you his plans?' He became pensive. 'That reminds me,' he said. 'How did you find Anthony?'

'You were careless. It is one of your many flaws. You told me his name when you went to see him in Jakarta.' Kirsten allowed herself a mild, contemptuous snigger. 'You even told me where he worked.'

'So I did. You're right. I was careless.' Carlo sipped from his bottle. 'I underestimated you, lady. That was a big mistake. I know you now though. That's your mistake.' He stared at her as he raised his bottle to his mouth. The wink, when it came, swallowed her pride whole and sent a shiver through her like the icy blast of an open refrigerator door. 'So, did you sleep with him or did Maurice discuss his future plans over lunch?' Carlo was watching for any reaction on Kirsten's face.

'He told me that night in Koh Phangan. He said that he liked to spend Christmas in Goa.'

'He said that? He just came out with it?'

'Why not? He had expected to kill me afterwards.'

'So why tell me this now? And why come all the way to Goa to tell me? You could have told Anthony over the phone.'

'I want to see what you do to him.'

'What I'll do to him?' Carlo laughed aloud and Kirsten watched beer trickle down the side of his mouth. 'You saw what he's like, for Christ's sake! I'm not going to *do* anything to him.'

'But...'

'But nothing.' Carlo noticed that Thomas was looking anxiously towards him, and he lowered his voice. 'Maurice is dead. Make no mistake, but it won't be me who finishes him. I'm no hit man, I know that for sure. I was careless in Thailand. More importantly I'm not making any hard cash while I chase that bastard halfway around Asia.'

Kirsten was frustrated. Involving hired killers would spoil everything. 'He's coming for you,' she said. 'He's coming here. You must do something.'

'I appreciate your concern,' said Carlo. 'But I'm not convinced that you're thinking about me here.' A snake-like grin spread across his face. 'You're running from him yourself. He's after you too.'

'He found us in Kathmandu. He wanted to kill us.'

'How did he find you?'

'I don't know.'

'And what happened?'

'He followed us to our hotel.'

Carlo sipped on his beer and leant backwards on his chair, lifting the front legs off the ground. 'So how did you escape?'

'We locked our door.'

Carlo shrugged and sighed. 'A door doesn't normally keep a man like Maurice out. Are you sure we're talking about the same man?'

Kirsten didn't reply.

'If you think he's following you, why try and hide in Goa when you know he's heading this way?'

'I told you. I want you to kill him.'

'And I told you, it won't be me who does the job. With any luck I won't be seeing him alive again.'

'Are you going to run?'

Carlo sat forward. 'No.'

'Then what?' Kirsten said, finding Carlo's reticence frustrating.

'What makes you think I'm gonna tell you?' He leant forward until his face was just inches from Kirsten. She could smell beer on his breath. 'Why am I even talking to you?'

'Because I can be useful to you.'

'In what way?'

'The same as before.'

'And what did I use you as before?'

'Bait.'

'Did I?'

Suddenly Kirsten exploded. She leapt to her feet and knocked her beer over. The gentle hum of conversation in the bar died as her bottle landed in the sand. 'Stop bullshitting me!' she shouted. 'We know what you did, we know how...'

Thomas put a hand on Kirsten's shoulder. The action was so powerful and smooth that she was seated before she realised what had happened. Carlo glowered at her, clenching his bottle tightly. 'Don't push your fucking luck,' he sneered. 'I set you up, but don't keep playing the innocent. You stole a lot of money from me. If you hadn't been so greedy, you wouldn't be here now.'

'You set us up to steal that money, and then you set us up as bait for Maurice. You planned everything.'

Carlo appeared to relax. He put the bottle back on the table. 'You said that you know I set you up in Thailand. What did you mean by that?'

'Andrew thinks that the policemen who arrested him worked for you. He thinks that they told Maurice that Andrew worked for you.'

Carlo laughed. 'I definitely underestimated you,' he said, and turned to Thomas. 'What do you think?'

Thomas shrugged. 'You don't need her. You've enough people out looking for him.'

'You see?' said Carlo. 'I don't need you for anything. I don't need bait. I don't need a cook, and I don't need a secretary.'

'You need a whore,' Kirsten sneered. 'I've done that for you before.'

'A whore!' Carlo stuttered, surprised but excited by the idea. 'A whore,' he repeated, turning again to Thomas. 'She's not wrong you know,' he said. 'Do you know of any man who doesn't need a whore?'

'Not one,' Thomas replied, hoping that some of the luck might go his way.

'Then lady,' said Carlo, leaning forward and returning his hand to her thigh. 'You're hired. When can you start?'

Chapter 33

Maurice grinned as a stranger stared back from the mirror. He took great satisfaction in the smoothness of his recently shaved, bald head. The key feature, apart from the obvious, was that, without hair, the face could belong to anybody. Certainly the face belonged to nobody; nobody, that is, that Carlo would have seen before. As a bonus, the new look made him appear ten years younger. This was the face Maurice was taking to Goa. It would be the last face Carlo looked upon.

He wore the clothes of a western backpacker; a green collar-less shirt, long striped cotton trousers that resembled pyjamas and a pair of cheap plastic flip-flops. He eyed with some satisfaction the green rucksack standing in the corner of the room, which he had bought that morning from a destitute Englishman. The disguise would do more than serve to fool Carlo; it would also ease his way into a group of backpackers heading for Goa. He looked like them now. Travelling in a crowd would be the second part of the disguise. Carlo would be looking for one man travelling alone, not a bald-headed backpacker travelling in a group. He fingered his scalp gently. The barber had done a perfect job.

He had taken a small ground-floor room in one of the most popular Madras backpacker hotels. The hotel, with its shaded courtyards, balconies, benches and hammocks, was a westerner's haven from everything Indian, and the hotel was always full, so full in fact that rickshaws queued outside, amongst the goats, for business. This was where Maurice stalked and charmed his future travelling companions; two Australian women and a Dutchman.

He found them through their noticeboard advertisement for a fourth person to share the cost of a first class cabin on a train to Vasco Da Gama in Goa. *Perfect*, Maurice thought, when he saw the advertisement. These people are afraid of what India has to offer. He imagined them recoiling from the filth of the streets and the sight of lepers and beggars, afraid even to look at them.

Maurice met them in their room on the first floor. They made their introductions. The two women, Amanda and Janine, were twin sisters, travelling in India for just six weeks on their way to work in London. They both wore sweatshirts and baggy military trousers with large pockets, and were it not for Amanda sporting a crew cut whilst Janine grew hers long, it would have been impossible to tell them apart. When they answered the door to Maurice, he felt them look him over with a mixture of delight and suspicion. He was there for an interview, he realised.

Peter, a seventeen-year-old, brown-haired Dutchman, had located the two women on the noticeboard just an hour before Maurice. He had obviously passed his interview and had been promoted to fellow panel member. He sat on the end of one of the room's two beds and smiled uncertainly. 'Hello,' he whispered, half looking at the floor, when Maurice greeted him.

'It's been a long time since I last auditioned for anything,' Maurice said to all three at once as he sat on a hard wooden chair. 'What's the part?'

'We're looking for a guardian angel,' said Janine.

'Somebody who knows about India,' Amanda interjected. 'We arrived from Singapore three days ago. India's more than we expected.'

'And you?' said Maurice to Peter.

'I'm just along for the ride,' he answered. 'I normally travel alone but I want to share a house in Goa with somebody. This is a good way to meet people.' He smiled at the two women and then slipped back into his shell.

Maurice held Peter in his gaze momentarily and then spoke to the women. 'Is that what you want?' he said.

'Probably,' they answered in unison.

'I've spent several years in India,' said Maurice, 'and I've even picked up some of the language. I know how to book a train ticket.'

The women laughed.

'It's harder than you think,' said Maurice, smiling kindly, enjoying the joke for their benefit. 'There are never any signs at the ticket counters, so you can queue for hours in the wrong place. Sometimes you can only buy first class tickets from one counter and second or third class tickets from another. Sometimes tourists have to find the stationmaster and buy from the tourist quota. If you really know what you're doing...' Maurice paused for effect. He realised that the two women were anxious about the forthcoming journey. 'You go to the tourist booking office and enjoy some western-style organisation and comfort.' He noted that the two women smiled, but that there was no reaction from Peter. 'It's easy if you know what you are doing.'

'Where are you from, Maurice?' Janine asked.

'France,' he replied.

'Are you going to stay in Goa over Christmas too?'

'If I find the right place.'

'Do you know somewhere?'

'I know of a few places, but it all depends on the cost.'

'Would you be interested in sharing?'

'Much cheaper,' said Amanda.

Maurice laughed. 'We shall see,' he said, knowing that the two women would be begging him to share with them by the time he'd finished. First he had to ensure that they found him indispensable.

Two days later Amanda looked up from her bag as a grey-haired man appeared at the door of their first class compartment and introduced himself politely, bowing slightly as he spoke. 'Good afternoon,' he said, 'I am the steward for your journey.' He stepped inside the door. 'Would you like to order your meals?'

'What do you have?' asked Amanda, inspecting him. His face was round and friendly with an almost permanent smile, but he hadn't shaved for a day or two and his short grey bristles gave him a rough chin. He wore a slightly faded check-grey suit, which might have been second hand, but his black leather shoes shone like new. He had tried hard to look perfect but hadn't quite managed it.

'Lunch, dinner and breakfast for seventy rupees. If you like, I can organise it for you.'

Amanda smiled. 'Yes, but what do you have? What food: omelettes; rice and curry, what exactly?'

'Oh I'm not sure, but if you pay me now, I can bring you menus.'

'Whoever heard of ordering a meal before seeing the menus?' Janine had finished packing her bag away and had stood up. 'We have to see the menus first,' she said.

'If you wish to see the menus first then I am afraid that I will not be able to assist you. The food is prepared at restaurants along the route and it is not possible to know what they will prepare. It depends on what is available. Ladies, we do not have your wonderful technology. However, if you wish to enjoy what is available on the train, I will be happy to assist you in this matter.' He smiled like a generous grandfather and became silent while his customers took time to consider. Seventy rupees was only a few dollars, after all.

'I'd like to try it,' said Amanda. 'We've got nothing to lose.' She looked at Janine and Peter, who was watching the activity on the station platform. Janine nodded in unconcerned agreement.

'Not for me,' said Peter without looking back into the train.

Amanda hesitated for a moment, then she took one hundred and fifty rupees from a money belt hidden against her waist, inside her green army trousers. 'Here you are,' she said, smiling 'You can keep the change.'

The steward pocketed the money. 'Thank you madams,' he said. 'I will be only five minutes.' He turned out of the compartment and walked swiftly back down the carriage.

Moments later, he returned, smiling grimly into the compartment. Maurice stood behind him.

'Have you given him any money?' Maurice asked.

'Please,' whimpered the steward, as Maurice gripped his left shoulder. 'It is only a few miserable rupees. It is nothing.'

'This man doesn't work for the railway,' said Maurice. 'I know him. He is an impostor.' Maurice laughed and his face lit up as if he was enjoying a joke. 'Did you give him any money?'

'I paid him for some meals,' said Amanda, her face beginning to redden with embarrassment.

'Perhaps you should return the lady's money,' Maurice said to the man. 'Then you can go.'

'Let him keep it,' said Amanda, the frustration of her humiliation burning her up. 'I don't care.'

Maurice released his grip and grinned as the man wriggled free and walked quickly through the train. 'Don't worry about it,' Maurice said to Amanda. 'Everybody gets ripped off in India, but it never costs much. It even happens to me sometimes, and I've been here for ages.'

'Thanks,' Amanda whispered, and she turned away from him. She sat opposite Peter and let out a heavy sigh. Janine grinned quietly to herself, not risking any jokes. Amanda had certainly been taken down a peg or two, she thought.

'You didn't want any lunch, Peter?' Maurice asked, genuinely interested.

'I'm hungry enough,' said Peter, 'but I didn't trust him.'

Maurice watched in amusement as the two women turned angrily towards Peter. 'You can't trust anybody out here,' he said. 'You will come to realise that in time.'

As the train rocked and jarred out of the station, the first class passengers relaxed. Amanda and Janine were thinking how useful Maurice was proving to be. Peter was thinking how good it would be to get to the beach. Maurice was thinking that gaining the trust of the two women would be easy, although he had to admit to himself that he was impressed by Peter's indifference.

At the same time, the middle-aged impostor was sitting in a restaurant just outside the station, waiting for a slap-up feast and counting the money that he had conned from Amanda, and the incredible three hundred rupees Maurice had paid him to do it.

Chapter 34

The Primrose Bar had become Andrew's favourite. There were others in Chapora Village but they seemed just like any other high street bar. The Primrose was halfway along a country lane, in the middle of nowhere, or so it seemed after dark. Although there was nothing special about the place itself, it was the best place to meet during the evenings, and it was definitely the place to gather before a party.

The bar was in a clearing, surrounded by trees, with a small field out the back, which was occasionally used for parties. The bar itself was just a concrete shop with a fridge and a counter. Few customers drank anything but water. Outside people gathered in a low-walled enclosure, sitting around tables or like wallflowers on the wall itself. Others sat on the surrounding grass, some dangled their legs over their hired motorbikes, and a few others, the ones who had taken too many drugs for too long, walked speedily about the place, repeating their paranoid gestures like wind-up dolls.

Almost everybody was smoking hashish. They gathered like pipe smokers, mixing their hashish with a little tobacco, popping it into their chillum bowl or rolling it up in special long papers. Chillums and joints were passed along the line; some were just smoking, others raised their chillum to their foreheads and chanted 'Boom Shiva,' before inhaling as deeply as their lungs would allow and passing the chillum on. Most chillums were simple clay pipes, but there were those who proudly passed around triple-cobra-headed pipes that glowed like distant cities in the dark when the hashish was inhaled and burned. All around, the sweet smelling smoke clouded the air and a gentle hum of conversation, unlike the loud roar of a drinking den, loaded the air.

The tribe had been using the place since they arrived three days before. They spent their mornings drinking black tea and smoking hashish on their verandah, and in the afternoons they went, via a small roadside café, to the beach, where they lazed and swam until sunset. They ate dinner in Chapora; usually fried prawns, shark, omelettes or curry, and then they lazed about some more on the verandah before strolling down the alleys to Primrose. The routine was numbing Andrew's mind but it had been ages since he had felt so relaxed or contented. Now that Kirsten seemed to have placed their relationship on hold, having spent the past three days on the beach alone, Sylvia was trying to take her place.

Apart from Kirsten, who Andrew hadn't seen all day, all the tribe members were at Primrose. They were all playing their customary roles. Simon waved away the offer of a joint because something he had eaten had wrecked his stomach, or so he said, and Henrik leant across him to pass it to Donna instead. She took a long, satisfying drag and passed it, without speaking, to Sylvia. Karen and Jessica were sitting just out of earshot, whispering and giggling.

As Henrik got the joint back, a Japanese guy whipped past them, did a strange dance and disappeared. 'I heard about somebody like him on the Bombay to Goa ferry,' said Henrik, taking a quick drag. 'He suddenly gave all his belongings to the guy sitting next to him, and jumped off the ferry into the sea. By the time the boat had turned around, he was gone.'

'Such is life,' said Donna.

'It's not life, it's just sad,' said Sylvia.

'Yeah,' said Simon, hardly able to speak at all.

'Another guy went berserk on the beach,' said Henrik. 'He killed a load of tourists with an axe.'

'Too many drugs,' Donna said, appearing slightly surprised by her comment, as if she had just worked everything out. 'There's nobody to help when you're so far from home.'

'Not if nobody knows where you are,' Andrew said, realising that nobody back home knew where he was. 'I suppose it's the risk we take.'

'Which reminds me,' said Simon to Henrik, suddenly regaining his strength. 'Have you found anyone with some acid for tomorrow night's party?'

'Don't worry,' said Henrik as he passed a new joint on to Donna and exhaled a cloud of smoke. 'Everything is organised. I just need your money.'

'Sixty rupees,' said Karen, as if she expected Henrik to rip them all off. 'That's what you said.'

'Actually, it's fifty-five,' said Henrik, smugly.

'Do you know where the party is?' Andrew asked.

'Not yet. Nobody will know until midnight.'

'That's crazy,' said Jessica. 'What's so complicated about a bloody party?'

'Nothing,' said Donna, awakening from her latest lungful of smoke. 'But unless you want an army of policemen dancing with you, it's best to keep the location secret until the last minute.'

The tribe became silent while they considered the prospect of a police raid.

They drifted away from Primrose shortly before one o'clock. Sylvia grabbed Andrew's arm and dragged him off the path when nobody was looking. In the shadows of a dark tree, she kissed him hard on the mouth. Andrew could feel her breasts pressed firmly against him and he knew that he wouldn't be able to resist this time, but as suddenly as she had grabbed him, she pulled away. 'Let's go for a swim,' she said.

'But what about Kirsten?'

'She's not my type.'

'Funny,' Andrew said, 'but I mean it: what if she is at home?'

'Andrew,' Sylvia said, 'she hardly talks to you anymore, you said that, and she didn't come home last night anyway, so why do you care?'

Andrew didn't have an answer to that. Kirsten really wasn't communicating with him anymore. She had even moved her mattress further away from his. 'Okay,' he said, unconvinced, and Sylvia led him towards the beach.

There were small groups of people on the beach so they headed along the quieter side, looking for a good spot for skinny-dipping. About two thirds of the way along, they passed a herd of bony cattle, permanent beach residents, and walked towards an outcrop of rocks. High above, Chapora Fort loomed, heavy and menacing, silhouetted against the moonlight.

Sylvia dropped her clothes on the sand and ran, yelping, down the beach, while Andrew was still struggling out of his T-shirt and trousers. He laid his clothes carefully on a rock to keep them free of sand and then waded into the water until it reached his waist and he began to lift in the swell. He could hear Sylvia splashing about but, even in the moonlight, he couldn't see her.

The water was cool, but the air around him was warm and he could feel his skin tightening. He felt invigorated and his mind was alive with flashes of nudity and fantasies. He desperately wanted Sylvia, but only physically. Every time he remembered how good she had looked when she was naked in the train carriage, he also imagined Kirsten. He was lost in thought when the panic came. He wasn't prepared and he staggered backwards as he felt the water surge below him. 'A shark!' he screamed and leapt high in the water, thrashing about with his hands and feet, kicking and punching, warding the shark off, fighting to get back into shallow water. He lost his balance and his head went underwater. He swallowed hard as he gasped for breath, still lashing out at the shark. A murky figure rose above him and he turned away, pushing back out of the water, beginning to run.

'What are you doing?' Sylvia spluttered. 'You almost broke my nose!'

Andrew stared at her, unable to respond. He tried to calm himself but his heart was beating rapidly and snot and salty water ran down his face. 'I thought you were a shark.'

'You thought that I was a shark?' Sylvia said, rubbing her nose. She laughed. 'Maybe I am,' she said. Suddenly she launched herself at Andrew and he found himself in retreat once again. The sand beneath his feet gave way and, as he tried to regain his balance, Sylvia leapt into his arms, wrapping her long, cold legs around him like an octopus. He was surprised by her strength but more so by the realisation that he was experiencing the same excitement he used to feel with Kirsten.

Wrapped together, they slid towards shallow water. Sylvia was kissing him and he felt as if he was being eaten alive. He grabbed her between the buttocks and slipped his fingers hard inside her. He could feel her breath in his mouth as she gasped with delight, and was surprised when she grabbed him between the legs and eased him inside her. As she rose high above him, his head was slammed back into the sand and once again his mouth filled with salt water and sand.

It was over in minutes.

Sylvia slid off him and slapped down into the water beside him, gasping and laughing at once. Everything had happened so quickly that Andrew felt as if he'd won a race. The excitement was simply too much to bear.

A figure was standing above them. Strangely, she was as naked as they were. What was of most interest to Andrew, though, was not her body but the expression of amusement on her face. 'Having a good time?' Kirsten said.

Sylvia raced back into the sea as Kirsten spoke, leaving Andrew to explain himself. 'I didn't think you cared,' he said.

Kirsten smiled. 'I don't really,' she said. 'I'm glad that you are happy. I would like for us to always be friends, but we are very different people.' She walked back up the beach and, as Andrew was admiring the way she moved, another figure, a man, emerged from the darkness with her clothes. When she reached the man, she turned back to Andrew and smiled, and something unsaid but clearly understood passed between them. The other figure was Carlo.

Chapter 35

Maurice looked around the house with an air of quiet satisfaction and returned outside to pay the old woman one month's rent and to take the keys. The woman thanked him and, taking the hand of her young grandson, she turned and walked back down the path to her own house on the other side of the mango orchard.

Inside the three-bedroomed house the others were organising their rooms, unpacking their bags and patting each other on the backs for having found a man like Maurice who could provide such a beautiful house. This house had been properly maintained; the paintwork was in perfect condition, there was clean glass in the windows, working plumbing to the indoor bathroom, a cooker and a fridge in the kitchen, furniture in the rooms and oil lamps for lighting. The verandah was small but there was room for six wicker chairs and a lovely glass-topped wicker table. There was a whiff of sea air because they were just five minutes from the beach. Across the path, in the orchard opposite the house, flycatchers and orioles flitted from branch to branch, swooping in flashes of red and gold as they hunted for insects amongst the dried grass and leaves. In some ways, thought Maurice, it was a shame that he would only be staying a few days.

The journey from Madras had passed comfortably and the train had arrived on time, just after seven o'clock that morning. Maurice spotted a thickset European man watching the arrival of the train over a cup of coffee and a newspaper in a restaurant across the road from the station. The man had looked up momentarily when Maurice and his group loaded their bags into a waiting taxi, but he returned to his newspaper without a second glance. The disguise had worked and, what's more, Maurice had the confirmation he needed that Carlo was expecting him. In the meantime, there was work to be done and fun to be had. He was sharing a house with two attractive women and one of them, Amanda, appeared to be flirting with him. It shouldn't be too difficult to convince her to help him with his research, he thought.

First of all, though, he needed to locate Carlo's house. He had taken the address from Anthony and, although he could spend hours creeping around, he preferred to locate the house quickly, because the owner of his house had informed him that there was going to be a party somewhere nearby that evening. There was always the chance that Carlo would attend, or at least the music might serve to cover his screams when Maurice cut off his head. To get close without drawing attention to himself, he would need the cover of his travelling companions, or at least one of them.

Amanda was the first out of the house. She had changed into a plain white T-shirt and a pair of baggy green military shorts. Maurice smiled to himself, thinking that Amanda should have been a soldier, especially with her close-cut hair. 'It's so beautiful here,' Amanda said, and a contented smile spread across her face. 'We're so lucky to have met you.'

'Think nothing of it,' Maurice replied. 'I'll change and then perhaps I'll show you around.'

'I'd love a swim,' said Amanda.

'An excellent idea,' said Maurice, 'I'll show you the way through the alleys. It's a pretty walk, better than following the road.' He walked into the house, leaving Amanda with her satisfied smile and notions of a romantic encounter.

Ten minutes later, Maurice left with Amanda. Janine and Peter both decided to take a few hours sleep, but they agreed to meet them on the beach afterwards. Maurice was wearing a baggy, white cotton shirt and a pair of light, Indian-made cotton trousers that were tied at the waist by an elastic chord. Like Amanda, he went barefoot. He carried his beachwear in a cloth bag with an elephant design on the back. Carlo would never expect to find him dressed like this and, with Amanda by his side, he was convinced that he looked like a typical western tourist holidaying in Goa. Even so, he had no intention of lingering outside Carlo's house for longer than necessary.

The house was a ten-minute walk along endless, straight, leafy alleys, bordered by crumbling stone walls and row upon row of coconut palm trees. A dark-skinned man wearing a thin white vest and a pair of red baggy shorts had climbed to the top of a tall palm and was holding on, partly obscured by the palm fronds wafting in a light breeze high around him. He was searching for ripe coconuts. Suddenly, with a hiss and a crash the first of the coconuts landed amongst a pile of coconut husks and dead leaves. 'Fascinating,' said Amanda, and she strayed close to Maurice.

'This is what I love about Goa,' Maurice said, smiling up at the man and demonstrating feelings of love that he simply didn't possess. 'Goa is truly paradise to romantics.'

'Absolutely,' said Amanda, gushing in awe of her worldly-wise companion.

Maurice captured her with a well-practised look of affection, knowing that she wouldn't stare directly back, but that equally she could hardly look away. 'You won't be disappointed,' he said. 'I know Goa well.'

Maurice spotted the house from nearly two hundred metres away and knew, at once, that he had found Carlo. The house resembled a hotel; a white concrete building spanning two floors, with an arched front door, large barred windows and a flat roof. It stood in a red sandy clearing and all surrounding fauna had been removed, except for a collection of potted plants beneath the ground-floor windows. Two motorbikes stood side-by-side out front. The entire property was surrounded by a six-foot stone wall, accessed via a large iron gate which was padlocked shut. Maurice was pleased; Carlo was nervous. He obviously didn't want any unexpected or unwelcome visitors walking up to his door.

Ten minutes later they were set up on the beach. Amanda stripped quickly and, without waiting for Maurice, she dashed into the sea. Maurice ignored her, thinking instead about Carlo's house and ways to penetrate his defences. The windows and doors would be locked shut, he had no doubt, and there was the added problem of the bodyguard. Without more time, he couldn't ascertain whether Carlo had others with him. If so, it would be impossible to storm the house. He would have to use an alternative method to flush Carlo out of hiding.

Chapter 36

Kirsten arrived at the post office in Panjim just after ten. She had taken a motorbike taxi from Chapora Village with an old man who told her that he was a careful driver, not like the young "wildcats" of today. The ferry across the Mandovi River had been only half full and she was able to take a seat and enjoy the view. From the river, Panjim was beautiful; terraces of picturesque, red-roofed buildings with tall arched windows and balconies, interspersed with palm trees and tall shrubs. There was little traffic, instead people were strolling in pairs or ambling along on rusty bicycles or chatting idly on riverside benches. Shopkeepers stood in doorways, greeting familiar faces as they passed by.

At the poste restante, Kirsten had to wait until four tourists were seen before her, but the wait was worth it. In Bombay, she had paid to have her mail forwarded to Panjim, and the letter had arrived. It was date stamped one week earlier, which meant that Maurice could already be in Goa. At the thought, she involuntarily spun around and scanned the shrubs alongside the river below the post office. There appeared to be nobody staring back. She walked to a bench above the river and, with a cursory glance around her, she sat.

Kirsten tore the envelope carefully along the top, puffed it open and, with her fingertips, she plucked the contents out. She was becoming stronger; she knew that, because this time the disgusting photographs had less effect on her. The previous set, the ones she'd received in New Delhi, had almost made her vomit. They were close-ups of the dead police clerk from Bangkok. This time the envelope contained a Polaroid photograph of a man's penis – Maurice's joke she supposed – plus Anthony's passport and his severed head. Kirsten had

228

never met Anthony and so, ironically, his passport identified him, even in death. Kirsten sighed to herself, considered what she had started, and smiled. She had finally manipulated a man, supposedly stronger than herself, to do her bidding. Her task was almost complete. All that remained was to witness the final act for herself.

With Maurice now probably in the area, she decided to arm herself. She headed into the centre of town, crossed over the Largo da Igreja, a pretty square beneath the Church of the Immaculate Conception, and disappeared down a narrow alley where she found a row of tiny stores, all selling implements for the home; plastic buckets of every size, crockery, cutlery, stationery, padlocks, hardware, bells and mosquito repellents. She bought a small, black-handled penknife with a three-inch blade for fifteen rupees. For a further five rupees, the owner of the shop had his son sharpen the knife until it was razor sharp. Kirsten tested the blade on a sheet of paper and left the shop satisfied that, given the opportunity, she could inflict considerable damage with it.

When she returned to Carlo's place an hour later, she had to call Thomas from the house to let her through the gate. He strolled out of the house and across the sand like a gatekeeper at a royal palace. Once she was inside, Thomas padlocked the gate again. He then took particular care, locking the front door behind them.

Carlo was on the phone. He appeared close to panic, but he tried hard to cover it up. 'Hello? Hello?' he was yelling into the phone. He had obviously finally reached whoever he was calling, but it was a lousy line. 'Can I speak to Anthony? Yes, Anthony … it's personal. I'm a friend of his.' There was a slight delay in the response and he sighed aloud. 'Who I am isn't important. Is he there?' Suddenly he slammed the phone down and stared at Thomas. 'They were trying to trace the call, I'm sure of it. Something is wrong. Why else would they do that?'

'What's the problem?' said Kirsten.

'Anthony isn't answering his calls.'

'Why don't you send somebody to check him out?' said Thomas, reassuringly. 'We could get somebody there in a few hours.'

Carlo sniffed. He stared at the floor momentarily. 'I'll have to pay for the flight,' he said. He thought again. 'Fuck Anthony,' he said. 'Maybe I'll just get the guy over here. I could do with his help.'

'I can do the job,' said Thomas, walking out of the room.

'Tough guy!' Kirsten joked.

Thomas ignored her but Carlo gave her a confident wink.

'He can do the job,' said Carlo, 'and you'd be safer trying not to piss him off.'

'If you're so worried, why don't you leave?'

'I'm not worried,' said Carlo, 'and I have a business to run.'

'You won't have if he finds you.'

Carlo stood abruptly and Thomas inched back into the room. 'You're very smart,' Carlo said, and Kirsten knew that she had pushed him too far. 'What I'd like to know is why are you so smart when you know what's coming? Why aren't you even a little nervous?' He stepped nearer to Kirsten. 'Something about you is bothering me.'

'I just don't share your fears,' said Kirsten, searching for a way out. 'I don't think that he can beat you.'

Carlo slapped her hard across the face and she stumbled backwards. She grabbed at a chair as she fell and pulled it over. 'That hurt?' Carlo asked, matter-of-fact. As Kirsten sat upright, he kicked her in the mouth and split her lip. As she spun on the floor she noticed that Thomas was smiling. Carlo picked her up by the throat and dragged her, choking, across the floor. He threw her into a seat. 'I don't want you leaving this place again unless I tell you to, okay?' Carlo was shouting again and he knew that his anxiety was obvious. He walked to the window and wiped sweat from his brow. Without looking back, he spoke to Thomas. 'Take a look outside,' he said. 'Check the back.' He waited until the front door clicked shut and Thomas had walked past the window. 'Don't make me look stupid in front of my people,' he said, turning towards Kirsten. 'I don't fucking need it.'

There had been another time in Kirsten's life when a big man appeared to have lost his strength. Her father had been released from prison after just twelve years and the first thing he did was come looking for her. She refused to see him, but when she caught a glimpse of his pathetic figure outside of her window, she found herself opening the door to him. He had aged so much; his hair was prematurely grey and his face had turned hard and leathery. He walked with a limp, the result of a knife attack in prison, and his confident, arrogant voice was reduced to a whisper. His eyes were so red; it seemed as if he had been crying forever. That was his power, and Kirsten had found herself forgiving him.

Kirsten was shaking as she held her mouth, feeling for the damage and trying to stop blood seeping onto her dress. The experience with her father had taught her not to give sympathy to a man when he was down. She would forgive Carlo nothing. Somehow, she thought, she would ensure that Thomas's padlocks were left open that night.

Carlo returned to the phone and dialled a number. He got through to an answerphone. 'Call me urgently,' he said abruptly, and replaced the telephone in its cradle. Then he crossed the floor to Kirsten and, dragging her by the arm, he led her upstairs.

Chapter 37

The rank, foetid aroma from the toilet beneath Andrew permeated the air like noxious gases forced from an erupting volcano, which was how his stomach felt whenever he was in there. The stench was so strong that he only had to visualise the toilet floor and he wanted to retch. Even so, it was still the only place he could find time to think. He only came down for a quick slash but he had a lot on his mind, so he adopted his version of the Indian squatting position; trousers around the ankles, knees bent, arms out before him for balance. After years of practice, he actually quite enjoyed the position. There was a skill to it and, like learning to use chopsticks, there was satisfaction to be derived from cultural adaptation.

Six feet beneath him, in a darkened hole beyond the crap-encrusted wooden platform, a soft beam of light travelled from the ground-level entrance used by the pigs to the stone wall directly below. Ahead of him, the thin curtain, acting as a door, shivered in the warm breeze, threatening to reveal him to his friends. Beneath the curtain he could see piles of coconut husks and fallen, feathery, palm fronds, and he could pick out strips of sunlight between the trees.

He was pretty stoned but he just couldn't get rid of the image from yesterday evening of Kirsten standing naked beside Carlo. He could hardly say anything at the time, seeing as she had just caught him shagging Sylvia, even though he had actually been thinking of Kirsten throughout. But Carlo of all people! Why him?

Of course, Andrew's biggest problem with Carlo was actually his biggest problem with himself: why Carlo and not him? After all this time, why had she gone back to him? It was unbelievable. At least he now knew who she had been getting those letters from. How the fuck did they get in touch with each other, he wondered?

Just when he had finally submitted to Sylvia's undoubted persuasive charms, Carlo had to turn up and make him jealous. Losing Kirsten, and it did seem as if he had finally done so, would have been more bearable had he not been aware that she was screwing somebody else, especially a somebody else who had ruined both of their lives once already. If Carlo had been good enough to keep away, Andrew might have got over Kirsten. Instead, he couldn't get her out of his mind, especially, funnily enough, when he was with Sylvia. Andrew needed Carlo out of the way. He needed him out of the way for good, and he knew how to do it: just one good photograph, a name and an address.

After a couple of lazy hours smoking on the verandah, the tribe actually made it to the beach. It was four o'clock in the afternoon, late enough to miss the worst of the sun. The beach was busier than usual. A large group of Indian women in a rainbow of brightly-coloured saris were splashing about, while their children were standing in circles, holding hands and playing games. A bus-load of Indian men had spread out, some with their trousers pulled up to their knees. They were paddling at the water's edge, their shadows glistening in the wet sand. Others were sneaking behind western women for a photograph to show their friends back home. The fewer clothes the women were wearing, the better. Every now and again the men were chased away.

As this was the last place Andrew had seen Kirsten, he was optimistically hoping that she might saunter along at some stage with her ape in tow. All he wanted was one photograph. Otherwise he may have to wait for the party and, to be honest, he didn't think that he'd risk losing his camera just for a bit of old fashioned spite.

The sun was hot and most of the tribe were in the sea, bobbing about or body surfing the bigger waves. Henrik and Donna were floating upright, rather close to each other, sharing a joint. In every sense, Andrew wanted to know what was going on beneath the surface. Only Simon was on the beach with Andrew, complaining about the heat, the sand flies and an enormous dead jellyfish he had found earlier. 'I told you it's not safe to swim here,' he said.

As usual, Andrew grunted and ignored him.

The Indian men were strolling back down the beach, probably to get their bus back to Bombay or wherever they had come from. Like all good colonialists, the tribe were only happy once the beach was theirs alone. One by one, they returned to familiar territorial borders, marked out by a collection of damp towels and sarongs. With the beach to themselves again, it was time to light up and prepare for sunset. Henrik was the first to oblige.

Surprisingly, once the tribe gathered for a smoke, Simon decided, against his better judgement, to take a swim. He hopped down the beach, all skin and bones, staring straight ahead, probably so that nobody would notice him. He carefully lowered himself into the water, trying hard to keep his hair dry, and drifted slowly out to sea. 'Hardly a Greek god,' said Jessica without a smile and Simon was forgotten as a wave lifted and then hid him as it rolled gently onto the beach to die.

Moments later, as if Andrew had experienced a time warp, Simon was standing above him, leaping about with an ugly expression on his face. 'Fuck! Fuck! Fuck!' he wailed, not speaking and not quite shouting. It was as if he had swallowed a red-hot chilli-pepper but didn't want to spit it out. 'I've been stung by a jellyfish,' he whimpered, and his mouth widened in horror as he began to accept that the excruciating pain wasn't going to go away unaided. 'Someone fucking help me!'

Donna was the first to react. Most of the others, suffering from hashish inhalation, were still too stoned to think properly. 'We've got to get him off the beach,' Donna said, and she began to pack her things. Simon tried to do the same but he couldn't stand still. Henrik eventually did it for him. It took two minutes more before they were all on their way to their favourite café where they hoped somebody might know what to do. They were all agreed that this could be serious for Simon. Jellyfish stings could be fatal.

It took another fifteen minutes to reach the café, by which time Simon was leaping about as if the ground were too hot to walk on. He was in serious agony and the rest of the tribe were beginning to come out in sympathy pains. The family running the café were suitably impressed by Simon's agony. The eldest son said that he had once been stung on the foot and had cried for hours. Mother issued a series of orders and the two sons were despatched to the surrounding fields with carrier bags. Meanwhile Simon was laid out across a table. The woman checked his back for signs of the wound but found nothing. Everyone gathered around but nobody spoke. 'Where were you stung?' the woman asked, and Simon turned his head to face her.

'On the arse,' he said, and he closed his eyes as the tears blurred his vision. Andrew was not certain whether they were tears of agony or embarrassment. Most of the tribe turned away and sat at surrounding tables. Some were grimacing in the same way football players share the agony of a player hit between the legs by the ball. Jessica ordered a drink. Sylvia gave Andrew a wry grin.

The brothers returned with two steaming carrier bags full of cow shit. Mother dug deep into a bag and came up with two handfuls of steaming shit. As one of the brothers pulled Simon's trunks around his thighs, Mother slapped her hands onto his cheeks and lathered the shit all over him. Andrew was the only one watching. The rest of the tribe were giving Simon a semblance of privacy during this moment of excruciating crisis. The woman spoke gently, attempted to calm squirming Simon. 'The dung will soak up the poison,' she said. 'It contains ammonia. The pain will soon be gone.'

Andrew for one didn't believe a word of it.

Fifteen minutes later, he was proven wrong however, and Simon had his trunks back around his arse and a T-shirt around his shoulders. Judging by the look on his face, he was still uncomfortable, but his life expectancy had somewhat lengthened, it seemed. Nonetheless the episode had ended their attempt on sunset, so they headed home. Henrik, Donna and most of the tribe were keeping Simon company, but Sylvia was coming on to Andrew for an afternoon of stoned passion. Since discovering that Kirsten was back in Carlo's arms, Andrew had adopted Sylvia as a Kirsten substitute. It helped to deaden the pain; all he had to do was think of Kirsten while he was making love to Sylvia. Pathetic he knew, but she was his nicotine patch now and he hoped that she might help ease him off his one serious addiction.

Chapter 38

Peter surprised the household by moving out unexpectedly. He didn't leave a note and he didn't steal anything. He was simply gone when Amanda and Janine returned from the beach.

'What do you mean *gone*?' Janine asked, unable to keep the obvious disappointment from her tone. 'He was going to take me to the party tonight.'

'I don't know,' Maurice answered, utilising his most bewildered voice. 'I came back just a short while ago and… nothing.'

'So how do you know he's gone? Have you checked his room?'

'Of course.'

'But how could you know that he'd left before you checked the room?'

'The door was open and the room was empty.' Maurice replied. He appeared offended. 'You don't think that I went into his room uninvited, do you?'

'Of course not,' said Amanda, coming to her sister's aid. 'But it is very strange. Why would he leave so suddenly? It doesn't make sense.'

'Peter was young and impetuous,' said Maurice. 'Perhaps he met somebody who offered him more than he was getting here.' He knew that Janine was fond of Peter; the comment was aimed to hurt her and to shut her up.

'Peter is young,' Janine countered. 'So he has gone. You don't have to talk about him in the past tense. He might still be at the party tonight.'

'I hope so,' said Maurice, 'because I would like to know what we have done to offend him.'

'Nothing I'm sure,' said Amanda. She smiled weakly at her sister and took her bag into her room.

'At least you can have a room to yourself now,' said Maurice, and he left Janine to her discomfort.

Janine felt suddenly alone. She had been looking forward to a dance with Peter and maybe getting to know him better. Although nothing had happened between them so far, Janine had hoped that there would be developments at the party. Why would he leave so suddenly, she wondered? They'd been getting along fine. Now she was part of a threesome and Amanda had clearly fallen for Maurice. Goa didn't seem so much fun now. What was worse, she thought, was that she didn't trust Maurice. Outwardly, everything about him seemed perfect; he was attractive in a tough sort of way, even with his bald head, he was charming and intelligent and he really knew his way around, but there was also something subtly unnerving about him. She thought momentarily of home and wished that she were on a flight to England with her sister.

This was already the longest time they had spent away from home; even when the sisters went to university, they had lived at home. Now Amanda was taking risks with a man she hardly knew, but in whom they had both placed their trust without question. It was the expected thing to do. Travel had its own rules. She solved her homesickness by grabbing a pile of postcards. She wrote them in her room, stretched out across her bed, plugged into the Walkman so that she couldn't hear her sister's laughter out on the verandah.

Outside, in the early evening warmth, Maurice was continuing his slow seduction of Amanda. He was setting an emotional, physical, trap and she was not just going to fall into it, she was going to leap headlong into his embrace, without knowing why. If he had his way, she was going to regret doing so for the rest of her life. Maurice had changed into a long pair of black cotton trousers and a black cotton shirt. He was wearing black Chinese slippers. He had shaved and splashed aftershave across his face. Seeing him dressed for a party, Amanda had showered and taken her favourite summer frock from the bottom of her bag. It was the frock she saved for aeroplane journeys.

Maurice had taken a bottle of Indian port from the kitchen and was pouring another round into two glasses. 'Another glass before dinner?' he said, referring to their planned visit to a restaurant. 'Are you sure that Janine won't join us?'

'She's not feeling well,' Amanda said. 'Something she ate, I guess.' She laughed. 'I must have a stronger stomach; I feel fine.'

'You're just more careful than your sister,' Maurice said. 'In fact, for twins, you are very different.'

'In some ways.'

'No really. Janine is very serious, but you are lots of fun and you take more risks than she does. You will enjoy your travels far more than she will, because taking risks leads to more experiences.'

Amanda blushed. Her ego needed help but she didn't want to enjoy herself at her sister's expense. 'Janine is kind. I can always rely on her.'

Maurice stopped her with a beaming, loving smile. 'I like Janine. It's just that for some reason I prefer your company.' He smiled again and sipped from his glass. 'I hope you enjoy mine.'

Amanda returned his smile. 'I don't know what we would have done without you.'

'I'm sure you'd have done just fine,' Maurice said. 'However, even you would never have found tonight's restaurant. It's my big secret. It's only used by local people and the food is legendary. You will love it.'

Amanda's face lit up. 'And how about the party?' she asked.

'The party will be fabulous,' Maurice replied. 'It will be a party to remember.'

Chapter 39

A ten-minute walk away, another household was preparing for the evening. Thomas was sitting in the lounge, playing with a small handgun he'd recently bought from a policeman in Bombay. The gun had been reported stolen, along with six others, by a shooting club. Although the culprits were eventually caught, the guns were never recovered, officially, and now they were on the market. Unfortunately, although the gun took six rounds, there were only four available as no ammunition had been stolen and the policeman had been unable to locate further stocks at short notice. Thomas wasn't concerned. Four rounds would be enough to take care of one, hopefully unarmed, man.

Carlo was upstairs, demonstrating his love and respect for Kirsten with his fists. One hard, unexpected punch to the stomach was enough to reduce her to a quaking mass at his feet. 'If our relationship has to be like this,' he said, caressing the knuckles of his right hand, 'then that's okay by me.' He walked to a window and checked for signs of Maurice. 'But I would prefer to be friends.'

Kirsten said nothing. She remained on the floor, pulling her knees close to her chest, knowing that he was watching her, that he was grinning at the sight of her naked legs, trying to catch a glimpse of her knickers, waiting for her to recover enough for him to rape her again, although he'd call it making love. She rubbed her stomach, trying not to vomit. Her head pounded and her mouth was dry. She longed for a glass of cold water. In her money belt, strapped around her waist, were her passport and her cash and a thin, hard object. She felt for it now and, although she wasn't convinced of its use, she felt with some comfort the black-handled penknife with its three-inch, razor-sharp blade.

'I wish you'd stop this crap,' said Carlo. 'You want me. I know you do. You love it. For Christ's sake this was your idea!'

'Fuck off!' Kirsten growled, not wishing to make things any easier for Carlo. 'You make me sick. Just fuck me if you want to, but do not expect me to like it. You are a pig and I do not enjoy your disgusting snuffling.'

'Don't try to wind me up,' said Carlo. 'You're whining like a baby.' He stared at her for a moment and Kirsten thought that he was going to hit her again. She opened her mouth as if to speak but Carlo stopped her. 'Just shut up,' he said and he stepped towards her. Kirsten rolled up tighter and closed her eyes.

Unexpectedly, as Kirsten waited for the blow to come, the door slammed shut and she realised that she was alone. She heard Carlo return downstairs. He was talking to Thomas. Then, for an instant, there was silence, until Kirsten heard the telephone click, and Carlo's voice boomed again.

Kirsten hauled herself up from the floor and walked to the window. It was almost dark outside although the lights from the house illuminated the area inside the wall and just beyond. Maurice would never get in unannounced. Things were getting complicated. Not for Andrew, though, she thought. He was probably out on the verandah with his friends, smoking himself into a stupor. He was free of this shit now. She was surprised by the realisation that she was pleased for him. In the strangest way, she was beginning to miss him.

She fingered the knife against her stomach and thought about ways of escape. The windows were barred, there was no way onto the roof and, although she could unlock the front door, she couldn't get past the padlocked gate, although if she had time, she could probably climb the wall. The only way out, she knew, was if Carlo and Thomas were asleep or dead. If Maurice didn't come tonight, she thought, then she would have to try and escape in the morning. Carlo was using her for sex like some people eat snacks or smoke cigarettes, and she had had enough. She had already considered cutting his throat while he slept, but the chances of doing it silently were slim, and there was no way she would be able to fight an animal like Thomas if he heard her do it.

Of course, the whole plan, everything she had worked towards these past two weeks, would be lost if Maurice didn't come soon. If Maurice didn't clash with Carlo while she was nearby, then one of them was bound to survive. Having Thomas around didn't make things easier. Somehow, he had to die too. She sighed. She was going to have to change her attitude towards Carlo if she was going to see him dead.

The door burst open and Kirsten swung around to find Thomas standing angrily before her. 'He wants you downstairs,' Thomas said. Before Kirsten could respond, Thomas was gone.

'I'm fucking sick of making pointless phone calls,' Carlo said when Kirsten appeared in the lounge. 'I'm also sick of Thomas's cooking. We're going out.'

Thomas insisted that, if they were going to eat out, they should at least eat at a restaurant outside of Chapora Village, hopefully somewhere where they wouldn't be noticed. He took his gun.

The restaurant they chose was beside the road to Vagator Beach, hidden behind a screen of pink Bougainvillea. There were eight moulded plastic tables but only two were in use. The atmosphere was relaxed, the scented air soaking up whispered conversation before it could reach alien ears. Thomas chose a table furthest from the entrance and sat facing the door. When the waiter arrived, a friendly man in his forties, he ordered immediately and insisted that Carlo and Kirsten do likewise. They allowed him his petty tyranny and quickly ordered shark steaks and some beer. Thomas asked for a pork vindaloo and insisted that it be served hot with freshly boiled rice, 'Not something that's been sitting with the flies all day.'

'Relax Thomas,' said Carlo, finding some amusement in his bodyguard's nervousness.

'Being here doesn't make any sense,' Thomas replied, miserably. 'I can't guarantee your safety out here.'

'Don't worry. If he gets me here you can still count on a good reference,' said Carlo, laughing at his own joke.

'If he gets you, he gets me,' said Thomas, and he lowered his eyes to the table, not wishing to continue the conversation.

Carlo sniffed and looked around the restaurant at nothing in particular. He smiled as he turned to Kirsten. 'You'll protect us, won't you?' he said to her. 'After all, you're pretty tough.'

'I don't think anybody can save you from him,' Kirsten replied and regretted it immediately.

'You're fucking weird,' Carlo said, shaking his head. Kirsten didn't answer, and Carlo took her lack of response to be one of embarrassment. 'Looks like we're all in this one together,' he said. 'He's not going to let any witnesses go free. You must realise that.' He winked at Kirsten and looked up as the waiter arrived with two beers and a glass of fruit juice for Thomas.

When the meals arrived half an hour later, there was silence rather than the usual excitement and culinary enthusiasm. The wait, relatively short as it was, had put paid to any attempt at false camaraderie. Kirsten and Thomas had nothing to say, and Carlo had given up trying.

Thomas took sanctuary in his meal, piling the rice high on his plate and adding the vindaloo in one go. Kirsten did likewise. Carlo, however, was instantly dissatisfied. 'This isn't shark,' he said, and he called the waiter over. 'This isn't shark,' he said. 'It's tuna. I ordered shark.'

'It is shark, sir, I can assure you. It was freshly caught today.' The waiter was a small man with a tired face and a thin moustache. He shuffled uneasily and tried to maintain a professional smile. There was a large gap between his two front teeth.

'I ain't arguing whether or not it's fresh. I'm saying that it ain't shark.'

'Does it matter?' asked Thomas. 'You're drawing attention to us.'

'Butt out,' said Carlo. 'I ordered shark.'

'I will ask the chef, sir,' said the waiter, blinking hard as he straightened his tie and retreated to the kitchen.

'Fucking...' said Carlo, trying to retain some composure. He knew that it didn't matter. Thomas was right, of course. He shouldn't draw attention to them. 'It doesn't really matter,' he agreed. 'I like tuna anyway.'

They ate in silence, Thomas shovelling his down; Kirsten and Carlo picking carefully between the fish bones. The waiter reappeared when they were halfway through the meal. 'The chef insists that your fish is shark,' he said to Carlo and he walked away without waiting for a response.

When the meal was finished, Thomas's plate was empty and his mood improved. 'That was bloody good,' he said, knowing that they would soon be returning home. 'I'll get the bill.'

'Thank you, Thomas,' said Carlo. Only Kirsten failed to derive any pleasure from the event or its conclusion.

The waiter approached the table uneasily when Thomas beckoned to him, but he smiled when Thomas asked for the bill.

'One second,' said Carlo, tugging the waiter's shirtsleeve. He pointed at a tidy pile of small bones at the side of his plate. 'What are these?' he asked.

'They're bones, sir,' said the waiter, confident that he was talking to an idiot.

'Correct,' said Carlo, and he stared Thomas down. 'Sharks don't have bones.'

'No sir,' said the waiter, happy to agree with anything that this lunatic said.

'Then how the fuck can it be shark?'

The waiter didn't respond. He had gone into a trance. There was nothing he could say and, other than run away, he didn't know how to save face. After an embarrassing moment's silence, he said that he would ask the chef again and he returned to the kitchen. As Thomas was about to ask Carlo to forget it, a shout came from the kitchen and the sound of flying iron pans joined the roar of argument. Thomas threw a pile of rupees on the table and stood sharply. 'Come on,' he said, and they left.

Chapter 40

Palm trees may seem like mere decoration to the uninformed, but for the insects and the birds and the monkeys these tall, graceful, coconut-bearing fruit trees are the essence of life. That was how Andrew felt, at least, when he watched the way the troop of monkeys were sitting in the early-evening light, beyond the mango trees, preening each other, preparing for their flight through the trees to their home for the night.

In India, because of their association with the monkey god, Hanuman, monkeys were sacred. They could be found everywhere, but they were especially noticeable around temples where they hung out waiting for gifts of food from worshippers and tourists. Although they could be aggressive and they stole anything they could get their claws into, including drying laundry, they were usually left alone, apart from the occasional gentle prod to move them along when they created too much of a nuisance.

In Africa, however, monkeys frequently made it to the cooking pot. Andrew remembered a time when he was renting a house with some friends in Central African Republic. One evening, during a card game, the owner knocked on the door and asked to store some meat in their fridge. An hour later, Andrew's curiosity got the better of him and he took a peep at her joint of meat. A near-human face stared back at him; hairs frozen crispy white, eyes and mouth wide open, teeth grimacing, two hands clenched like fists, knuckles gleaming frostily. 'There's a fucking monkey in the fridge!' Andrew had screamed as he retreated, and the game of cards was cancelled for the evening.

He put the thought out of his mind when Donna announced that the monkeys were climbing into the trees. Suddenly, they were on the move, high above; one by one, they hurled themselves along their arboreal pathway, like arrows from a bow. Palm fronds hissed violently as each tree catapulted its passengers through the air onto the next. The tribe stood motionless, staring at the great natural spectacle above their doorstep. Nobody spoke. There was a genuine excitement and a momentary sense of freedom as the graceful, powerful beasts walked effortlessly, pleasurably, across the naked air.

'Fantastic,' Henrik said, as the monkeys disappeared into the night. He passed Andrew a joint. 'That's worth celebrating,' he said. 'Monkeys can fly!'

'Of course they can.'

'I never saw them do that in a zoo.'

'You smoke too much,' said Donna, sitting beside him. 'There's no room for flying in a zoo.'

'And that includes birds,' said Sylvia, and they all smiled, happy in their hashish, that they had shared a lesson in the University of Life today.

Much later, having eaten in Chapora Village and having enjoyed some after-dinner smokes out on the verandah, they made it along to the Primrose Bar. It was a difficult walk after dark because of all the tree roots snaking across the path, but they arrived in one piece. Simon, however, played heavily on his jellyfish sting, and remained at home to read.

By midnight, when they arrived, Primrose was packed and kicking and there was nowhere to sit. The queue to the bar stretched out into the open. Motorbikes were backed up as far as the dirt road. Tonight, more than ever, there was a huge fleet of motorbike taxis alongside all the rented bikes. The locals were obviously expecting a major event. Henrik refused to be daunted by the queue and he left the tribe to roll a few joints while he bought some drinks.

Watching Henrik in the queue, Andrew had to laugh. He was sporting a truly bizarre haircut; a shaved head with island tufts of hair all over the place and a question mark on the back of his head. He called it his party haircut. The rest of them had all shaved their heads, but nothing fancy, just baldies. They had the haircuts done at a one-chair, pink-walled barbers, in Chapora Village after dinner. They were all stoned, of course, so it had seemed like a good idea. Now, in the dark, it was difficult to tell them apart. Mind you it would be handy for later, Andrew thought, because their bald heads should stand out in the crowds if any of them got lost.

By the time Henrik found them again, they were sitting beneath an old tree in the shadows beyond the motorbikes and they had been through a lot of hash. Time was moving on and, if they were going to be ripe for the party, they needed to organise some LSD soon. Everyone was up for it; Henrik could tell by their eager faces and so he passed out the drinks quickly, laid his bottle of beer in the dirt and dug into his pocket for a small plastic bag. The tribe were sitting in a circle, their friendship bonded on the road and they were all excited, preparing as they were, to make a grand commitment to each other. This was not something to do alone. Henrik passed around tiny pieces of blotting paper and returned Simon's to the bag for later. They each held a piece on a fingertip and raised it before their faces. Henrik looked around, smiling like a witch, and he swiped his drug into his mouth with the tip of his tongue. He was a sacrificial lamb, a party animal. A sigh filled the air and the rest of them followed suit.

Across the dried grass, the pre-party warm up went on. Motorbike taxis driven by laughing, grinning Goan men with small moustaches and bright red betel juice teeth were delivering other tribes to the rendezvous at Primrose. People crowded into the grounds, kicking up dust, billowing smoke, swaggering, strutting, ambling, dancing, doing what people back home never did. Chillums passed along lines of people sitting on the walls, one almighty cloud of smoke each, glowing sacrifices, glowing celebrations. You can't pick your family, but you can pick your friends. Everybody had picked their friends. They had met on buses, on trains, in hotels, in restaurants, on mountain paths, on camel trecks and elephant treks, in airports, on boats, in shops and on beaches and bars. Everyone trusted everyone implicitly. Travellers had a code.

The tribe was silent; nobody was speaking. They were leaning back, resting on their palms, legs stretched out straight before them, feet touching at the centre. They were smiling and enjoying a series of private thoughts all centred around their union. If it wasn't for the fact that just about everybody at Primrose was stoned, they would have looked pretty odd. What made it so easy to be weird in Goa was the fact that everybody was happy to be themselves. Nobody was weird, not for the moment at least, nobody wanted to be uncool.

Goa was so refreshing after all those fashion conscious beaches and strutting streets in Thailand. Goa was a nutters' paradise where everyone got on with their own thing during the day and then crawled into the darkness to cling to the warmth and strength of tribalism. Andrew was going to miss it all when he moved on. Sylvia was sitting beside him with her head resting against his right shoulder. She was watching a group of people who had detached themselves from the rest and were heading out onto the path. 'They're going to the party,' she said dreamily. 'We should follow them.'

'No need,' said Henrik, looking pleased with himself. 'I know where it is.' Realising that the tribe demanded an explanation he added: 'I asked when I was getting the drinks. It's down by the beach.'

'Shouldn't we go then?' Andrew asked.

'I tell you what we should do,' said Donna. 'We should wait until the acid is working, then we can drift along the path together. Just think what it will be like to arrive at a party in full swing: all those lights, and the crowds and the music.'

'Wow!' said Karen, at the thought and she sent a sexually-loaded smile to Jessica, who was so obviously ecstatic that she didn't have a bad word for anybody.

'Gonna be some party,' said Henrik, and they all smiled on in silence.

An hour later, Primrose was closing down as most people had gone. The tribe had let everybody go ahead of them because they were enjoying themselves. They were all buzzing like kids in an autumnal field full of shiny conkers. They had taken more than they could handle and were letting it ooze through them, all butterflies, tickling throats and expectation.

An energy, something like the devil himself, was surging through Andrew's body, enlivening his imagination and giving him physical strength. He wanted to possess somebody and that somebody was Sylvia. She was walking just ahead of him, peering into the surrounding darkness. She was wearing a sleeveless, purple waistcoat, a pair of light brown leather sandals and an Indonesian Sarong wrapped around her waist like a miniskirt. It clung to her backside like cling-film. The material was so light that Andrew thought that his hot breath could probably render it transparent. In his dreams he was only three buttons away from removing her waistcoat.

The others were a few metres ahead, laughing and fantasising, strolling slowly, holding hands, moving to the distant rhythm. They were walking in an urban forest of palm trees and mango trees and gardens and stone walls and winding tree roots and fallen leaves and chirping insects and swooping bats and darkness. At random there was the sound of a distant barking dog or a whispered conversation. Somewhere in the forest, directly ahead of them, there was a sound so loud that only distance hid it. Andrew was concentrating hard to locate it. As they walked, the distance lessened, and something warm and beckoning pressed lightly against his ears.

Music.

They turned a corner and headed towards the light boom, boom, boom, and, as they did, there was a momentary sight of people moving in the shadows. They followed the path to the end and there were more people. They turned again. The path was bigger and the sound louder. There was a small crowd ahead and, looking back, Andrew could see that there was a thin line of people following them. They had found it.

A quarter of a mile further on and they were really amongst them. The crowd had grown and motorbikes were constantly flying past. The path was a procession of latter-day clowns and dancers, actors and jesters, all singing, all dancing, all laughing. Music was beating the air with a fierce intensity. Even the earth beneath their feet was rumbling. The darkness was giving up its secret.

A blast of light and a rush of strobes punched Andrew, like a physical rush, as they turned from the path and faced the party head on. The tribe closed up, wagon-train style, ensuring that they were all safe, all confident, all together. There were 500 backpackers, hippies, tourists and travellers parading before them, and there were plenty of local Goans, some working, making cash, and some there to party, and some to watch. Chai ladies, local Goan women, were setting up tea stalls on mats outside the gates, where tired partygoers could take time out to sip hot tea out of small glasses, eat cakes, smoke a chillum or stop to talk. A light aroma of woodsmoke mingled with the smell of hashish burning in clay pipes, hot glowing embers lighting up like fireflies, clouds of smoke billowing from mouths raised in reverence to the night sky. So much was hitting Andrew at once that he couldn't take it all in. There was a sea of motorbikes, most belonging to Goan motorbike taxi drivers, who were having their own party because they were making good money tonight. They were standing with their machines, laughing and smoking and spitting streaks of bright red betal juice across the dust.

The taxi-drivers' mood was infectious. Andrew developed a smile, which seemed to have its infancy in his stomach. It grew, spreading outwards and upwards towards his face, until the walls of his mouth were forced apart. His eyes opened wide, hypnotised and staring. He was hooked, trapped in a fantastic dream.

Chapter 41

Maurice held Amanda tightly around the waist and kissed her as he gently dropped a heavy canvas bag over the low stone wall opposite Carlo's house. He held tightly onto the straps until he felt the weight of the bag touch earth. He couldn't afford to have the bottles break, not even one of them. Amanda smiled as she turned to kiss his mouth and Maurice had to tighten his hold on her. Earlier, on the verandah, Amanda had finished a bottle of Indian port, thinking that Maurice had drunk at least half of it. In fact, Maurice had drunk none at all. Alcohol was one of his favourite weapons. He saw no reason to use it on himself.

Janine had asked Amanda not to go to the party, but Amanda had ignored her, saying that if Janine was worried about her, then she should come with her. Janine was too sick to go anywhere though, let alone a party. She blamed her condition on one of several meals she'd eaten that day, although she couldn't say which.

Ten minutes after stashing his bag Maurice arrived at the party. Amanda was beside him, barely able to stand. Maurice's heart was pounding. There were so many tourists, he thought, their money belts stuffed full of dollars and credit cards and passports. There was enough here for him to live off for years. Hippies were in the majority, hundreds of them, many dressed like locals. The women were wearing saris and sarongs; the men were dressed in baggy cotton trousers, one was even wearing a turban. For a second Maurice was tempted to forgo the pleasure of cooking Carlo's corpse and settling for some easy pickings, but the need to rid himself of his nemesis won him over.

Amanda staggered off to the bar. She looked back over her shoulder, grinning inanely before disappearing amongst a seething crowd crushing forwards against a row of tables, which had been set up like sandbags against a rising torrent. Money changed hands like paper flapping at a stock exchange and the lucky ones forced their way out, shoulders first, escaping with their drinks and their lives and their self-satisfied smiles.

Across the field, beyond the crowded dancefloor, two stacks of speakers, eight feet in height, were pounding out the Acid House beat, repetative, fast, and mesmerising. Maurice scanned the huge crowd, searching for familiar faces, searching, just for the fun of it, for potential victims, but he knew it was a pointless task and he drew the expected blank.

'Got you a drink,' Amanda said, trying hard to focus. 'Do you want to dance?'

Maurice took the water and sighed, ignoring Amanda's question completely. He moved away from her and waited for her to respond to his rudeness. Amanda blinked, not quite sure whether or not Maurice's behaviour was strange. Unsteadily, she looked around the party grounds, trying to take in something that she couldn't quite understand. Maurice slipped away.

When Amanda turned to speak again Maurice was gone. She closed her eyes and took a sip from her drink, but when she opened them, he still wasn't there. She concentrated hard; she knew that she was drunk, but she couldn't see him anywhere. She giggled nervously and remembered her sister's warnings.

And then he was back, grinning like a child. 'It's a great party,' he said. 'I was just looking around. How are you feeling?'

'Nice,' said Amanda, relieved that she had just been imagining things. 'I thought that you'd left me.'

Maurice laughed gently. 'Leave you?' he said. 'Why would I do that?' He smiled at her momentarily and then kissed her gently on the mouth. He could manipulate her any way he wanted now, but he didn't need her any more. He had used her as a disguise but now, in the darkness, he would be able to approach his target without her. He didn't need much more time. Carlo hadn't come to the party. He was probably too nervous. All Maurice wanted now was for Carlo and his household to go to bed. 'I've had an idea,' he said to Amanda, looking deep into her eyes. 'Let's go down to the beach where we can be alone. It's such a beautiful night.'

Amanda was delighted. This incredible man could have anything from her, she thought. She threw the last of her drink to the back of her throat in a defiant gesture. 'Why not?' she said.

As they turned towards the gate they encountered Janine, who was staggering towards them, clutching something in her hand. She was wearing an old T-shirt and a pair of shorts. Her long hair was matted with sweat. Amanda was horrified; Janine was about to ruin her perfect night. 'What are you doing here?' Amanda growled. 'You should have stayed in bed. You're ill. Why don't you leave me alone?'

'There's no need…' said Maurice, but Janine cut him off.

'You bastard!' she yelled. 'What have you done with him?'

'Janine!' Amanda yelped. 'What are you doing?'

'This,' Janine interrupted. 'This…' She thrust Peter's passport into Maurice's face. 'This was in Maurice's room. It was in his bag. It's Peter's passport!' Janine was screaming now and people were staring. 'What have you fucking done with him?'

'I don't know what you mean,' said Maurice. 'I haven't seen that passport before.'

Janine turned to face the small crowd, now watching them with unease. She was trembling as nausea washed through her in waves. 'This man is a murderer!' she screamed, her face reddening with anger and pain. 'This is my friend's passport, and I found it in his bag.' She turned back towards Maurice. 'No wonder you said that he had left unexpectedly. You've killed him; I know you have.'

The crowd was pressing in on them and Maurice was becoming uncomfortable. Janine shouldn't have been able to get to the party. He had given her a large enough dose to knock her out for hours. He turned to Amanda. 'She's delirious,' he said. 'She has a fever. I don't know where she found that passport, but it wasn't in my room.'

'I don't know what to think,' said Amanda vaguely, overpowered by confusion..

'You're drunk Amanda,' Janine sneered. 'You've never been drunk before. He got you drunk.' She waved the passport at Maurice. 'Why would you get my sister drunk? Why would you have somebody's passport? What kind of games are you playing?'

Maurice laughed weakly. Peter's passport was getting the attention Janine needed. If the crowd tried to detain him and call the police, he wouldn't be able to fight them all off, even with his knife. He was shaking with anger, losing his calm, losing face. He should have killed her before now. He made his move and side-stepped around her. As she turned towards him, he faced her with such anger that surrounding people recoiled. He raised his hand to hit her, but he stopped himself. He screamed something in French, shoved his way through the crowd and headed for the gate.

'Somebody call the police!' Janine begged. 'Murderer!' she yelled, and spittle ran down her face. 'Murderer! Murderer!' But nobody moved. 'Why don't you do something? Somebody call the police!'

Andrew was dreaming… it was wonderful… he was dreaming… he had to be. He was lying in the sand watching Sylvia dance. There was a palm tree high above him and it was whistling in the breeze, whistling like a breeze, whistling at Sylvia. Each time the strobe illuminated his goddess, the palm tree leant down and carressed her with its fronds; its big, soft palm leaves. He could hear the tree breathing and panting. It was a crazy tree, a jealous tree, and he was certain that it was about to speak. It wanted her. Andrew wanted her. Sylvia danced, unaware of the eyes upon her, unaware of the heat emanating from her, unaware that Andrew was watching her making love to herself, her naked feet patting the hard sand, footprints for its memory.

He was fully aware that he had taken far too many drugs for his own good but it was difficult to believe that the acid was inducing this. This was too real. He had Sylvia's sandals in his hand. He was looking after them while she danced. Her sarong had risen up her thighs and the buttons of her waistcoat were opening, one by one. She was smiling invitingly at him. The funny thing was that, no matter how many waistcoat buttons pinged open, the same amount always remained secure.

They had found a great spot at the far side of the party near the speakers. They were booming like crazy, sending out signals that everyone followed. There was a skinny guy in white Y-fronts marching around like a madman. He stormed up to a stack of speakers, shook his head around, trying to knock it off, then he marched up to the other stack and repeated the exercise. Sylvia was looking at Andrew now with a wicked expression on her face. She wanted him as much as he wanted her. He noticed, with some satisfaction, that she was not looking up at the jealous palm tree.

Suddenly a pair of hands clasped around his eyes. He grabbed the hands but they wouldn't release him. He turned and the hands let go.

'Thanks for everything,' said Henrik, and Andrew had no idea what he was thanking him for.

'Thanks for what?'

'I just want to thank you,' he said, angrily. The acid hadn't agreed with him. 'There's no need to make a big deal out of it!'

'Sorry.'

'That's okay.'

'Where's Donna?'

'I don't know,' said Henrik, and he looked up at Sylvia. 'Have you seen Donna?'

Sylvia just smiled.

'Have you seen Donna?' Henrik asked some guy Andrew had never seen before.

'Donna!' Henrik shouted.

'Henrik,' Andrew said gently, and grabbed hold of his arm. 'Don't worry about her. She's fine.' Henrik's paranoia was ruining his trip. 'Stay with me until she comes back. Come and watch Sylvia. She's really something.'

'Yeah,' Henrik said, and he settled next to Andrew and tried to smile. 'She's lovely,' he said, and Andrew drifted back into heaven.

Strangely, Sylvia wasn't there anymore but, somehow, Kirsten was. Kirsten was always fantastic to watch; elegant, sensual and imaginative.

She danced like she made love. Looking at her now, Andrew realised that she would always be the one for him. She gave him an excitement no other woman, not even Sylvia, could give. He was tempted to get up and dance with her, but Kirsten had gone, and Sylvia was back again.

There was a wonderful sexy feeling in Andrew's stomach. Sylvia was beautiful. She looked a lot like Kirsten. She had the same build and she was noisier in bed too. She was lovely. Everybody was lovely.

Henrik leapt up. Donna was back. Karen and Jessica were with her. They were all together again. Donna had a pocket full of joints that she had made up on the verandah earlier. She took one out and lit it. She sat in the sand and dragged hard on the joint, a hot glow burning along the paper like a lit fuse. Without looking to her side, she passed the joint to Henrik. Moments later, she exhaled and smoke rushed from her pouted mouth like a blast of history, releasing a genie from a bottle. Sylvia was the genie. She knelt above Andrew, pulling the sarong high to her thighs. She spread her body across his and kissed him. 'Let's go to the beach for a while,' she said.

Andrew reacted immediately, by his current standards, clambering awkwardly up Sylvia's legs as she stood. They hugged, linked arms and smiled at the other members of the tribe as they headed for the party's exit. The crowd was heavier the further they went. Near the entrance it became an impenetrable mass, surging into a central nucleus, as if there was something drawing it in.

'Hang on,' Andrew said. 'I'm going to have a look.'

Surprisingly, although he was using a modicum of force to get through the crowd, nobody argued with him. Like zombies, people moved to one side, allowing him through, and he began to think that perhaps there was nothing to see after all. However as he pushed his way to the front he could hear raised voices and the murmurings of the inner circle. Then, to his horror, he realised the cause. It took more than a few blinks of the eye for him to finally accept that the man walking away through the gate was Maurice. With great reluctance, and not a little resistance from Sylvia, Andrew finally accepted that he had to follow him.

Chapter 42

Maurice moved swiftly. Once he was out of sight, he broke into a jog. Everything had gone wrong. He should have given Janine enough to kill her, he realised that now. What was he trying to do? There had been nothing to gain from keeping her alive. He had looked forward to humiliating Amanda on the beach. He clenched his fists at the thought of what he had lost because of his stupidity. Worse still, he had to act quickly now, so that he could get rid of Carlo, gather his things and get away before the police arrived. Annoyingly he would have to return to the house and pack before he could pay Carlo a visit. He couldn't afford to leave anything behind that might identify him. He would have to stash his bag. To be certain of escape, he would have to leave Goa as soon as the job was done.

He ran to the house, not fast, not in panic, but an easy jog, long, careful strides. He arrived, barely breathless, and packed carefully, making sure that he forgot nothing. He slung the pack over his shoulder and locked the front door behind him, leaving the key in the lock. Then he found a rock and smashed the key in the lock, ensuring that it couldn't be removed. The delay in opening the door could give him valuable minutes.

He jogged to Carlo's house and climbed over the wall opposite, finishing the journey on his belly. When he reached the stashed bag, he dumped his pack beside it and opened the bag. He took six petrol-filled bottles from the bag and stood them side-by-side against the wall, careful to ensure that they wouldn't spill. He removed the bottle lids and replaced them with thick strips of muslin. One by one he carefully put each of the bottles back in the bag. He removed a cigarette lighter from a side pouch and put it in his pocket. Then he peered over the top of the wall.

The house was in darkness. It was two o'clock. In the distance, through the trees, the party boomed with authority. He sighed with pleasure. The time had come.

He crept from behind the wall and went around to the back of the house where there was more cover. He climbed the wall and dropped gently to the sand on the other side, lowering the bag by its straps first. Stealthily, he moved to the back door and found it locked tight. From the bag he took a chain and a padlock. He draped the chain around the door handle, pulled it around a down-pipe from the gutter above and padlocked the chain. Nobody would leave the house through this door tonight. The ground floor windows were all barred. He crept around to the front of the house and found the front door locked. This time there was nothing to chain the door handle to, but he had done his homework. He wheeled one of the motorbikes across the sand and rested it against the door. Then he did the same with the other bike and locked them together with a small padlock and chain. Then he chained the door handle to the motorbike handlebars. It would take a lot of pulling to open the door now.

Maurice thought about what he was about to do. It had taken him so long to reach this stage. Carlo had manipulated him over the years, caused him to make terrible mistakes, cost him his child, stolen from him. Carlo deserved this. He went to the window to the left of the door and peered inside. He took a bottle from his bag. Then he smashed the glass with an elbow and lit the fuse in the neck of the bottle. He slipped the bottle through the gap in the glass and flung it towards the open door to the hallway. The bottle exploded with a flash and a surge of heat, and Maurice saw the flames climb the wall and spread across the floor.

He moved fast, running to the window on the other side of the door. Again he smashed the glass and hurled the bomb inside. He was already on his way to the back of the house when he heard the explosion. This time he hurled a bomb against a window on the top floor. It smashed through the glass and exploded somewhere inside. There were screams and shouts from inside as the occupants awoke to an inferno. Maurice ran back to the front, his body shaking with excitement. At a window above the door he caught a glimpse of a face. It was Kirsten. She was here. Another explosion ripped through the night and Maurice felt an excruciating pain in his shoulder that he couldn't explain. The force of the blow spun the bag from his hand and knocked him backwards. He looked back to where he had seen Kirsten's face, only to see another. A man was pointing a gun at him.

Maurice staggered away from the line of fire, reached for the bag and took another bottle from it. Painfully, he hurled it up at the window and watched it explode against the wall. Flames billowed into the darkened sky and licked at the window frame. Black smoke obscured the glass.

Maurice had just two more bombs. He wanted to make them count but the pain in his shoulder was hindering him. His left arm hung limp and useless beside him. He couldn't concentrate. Carlo had never used guns before and he hadn't expected him to use one now, but the gorilla had changed the equation. The man had to be a hired bodyguard. Maurice should have expected a gun. In anger, he hurled the last two bombs at the front door. They exploded, engulfing the motorbikes in billowing orange and black flames and smoke. Moments later he struggled over the back wall and dragged himself back to his rucksack to watch the house burn.

Carlo, Thomas and Kirsten were trapped on the top floor at the front of the house. The ground floor was ablaze and flames were climbing the stairs. Heavy black smoke was pressing against the door, seeping beneath it, choking and covering them in soot. Carlo had been burnt by the exploding bottle hurled through his bedroom at the back. The skin on the right side of his face was raw where exploding petrol had sprayed him. His eye, his winking eye, was burnt shut. The hair on the right side of his head was shriveled and curled. He ignored the pain as best he could and attempted to plan a way out. The wall outside their window was burning hard and the glass in the window had shattered. The heat was intense. It was impossible to grip the iron bars across the window.

'Are you certain that he won't have a gun?' Thomas shouted above the roar of the flames. 'We're fucked if he has.'

'I've never seen him with one,' Carlo hissed. 'Either way, we're dead if we stay in here.'

Kirsten said nothing. She was experiencing an incredible conflict. Maurice had come as she had planned. This was her doing. Carlo wouldn't live to see morning but, probably, she would die too. Her death didn't bother her so much, but the thought of Maurice surviving, grieved her intensely. Somehow she had to survive this. She had to ensure that Maurice died too.

'Can't we dig the bars out somehow?' Kirsten said.

'With what?' said Carlo.

'Knives or something.'

'Knives! If you can't come up with something better, then shut the fuck up.'

'She might be right, though,' said Thomas.

'We need to get out through the ground floor,' said Carlo. 'If we jump from here, we'll break our fucking legs.'

'It's an inferno down there. There's no way out that way.' Thomas pointed at the door. 'The landing is probably burning now. This room will be full of smoke in no time.'

'I've got a penknife,' said Kirsten, and she took it from her money belt.

'Fucking hell,' said Carlo, with a sigh. He took the knife, opened it up and passed it to Thomas. 'You dig,' he said.

Thomas began scraping the wall between the bricks. To everybody's surprise, the knife went in without difficulty and chalky paste fell away like mature cheese. With the brick loose, Thomas stood back to the side. He raised his foot to the brick and kicked it out, exposing the bar.

'You're beautiful!' Carlo yelled. 'Don't stop now.'

Thomas kicked again and the bar moved. It was loose, resting in the hole through the brick on the other side. Grabbing the hot bar with his hands, Thomas pulled and screamed at once. With the bar coming away, he leant back into the room and pulled it back on itself. The last brick holding it in place came away and the bar fell with an echoing clang, to the floor.

As Thomas began work on the second bar, the motorbikes' petrol tanks exploded and blew the front door away. The house rocked and a wall of flame engulfed the front of the house, sending a wave of heat and stinking smoke into the room. Kirsten and Carlo stood away from the window, leaving Thomas spluttering and gasping as he continued to pick at the wall.

The second bar came away quicker than the first, the wall weakened by the heat. With the window fully open, there was little left to do but to jump.

'You go first, Thomas,' said Carlo. 'Leave the gun with me until you hit the ground. I'll cover you. When you're ready I'll throw it down to you.'

Thomas nodded and climbed into the window. He took one look ahead, one quick glance down and jumped. Carlo leapt into the space and pointed the gun out across the flames towards the path beyond the wall. He could see nothing.

'Throw it down!' shouted Thomas, somewhere beyond the smoke, and Carlo hurled the gun towards him. 'I've got it!' Thomas shouted up to them moments later. 'I'm covering you. Get down here.'

Carlo climbed into the window and leapt instantly without looking. He hit the ground heavily and yelped as he rolled forward. 'I've twisted my fucking ankle,' he growled at Thomas, who had stooped to help him up.

Kirsten could see nothing through the smoke. No way was she jumping into that smoke-filled void. She stepped back into the room to think. As she did so, she spotted her knife lying on the floor. She dusted it off and put it back in her money belt. Then, cautiously, she opened the door to the hallway. Incredibly, the flames had died down. The petrol had burnt itself out and the hallway and stairs were just a hot, smoking, scorched, wreck. She ran through the door and down the blackened stairs to the ground floor. Nothing was recognisable.

The plaster walls were gone and nothing remained intact. There was no front door.

'I don't know why you didn't just use the door,' she said, as she walked past the wrecked motorbikes, into the open.

The two men just stared at her.

Andrew had followed Maurice with some difficulty and, in the end, he had almost run smack into the back of him. Since then he had been watching events unfold without understanding any of it. Nothing made sense. Now seeing Kirsten appear through the door, he knew that this was real. He yelled out to her but wasn't certain that he had spoken. The voice he heard sounded nothing like his own.

But Kirsten looked up and saw him cowering beside the wall. To Andrew's delight she seemed pleased to see him. To his horror, though, moments later, he had Carlo's arm draped over one shoulder and was helping to carry him to their house. He had become a human mule. Strange images and sensations aside, he was now convinced that his peaceful sojourn to the beaches of Goa had taken an unexpected turn for the worse.

Chapter 43

Simon was still rubbing sleep from his eyes when Carlo shoved him hard in the ribs and sent him tumbling backwards in a heap. 'What was that for?' Simon squealed as he picked himself up.

'We've had a bad night,' Kirsten replied on behalf of Carlo, who wasn't in any mood to be polite.

By the time they had opened the gate and were out onto the path opposite Carlo's house, a crowd of locals had gathered to watch the smoking house. It was no longer burning but there was no way that anybody could live in it. The best option, they knew, was to get away fast, before the police arrived and before Maurice could take advantage of their vulnerability. The safest place for the night was Andrew's place. In the dark it was impossible to see anything and the journey had been tense. Only Andrew, who was gasping under Carlo's weight and gabbling unintelligibly, seemed unaware that the danger of Maurice was real.

When they reached the house, Kirsten had gone in first and found only Simon at home, asleep in his room. When Kirsten gave the all clear, Thomas refused to help Carlo inside, saying that it would be the perfect signal to Maurice to rush them. Kirsten and Andrew dragged him in. Finally, with a last look across the path, Thomas backed into the house and locked the door from the inside.

Simon had been surprised to find two strangers in the house with Andrew, who was utterly stoned, and Kirsten, who he hadn't seen in days. It was after three o'clock and all he wanted was a crap, but Carlo had stopped him opening the door and told him to take a crap in the morning.

'Fuck off!' Simon had answered, quite reasonably, so Carlo made sure that Simon got the message in his own way.

Thomas returned from his tour of the house, gun in hand. 'All secure,' he said. He gave the front door another shove, just to be certain. 'Nobody is getting in here tonight. Who else lives here, though? There are mattresses everywhere.'

'They are all at the party,' Simon said, helpfully. 'They won't be back tonight.'

'You're sure you hit him?' Carlo said, ignoring Simon and gently caressing the burnt side of his face, which was beginning to hurt like hell.

'Pretty sure,' said Thomas, 'but there was a lot of smoke.'

'Then there's a chance that he'll bleed to death anyway,' Carlo said, with a hint of hope in his voice. 'Maybe this will still go in our favour.'

'As long as he has no more petrol bombs,' said Thomas, looking at the windows. 'We should stay in one room tonight. Stick close and keep the doors shut.'

'No way,' said Carlo. 'I want that bitch and her junkie boyfriend out of here.'

Kirsten ignored the remark. She had decided to observe proceedings and to keep as low a profile as possible. She was amused by the confusion, the helplessness, the pathetic pretence at bravado, and Simon's bemused compliance was the best part of all. He was standing now, in his boxer shorts, watching Thomas pacing about the lounge. He had obviously calculated that it was best to say nothing. He had no influence over events, as usual, but clearly he was also trying to figure out whether it was Carlo or Thomas who was the biggest threat.

'You just concentrate on controlling your bowels,' said Carlo, noticing the quizzical expression on Simon's face. 'We'll be leaving as soon as it gets light.'

'Somebody is after them,' said Kirsten, in explanation. 'He's probably outside right now.'

Carlo stared at her, angered by the unmistakable sarcasm in her voice. 'One more smart-arsed comment and you're going out the door,' he said. 'Just keep out of my way. Find a bedroom. It would be real nice if I never saw your face again.'

'You've got the gun,' said Kirsten, failing to maintain her low profile. 'He hasn't. He would have shot us by now if he had.'

'We've got a gun with three fucking bullets in it,' Carlo snarled, anger and pain flooding through him together. He turned to Thomas. 'Even so,' he said. 'If she says another word, use one on her. It will be bloody well worth it.'

Thomas smiled and Kirsten decided to comply. Seeing as Andrew had already walked automatically to his room she decided to follow.

'Right,' said Thomas, suddenly animated, big decisions made. 'Simon, I want you to find some things for us to sleep on – mattresses, sheets etc. Bring them into the lounge. We need to get comfortable. Then I want you to go through your friends' bags and find their first-aid equipment, so we can patch Carlo up.' He thought for a moment. 'Kirsten,' he ordered, 'before you disappear, see if you can find something nasty in the kitchen that we can use for weapons; knives, hammers, anything. Bring them here.'

An hour later, Simon was lying silently in the corner of the room, pretending to be asleep. He didn't know what was going on, but there was some kind of danger, best avoided through anonymity. Sleep was the safest place to be, so long as he didn't crap in his bed during the night. Occasionally he actually pretended to snore.

Thomas was sitting in a chair inside the front door, gun in his lap, eyes opening and closing as he tried to remain alert. He was paid handsomely to keep Carlo alive, and this threat from Maurice would extend his earning potential by some months. Carlo wouldn't let him go until he had at least recovered physically. Judging by the ferocity of Maurice's attack, Carlo would be a fool to let him go at all. Danger wasn't a problem for Thomas; he'd faced plenty over the years. Tonight he was feeling pretty good; fully employed and getting wealthier by the minute.

Carlo was lying on his back, keeping his burnt face from rubbing. He stared at the ceiling, breathing steadily, imagining what Maurice was up to. If Thomas had shot him, then there was a good chance that he had backed off or even staggered back into the trees and bled to death like any normal person would do. But Thomas couldn't be certain, not through a pall of smoke. The simple truth, though, was that Maurice was a hard man to kill. He made mistakes, just like anyone, but he had more luck than most, and he knew when to quit. Horribly, Carlo also realised that Anthony's disappearance and Maurice's arrival had to be connected. Anthony was the only person he had told where he was. Maurice must have found him. Anthony, for all his weaknesses, was Carlo's only true friend. He closed his eyes and shivered with anger.

Kirsten was kneeling across Andrew's confused body, smiling contentedly to herself. She had created this chaos. She was responsible for Carlo's agony. She listened to the distant music and wondered what Andrew was thinking. He was on another planet, although he probably didn't realise it. He was staring wildly off into space. He wasn't a bad man and he made her laugh, but he was weak and he was naïve. But he represented normality for her. He enjoyed the simple life, he threatened nobody, least of all her, and he loved her, made her feel important. Andrew was her one ego trip and, even though he had little money left, she needed him as much as he needed her. If this was over by morning, and they were still alive, she would take him away with her.

First, though, she had to ensure that Carlo was dead. The obvious way to do that was to open the front door and invite Maurice inside, but with Thomas by the door, that wasn't going to happen. She thought about killing him herself, stabbing him to death with her penknife or grabbing the gun from Thomas and shooting them both dead, but she'd never used a gun before. Of course, it was possible that the others would return from the party before dawn. That would create plenty of confusion and Maurice might take advantage of that. Probably, though, Carlo was right and Maurice had failed again, letting Carlo off the hook. She sighed and remembered the attack on the beach on Ko Phangan. This was her last chance, she knew it. If Carlo escaped tonight, she would never have her revenge. The thought appalled her.

She closed her eyes and, even though he was high on LSD, she decided to see if she could entice Andrew to make love to her one last time.

Andrew couldn't decide whether the woman making love to him was Sylvia or Kirsten. She was laughing, her face contorted and red, her eyes bulging, wild and hungry, sweat dripping from her forehead and splashing like huge, exploding raindrops onto his face. She danced in slow motion, cobra-like, tantalising, entrancing, eating him alive. All evening Andrew had enjoyed brief flashes of reality, but now it was too late. He couldn't even be sure that he was tripping. The images he'd seen earlier of people like Maurice and Carlo were consigned to history. The strangest things were happening to him now. There were times when he wasn't exactly certain that he was Andrew at all.

He reached up and took the woman's breasts in his hands. He could feel her nipples growing and growing. She was sighing like a warm breeze. She licked her lips and Andrew watched as her tongue unwrapped and reached out to him like a snake. She lay upon him and kissed him. Andrew reached out for her hot, wet, backside and, as he grabbed her, he felt her knees press hard into his ribs, gripping him tightly, holding him so that she could pick the flesh from his bones. He felt her tongue in his mouth and he found that he could hardly breathe. Above them both, the sky was on fire.

Andrew gave into the force above him. He closed his eyes and took shelter in a kaleidoscope world where naked women, joined at their waists, danced in an ocean of stars and bubbles, all green, red and blue. There was music in there, playing slowly in a slow-motion world, and there were answers to all the questions he had ever asked. Everything was so perfectly simple. Outside his body, even with his eyes closed, he could feel this incredible woman moving over him, back and forth, gently, softly, lovingly.

Chapter 44

Thomas woke with a start when he heard Simon at the door. 'What are you doing?' he asked, sleepily.

'You said that I could take a crap in the morning. It's morning.'

'What time is it?'

'Six.'

'You're right,' said Thomas. 'It is morning.'

Carlo was roused by the conversation. 'What time is it?' he asked.

'Six,' said Thomas.

'Daylight?'

Thomas unlocked the front door cautiously and sent Simon onto the verandah, while he remained inside, gun ready. Daylight lit up the lounge. Kirsten woke with a start when she heard people moving about. She sat upright and found Andrew curled like a foetus in the corner of the room, barely visible beneath a pile of clothes and sheets which he'd pulled across him like a tortoise hiding in straw. He was awake, Kirsten realised, his eyes fixed upon her impassively. He hadn't been able to sleep all night because of the LSD. He was still tripping. In the lounge the rest of the household was on its feet.

'Good morning,' Carlo said to nobody in particular, and he grinned like a man walking away from a near-fatal accident. 'I have to say that I feel lucky today. As soon as I can, I'm on a flight to Hong Kong. I need to start living again.'

Thomas looked anxiously at him.

'Don't worry,' said Carlo. 'You're coming with me.'

'Can I take a crap now?' asked a voice from the verandah, and Carlo laughed aloud.

'I'll go with him,' said Thomas. 'I'll use him as a lookout while I'm in there.'

'Check around while you're out there,' said Carlo. 'Knock hard when you come back.'

As they walked around the side of the house, they heard Carlo padlocking the door from the inside. Thomas grinned to himself and followed Simon towards the toilet. The morning was fresh, dew clung lightly to the thin grass, the sun was reaching above the trees, streams of light searching amongst the undergrowth, warming insects, waking them. Thomas felt great. He was on his way to Hong Kong, one of the most vibrant places in Asia. Carlo would be paying him well. Maurice, he decided, was the best thing to happen to him in years.

He was in such a good mood that he allowed Simon to go first. While he listened to Simon's grunted complaints about the smell and his relieved sighs, he checked the alley behind the toilet and nosed around the surrounding trees. Maurice was nowhere to be seen. He had gone.

When Simon reappeared from the toilet with a huge grin on his face, Thomas told him to wait for him. He was even tempted to pass the gun to Simon, but decided against it. The toilet was one of the reasons he looked forward to Hong Kong. There was barely enough room to stand straight, especially for him, and he hated to think what it must be like to squat down inside one of these things. He shoved the gun as deep into his pocket as possible, then he undid his trousers, positioned his feet as wide apart as possible on the slippery wooden planks and aimed into the hole below. As he did so, two hands reached up from the darkness and grabbed him by the ankles. Before he could remove the look of surprise from his face, he was falling into the hole.

Thomas groaned as his chest wedged tight in the hole. He was hanging, suspended by his arms, a metre above the toilet floor. 'Simon!' he growled. 'For fuck's sake, Simon!' But Simon had drifted away in an early-morning trance and was leaning peacefully, half asleep, against the base of a palm tree.

Thomas lashed out with his feet, kicking wildly at whoever was down there. He couldn't reach the gun, which was below him now. Desperately, he grabbed at the wooden planks, trying to extricate himself, but there was nothing to grip.

Maurice was holding his nose where Thomas had just kicked him. Blood cascaded over him. The pain in his shoulder and the gas-like stench of excrement made him want to vomit. He had little strength left. On the floor beside him was his bag of tricks. He opened it and removed his knife. Then he crawled around to the side of Thomas's dangling frame and looked up. He saw the gun. He considered tugging the gun from Thomas's pocket, but decided against it as it would probably induce a flurry of kicking again. Instead he positioned himself on his knees and took the knife in both hands. He leaned backwards and raised the knife above his head. With all his remaining strength he lunged forwards, ramming the knife into Thomas's side until only the hilt was visible. Thomas somehow kicked him square on the nose and shattered it, but Maurice held on as huge droplets of blood flowed freely over his chin and ran into his gasping mouth. As if the knife was keeping Maurice from toppling over a cliff, he gripped it tightly with both hands and fell to his knees. The blade tore downwards through Thomas's body, tearing through his finely toned muscles, spilling out his life like bloody afterbirth. While Thomas kicked and twitched, Maurice hung onto the knife, tugging at it, sawing with it, tearing into the belt which held Thomas's trousers up. As the knife finally severed the belt Maurice toppled backwards, landing heavily on the slippery toilet floor. Above ground Thomas, his eyes stunned in agonised terror, opened his mouth to scream, spewed blood and bile, and died.

Maurice was exhausted. He had spent the entire night in the hole, waiting for somebody to make a mistake. He was covered in human shit, some of which had dried like mud on his clothes, and he had lost a lot of blood. His shoulder was numb and now his nose was broken. It crossed his mind that this was a good time to retire from the scene. He could find Carlo another time. But then he remembered the gun. The gun would make all the difference.

Moments later, Maurice was standing above Simon with the gun pointing downwards. He held his bag in his other hand. His knife remained in the toilet with Thomas's gutted corpse. He kicked Simon hard between the legs and Simon woke with the shocked realisation that his balls had been crushed. He doubled up in agony and began to moan. Maurice gave him enough time to recover and ordered him to his feet. Simon held onto the tree as he dragged himself upright and stared, in disbelief, at the gun in Maurice's hand and the crazy expression of hatred on his face.

'I want you to get me into the house,' Maurice said, and it didn't even cross Simon's mind that he should object.

Simon walked ahead of Maurice, carrying his bag, a cloud of uncontrollable panic programming his actions. Maurice didn't have to say anymore: Simon knew exactly which role to play. He had cut himself off from the present and was planning his homecoming. The first night home he would phone all of his friends and get them down the pub. He would spend the evening regaling them with tales of his great adventures, including this one, and they would get him drunk on free beer. The blokes would shake his hands and pat him on the back and the girls would hug him and kiss him and, for an evening, he would be a hero. He couldn't wait. Just as soon as this was over he was flying home.

'Ask them to let you in,' Maurice whispered in Simon's ear as they stepped onto the verandah.

'We're back,' Simon stuttered. He swallowed hard and tried again. 'We're back,' he said, louder this time, and he knocked on the door.

Immediately there was the sound of a key in a padlock and the unwrapping of a chain. 'What took you so…?' said Kirsten, as Simon flew into her and shoved her backwards. Maurice stood in the doorway, looking as if he was about to collapse. Blood and sweat dripped from his hot, fevered face. Simon had stopped and was standing rigid just a metre in front of him, obscuring his view of the room. He had dropped the bag beside the door. Kirsten had instinctively stepped away and was now standing unthreateningly to the side, out of reach. Without hesitation, Maurice pushed the barrel of the gun into the scruffy red hair at the back of Simon's head and, with the gentle squeeze of a finger, he blew out his brains, splattering Kirsten with blood, flesh and scraps of sticky, bloody skull. As Simon's body shrunk to the floor, Maurice came face-to-face with Carlo, who was advancing painfully towards him, a rusting carving knife in his right hand. Maurice fired two shots at him and stopped him dead.

'Got you,' Maurice said, and he grimaced as he struggled to raise a well-earned smile.

Carlo was finished. He was flat on his back, gasping for breath. He had raised one hand to his mouth. The other was clawing at the floor. He simply couldn't understand what had happened to him. One of the bullets had hit him in the mouth and had shattered his teeth, exiting through the back of his neck, leaving a large hole, through which blood was spreading across the floor. The other bullet had hit him in the chest, breaking two ribs, before coming to rest against a third.

'Nice to see you again,' Maurice said to Kirsten, who had sat in a chair and was smiling contentedly to herself.

'Finally,' Kirsten replied. 'It seems so long since we first met.'

'And how are your two friends, Annabel and Jonathon?'

'Well they're dead of course. Your poison is quite effective... sometimes.'

'And Andrew?'

'I don't see so much of Andrew now. He's around somewhere I imagine. This is his house, you know.'

'I didn't know.' He made a point of examining the room. 'I don't suppose that he's home.'

'He's at the party,' Kirsten said. 'He's probably face down in the sand by now.'

'Maybe he'll come home soon.'

'If he does, he won't be alone.' Kirsten smiled. She couldn't believe that Maurice hadn't bothered to check. 'Looking at you I doubt that you will live that long anyway. It seems to me that you're not at all well.'

'No. I have had some bad luck.'

Kirsten smiled.

'You shouldn't smile,' Maurice said, unable to disguise the physical pain that he was enduring. 'You have been careless. You led me here with your childish games, yet you are unprepared.'

'Unprepared?'

'I have quite a weapon here,' Maurice said, waving the gun gently from side-to-side.

Kirsten smiled again, knowing full well that the gun was empty. 'Clever old Maurice,' she said. 'Did it ever cross your mind that you were not my target? Did it cross your mind that you have spent the night lying in shit with a bullet in your shoulder while I slept comfortably on a mattress? Did it ever cross your mind that all I've had to do is write letters, while you did all of the work, spent so much money, and took all the risks?'

'But there will be a price to pay,' Maurice said, anger rising above the cool menace. He knelt and picked up the padlock and chain. He locked the door awkwardly with one hand and turned back to face Kirsten, who was still smiling at him. Angrily, he took a chair, placed it across Carlo's face and sat on it, pinning him to the floor. He needed to reassert his control. 'Your good friend, Anthony is dead,' he said to him, forcing a grin, watching for recognition. 'I drowned him in his bath and cut off his head.'

Carlo closed his one good eye, the other still burnt shut like a grimacing wink. Kirsten imagined that he was crying, and the smile on her face broadened further.

'Of course he was terrified,' Maurice continued. 'When he learnt my identity, he cried with fear. You would have been proud of me; after all, it was you who taught me everything I know.' Maurice was enjoying himself now, so much so, that he was almost oblivious to his agony and weakness. 'Of course, that isn't all,' he taunted. 'Have you asked yourself how I found Anthony?'

Carlo reached up and grabbed Maurice weakly by the throat, but his hand fell away again and Maurice laughed. 'Why, Kirsten told me,' Maurice said, his face lighting up with joy. 'She told me many things, in fact. But it must have been you who told her in the first place. How else could she have known?'

'It's true,' Kirsten said, ensuring that Carlo had no doubt that he was the cause of his friend's death. 'As I mentioned before, you told me the same day you fucked me like a dog in Jakarta. The same day I decided that I would see you dead.' She stood and approached them. 'Of course, Maurice still thinks that he has created this beautiful moment. He is too arrogant to see the truth.'

'Oh no,' said Maurice. 'That is not so. I know what you have done, and I know why. But I know more than you think.' He waved the gun at her and Kirsten, thoroughly enjoying herself, happily returned to her seat.

'You see,' Maurice said. 'In Kathmandu, I realised that you were not the innocent tourist that we had all taken you for. You were far too manipulative.' He stopped for a moment while a sea of fire washed through his body, and his nose and shoulder throbbed again. 'I made enquiries, you know. I have contacts in the most useful of places, even in Germany. I know all about you.' He hesitated so that he could enjoy Kirsten's surprise. There was no doubt in his mind that she had brought him this far for a purpose, but it was important to him that she should know that he had followed her willingly. 'Life has been so unkind to you. Your parents are both dead. Did you ever tell Carlo how they died?'

Kirsten fidgeted uncomfortably. It didn't matter that he knew her history and it wouldn't matter a damn if he told Carlo, but she didn't like strangers talking about her mother. 'He wouldn't have believed me,' she said.

'No,' said Maurice, 'but he didn't see you in the shower in Kathmandu.' He laughed aloud. 'Wow!' he shrieked. 'That was when I realised you were capable of anything.'

Carlo was listening, although his eyes were shut. He had no idea what Maurice was talking about, but he knew that Kirsten was the only chance he had left. His mind began to cloud over and he realised that he was losing consciousness. Just one last effort, he thought, and he reached above the chair and grabbed Maurice by the shoulder.

Maurice was taken by surprise, his arrogance disarming him, and Carlo was able to drag him forwards over the chair. Immediately, however, Maurice smashed the gun into Carlo's face and pulled himself upright. As he did so, he felt the sharp blade of Kirsten's penknife against his throat.

Kirsten pulled him backwards and looked into his eyes until she received a glint of recognition. 'Women have rights too,' she said, remembering her father's words. She remembered that day in Berlin when, a week after he had come to stay, her father had returned home drunk. With tears in his cruel eyes, he had forced himself upon her. She shook now at the memory, and she recalled how, with a knife similar to one she now carried, she had struck her father in the belly and torn him to pieces. She remembered screaming for her dead mother's help and how, in those final shocking moments, her father had cried for forgiveness and died with his arms wrapped around her legs. How could she ever return to Germany after that, she thought with bitterness? Her father had seen to it that she couldn't even visit her mother's grave.

She looked again into Maurice's eyes and imagined her father staring back at her. Hatred boiled inside her, hatred enough to do it again. Without further contemplation, with her tiny little penknife clenched tightly in her fist, she ripped open his throat, pulled him sharply backwards across the room and hurled his gasping body to the floor.

While Maurice grasped at his throat, trying desperately to stem the flow of blood, Kirsten turned her attention to Carlo. He was outstretched across the floor, possibly dead already, she couldn't tell. She poked nervously at his face with her foot but he didn't move. She kicked him and stepped quickly backwards but he didn't move. She kicked him hard, hard enough to kick a severed head across the room. Then she kicked his head again, and again, and again, screaming now with rage and exhilaration, realising her dream, taking her revenge, capturing for herself that power and control lost to her since the age of eight. She screamed at her father, screamed at her mother, screamed at Carlo, screamed at everybody who had ever taken her mother's name in vain, screamed at those who had told her to forgive, forgive, forgive. She kicked and kicked and kicked until something seemed to snap, both inside her and inside Carlo's head, something that turned his head limp like a deflated football; useless, soft and unwanted and reduced her to a gasping, spitting, doubled-up hag.

Maurice had watched Kirsten's despatch of Carlo with dread. She hadn't cut him seriously enough to kill him, not quickly at least, but the combination of injuries had left him simply too weak to fight back. He was slumped against the wall beside the door, holding his neck, resigned to what was to come.

Kirsten was exhausted. She hadn't planned to kick anybody to death and she really hadn't been prepared for the physical exertion it took. She bent forward, head bowed, hands clasping her knees. Had there been a bed nearby she would have gladly fallen onto it, and it was a while before she thought of Maurice again. He was a beaten wreck of a man, blood-soaked, frightened and pathetic. He was her final victory; the greatest test of her resolve.

Kirsten saw his bag on the far side of the door, caked in shit. She walked to it, stepping over Simon's body as she did so, and kneeled to open it. True to form, Maurice carried the tools of his trade inside the bag. She found his instamatic camera, the one item she wanted, inside a plastic bag. She took the camera from the bag and approached Maurice. 'I need your passport,' she said to him, kicking at the soles of his feet menacingly as she did so. Maurice didn't have the will to resist. He needed this to end. He pointed at his waist where he kept his passport inside a money belt. Kirsten placed the camera on the floor and, as she bent to unzip his trousers, she considered the irony of Maurice wearing a money belt. He hated backpackers yet he had developed many of their habits. The money belt probably wasn't even his own, she realised, undoing it. It was made in Holland. It was then that she was struck by a wonderful, final irony.

'I win,' she said, staring down at Maurice. 'Now you belong to me.' She made a show of returning the passport to the money belt and zipping it up again. 'You can keep it,' she said. 'I don't want you. You're simply not good enough.'

Maurice stared at her impassively.

'I have a better idea,' Kirsten said, kneeling beside him. She draped the money belt over his head and lowered it around his neck. Then she crawled in front of him and pulled his open trousers down to his knees, zipping them up again to prevent him struggling free once he realised what was coming. 'Humiliating, isn't it?' she said.

Kirsten took her time, working out how the instamatic camera worked. A photograph would be much easier to carry around than a passport. She needed just one picture for old time's sake. It would be something to restore her confidence at times in the future when things were hard. She imagined taking out the photograph sometime and showing it to a surprised audience. She could jokingly tell them that he was her ex-boyfriend. Maurice appeared quite ridiculous to her now. He didn't seem to care that he was being mocked. When she took the photograph he actually smiled.

Kirsten didn't have much time if she was going to get away. The gunshots would have woken the family next door and, even if they had ignored them, they could never have ignored the screaming. Her bag was already packed, so she only had to pack Andrew's. She had no time to wash off the blood before she left. She would do that in the sea.

She left Maurice to his own devices while she gathered up her rucksack and Andrew's belongings. She unlocked the front door and placed the two bags, the padlock and the chain outside. Then she returned to the house and gathered up the belongings of the other residents, piling them up in the room with Carlo, Simon and Maurice. In the kitchen she found a small camping stove, a box of matches and a bottle of fuel. She placed the fuel and the matches beside the pile of belongings.

She checked the house one last time, ensuring that all the windows were locked tight and that nothing belonging to her or Andrew remained. Then, finally, she plucked Andrew from the corner of the bedroom where he had now completely buried himself in the pile of clothes. She tidied him up a little, kissed him on the forehead and walked him through the carnage, which he seemed not to notice. They went out onto the verandah and into a beautiful fresh day.

Then, she walked around the lounge one last time and returned to Maurice, who had been following her with his eyes the whole time. As she stood beside him she heard him speak.

'What was that?' she said, bending beside him, threading the belt through the buckle until his neck was in a noose.

'Thank you,' Maurice said.

Kirsten looked at him momentarily, wondering what he could have possibly meant, then she put a foot on his neck and, tightening the noose, she pulled and pulled and pulled until the blood drained from her fingers and her knuckles turned white.